The Harvest of Chronos

D1146906

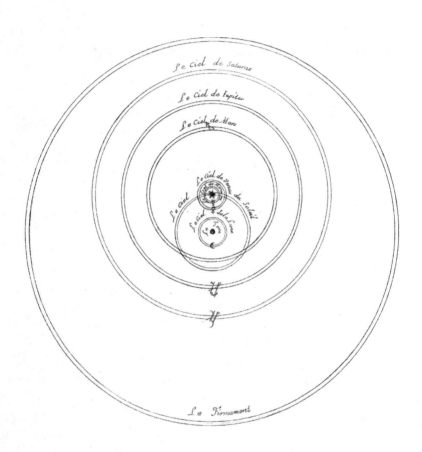

MOJCA KUMERDEJ

THE HARVEST
OF CHRONOS

Translated from the Slovene by Rawley Grau

istrosbooks

CONTENTS

A Brief Note on Time and Place

Mojca Kumerdej's novel *The Harvest of Chronos* is set in the year 1600 during the Catholic Counter-Reformation in the territory of what is today the Republic of Slovenia – an intersection of history and geography that may require some context for twenty-first-century readers.

Exactly five hundred years ago (almost to the day, as I write this) and eighty-three years before the novel begins, the German monk and theology professor Martin Luther, according to a famous but disputed legend, nailed his *Ninety-five Theses* on the door of a church in the Saxon town of Wittenberg, in northern Germany. The *Theses* laid out his objections to certain practices of the Roman Catholic Church, and their publication is generally considered the beginning of the Protestant Reformation, which over the following decades developed from a movement to reform the Catholic Church to the establishment of a number of breakaway churches with differing structures, practices, and doctrines.

Luther had published his *Theses* primarily to protest the Catholic practice of selling indulgences, that is, the idea that you could purchase a reduction in the time you or a loved one would have to spend in purgatory before being admitted to heaven. But other practices were equally abhorrent to Luther and his followers. Lutherans insisted on the importance of taking Holy Communion 'in both kinds', that is, with all communicants being given both bread and wine, as the body and blood of Christ. In the Catholic Church, however, the Lord's Supper was offered to lay believers only 'in one kind': while the clergy took both wine and bread, the laity were only permitted to receive the bread, which was placed by the priest on the communicant's tongue. But most importantly, Protestants rejected the idea of papal authority and, by extension, the authority of priests in general; they believed in the priesthood of all believers and elevated the Bible as the primary if not sole basis for doctrine and personal faith. Consequently, the translation of the Bible into the vernacular languages and the promotion of universal literacy were central priorities. At the same time, the emphasis on the individual's direct access to God meant a rejection of the role of the Virgin Mary and the saints as intercessors.

But the Protestants were also divided among themselves. Besides the Lutherans, the other major Protestant group were the followers of the Geneva-based theologian John Calvin, who most famously put forward the controversial doctrine of predestination, the belief that God has preordained some people for eternal life and others for eternal damnation. There were other sects as well, such as the Anabaptists and the Flacians (whose founder, Matthias Flacius, was a Croat from Istria, born Matija Vlačić), as well as smaller, more radical groups, some of which appear in the novel as Leapers, Founders, and Ecstatics.

By the middle of the sixteenth century, Lutheranism had gained a strong foothold among the nobility and burghers in the Habsburg domain known as Inner Austria, in the south-eastern corner of the Holy Roman Empire. Squeezed between the Venetian Republic on the west and Hungary and the still-expanding Ottoman Empire on the east, Inner Austria comprised the Duchies of Carinthia, Styria, and Carniola, as well as the Princely County of Gorizia, the City of Trieste, and a large part of the Istrian Peninsula. Roughly a third of this territory was inhabited by speakers of the South Slavic language that today we call Slovene.

The main proponent of Lutheranism among Slovene speakers was Primož Trubar (1508–1586), who served as a Catholic priest in Carniola and Styria until 1548, when he was expelled from the region because of his Lutheran views. He fled to Germany, where he began publishing books in Slovene, most importantly, his *Catechism*, with explanations of the basic Lutheran doctrines as well as hymns and a litany for worship, and the *Abecedarium*, an 'ABC book' for learning to read and write. Published in Tübingen in 1550, these were the first books ever to be printed in Slovene. Although Trubar also produced translations of the New Testament, it was his younger colleague, Jurij Dalmatin (c. 1547–1589), who translated the entire Bible into Slovene, which was printed in Wittenberg in 1583. Meanwhile, the Slovene Protestant preacher Adam Bohorič (c. 1520–1598) wrote the first grammar for the language (1584) and devised the alphabet used by Trubar and Dalmatin (the Bohorič script was eventually replaced in the mid-nineteenth century by the modern Slovene alphabet).

While it is impossible to overstate the importance of the Protestant Reformers' role in the formation of the Slovene literary language, no less important was their contribution to the creation of the Slovene national identity. It is no accident that Trubar begins his *Catechism* with the words: 'For all Slovenes I ask grace, peace, mercy and the true knowledge of God through Jesus Christ.' His appeal to 'all Slovenes' – *vsem Slovencem* – is breathtaking: it is as if he is naming a people and thereby envisioning a nation, even if that nation would not be realized as political fact until hundreds of years later. While it would be wrong to view Mojca Kumerdej's novel as engaged in the formation of a national mythos – her concerns are much broader than this – the anxiety of an inchoate populace that, for good or for ill, is striving to define and assert its identity is a significant element in the matrix of power she describes.

The novel unfolds against the background of a new stage in the Catholic response to Protestantism in Inner Austria, when after decades of reluctant compromise with the powerful Lutheran elites in the noble and burgher classes (the Provincial Estates) – a compromise marked by agreements such as the Peace of Augsburg (1555) and the Pacification of Bruck (1578), which assured the feudal gentry and the towns the right to choose their own religion – the Catholic Church launched a ruthless crackdown, burning Protestant books, forcing conversions, and expelling anyone who refused to swear allegiance to the Church. These efforts were undertaken with the full support of the Prince of Inner Austria, Archduke Ferdinand II (1578–1637), a fervent Catholic whose later actions to impose his religion, first as King of Bohemia and then as Holy Roman Emperor, would eventually trigger the Thirty Years' War (1618–1648), one of the longest and deadliest wars in European history. In the end, Protestantism was completely eradicated in the Slovene lands, with the exception of the Trans-Mura (Prekmurje) region, then in Hungary but now the north-eastern corner of Slovenia, where a significant part of the population has remained Lutheran.

The social and philosophical conflicts Kumerdej portrays – between competing religions, folk beliefs (including the belief in witches and sorcery), scientific rationalism, humanism, scepticism, and mysticism – are underlaid with political questions about power, violence, patriarchy, misogyny, xenophobia, and populism. Who is in control? Who is manipulating whom? Who determines what is good and what is evil? And then there is the question of time itself, the harvest that is reaped (or raped?) by Chronos: are we moving forward or are we spinning in a void on the edge of the universe? For ultimately, this is a novel where centuries collide and collapse into each other, and behind the veil of the past we see our own century flickering, but whether as hope, doom, or simply illusion, it is impossible to say.

— Rawley Grau
Ljubljana, October 2017

T hen I looked, and there was a white cloud, and seated on the cloud was one like the Son of Man, with a golden crown on his head, and a sharp sickle in his hand.

Another angel came out of the temple, calling with a loud voice to the one who sat on the cloud, 'Use your sickle and reap, for the hour to reap has come, because the harvest of the earth is fully ripe.' So the one who sat on the cloud swung his sickle over the earth, and the earth was reaped.

— Revelation 14:14–16

IN SYNCOPATED RHYTHM

Hills of tender green were scattered about in syncopated rhythm, and the late-morning sun, which bathed the land in apricot light, announced that the cold which had paralysed the province right up to the first days of April was slowly releasing its icy grip. On a distant ridge, a little village was bashfully uncovering itself, wedged into a rounded slope and pierced through by the bell tower of a church. The bright-green forests revealed that the trees within them were mostly ancient beeches interspersed with lindens – trees that in these parts and those times held special importance for the populace. The hard wood of the beech tree had economic importance, for it produced the most bountiful warmth in household hearths. But for other fires, not meant for heating homes, it was best to use faster-burning woods drenched in animal fat, which were then tossed into a pile. On some occasions, linden trees were involved. To be sure, when it blossoms the linden gives off a heady perfume and its dried flowers have the power to soothe coughs and reduce fever, but the wood of the tree, with its particular softness, is also ideal for carving gods. And carving and cavorting with lindenwood gods was sufficient reason, in the late sixteenth century, for the carvers and cavorters to roast at the stake and be burned to the bone.

The old trees kept watch over memories from an age the local populace did not remember first-hand but that still rustled in secret among them. The little villages, sprinkled with modest churches, were watched over by the tall and mighty old trees, and, not infrequently, an oak might hold the foundation and walls of a church in the tight grip of its roots. As evening approached, the little churches would ring their bells and announce to honest folk that it was time to milk whatever there was to be milked and to fill their stomachs with whatever there was to fill them, so they wouldn't churn and growl until morning, and then to go to bed and, before falling asleep, if their bodies allowed it, make a new Christian – a Catholic one, not a Lutheran! And then the churches, too, would shut their eyes and still their bells in a well-deserved slumber. That was how things were supposed to be. That was what was demanded and expected of a God-fearing people.

But not everybody kept these customs. Just as eyelids should be shutting out the visible world, the hours arrive when the dark world awakens and with it the ancient forces that supposedly lay vanquished and rotting beneath the little churches. When the evening bells have finished chiming and diligent hands have done what remains to be done, all in keeping with secular and religious law, there are a few who then start lifting the heavy lids off household chests, opening cabinets, pulling up a floorboard or unscrewing a panel in the wall, and as they look to see if anyone is watching, they take out various dried and fresh herbs, clay pots and bowls, glass jars large and small, roots, ointments, desiccated toads, insects and snake heads, which they place all around them, preferably on the floor, lest what they do be noticed by an intrusive eye from behind the curtained window and tightly closed shutters. Or perhaps, sitting or crouching amid all this paraphernalia in a windowless black kitchen by the light of a candle, they begin to consider what mischief might be made that evening. Would it be a good idea, is it the proper time, to take revenge on a neighbour – although they could just as easily do him evil for no other reason than the pure pleasure of it? Is tonight the night for wreaking havoc on a henhouse and binding the fowls' guts so they never again lay a single egg? Oh, right! They could see if that woman has already given birth, and if she hasn't, or is only now in labour, they could twist the umbilical cord around the little head in her belly so that not even the most skilful midwife would be able to disentangle the child.

There were, to be sure, more than a few midwives among those who hatched such schemes and nursed such dismal thoughts – the very women the populace was obliged to trust on such a sensitive and important occasion as the birth of a child. It would not be the first time that, right after a woman gives birth, the midwife hurries outside with the newborn, lifts him in the air and thunders out curses, summoning her dark master and offering him the baby as a gift. And her master willingly accepts these unbaptized little souls. Sometimes he will take both body and soul, and people then wonder why the child died so unexpectedly when there was nothing at all wrong with the mother's belly, either during the birth or before it. Sometimes the hornèd one leaves the body alone for a time, bringing up the soul inside as his very own child, who does evil at his bidding. Some of them really are his children, although this is not always apparent at first glance. The child seems healthy and active enough, no naughtier than other naughty children. But eventually, the observant eye begins to detect certain suspicious and revealing signs. For instance, farm animals are afraid of the child, while foxes and wolves approach him boldly and roll on their backs at his feet like a pet cat or dog. Or when he walks past a crucifix, it tilts and turns so that if the Saviour really was nailed to it, all the blood would rush to his head. Accidents start happening in the family and no one can say why – and this in a family that is devout, where everyone has a good, pure heart and harsh words are never spoken and the rod always spared, unless the punishment is well-founded and necessary, a family who crawl on their knees in the great processions around the altar and even give to the church a little more than they are able to, who have no dispute with their neighbours or with anyone else in the village, not the priest or the count or any other authority. And then one day the mother slips and falls on her back and cannot get out of bed any more. And a few weeks later, one of the children breaks out in a festering rash, and even after the barber has let his blood and applied leeches to cleanse the poisons from the body, the child gets weaker and his skin turns sallow, until eventually, pale, ashen and emaciated, he sleeps the sleep of eternity. And that's not the end of it. The family has not yet fully recovered when another son falls out of the cherry tree, hurting himself so badly he's no good for anything until the following spring; with his broken fingers, he can't even crack nuts or do the other small chores by which the populace gets through the long, cold, dark winter hours.

And to make matters worse, after a night in spring the fifteen-year-old daughter throws up her morning porridge and bores her eyes into the floor; and when someone asks her what's wrong, she bursts into tears, clasps her hands in prayer and falls on her knees, begging Mary for help, because she doesn't know what's wrong. And she does well to pray to Mary, who more than any saint, male or female, let alone Jesus or God, understands why a teenage girl might first feel sick in the morning and then, despite not eating very much, grow larger by the day. 'Tell me his name!' The father is pummelling his daughter, who bears the blows meekly through her tears, for she knows she has honestly earned them and is now paying the price for her short and sinful life. 'His name! His name!' the father shouts, bellows, thrashes her. 'You have defiled our family's name! Never in recent generations has anyone in our family whored herself so young!' (This, in fact, may not be true, for who knows whose seed a woman carries? Sometimes the woman herself doesn't know, and in those days, the man she names as the father could as easily doubt her as take her at her word.) And because her father's hand does not relent, the girl agrees to tell him, to show him, everything. He cracks his knuckles and looks around. Should he grab the musket, which he uses from time to time for poaching deer on the count's hunting ground? Or should he take the sickle, the axe, maybe the scythe? Or merely a knife and with threatening looks make his daughter understand that she'd better not dally with the information. He moves a step closer, grabs her head and turns it towards the picture of the Virgin Mary that is hanging on the wall, and the daughter blurts out the first name that comes to her.

'Who? I don't know him! He's not from our village!'

'Of course he isn't!' the daughter weeps. 'It didn't happen in our village!' While her young brain is weaving a story, the father holds his head in his hands, turning it right and left and roaring like a bear that she must have seduced him, she must have offered herself to him, since he's seen the way she struts around showing herself off, even in front of those seven oddities on the Kostanšek farm, who most people, when they see them, turn away from and cross themselves.

'But it's not my fault! I was forced to do it!' And so the daughter begins her tearful narrative.

'One night, after saying my prayers – the Our Father, the Hail Mary, the Angel of God – I fell asleep listening to the breathing of my brothers and sisters sleeping next to me. But then, all of a sudden, I wake up.

I open my eyes and look out of the window at the moon; it's glowing with a strange reddish colour and is so big it's like it's trying to break into the room. That's scary enough. But then I go numb with horror when a shadow darts across the glowing moon and covers it in darkness. A moment later, a hideous crone is standing in front of me, and her twisted fingers are reaching for my face and she's laughing through her jagged teeth. Her hair is all tangled and she's laughing and laughing and grabbing at me with her crooked fingers. I try to turn away, I really do, but right beside my bed the hag keeps shifting from one foot to the other with a broom between her legs. I want to cry, but nothing comes out of me. Then she takes the broom in her hands like this' – the girl demonstrates – 'and does like this.' And to make clearer what she's saying, she slides the invisible broomstick between her legs. 'The old hag is rubbing it up and down and back and forth and back and forth and … Yuck! I'm so disgusted I cover my face with my hands, only my fingers are open just wide enough to see what she means to do with me. The hag keeps rubbing and rubbing until the stick is dripping wet, as if it's slathered in hot pig's fat. Then she grabs me, shoves the broomstick between my thighs and, with one hand clutching my body so I can't move, let alone wriggle out of her grasp, with the other she grips the greasy, slimy stick, and all at once we're flying through the closed window, right past the picture of the Virgin Mary, who turns her eyes away in shame. Help me, Mary, help me, I sob, but the Virgin only clasps her hands more tightly and sheds a tear, so I realize that if Mary can't help me, only God can. And I will need God's help, because wherever I'm flying on this broom, this wild night, it will very probably be hell. And so it was!

'We go off to a mountain – that one there' – the girl points through the window at a hill not very far away. 'There's a clearing up there where you have a good view down – you can even see our house and our field – and a cold stream runs through it. From the air I see people in the clearing, a little way from the stream, people I don't know, men and women staring up at the sky as if they're waiting for us, and – oh, it's horrible! – they're all naked, stark naked, with their arms lifted in the air towards us. When we land on the ground, it starts. No order at all, everyone together, like in our pigsty if not worse, doing things with each other that not even animals do, and meanwhile they take me to the middle of the clearing, where a strange altar has been set up. It's covered in bearskins, or maybe sheepskins, I don't remember very well since I was shaking all over with fear, and I was also a little dizzy from the broom ride.

'There they undressed me and poured something awful into my mouth; then they pushed me down on to those foul-smelling skins just as everything around started glowing red. The earth opens up and out flies someone with big horns on his head and a tail on his backside, which he's whipping left and right like a dog, and there's a kind of filthy ooze dripping from his mouth. It's looking bad for me, as bad as it can get, I think, and I'm terrified. The hornèd one is standing over me stomping his hoofs, like this and like this' – she reaches her arms out towards her father's face and beats her fists together. 'Then he opens his mouth up wide, and a long burning tongue hisses out and licks my naked skin, and it stings something terrible. Next, they bring a man over, and the evil one pushes him on top of me and then, dear God, it happens, and it lasts and lasts until the only thing I want – me, a poor girl forced into sin against her will – is to die right then and there, even without confession, even in that vestibule of hell. But suddenly, a ray of wondrous blue pierces the red glow and turns everything around me green, until finally there's nothing but a heavenly blue sky. Then a strong wind blows away all those wicked people, all those bodies, and the hornèd one is swallowed up by the earth, just as earlier it had spat him out. In that heavenly light, I'm the only one left in the clearing when an enormous white bird appears, flapping his wings above me and cooing and cooing. "Birdie, oh birdie, who are you?" I ask, and he flies down right next to me, his wing tenderly brushing against me, and he says, "I am the Holy Spirit, dear sinner, a sinner by no fault of your own." What happened to me next I don't know, since I woke up in the morning on my own straw mattress and, miraculously, I didn't have a single flea bite.'

Her father, for some time now, has been holding in his hand neither a farm tool nor a weapon, but a nearly empty flask of marc brandy. By the time the girl finishes her story, there's a whip in his right hand, and with his left he tips the last drops out of the flask and then grabs his daughter and starts thrashing and thrashing her. The girl whimpers softly and waits for it to be over, when she catches sight of her mother in the corner, kneeling beneath Mary's picture and rigidly moving her lips. When the father, teetering, has finished beating her – the drink is affecting his balance, allowing the daughter to avoid a few blows – he shouts, 'Now get out of my sight and think again about your story. A name … I want a name! … You will tell me a name! And if you start babbling that rubbish to me again, don't doubt I will tan your hide all the way to kingdom come and that Holy Spirit of yours!'

Aching with pains she then only vaguely feels – the real pain will come later when she's lying on the hay – the girl, as she leaves the house to go to the barn, glances over at her mother, whose woebegone face is streaming with tears as she rattles off prayers beneath Mary's picture, and it dawns on her, fine, none of it was really necessary. But why are you grovelling to Mary? What's done is done. I hope you're praying for the baby, your grandchild, that things will be well and it will all work out somehow. That some loser of a man will marry me, if only to get his nuts off on a regular basis. But honestly, she thinks, have I really thrown my life away with that unpleasant little adventure? Maybe, but then again maybe not and all I've really done is hurry life along a bit. I've had my fill of whoring, which would hardly be the case if I had waited for a suitor to come along and been innocent when I married – which in our cottages is not very likely. Anyway, it wouldn't be my decision who I married. Papa would put his fist down and shake hands with whoever he thought was the best choice. I'm not the first or the last girl to make this pilgrimage in her rosy years. And as for *him* marrying me, well, he's hardly the Holy Spirit, although at times it felt like the gates of heaven opened when I was with him, and the idea that he would leave his wife, children and farm for me and the baby, or even that he'd acknowledge the baby as his – that's not going to happen, of course.

When I told him two weeks ago how things stood, he just shrugged his shoulders, turned around and tried to walk away.

'So what are we going to do?' I asked.

'What do you mean *we*? There is no *we*,' he said with a shrug. 'What you do with your bastard child is all down to you.'

'All down to me? It's you who were all over me! I didn't make this baby by myself, you know.'

'No, not by yourself. But who with, that's something you'll have to figure out.'

Oh, I just cried and cried. It's all over, I thought. My life is finished. My father will kill us, me and my baby. But what's done is done. I'll keep it a secret a little while longer. I'll bind my belly tight, and by the time he discovers the truth, the child inside will be strong enough to grab on to my heart with his little hands, avoid the blows, kick back at them and maybe live.

That part of the story my baby and I have just survived. But – she thinks as she settles herself on the hay and strokes her belly – does it all have to be so predictable? Do I really have to end up just another big-bellied waif? It'll be hard finding any sort of husband for a girl with a bastard child: she's good to bed but not to wed – that's what the men will be spouting to each other – if she started so young, you can be sure that as soon as you turn your back or go away for a while, she'll jump the first man she sees and plant horns on your head. So is that how it has to be? Hmm. Maybe not. Baby and me – we don't have to give up so easily. In fact, we could strike back and make a rather nice life for ourselves. 'So watch out, everyone, watch out! Revenge is on the way!' she says out loud. Lying in the hay and grimacing in pain, she stretches her limbs like a cat as a smile forms on her face. Her fingers touch the corners of her lips, and she thinks her face has nearly forgotten how to contract and extend its muscles in laughter. But this was not a smile of satisfaction, let alone one of reconciliation with the world and with her fate. This was a smile that since antiquity has spread across the faces of generals preparing for military action as they survey the enemy in the distance while glancing from time to time at their own soldiers, who from that moment on are nothing but nameless particles in the organism they will soon unleash, which will destroy the enemy to the last man. The father of her bastard child she will tackle methodically, and not even his wife will escape without consequences, not even his children – well, she'll have to think about the children. Her attacks must be planned with a clear head, her goals carefully chosen. It makes no sense to strike in all directions; that will only turn people's stomachs. But if in your battles you carefully cultivate a certain purpose, shifting it back and forth between the front lines and the rear, people will come to view the war first as understandable, then as acceptable and later as inevitable, until finally it seems well warranted and just.

In the war she is preparing she will at first be alone, but, like any good commander, she will gradually subjugate both individuals and the populace, who will be unwittingly enlisted in her army. She will play the helpless victim, which means she must choose her targets carefully if she wants to create the impression of a process driven by justice and humility before God. So she probably won't go after the children. Anyway, his pock-faced daughter (who is her own age) is so ugly there's little chance she'll ever know passion, let alone love. And the other three children are still little so it wouldn't do to make them suffer – that could bring down vengeance on her and her baby.

'But why not use this opportunity and take care of everything that pains me in life?' she thinks. 'Sure, I've been a whore, but he wasn't my first. Before him, years before, my own father got drunk and had his way with me right in our cottage. He was the first, and the next was my mother's brother. And then there was the farmhand who grabbed my hair and pressed me up against one of the beams in the barn, and there was another time when some mowers pushed me into the hay and I don't even remember how many there were. I know people do such things, but did I have to put up with it all? No! Nobody should do that to a child! It's a sin, even if our priest never talks about it. And every time it happened, it hurt so much and I was so scared, I didn't think I'd survive. But I did! And because I did, I'll see to it that this wrong is put right. And I should do something about my mother, too, since she knew what was going on and even caught us at it a few times. But she did nothing. She just turned around and bustled into the house, kneeled down before Mary and prayed. So why didn't you say anything to them? I used to ask her in my thoughts and from somewhere I'd hear her whining, "But I was afraid, I was so afraaiiid … It happened to me, too, you know, the same thing, when I was a child. Women are put in this world to kneel, and, whether on our knees or our backs, we must patiently bear it."

'Oh, is that right? Well, I couldn't agree less! Surely, Mother, when you were a child and they were doing to you what they did to me, didn't you pray to grow up as fast as you could and be married off to a man who wasn't the brute men usually are? I have almost all of the names written down, not so I wouldn't forget them but so I'd preserve that memory of being unglued from my body in the midst of my pain and having a revelation, a revelation that sounds like this: *We don't have to accept what other people force us into.* So anything that has ever been taken from me by force from this moment on becomes my weapon. I've heard and read that there are women who know how to rule entire kingdoms with their pussies. If that's true – and I believe it is – then I, too, will create my own fiefdom. I used to blame myself a little for being naïve enough to think that if a man is nice to me the way *he* was, that if he doesn't beat me or take me by force, it means he loves me. I know now it's no good believing anyone, that I shouldn't surrender so trustingly to pretty words or comforting arms, that I should never surrender and must always maintain control. Well, Mother, tell me because I'm curious: did the Virgin lay it on your heart, as you kneeled there snivelling beneath her picture, to patiently bear it the way you've done all your life? Or did she maybe point her hand in the direction of the man, your husband, who at that very moment was sticking it into me, and then look at you and say, "Now, Mother, go to the barn and take the pitchfork, or if the pitchfork is not at hand, take the sickle, and return to the house and swing it with all your might over the bed, only be sure that it is him you strike down and that she survives." And if you later explained to people that he had taken his own daughter countless times, they would believe you, and I would have told them everything, too, and you and I would have run the farm together in peace.

'But no, Mother, you have less sense than our entire henhouse! Whenever I suffered these unmentionable things, you would send me ugly looks as if to say, "It's your own fault! Ever since you were a little girl you've had something of the whore in you. Even as a child you would point your finger at things – 'Oh, look, Mother, look at the bull on top of the cow! And that bitch is in heat again!' or, 'What's that sticking out the farmhand's trousers? That thing he sometimes scratches so much it makes him grimace like he's hurting all over, and then, when the pain passes, there's a sort of white blood dripping off his hand? What's the farmhand got in his trousers that I don't have?'" And you would slap my face every time and yell at me and tell me not to look at such things, not to talk about them, because they're disgusting and unsuitable for girls. Oh, but I will talk, and how I will talk! And I'll point my finger at everyone who has ever done anything bad to me.

'The more I think about it, the more I'm convinced I don't have to meekly surrender. And what looks like my doom doesn't have to be my destiny – my destiny is to turn things around to what's best for me and my baby. If that's God's will, too, so much the better, although I'm not going to rely on God. Why should I wait around for some-one to marry a disgraced girl with a bastard child out of pity? From now on, it's me who does the choosing. My visits to the sacristy have served me very well. The priest always reimbursed me for my nice little favours by slipping a kreutzer in my blouse or giving me some little book to read. Back when he didn't like Mary all that much he used to teach some of us children to read and write during our Sunday classes. I learned to read and write Slovene and German, and I took good care of the books he gave me. I'd read them at home in secret, so nobody could accuse me of wasting time on nonsense; then, at our next appointment, I would give them back to him and earn myself a new little book with my good works, which might not get me into heaven but they'd always get me a book and a coin, the priest said, who ever since that visit by the Church official has started giving us communion under one kind again. But I'll leave the priest alone; that way he'll stand up for me and support me. After all, when he hears my confession, he'll be scared that he, too, might end up among the people I'm accusing, my tormenters and persecutors.

'But what if nobody believes me? Oh, it'll be hard for them not to! May is coming, and every day I'll put flowers around the church altar and crawl on my knees from saint to saint with the rosary in my hand (I'll wrap my knees in wadding so it won't hurt), and during these scenes it'll look like I'm praying, but what I'll really be doing when I open my mouth is spinning the story I'll use to bring justice to my life. I'll keep the Holy Spirit in it, since I know that will make a strong impression on the community and the judge. White doves look like little angels and the souls of innocent babes, so whoever hears me talking will connect the bird to the baby in my belly, and to me, too, since I'll look just like a wounded little sparrow. But birds don't live on seeds alone; they'd rather peck on grasshoppers, worms and the flesh of other animals. And if a bird doesn't watch out for herself, she'll soon become someone else's quarry.

'So starting tomorrow, I'll be good, pious and humble, or so it will seem. Now that spring's here, I can easily sleep in barns and mangers, but I'll need to get everything done by winter. And you who gave me this baby, you'd better be ready. Things are going to get hot for you, you selfish pervert, so hot that everything you have, everything you have ever known, will be going up in flames. Your life will turn to charcoal before my eyes, and my child, who from this day forth is mine and mine alone, will be joyfully kicking inside me while his father burns at the stake. As for *my* father, and my uncle and mother, too, I'll weave them into the prologue of my tale and so be free of everyone who's hurt me. And then with my baby and my little brother and sister, I'll stay on the farm and run it myself, probably no worse than my parents are doing now. I'll bring my brother up to be someone who doesn't do the things men have done to me, and I'll bring up my sister to follow me, and not our mother, in her actions and decisions.'

After weeks of not sleeping, she felt herself being slowly lulled to sleep as she lay there on the hay. Tomorrow was a new day, and with it a new life would begin. 'Good night, little baby,' she said out loud. 'Good night, angel of God, my guardian dear. And you, too, Virgin, who endured what I must endure and accepted it all without complaint – but since it was God you were dealing with, I guess you had no choice. Good night to you, too, Holy Spirit, who I hope will be able to help me. But not to you, God the Father, since you take the side of men and fathers and let them do to us whatever they feel like, even horrible things. Good night to you, Baby Jesus, who will soon have a little brother. But grown-up Jesus, I'm not talking to you right now because of my problems with men, since, even if you're special, you're still a man. And good night to you, by which I mean me: you're not to blame for anything, and you're going to be a good mother to your baby and to your brother and sister, too, and when all of this is behind you, you'll be the owner of a farm, and, with the good sense you have, which is not very common around here, you'll find yourself a good husband, a father for the tiny tot and the other two little ones – and Jesus, I'm expecting you to help me with this because I want him to be like you – kind and tall and strong, and good-looking, too, with long wavy hair. Good night, world … good night, moon … good niiii …'

DARK SOUNDS

The province was beset by catastrophes of a moral, meteorological and medical nature. It was just as in the Old Testament, the populace was starting to realize. After the bitter winter, the snow was melting, which in early March led to rising waters. This was followed by cold rains, and people were hacking and wheezing and spitting out gobs of phlegm. Then there was an unexpected warm spell, and the germs that had spent the winter in idle numbness now revived and attacked people's bowels, ears, throats and lungs, and did not spare the livestock either. Two years earlier, the oaks had been full of acorns, so the following year the mouse colonies increased, with mice running freely through yards, barns and houses and even scurrying out of drawers and chests, but the year of the mice forecast an even worse torment waiting for the populace this spring – snakes. Overfed on fat mice and rats from the year before, with the first warm rays of the sun they were slithering about between people's feet – long ones, thick ones, short ones, thin ones – and few could avoid them. Some snakes would strike at any feet they feared might trample them. And certain ones – such was the opinion of more than a few – were biting people out of sheer malice. After all, not only people and – well, we won't mention who – can be evil; animals can, too, since he whose name is not to be written or spoken can sometimes assume their form.

Even before the real summer starts there will be a brutal heat wave – such was the prediction of both folk wisdom and astrology. Fires will break out (but surely not without help?), after which swarms of strange insects, like grasshoppers only bigger, will attack and devour the few crops that have taken root in the fields. The countryside will suffer scarcities, and it will be worse in the towns, where prices will surge. And to ensure that the catastrophes reach biblical proportions, an epidemic of dysentery will break out, with such excruciating stomach pains that some people will even die. And plague will arrive and claim a fifth of the village, and then typhus, putrid fever and again dysentery, and again plague, and meanwhile the Turks will invade and there will be an outbreak of the black pox, and as people from all this misery begin to dance the dance of St Vitus, typhus will reappear, and then plague again …

Maybe all these things really did happen, but probably not all in the space of a year or two. The human mind, looking back at the past, tends to compress events, reshaping them in rich and colourful ways and exaggerating many things. Exaggeration proves particularly useful when it is good to justify some past action. And as for what is good, well, the populace are experts in such matters. Common sense tells them clearly what is and isn't good, especially when the deed marks the boundary between life and death, when it cuts into a body. Plainly, there was no other choice; it's better for everyone this way – these are the usual explanations after such irrevocable actions, some of which are simply erased by human memory. Words like *simply* and *plainly* are very convenient for justifying violence, for they reinforce the logic and underscore the inevitability of what was done. And erasing memory is good not bad. Living with too much badness is exhausting and painful for human beings; it can arouse feelings of guilt and unease, which, in turn, can develop into severe anxiety. We should be grateful to the mind of God and the way he structured the human brain: everything is constantly being filtered so the bad things don't clog our thoughts. Exaggerating, mitigating, erasing, inflating or in some other way transforming events – all this the human mind can do. But the human mind and the mind of God are not the only minds. There is another one, too, one that speaks deceitfully to the populace, seducing them, leading them astray …

'So how do we know that what we did was right?' the populace wonders.

'That we didn't make a mistake?'

'That we did what we did because it was the command of God and that we didn't maybe fall into a trap?'

'Yes, how do we know when it's God speaking to us and not perhaps ...'

'Perhaps ...?'

'The other one ...'

'You can tell who is speaking by the voice.'

'But is it really always possible to tell the two of them apart?'

'The two of them?'

'Because sometimes we might believe and be entirely convinced that it's God speaking to us, when, in fact, it's ...'

'Who?'

'His impersonator ... the evil-toned ... dark-timbred one ... who pretends to be what he's not ...'

'Devout people can tell good from evil!'

'But can they always? And, if so, how? How did Abraham in the Old Testament, to whom God gave a son in his old age and then commanded him to take his son to Mount Moriah and offer him there as a sacrifice, the way animals are sacrificed – how could Abraham tell that it was God's voice and not some other's? How could he seize the knife without hesitating, ready to plunge it into the heart of his son, because that was what God wanted of him?'

'He who believes is not afraid and does everything God expects of him.'

'But what if the angel had not stopped his hand at the very last moment and placed a sacrificial animal before him?'

'The fact that the angel did stop the Abraham's hand and put the ram before him proves that this was the voice of God.'

'That might be comforting in hindsight, but at the time, when you hear such a dreadful command and everything is still open and there's an endless gaping void in front of you ... What if the void really is empty and there's no meaning in it at all?'

'Where there is faith, there can be no meaningless void!'

'But to kill a child? What sort of God can demand of a father his son's death ...'

'If not a God who was able to send even his own son to his death?'

*

'Quiet! Let's not impose on creation by trying to understand more than we need to, more than we are meant to. Let's not undermine the plans of God with doubt and inappropriate questions! Some things are beyond us, beyond our understanding, and can only be accepted!'

'But how can we know for sure what God wants from us? That he wants anything from us? How can we know that the voice that speaks to us is not our own madness?'

'We know because we believe! That's all there is to it! For all that we are and for all that we have, we must be thankful to God. Without him we would not exist, we who are created in God's image ...'

'That's well and good, but there are some – not many to be sure – but some who believe that the mind of God is not necessary for us to exist. That we are what we are, in all our sad imperfection, because the cold laws of nature have spewed us forth – the laws of nature, which care nothing for man and have no conception of God or anything else and which, like automatons out of control, keep creating and grinding on in a void. And while we may believe that we are created in the image of God, in fact, we are nothing but grains poured into this mad machinery, of no more importance than animals or water or stones or stars. For there are some who are able to live without God, who neither dread nor fear the idea of a world that grinds on without meaning from beginning to end. And one fine day, these people say, which, in fact, won't be fine but bitter, the end will come and the machinery stop, because this is what the laws of nature want. Or, even worse, whether they want it or not, they will keep on mindlessly crushing the grains until they themselves collapse and disappear, with the world in tow, just as they once arose out of nothing ...'

'Utterly impossible! Something cannot arise out of nothing and vanish into nothing. It can't! It can't! It can't! There is no nature without God! God created nature, and nothing in nature happens that he himself has not ordained!'

'What about miracles?'

'Miracles are God's way of revealing his greatness to us, by inflating nature and giving it a little twist.'

'But what if there are no miracles and these are merely natural phenomena that seem strange to us because we don't fully comprehend them?'

'What if ... but ... yet ... still ... All these speculations – none of it gets you anywhere!'

'But some people live with the absence of meaning ... are able to live ...'

'But not for long! Because we will find them; we will ferret them out. And then we'll see how they sing and dance that tune of theirs in Spanish boots!'

'But what if the only reason we have God is because we're afraid? And it's only out of fear that we prattle on about how he created us, how he watches over us? And we do everything in his name because we dread the thing that might well be the truth, namely, that it doesn't matter if we are good or evil, that it makes no difference at all whether we exist or don't exist?'

'Silence! If you're going to blather on about this, keep your voice down. The walls have enormous ears with falcon-sharp eyes attached to them. It's best to ponder these things in silence ..."

In silence ... now let us think without speaking:

All thoughts we ponder deep in our minds and say nothing because we are afraid. We are afraid of the Creator, and even more afraid that there is no Creator and that all the stories about God are inventions by which our masters oppress us and, mainly, by which we oppress ourselves. We are afraid of everything – of nature, God, the count, the prince, the emperor, all those bishops and vicars, visitations, faith commissions, preachers, Leapers, Founders and mercenaries, as well as the Turks, natural and supernatural catastrophes and ominous astrological forecasts; we are afraid of foreigners, we are afraid of each other, we are afraid of our very selves ...

And now let us think and again speak out loud:

Worst of all is when you do everything, and do it exactly as God commands, and he still pays no attention to you. You ask, you beg, you grovel before him, but he just seems to close his eyes and shut his ears, and meanwhile some new misfortune befalls you and you haven't even recovered from the last one. And when there's a new catastrophe on the horizon, meant not just for you but for those closest to you, too, good fortune steers well clear, while those other people, who commit outrages against God's law, live in peace and stuff their faces, since, for reasons we can't comprehend, life delivers the biggest and juiciest cuts to their table. And we keep waiting and waiting, wondering what's going on and understanding nothing. Why do bad things happen to us, who are neither responsible nor guilty? Why does sickness spare them, who are the embodiment of human evil (if it really is human) and instead attacks a good husband and father, who toils from morning till night to feed his family? Why does it ambush the mother whose dried-out breasts are suckling her tenth child – a child that like six children before him will probably breathe his last not long after breathing his first? Why? Why do these things happen to us, who are just and honest, but to certain others never at all?

Living among the populace are certain individuals, and it's because of them that you have to be constantly on your guard. Things that apply to ordinary suffering mortals do not apply to them – and for several reasons. First, they suffer less than the majority. Second, the majority suffer precisely because of these individuals, who (and this is the third reason) make the majority suffer simply for their own amusement, doing evil to kill the boredom of their lives as merrily as possible. And meanwhile, honest people suffer because, sadly, by some inexplicable rule, righteousness and suffering go hand in hand, as the ancient Greeks tell us. But the populace knew nothing about the ancient Greeks, since what they needed to know was not much more than working the fields, raising livestock, making handicrafts and fabricating lots of ideas and theories that would curl their God's hair. If he had hair, that is, long grey hair, just like his beard, which is the way the populace imagined their God. But he doesn't have a beard or hair because God is a concept, which is something very few people thought in those days – or rather, God does not have hair or a beard for the simple reason that (and in those days only the very boldest people thought this, in secret) God ... simply ... does not ... exist.

There is no God – *nada*, as travellers in the past expressed it, who, fleeing the Inquisition in Spain, passed through these parts on their way to the Holy Land, but then they got bogged down in the Ottoman Empire, many of them in Bosnia. *Nada* was what the mercenary soldiers said in the Spanish tongue, coming back from the wars in Spain. The local populace, with sidelong glances at all these Spanish speakers, thought they were saying the Slovene word for hope. *Nada*, *nada* – always this *nada*. But it wasn't *hope* they meant, but *nothing*, which is what the Spanish word means. The few people who understood Spanish wondered if some words might not contain the hidden truth of similar-sounding words from other languages. If so, then *nada* – hope – is pure ordinary nothing, as it fairly often turns out to be in life. And to hope for nothing, therefore, is more realistic than to hope for something, because you won't be disappointed when your *nada* proves to be nothing more than a worthless piece of nothing. And *nada*, nothing, was all that remained to those whom the populace saw as guilty, who found themselves in the grip of the people's justice.

We have, to be sure, gone somewhat off track, but not astray. What we have said does, in fact, relate to those insidious manipulators mentioned earlier. The ones who look most innocent are actually the very worst. It is not easy to recognize them, for they disguise themselves in the skin of youth, or maybe the skin of old age, an utterly desiccated, wrinkled skin – since he doesn't choose the form of his appearance … Oops, we wrote 'he' – we are intentionally not writing his name, let alone pronouncing it, lest that pervert think too highly of himself. But if we had to write it – and there are some among us who can, although not many – we would never capitalize it; we'd write it all in lower case, in sloppy handwriting, and do our best to make it a disgusting scrawl … ughhh … aarrgh – he knows somebody is talking about him, he's kicking and stomping, so from now on we'll have to be more careful, think more slowly … We should zealously try to humiliate him with our scrawl. So, unless it's truly necessary, rather than saying his name, let's just clear our throats, cough, maybe whistle as we meaningfully roll our eyes, then spit out a juicy one on the ground.

All these catastrophes, all these vermin crawling out of the earth or tumbling from the sky, there must be a reason for them. We don't believe God would torture us right and left just because he felt like it – that he'd torture *us*, who every Lord's Day, even in thick snow or pounding heat, fly off to church – well, not literally *fly*, since we're honest folk and don't keep to hidden ways, let alone fly through the air like the ones we're talking about. No, our Creator is not, and cannot be, the one putting us through so many torments. We are devout people, so it simply cannot be God who is poisoning our lives so randomly, burdening us with so many terrible afflictions and punishments, which, considering the degree of our sinfulness, we do not deserve. We are honest folk who love God – we give to the Church whatever God demands, and what the count wants we give to him, and what the prince wants, the Archduke Ferdinand, we give to him as well, although we also keep something back from all of the above, since they ask too much from us. And besides all these, there is also the emperor above us, who is so far away we can hardly imagine him and we're only aware of his existence when we must render unto him that which is his. Which mainly means our lives, which the provincial armies throughout the empire enlist and send to war, the causes and purposes of which are unknown to us and don't really concern us, except when it comes to fighting our land's hereditary enemy, the Turks, who have been capturing, raping, pillaging and slaughtering us for some two hundred years.

Nevertheless, we have worked out methods for determining what is good and just and what isn't entirely that. On feast days we process around the church, staggering beneath a heavy banner, and venerate especially our Virgin, all the way from when she was not yet a mother but Mary Immaculate (to whom our church is consecrated) to when she became a mother and was finally assumed into heaven. A wooden statue of her, beautifully painted, stands on our main altar, while carved into the side altar is an image where Mary is kneeling before her mother, St Anne, and offering her a large white lily. In December, when it's cold in our province and our feet are sinking into snow or cold mud, we piously trudge to her shrine and, no matter if the weather is fair or foul, wrap our Virgin in pine needles and worthily venerate her, as good Catholics should, and on all her other feast days, too, we show her great honour. Mary the Queen of May we adorn with lilies of the valley, while she who was assumed into heaven by her son Jesus is presented with large roses. All this we do in humble faith, and we could list many other things, too, so it's hard to believe that God the Father would treat us like naughty brats. Sure, in a way we can understand that he might as a reminder send us hail or drought or freezing cold, but at most all three in one year. Everything else, however, and almost at the same time – dysentery, rats, snakes, the plague, the black pox, Turks, mice, ice storms, special levies and tributes – no, all these things coming so thick and fast, they can't be the Creator's doing. And if not his, then they can only be the doing of someone created by God who later went his own dark way. And he does not do these things alone, oh no, not alone, for in every populace somebody can be found – and it's usually more than one – who is willing to be his accomplice. Sometimes the entire populace will bow down to him, the way Sodom and Gomorrah did. But not us, we're not like that, not most of us anyway, although there are a few among us who are different, and not many of these are men, which means that most are women – young, old, some almost children – women who like nothing better than cavorting with him whose name we will not pronounce, since we all know who we're talking about. They're the ones you need to keep an eye on, observing their behaviour and habits, listening carefully to how they talk. Do they pronounce their words in a strange way? Do they keep clearing their throat when they speak, make peculiar gestures, purse their lips and wink suspiciously? You need to see what they're up to when they think nobody is watching. So it's sometimes a good idea to follow one of them – carefully, of course, so she doesn't notice that your eyes are glued to her back, and that's not so simple, since such individuals in particular have extremely sharp senses and are quick to feel it when somebody is watching them from behind and following them. This sort of awareness goes beyond human powers. And how could it be otherwise, when they have the help of somebody whispering in their ear, constantly warning them – which is why they're able to slink among us like foxes. When bad things happen, sickness or accidents, it's a good idea, too, to have a look around, go for a stroll at night near their dwellings and see if there's a light burning inside, peek through a crack in the window, press your ear to the wall and, later, ask the people who live with them a few questions, incidentally, as it were. Regarding health, for example, or the livestock, or the field: Are the crops doing well or not so well? Is there anything unusual sprouting up? Are they maybe having an exceptionally good yield this year, even though nature has ravaged all the other farms in the area? The family of the individual may not realize that evil resides among them, so if any of their answers seem suspicious, it's good to give them a hint, to wake them up a bit and get them on our side. Who better than the relatives of the depraved to keep track of the unusual activities and habits of these witches? And witches – *vešče* we say in our language – is just the right word for them, because at night, when honest folk are asleep, they fly around like moths (which we also call *vešče*). So it's for the welfare of the community to check regularly and see if there's any strange glow coming from a neighbour's yard or house, any strange barks, noises, commotion, anything that can't be attributed to people who always cross themselves before the crucifix and light incense on Three Kings' Day to expel evil from their homes. But what can we do when those other ones are not without power of their own? We can light incense and sprinkle holy water as much as we want, but sometimes nothing seems to work.

So why doesn't our beloved Creator deal with the lot of them in one fell swoop? We ask the priest about this from time to time. If anybody knows who is cavorting with evil, then surely it's God. Why do we honest people have to suffer to the end of our strength because of them, when the Creator could fry them all with a single look? Why do we have to deal with this, when instead we could be devoting our time to other things, to worshipping God and his Son and venerating the Virgin Mary? We could devote more time to working our fields and raising our animals, or, some of us, to our trades, or the more industrious among us, who sell produce, cloth and other goods to the nearby town, to our commercial enterprises. We could take better care of our children, making sure they are healthy and well-fed, since hungry children are no use at all. This is what we ask our priest, and then, since we ourselves have no book learning, but we're not dolts either, we wait and wait for the learned man to finally explain the things that are causing us no end of torment.

And our priest looks up at the sky, clears his throat and tells us, 'God is mysterious and beyond comprehension, even more so for simple folks like you. He alone knows what, if any, plan he has for you. And so, my children, you must be obedient. Not for a moment should you think of looking in rage at the sky and, God forbid, shaking your fist at him, because not even Job, when he complained to God ...' 'Job? What Job? He's not from our village!' we say, glancing at each other, but the priest snaps back, 'Job from the Old Testament, you stupid peasants, who was a Jew and grumbled at God, but it didn't help him, not in the least. On the contrary, God sent Job even more misfortunes so he'd come to his senses and prove how strong his faith was. So just you leave God alone. Do what I tell you, obey the Ten Commandments, avoid the seven deadly sins and in general try not to make God angry, since it's best he doesn't know that you exist ...'

'What are you saying? Aren't we part of his creation, too?'

'Well, at least don't remind him of your pitiful insignificant lives. Accept what life gives you, in all humility, without complaining or grumbling about it. When you're hungry, know that there's a full table waiting for you in heaven, and anyway, an overfed man is no good for anything. When you're sick, remember that there is neither sickness nor pain on the other side, and when the stench of rot strikes your nostrils, know that death reaps its victims only in this vale of tears, but after death there is everlasting life. So don't squander your opportunities, lest at the Last Judgement Jesus places you not on his right but on his left, and lest, at the very gates of heaven, St Peter boots some of you into seething cauldrons of scalding-hot fat. And as for the ones you've been asking me about, know that the flames of hell are waiting in constant readiness for them, like frothing maws, to grab them after death and burn them to a crisp.'

That's the sort of thing the parish priest fills our ears with. We ask him something, and he prattles on and on without ever giving us a straight answer. Did we go to school, or did you? we think, looking him up and down and saying nothing. It's true, we're simple people and we don't understand everything. Only a few of us know how to read, and they learned it from a different priest in a different, smaller church, who professes a somewhat different Christian teaching, and, if anyone stays on after the sermon, he tosses on the pew a few copies of Trubar's *Abecedarium* and *Catechism*, and they lick their fingers and move them slowly from letter to letter, and sometimes they sing something, too. And even if most us can't read or write, we're very good at arithmetic, which is a practical, useful subject, and anyway, what we know and what we can do is quite enough for us.

The parish priest may be our shepherd and we his flock, but that doesn't mean we're just ordinary sheep that the Church, counts, princes, stewards, tax collectors and parish priests can fleece any way they like. We might be meek, but beneath our sheep's clothing our blood can boil so we start frothing at the mouth, ready to attack. We need to be treated decently, properly, which the authorities don't understand, and the same is true of our town, which we call *our* town because it's the one nearest us and we do a lot of trade there, but the townsfolk just laugh at us and think we're ignorant yokels. But not only do we know arithmetic, and are quick at it, we're also quick at making connections between events, things and people and recognizing the root cause and meaning of something. It's true that in some cases we don't fully understand the cause, and it can happen that when we're speculating and looking for connections we make mistakes. But, since we have faith that God forgives our mistakes, we take a lot of things into our own hands without fear and asking God's forgiveness in advance.

After all, who says the parish priest is always right? What makes him more right than us? He tells us we're equal in the eyes of God – well, maybe he's thinking of the Last Judgement, we can't say, but we're not endlessly patient, and we often ask ourselves why we always have to be the poor wretches who get invited to the Creator's banquet only after death, while in the here and now there are half-eaten legs of veal and pork ribs falling from the count's overladen table, game meat, too, from game we're not allowed to just go into the woods and hunt for ourselves, since everything in the woods belongs to the count? And why does everything have to belong to the count? Game, woods, sheep, cows, pigs, fish ponds, quail, and us, too, the populace, while we're barely surviving hand to mouth, with our empty tables and louse-ridden mattresses, with maybe an ox for working the field, a goat and a sheep – cows are a luxury – and from all of this we are also required to set aside tax payments for the count, the prince, the Church and the emperor? We don't doubt that such is the will of the secular authorities, but is it the will of God? We're not so sure about that. And is it our will? Absolutely not! Why can't we be the ones who live in trepidation of not being able to squeeze ourselves into heaven through the eye of a needle? We'd much rather live with fears like that than worry that one day soon we'll have nothing to mix in the pot but water and air. We'd even prefer the priest's position, since he's well-fed and lives in comfort at our expense. He's got two farmhands who work the land for him and a housekeeper who, people say, works everything else. The question is whether *he* will be able to wriggle through heaven's gates, if only because the eye of God can see even beneath the blankets where the priest likes to dispense indulgences.

So we pay close attention to everything we hear, everything we see. And we see not only with open eyes, but, lying in our beds, we also see beneath the skin, as we sleep and dream. And what we see in our dreams is not by chance. Sometimes a person dreams things they'd never tell another soul, not even the priest in confession – that village blabbermouth least of all! Sometimes a person dreams horrible things, disgusting things, all of the deadly sins, each of the Ten Commandments broken – even if many of these things would never cross our minds when we're awake, for we know that just as we watch others, God, too, constantly keeps his eye on us and sees even into our minds, so we are careful not only in our speech and behaviour but also in our thoughts and ruminations. And when we dream such dreams night after night and wake up in the morning not rested but worn out, as if we'd been pummelled all through the night, then it's good to look around, say a word to someone, ask questions and chat with someone about what might be the cause. That's how it is and how it was, and that's how it will always be in our land, where we honest folk live.

THE SCAPEGOAT

And that's how it was, too, a few years earlier, when the populace made a certain widow the scapegoat for a number of seemingly natural catastrophes. She was known to brew concoctions from plants and animals, and people said she had brewed a young man into her concoctions, someone who had been coming to her place for months and then simply vanished. He wasn't the only young man who had got himself involved with the hag (which is what most people called her), who surely had her own twisted reasons for never remarrying after her husband's death. Indeed, it's quite possible that these reasons were somehow connected to the death that had suddenly and under extremely suspicious circumstances struck down her husband. The death was said to have occurred when he was on the privy, or headed there, which (probably not coincidentally) was in early autumn, when the woods and meadows abound with mushrooms along their margins, in particular the tender-fleshed parasol mushroom. But there are others, too: one that is very similar to the parasol, when it is still small and demurely closed, is the green fly mushroom (as it is known here), whose only good quality is said to be its excellent flavour, but for anyone who has ever tasted it, it was also the last flavour they tasted, for within days they had departed this world. Not unlike the way her husband departed the world. He was a miller, around forty, and a healthy, hard-working and honest master. But don't we say the same thing of everyone who dies, that he was hard-working and honest? People fear to speak ill of the dead, and not because God might hear but because the dead person might hear and, in fury at the gossips below, return to earth to make them shut their big mouths for good. Especially if the sinful soul is still wandering about, lurking in churchyards or dark, dank hollows, or on the riverbank, luring people into the water – a soul whose body was never properly interred and who is still waiting for someone to discover the now unrecognizable corpse and give it a decent burial.

And so people sang the praises of the late miller, who had crapped out his soul (so the story went that spread among the populace) – a soul very likely mixed with mushrooms remarkably similar to the delicious parasols, which in those days perhaps were not even called that but had an entirely different name.

As the priest intoned his prayers above the open grave and made the sign of the cross in the air, most of the mourners were glancing at the widow to see if she was sad enough, and sincerely sad, as befits a new widow. Did her breast heave with bitter sorrow? Was a tear trickling down her cheek? Or did her countenance possibly betray some other emotion? Well, not delight exactly – in such circumstances only a madwoman would display that – but, for instance, relief?

The thirty-five-year-old widow was, relative to her widowhood, too erect, not stooped enough, and her protruding lips were hardly pressed in woe but limp and relaxed. The miller's death had been no great loss for the village; there was another miller working there who was both easier to do business with and better at his job. What's more, people weren't afraid of him, as they had been of the deceased miller – even horses, which are sensitive animals, could tell he was a highly strung man, not to say a boor. But a community must have order. There are rules to be respected and customs to be upheld, which are well known and clear to the populace of these parts. And one such custom is that the woman is in charge in the kitchen, in raising and caring for young children, in looking after blood relatives and in-laws, and in various other tasks that hold the community together, but the public representative of the property and the house, even if it's just a flea-bitten cottage, is the master, that is to say, the man.

By the time the Requiem Mass was held, a week after the departed's death, a theory had developed which said that the miller had died a natural death only in so far as mushrooms are part of nature, and that the deadly recipe had been literally cooked up by the new widow. The miller's two maidservants, when cross-examined by the populace, did not have much to say.

'It's true we had mushrooms a few times in September,' the girls admitted and listed the different sorts, 'parasols, foxes, georgies, buttercaps, little doves and hoofs and claws and deadman trumpets ...'

'*What* sort of trumpets?' the populace asked in alarm.

'Deadman trumpets. That's what they're called,' the girls said, at once regretting that they had mentioned the mushroom's name at all. 'They're black and look a bit like they're rotting, but they taste good. Although it's best to use them as flavouring. You wouldn't cook them like you do parasols or georgies.'

'Well, maybe they don't taste bad but still, someone could probably get sick from eating them, couldn't they?' The populace had their suspicions.

'No, if they're fresh picked and properly dried and prepared, and if you don't eat them late at night before you go to bed, they're fine,' the girls replied.

'But if something has death in its name, it can't be entirely good, since that small piece of it revealed in the name would surely be fatal. Anything that has something bad in its name, especially if it's death, must be dangerous, and besides, deadly things have their doubles ...'

'But don't we all?' the girls asked.

'That's true. We good people do have doubles, who to look at aren't very different from us, although in truth they are evil. And various herbs, too, or *zeli* – a word that itself contains "evil" – *zlo* – as well as many sorts of mushrooms, which most people don't even know about and only a few can recognize – all these things can be very bad for you, fatal even.'

'But we didn't eat just mushrooms!' the girls tried to soften what they had said. 'We had lots of buckwheat and barley porridge and plenty of things we sautéed in fat; we wrung the necks of chickens, roasted dozens of trout and cooked up a whole bunch of carp. And there was no lack of milk and gruel, cheese and curds. We also ate cabbage and beans, kohlrabi and carrots and, of course, our daily bread.'

'What did you girls have to eat right before the miller's death? Mushrooms? And what did the mill hands eat? And *her*? What did *she* eat? And what was that story about her children? Or was it only one child? Well, we know about one child for sure. A few months after he was born – it's been eight years now – the miller's son, asleep in the crib, released a little trickle of blood.'

'Is that really true? How did it happen?' The populace looked at each other.

Indeed, it was true. And nobody knows why the child died. It was she who found him in the crib, already somewhat blue and rigid. The miller lost his head at the time, and whenever it flashed before his eyes how she had come to him pressing his son to her heart with a big black fly buzzing around the boy, he would always give her a few hard smacks. Where in God's name had she been? How could she have left her newborn baby when by then she had two maidservants to help her? So she didn't need to be turning the hay or whatever it was she was doing that day. She should have been looking after his son and nothing else, since when the miller grew old it was the boy who would take over the property and care for him in his old age, and in the end give him a decent burial.

At first there had been no son. There had been a daughter, who died the day after she was born. But losing a daughter is different from losing a son. A son bears the master's seed and carries the family line forward, while a daughter, except for helping her mother with the housekeeping, is nothing but an expense from childhood to marriage (if she doesn't make a whore of herself first), and to get rid of her you have to prepare a dowry, unless you hire her out on day wages when she's little. That son, the never-to-be future master of the property, had died suddenly in his crib, and a second never appeared. Well, there was another daughter, but she also died very young when a strange childhood illness was ravaging the region. A little girl in the village died, and her friends came to bid her a last farewell. She was lying in an open coffin on the bier. Her friends sat beside her, caressed her and wept, and, before leaving, kissed her cheek. A week after the funeral, at the Requiem Mass, there were whispers going around that these same three little girls were now sick in bed and that the barber, offering not a shred of hope, had told the parents to summon the priest. One of the girls was the miller's daughter, and he was shaken by her death. More and more he suspected that his family's misfortunes were no accident; death, after all, doesn't just come and strike down for no reason everything that's his. So he started looking around, watching for whatever, or rather, whoever, was destroying his offspring and bringing misery and death into his home – if he didn't do something soon, his property would remain without an heir and eventually pass into the hands of strangers. In such situations, even a daughter is welcome: someone marries her with her dowry and moves in, and with the arrival of the bridegroom the name of the house – which went back to God knows what ancestor – does not change.

For the first time in years the miller shed a tear. He took a few kreutzers from his purse and set off to the inn, where he replayed all his troubles, at length and with much repetition, for the company assembled there.

'You're right,' they said, patting his shoulder. 'Someone is doing this to you on purpose. We'll track them down together. And, since we're not animals, we'll report them to the authorities, and they'll be judged strictly and fairly. Maybe someone's jealous of you because you're a miller and make a good living for yourself and your family. Or maybe they're jealous because you're a handsome fellow and in good health. Or maybe they put it all together and came up with the following plan: The miller is doing pretty well for himself with his business and everything he owns. Still, it will be hard to cast a spell that damages his body – he's strong as an ox – but it might be fun to take it all away from him, then we could find another way to finish him off.'

But who could have such a motive? The count and the authorities, right up to the highest power, would have gone about it differently. Nor did either of his brothers have a motive – the older brother had been impaled by the Turks in the Battle of Sisak in 1593, while the younger, who had mental problems and lived off his charity, would only be harmed by the miller's death. So who, then?

'Well, there's one person in particular who would profit from such wickedness …'

'But do we need to say who? To say it out loud?'

'No, no,' the miller said, holding his head in his hands.

'So you know?'

43

'Yes, but please don't say out loud what I dread the most – that night after night I am lying in bed with a murderess, and whenever I sire an heir, or fine, an heiress, she kills them, one by one.'

'So you thought it might be her?'

'Didn't you?' The miller glanced at the men around him.

'Yes, of course. And really, who else could it be?'

The miller drained his glass and hurled it to the floor, as if to say, that's exactly what I'll do to her; I'll smash her so hard she'll fly across the floor and blood will flow.

'You're right. She's your wife, and you can do whatever you want to her. And we'll support you; we'll testify that you caught her murdering your children and she tried to kill you, too, deviously, from behind, which is hardly surprising since she's a woman, but at the last moment you turned around and dealt her a deadly blow with your arm.'

Yes, yes, that will be best for everybody. The damned witch! It's not easy getting rid of these evil women.

The populace loves children. More precisely, the populace doesn't like people who don't like children. This has nothing to do with sentimentality, which would require you to hold them in your arms, cuddle them, spoil them with the kind of protective parental love people would know how to show centuries later. The populace loves children because children are the vessels for the seed by which humanity continues into the future. Children are entrusted with the mission of carrying on our traditions and customs, so the more children the better – that way, the populace reasons, we have a better chance of not simply vanishing. What if there's a terrible plague or some other disease that wipes every last one of us off the face of the earth, as if we never existed and meant nothing at all? Well, our Creator would know about us, but down here on earth nobody would be following our traditions and taking care of our farms, taking care of everything we had made and that, unfortunately, couldn't take with us after death – debts, diseases and other troubles, of course, we would gladly leave behind in this world. But there would be nobody left to look after our graves. They would soon be overgrown and, a few decades later, cows would be walking and crapping on them, and a few centuries later new settlements would rise on top of our bones, populated by strangers with none of our blood and none of our customs; they would be living on top of our bones, and their lives would have no connection to us.

The same thing, however, must have happened to the people who lived on our land before us. They weren't Christians like us. They had their own gods, customs and traditions, and they carved them on their tombstones, which not long ago the river disgorged. An entire grave-yard opened up right here among our houses, yawning graves filled with grey bones in our kitchen gardens and fields, and we had no idea whose bones they were or what all those symbols and images could mean that were chiselled into the stone – oh, they must have lived very well, lacking nothing, to make such tombstones. But what about us? How can we sleep peacefully and be fruitful and multiply on top of an ancient graveyard, which is probably haunted, too? Because there are no crosses on these graves. One of the stones has strange spirals carved on it, while others have weird horses with long fishtails, and fish, too, which maybe are not really fish but dolphins, as we were told by some merchants from Trieste who have been living in our prov-ince – they used to watch them through the window, in the Gulf of Trieste, leaping in unison out of the water, and their faces were so adorable, like some sort of merfolk.

'So,' the populace asks themselves, 'are these the same mermaids that galley slaves talk about, who show themselves to sailors, sing to them and drive them wild with their firm breasts when they lift them-selves above the surface of the water, although from the waist down they're no different from cold, scaly fish?'

'No, no, no,' the Triestine merchants reply. 'Dolphins are wonder-ful, good creatures, who often circle around castaways and swim with them all the way to land. They are such incredibly magical animals that the ancient peoples would depict them on tombstones as guides who lead the departed to the realms on the other side, along with hippocamps – those horses with the fishtails.'

Such things are terribly confusing for us. We've been here for-ever, well, almost forever, and as natives we enjoy certain rights that foreigners don't have. But then the river floods or a ploughman digs too deep and the ploughshare gets bent when it strikes a stone, which turns out to be a tombstone from some past people we know nothing about except what the Triestine merchants tell us.

So would it be a good idea, we ask ourselves, if we collected all those bones scattered in our gardens and washed and buried them? And, if so, then where and how? Since they weren't Christians, we can't bury them in our churchyard, and to bury them just anywhere doesn't seem right. Because maybe these graves are from before Jesus was born. And we're not sure if Jesus, by dying and rising again from the dead, saved people who lived before him or if people who follow a different religion also go to heaven after they die. We're terrified that these disinterred dead people will start haunting us out of anger, that they'll wreck our barns and ruin the crops in our fields and kitchen gardens, that they'll infect us with ancient diseases which lingered on after they died, and that they'll turn up in our bedrooms and come out of our bureaus and chests and grab us with their skeleton arms.

'But the world didn't begin with you, or with Jesus, or even with the people who came before you. The world has been around – oh my goodness! – a long, long time. It says that right in the Bible,' the Triestine merchants tell us.

'Oh, really?' We look at them and remember that they are foreigners, and odd ones at that. 'You should be careful, you Triestine merchants. How do you know so much about these old tombstones? We find that rather suspicious.'

'We have lots of these stones on the coast, as many as you could want – stones from the pagan Romans,' they reply.

'What do you mean, *pagan* Romans? Rome is where the pope lives!'

'Well, there wasn't always a pope in Rome. And there was Rome before there was a pope; it's where the pagan Romans lived, and they only gradually became Christians, sometimes by force.'

And then we look at the stones and at the bones scattered around. We look at the old walls, and the strange spirals and circles, and the old ironwork, spears and jewellery – which our women would gladly wear around their necks if they weren't afraid it might hold some ancient spell. And it's all terribly frightening and makes us sad, too. Because what if something horrible did happen to us, and our entire village suddenly disappeared? What would be left of us? Our houses, which are mostly wood, would sooner or later rot away, same as us, and that goes for our crosses, too, since we don't have money for chiselled tombstones that last forever. Everything we have, even our own life, is temporary and fragile. So will the people who come after us, those foreigners, be as confused as we are? Will they wonder what they should do with *our* bones if, by chance, the river disgorges them? 'Who were these people?' they'll ask. 'What were they like?' Sure, we'll be up in heaven with the blessed, but what about our bones? Nobody will know anything about our customs or how we lived.

'And, more to the point, what about you, Triestine merchants? Where do you bury *your* dead? That time when one of your sons unexpectedly died, you didn't bury him in the village churchyard or even a little further away by the prayer hall. Instead, very quickly, the day after he died, you took him over there, to the remains of those other graves, where nobody has buried their dead for decades – that graveyard without crosses, where nobody ever brought flowers either; all they did in the old days was put little stones on the graves.'

'We mean you no harm,' the Triestine merchants tell us. 'We've even reduced our interest rates for you – it's disgraceful how low we made them. And with the edicts on trade routes for wine and other goods, you wouldn't be able to sell your crops and products to Gorizia and Trieste, let alone farther into Italy, without us. And you couldn't get goods by other routes, from west or east, or, if you did, they would be a lot more expensive.'

'That may be true, but we're warning you all the same: don't you dare try to confiscate our houses if our business dealings go belly up and we can't pay our debts on time, and with interest. Don't even think about it, you … merchants, whoever you are and wherever you're from.'

But that's not all that nags and gnaws at us. We're also very worried about the lack of order in our community. We're worried about women who first turn wanton and then try to conceal their expectant condition from everyone else, even from their own husbands, their lords and masters. If they're not able to beforehand, then right after the birth they do away with the child in secret. An honest man has no idea what women are capable of doing. Supposedly, in the olden days in our country, if it seemed like a family couldn't feed another child or if a child was born weak and sickly, they'd get rid of it. But such times are long past. We don't put an end to newborns; much less do we let the women who bring them into the world make decisions about the child's life. And they're not alone in their secretive doings. It's well known that midwives have ways of making sure the birth never takes place. What things don't you find in their cupboards? All sorts of potions and creams and different implements, which they use to prevent the child from happening. Of course, we never summon the physician when a woman is giving birth – we can't afford him – or even the barber, who is a man and knows more about straightening bones than delivering babies. And some young married women, despite their strong and healthy appearance, are simply not able to bring a baby into the world, no matter how much everyone wants it. In such cases, it's good to make sure there isn't some midwife involved whose little tricks are helping the woman deny offspring to her husband, the man with whom she is obliged to lie down in bed and do, or let be done, what is expected of a wife.

So a wife still in her youth might wait patiently for her husband to slip on the ice one winter's day and crack his head, which then becomes hopelessly inflamed, or for some illness to come and claim his life while leaving hers untouched, or for mushrooms to start sprouting one August day, the kind of mushrooms you have to know how to recognize, how to pick, prepare and serve them, all without forgetting which plate is whose.

This last possibility, the populace speculated, is what most likely befell the miller. Not only was the widow left with a small bit of land and the mill, but, in addition to the mill hands and maidservants, she began employing young men who at home had never displayed any joy in work but now, on her property, picked up their tools with such zeal that the very sight of it was suspicious. They never complained about the weather and worked no matter if it was foul or fair. They never complained about the money, but rose at the crack of dawn, left for her fields, worked until evening and returned home late. From time to time, a young man might not even come back the same day but a day or two later, and a few never came back at all. More precisely, two never came back, but two is enough for it to seem like it might become a habit and, with repetition, a rule. The populace gave the situation some thought and resolved to act decisively.

Even before the two boys' disappearance, the family of one of them took their son firmly in hand. They waited just long enough for him to put the money he had earned at the widow's down on the table and then interrogated him, reproaching him for doing day-work for strangers, and especially for a woman who was a stranger.

'How is she a stranger?' the youth defended himself. 'She's from our village.'

'Even so, she's a stranger to us, and, besides, there's plenty of work for you to do at home!' His loved ones persisted, attacking him with the subject of his betrothed, who, they said, was in tears from feeling abandoned and in doubt. And then they told him about the various rumours and promised to do everything they could to protect him.

'Protect me from whom?'

'From her! So nothing bad happens to you, too – so you don't, for example, eat those deadman mushrooms.'

The other boy, too, felt the pressure of his relatives, who even threatened to register him with the provincial army and arrange it so he was conscripted as 'every fifth or third son'.

But clearly the families' intervention was too late. The hag's spell had already seeped into the boys' brains and entirely corrupted them. They came home less and less and then vanished into thin air. One of them, apparently, later sent a letter from somewhere, which the priest read to the family (what, the hag even taught them to write?), and that, basically, was everything that spread among the populace – and stories spread among the populace like mushrooms in the undergrowth.

'There must be some perverted reason why she didn't remarry after her husband's death and instead squeezed the life juices out of her young helpers, who rather than work at home preferred to till *her* fields, which, amazingly, haven't suffered any terrible catastrophe, unlike the fields of us honest villagers. People say she can predict the weather and even command it …' Thus the populace aired their thoughts, first refuting and then justifying them again.

'But astrologers predict the weather, too …'

'Sure, but they're educated; she isn't.'

'That's not entirely true. There was a preacher here who taught her how to read and write; he was even ready to marry her …'

'So the preacher is why she poisoned her husband?'

'No, no. The preacher came later, after her husband was well and truly buried, if not rotting in his grave like those black deadman …'

'Trumpets?'

'Those deadman trumpets, which trump even from the grave?'

'But maybe it wasn't them.'

'Not the trumpets? Not the preacher? Not her own hand which did the poor fellow in?'

'But the miller, that greedy miser, wasn't a poor fellow; he was an oaf!'

'Yes, he was an oaf. But in the end he was a poor bastard who lived with a witch and didn't realize it until it was too late.'

'And later, too, when he was already in his grave, she used witchery to get whatever she wanted. If she needed rain, it rained. If she wished ill on a neighbour, his cow got sick and died. That big storm – you remember that storm, which blew off half our roofs and there was lightning everywhere and five people were killed? – well, it was obliging enough to skirt around her fields and property.'

'That preacher of hers – and we let him give us communion, too, back then, since back then we took communion from every priest who came around – well, people say he'd have married her if he hadn't gone off to Württemberg because the authorities were chasing him and the other preachers out of the province. So why didn't she go with him?'

'If he had taken that witch with him to the German lands, she would have met the same fate she can expect here with us. All we Christian peoples have at least one thing in common that sets us apart from the Turks and the Jews – we know how to detect witches and have methods for getting rid of them. Which is why, after all these disasters from the Evil One, we had to take action and denounce her.'

At the castle, the criminal judge had the screws put on her in a dank dungeon so that, with the help of a well-tested method based on pincers for peeling off fingernails and a device for breaking and crushing limbs, she would spit out the truth and confess to the commission in attendance that the devil himself had minted the coins with which she paid her young workers and that it was not just labour she extracted from the youths but also, by means of spells, their life force and will – so that once and for all they could get rid of the hag and be free of the shackles of her inhuman power.

'What happened to her husband and to those two boys will happen to you, too,' parents warned their sons. 'One night you'll go to bed and close your eyes and never open them again, because the moment you shut your eyelids, her hornèd companion will come to your bed and suck your soul out through your guts or through your head and then dance off with it to his dark kingdom. Your heart and any other useful organs, even your brain, she will boil up and mix in with those trumpets fried in pig's fat; then she'll go on poisoning honest men and leeching them to herself so they can't resist, can't escape from beneath her wings – yes, yes, her wings – for we know what the old hag binds them with. No normal man would desire her unless he was drunk. Nobody wants an old woman for that sort of thing. Old women are good for doing the cooking and watching the children – the grandchildren, to be precise – and for certain kinds of farm work and craftwork, but for the things we healthy men so badly want, old women are no good. We know this because we're strong and healthy, since everyone knows that men don't age as fast as women. We men aren't old until we're very old, while women get old even when they think they're still young.'

'That's true. We women know this, both those of us who are young and those who are her age or older. Only we know that we're old, while she lives as if she's young, as if she wasn't one of us. And she isn't!'

'But even though she's nearly forty, she has hardly any grey hair – now, why is that?'

'It's because of dyes made from stones and plants,' she stammered in the dungeon as they popped the joints in her arms.

'And why doesn't she have bristles on her chin like we do? Why does her skin look so young?'

'It's because of creams made from herbs,' she cried out in the dungeon.

'Sure, herbs – *zeli* – but if you stir the word a little, the way she stirs those potions of hers, you get …'

'Oooh! Nothing good, nothing good at all! Pure evil – *zlo!*'

During the interrogation, a physician, using a kind of metal horn, examined her for traces of the devil's seed; he determined that, in his expert view, such traces did exist in a certain greenish, odoriferous mucus. Another piece of important evidence was the birthmark below her right breast. Such a mark is a third nipple, by which the devil imbibes the witch's milk, which is full of the potions witches pour into themselves so they can suckle innocent young boys and bewitched men. The commission – which besides the judge also included the physician and other honest men from the district – ruled that they had all the evidence they needed to show that the woman was the devil's whore and that everything she had done was with the sole purpose of leading faithful Christians into sin and bringing harm to the community, even if that meant harnessing nature with the devil's help and turning its forces against them.

The witch was given one last chance to prove her innocence. They hung a stone cross around the neck of the shattered, broken woman and pushed her off a bridge into the river, following the common-sense logic that, if she was guilty, she would sink with the stone. And if, on the contrary, she rose out of the water with the stone still around her neck, it would mean that supernatural forces were at work. But such forces could be either good or evil. For them to be good, however – in the event that the witch did not sink with the stone – an additional miracle must occur in which the grace of God was evident beyond all doubt. What sort of miracle this might be was difficult to predict, but, when it happened, the shining glory of the Holy Spirit would make it clear to all who were present.

But it didn't happen. There was no miracle. The body of the accused sank.

As the bubbles rose to the surface from the bottom of the river, fewer and fewer each moment, a snake appeared out of nowhere. As it swam across the water, its body formed beautiful arcs and it kept its head upright above the surface.

'Look! Look!' somebody shouted. 'The evil spirit has swum out of her body!'

'You mean it survived?'

'The devil must have summoned it to himself. Now that it can't live in her body any more, the witch is of no use to it. Such forces aren't so easily destroyed. You can only destroy the body in which they sojourn. You can't drown them; you have to burn them to death. An evil spirit is only destroyed by fire.'

After the little snake swam beneath the bridge and then, miraculously, never appeared on the other side, which the populace took to mean that the hornèd one had pulled it down to hell, a gentle white swan appeared on the river – a female swan, they decided, since it did not seem brawny or aggressive, the way only male swans, protective of their offspring, are known to be. She was swimming peacefully towards the bridge, but then she turned around beneath it, unlike the snake. After that, she started swimming back and forth on the water, occasionally looking at the people watching her, who were waiting to see what would happen.

'If that's her soul, it's not very small.'

'Well, her body wasn't exactly tiny or delicate.'

'What will happen now? Where will the swan go?'

'She'll probably fly into the sky.'

'But look at her eyes! Why is she looking at us so strangely?'

'What do you mean, strangely?'

'As if her eyes were a little moist.'

'Well, she's swimming in water, and there's lots of moisture in water.'

'No, no. That look of hers ... Doesn't it seem like her eyes are accusing us?'

'Accusing us of what? Does anyone really believe that we didn't do the right thing? After all, the witch confessed!'

'But who wouldn't confess after such brutal torture! Maybe she only confessed to make the pain stop ...'

' ... and knew that God would see her heart and in the end separate the truth from the lies and take good care of her when she died ...'

'Well, even if that's true and there is some sort of reproach in the swan's eyes, there's also mercy and forgiveness there. If in anything we did we were by chance mistaken, she – that is, her soul in the form of the swan – forgives us our mistake, for we acted in good faith, believing that what we did was just, honourable and good.'

'So you think there could also be mercy and forgiveness in her eyes?'

'Oh, yes, no doubt about it. Now her soul will swim off peacefully, up or down the river, to the other side, and if she herself is forgiven – since she's not going to the other world completely sinless; nobody, except the littlest children, is without sin when they go to other side – then if we did make a mistake, God will forgive us, too.'

'But we didn't …'

'Of course we didn't, but still, just in case …' This is what the populace was thinking as the swan spread her wide wings, toddled across the water on her red feet and, after a few yards, lifted herself off the surface and rose into the air; then, circling twice above the bridge, she flew into the distance, an ever smaller dot on the horizon until she completely vanished.

'Vanished just like …'

' … like everything vanishes.'

If God had wanted to, he could have prevented her death – a few isolated voices quietly speculated. But clearly, he had decided to snatch the poor woman from her torturers' cruel hands and call her to himself, and then, years later, he would send that community of purportedly honest men and women a punishment they would be talking about for a long time. A punishment designed not to look like a punishment at first but like yet another opportunity for the populace, led by the secular and religious authorities, to go completely wild, and then afterwards they could celebrate their methods from the pulpit and boast of what had happened as a lesson to sinners far and wide. But perhaps the worst part of the punishment was that nobody ever fully agreed on what had actually happened during those cruel events. For the story, which was told in various versions, sounded completely unbelievable – almost as unbelievable as the atrocities that came centuries later would have sounded to people back then.

SUDDENLY, A CRACK

The ancient trees passed by slowly by, to the syncopated rattle of the carriage, and with them the fading old world was also passing, a world regarded as dismal, shadowy, dark-sounding, with other onomatopoeic tones as well. But the world of the churches could in truth (and truth was in the crosshairs of the little churches), even during the day, no matter how blazing the sun, produce such an oily-black gloom that the ancient trees, even at night when the churches slept, were unable to thicken it in the dense mesh of their branches. Not for a very long time now. What had existed centuries ago in the places where the little churches were standing (for among these same long-lived trees there had been other temples) many people knew, but no one could say for sure. So stories circulated, cruel fables and fairy tales, woven by memory and the imagination in who knows what proportions.

Sunlight bounced off the amethyst that was set in a massive gold ring, which bit into the fleshy ring finger of a left hand. The hand opened the carriage curtain slightly, clenched and unclenched its swollen arthritic joints a few times, and rose to a mouth, which let out a harsh little cough through pursed lips.

'Have you been in these parts before, Julian?' the prince-bishop asks the young man sitting across from him.

'It's my first time here, sir,' the travelling companion replies.

'Do you think it beautiful?'

'How can it not be? Nature is the work of the Creator and is beautiful everywhere,' says Julian.

'Well, nature is generous in some places but bleak and harsh in others; in some places it is soft and round but in others sharp and jagged. And here it is round, so it's as if we're sitting still, while hills and wonderful little valleys roll past. Don't you agree, Julian?'

'You are right, sir.'

'But Julian, never let nature become aware of you. No matter how wonderfully beautiful it might be, it can bristle in an instant, fly into a rage, thrash the trees and shake the earth until in places it opens up and swallows innocent and guilty alike; it can move mountains, flood valleys ...'

'But if such be the will of God ...'

'Yes, of course. The will of God. But nature can rage even without God willing it. Some say nature can go mad entirely on its own and that there are those who can make it serve their most wicked intentions ... Do *you* believe this?' the prince-bishop asks.

'That's what people say ...'

'But you, Julian, you have an open mind – do you think it likely that a person can have so much power that he's able to interject his sinister will into the laws of nature, to cause drought to appear and dry up what has been sown or make a cloud come whirling down to earth and flatten everything in its path?'

'It's said that there are people who can do such things, but not ...'

'But not on their own? Of course not on their own but, it is said, with help from another quarter. And that is why we are here, Julian – for we know how to judge whether such people, people with extraordinary abilities and dark intentions, are hiding among the populace ...'

'Yes, sir.'

'So do you believe that we are indeed able to divide the wheat from the chaff? To detect rye mould even in new sprouts?'

'Such is our task ...' Julian replies.

'Yes, our task. But a person has some tasks he is sure he can do and is called to do and others which he may feel have nothing at all to do with him. Well, let's put that aside for now. Why don't you take a nap? We have a great deal of work to do in the next few days,' the prince-bishop says and looks out of the window. 'Not long ago certain writings came into my hands in which the author argues that nature behaves solely and exclusively in accordance with the natural laws created by God, and that miracles do not exist and are, in truth, merely unusual phenomena which the finite mind of man is unable to grasp. It may well be true that miracles don't exist, but that nature never goes mad, well, I'm not convinced. One moment it can be benevolent and calm and the very next run riot, whether in keeping with nature's laws or opposed to them – and the very same thing can happen with human nature. Everything is fine and lovely and then, in a single moment, it skids off track ... What do you think, Julian?' the prince-bishop asks, turning again to his travelling companion. 'Ah, yes, enjoy your little catnap. When we arrive in the late afternoon, there will be a splendid supper waiting for us. Count Friedrich is a generous and hospitable man, and he will be so even more when he hears of the nature of our visit. Hahaha, wherever you turn there's always some sort of nature. Just one more task and my work is done. Not here ... somewhere else ... not as I am now ... merely similar ...'

Slowly, in a syncopated rhythm with the accent on the first, fourth and sixth beats, the carriage moves across the softly illuminated land-scape, as the hand sticking out of the window alternately squeezes into a fist and opens again. The person opposite, his lips slightly parted, is asleep and gently snoring, unaware, the prince-bishop thinks, of how quickly his tender, youthful features will be wrinkled by time. He is unaware that man's greatest enemy is not the swarm of dark forces hurtling through the Holy Roman Empire and flying across the Hereditary Lands of Inner Austria; he is unaware that man's worst enemy is not the devil, who leads men and women into temp-tation and sin, nor the Protestant preachers who serve communion in both kinds, nor the Turks, who for centuries have been striking terror into the hearts of the local populace, nor the naked madwomen who rub their exposed loins on broomsticks, nor the simple folk who cook up potions and creams for the populace, who can't afford even barber-surgeons let alone real physicians. No, man's greatest enemy is time. Tossed into its mill at birth, man kicks and struggles, but all in vain. Against so powerful a foe the battle is lost before it starts – the cruel and voracious god Chronos, who sires children only to chomp them in his teeth and, in the end, whether that end comes quick or slow, he grinds them up, swallows them whole or spits them out. And young Julian, his milky-white hands swaying in the lap of his cassock, is still at an age when he believes everything is possible. Such as changing the world for the better. Yes, passion, visions and utopias – these, too, are part of that ancient deity's dark plan, which is why a creature flush with the juices of life is so succulent, right until the juices start drying up and disappear altogether. And in the end – well, what about the end? Most people believe that only the body ends, after which there is another life. Some, a very few, believe that everything begins and ends with the body. We know what we believe – or could it be the other way around, and we believe what we think we know?

The carriage trundles on in its syncopated rhythm across the landscape, above which a dark cloud is gathering, the prince-bishop notices. Is it going to rain? he wonders as he leans slightly out of the window and knocks on the carriage frame, but the shape of the coach-man sitting in front of him makes no response. It might rain, the prince-bishop thinks, or it might not. Does it matter? Did he ask the question for no particular reason, without really being interested in the answer, without thought? Is there not, perhaps, in many questions, statements and comments a certain automatism unworthy of man, who as a spiritual creature is supposed to possess free will and the ability to make his own decisions? Are we really little more than those mechanical toys that move their limbs, the ballerinas that spin when you wind them up, the metal dogs that wag their tails and yap at you?

He sticks his arm out of the window, extending it all the way, as if trying to check for rain. *As if*, he thinks, but is this really what I wanted to do, or did I stick my arm out and only then, after a delay, realize something that my body knew before me? He rotates the palm of his extended hand towards himself and feels the cold spray of tiny droplets in the air. He then spreads his fingers apart a little and is looking through the gaps when, suddenly, a strange scene appears to him. A miracle, perhaps? What would those writings say, which he had recently been reading?

In a meadow in front of the forest's edge he sees an enormous stag with many-branched antlers wobbling forward as it tries with its last strength to keep its balance. The animal falters as its knee gives way and then, with all the strength it can muster, lifts itself again, and then again it lurches forward and rights itself, with ever greater difficulty. Had there been a shot? He had heard no bang. But there is a dim buzzing noise that pierces the landscape, a sound he does not recognize. Thunder, maybe a storm, he thinks, when he notices that the landscape is bathed in a metallic light, no longer orange but a dense saturation of dark red and leaden grey. What a sight! What a magnificent, majestic sight! And suddenly, the moving canvas of the landscape is rent, and in the distance, beyond the little forest in front of which the animal is struggling, he sees something else he does not recognize. A different or at least an altered landscape has folded itself through the opening. In the distance he sees something that is very likely a city, with strangely tall towers – thick rectangular boxes jutting into the sky. The landscape is criss-crossed with thin lines – could they be wires? He leans out of the carriage and is looking up at the sky – a roaring vessel is flying overhead (could that be the sound, the strange thunder?) – when, alongside the carriage, on the grass next to the road, a vehicle appears that is neither a cart nor a carriage, and lying beneath it, to judge by the shoes, is a man, while a girl, standing, leans against the side of the vehicle. She is dressed indecently, in short trousers that reveal her firm, sun-browned thighs, and her fair hair spills luxuriantly over nearly naked breasts. She sees him; from the way she looks at him there can be no doubt that she sees him. When, in a strangely protracted moment, the girl strikes her hand against the frame of the vehicle, the sound reverberates metallically. She quickly bends over, her hair cascading across the silver metal, and calls for the man to look, since she's not sure if what she is seeing is real. She then jolts back up and covers her face with her hand; the prince-bishop can't tell if she's laughing, astonished or terrified. 'I'm losing my mind again,' the girl says, 'I'm losing my mind; it's been a while, but I'm getting that feeling again.' And she removes her hand from her face, which now beams with a euphoric smile. Is that sweat, or are tears trickling down her cheeks? the prince-bishop wonders. And as the supine male figure wriggles out from underneath the vehicle, the scene starts to flash and fade and flicker out, just as pictures will flicker out on other canvases centuries later. 'All these colours, these intense colours and sounds, it's like they're flowing through me and I am in everything and everything's in me,' he hears her say, and the scene vanishes.

What was that? Did you see what I saw? he would like to ask Julian, who is still asleep. The landscape had been rent in a single moment, and a new one, entirely altered, had lain open before him. Had he slipped into a parallel world and become wedged between two overlapping times? There is no more buzzing, no more unfamiliar sounds. And when he looks back at the edge of the wood, there is no enormous animal there, only a brown spot, which becomes smaller and smaller until it vanishes. He brings his right hand, clenched in a fist, up to his face and presses the violet amethyst against his lip. What was all this? Where did it come from? Did it take shape in my head and merge into the landscape, an optical illusion appearing as exterior reality? Or did that other landscape pass through me in some duality of time and two temporalities collide? … Did my present and the present of the fair-haired girl divide into the future for me and the past for her? Did time crack open and eternity pass through it, folding into something alien to itself? Do miracles really not exist? Are there only laws of nature ordained by God? Maybe … but maybe not. And the girl – didn't the girl think she was going mad? What was this? Did I fall asleep? Was it a dream? Did it even happen?

DOUBT ... DOUBT ... DOUBT ...

What's hardest is spotting those who, to look at, are no different from us at all. They do nothing in particular to make you suspect there's anything malevolent in their activities. On feast days they crawl on their knees around the altar, just like we do, and give to the Church no more and no less than we do ourselves on average. And when they go about their work, they do it no better and no worse than we do. They resemble us in every way, but in reality they are very different. Just because you find them in bed at night when you go to their house in secret and peek in, it doesn't mean they are really lying there on the mattress. Not entirely. Because while their body is sleeping, their soul could be flying off to one of those ill-famed places where people of their ilk like to gather, people who do us harm and make our lives much worse than they could be otherwise. They're the ones, the ones you can't catch in the body, who are the most powerful of all, since they're able to travel outside their body. They don't need a broom, and they don't have to depend on creams that make their body float above the bed or above the floor. Their body can sleep – and be truly asleep and even snoring – while they fly around doing evil. Even when they do quite ordinary things, it doesn't mean they're all there, working, their soul included – since they can make it so their body moves and speaks while their little soul is somewhere else entirely.

So how can we prove that such people are part of the evil host, when there's no external evidence or facts?

Well, it's hard, but not impossible. For where there is faith, everything is possible. The one who truly believes won't be taken in by some evil spirit, no matter what alluring enticements it tempts him with. Who among us is devout and who isn't – here there can be no doubt. For wherever doubt appears, faith starts leaking out and has to be verified. Where doubt bores a hole, evil makes its home.

Verify. Verify. Verify.

Apart from God, nothing is entirely certain. For there are forces that don the likeness of God, that disguise themselves as God's voice and God's words ...

'But what does the voice of God even sound like?'

'It is terrible, true and strict – but beyond this, it is hard to say anything about it. God usually speaks to man not through the ears but through the heart, and what he says we first feel, and the moment we feel it, we understand. And whosoever's heart is uncorrupted, pure and clean, he will know when it is God speaking to his heart and when a worm is residing there. For a worm bores holes in the heart, that tender yet strong piece of meat which is the nest of the soul. The worm burrows in, nibbles at it with sharp teeth – and it hurts, oh, how it hurts, when the worm sinks its teeth in the heart and with every nibble gnaws off a little piece of faith and hollows out a place for doubt. Doubt. Doubt. Doubt. Always and everywhere, that accursed doubt.'

Report from the Patriarch of
Aquileia to the Holy See

In the period from April to the middle of September in the year of Our Lord 1596, I performed visitations in the Hereditary Lands of Inner Austria. Let me begin by noting the appalling disorder rampant throughout the provinces; I have, therefore, instructed the lesser Church authorities to deal quickly with this issue using all available means. I should stress that this will not be easy: so widespread are the various excesses that in some places they have become entirely routine practice. In the present report I do little more than mention certain forms of heresy, which require a separate discussion. My visitations, performed over a period of several weeks in the company of a retinue of aides and soldiers, were primarily intended to verify the work of the Catholic clergy, in which endeavour I frequently encountered heretical apostates and, at times, in place of God's shepherds, people of entirely different professions and profiles.

The first stop on my visitations was a place called Mirna – a small settlement, more village than market town, even if it does pride itself on possessing market rights. As our road took us past the local church, dedicated to St Andrew, I ordered my retinue to stop. It was a Sunday, and I expected at the very least to see fresh flowers on the main altar. But that the House of God should not be open on the Lord's Day – this was something I had not foreseen! After the soldiers dismounted and I set off for the church with my aides, it became clearer with every step that God's house was poorly cared for. The main door was densely overgrown with a vine that would surely have been ripped off the wall had one of us even tried to open it. I asked my retinue how much time it would take for such a plant to grow so profusely that it covered the entire front of the church, but they just stared at me stupidly and mumbled something. I mention this only because it shows how little I could rely on my retinue for the explanation of natural phenomena.

Surely one of them might have known something about a rather common plant and its cycle of growth. I stress this because, among other things, the description of the visitator's tasks includes elucidating natural, unnatural and supernatural phenomena, so I advise my successors to include nature experts in their retinue. The Dominican and Benedictine monasteries have been educating such people for centuries; the universities and Jesuit colleges also do this quite thoroughly.

Let me continue. When we were looking at the grounds around St Andrew's Church, I saw further that some kind of red weed had grown into the cracks in the walls and that swallows were chirping noisily in a nest above the church door; they had clearly not been disturbed in a long time. Indeed, our visitation may well have been the first disturbing event to upset the swallows' peaceful existence in Mirna (whose very name means 'peaceful'). Someone proposed that we break into the bolted church, but instead, I ordered some soldiers to brace their backs against the church wall and lift me up so I could examine the interior. I saw nothing. The glass in the window was so filthy I saw only my own distorted reflection. I gave orders to proceed to the presbytery, which, as my retinue informed me, was next to the main square.

We knocked at the door and an elderly woman stuck her head out; she was so surprised and frightened to see me that she could hardly answer my questions.

'The priest's not here, not at home ...' she says in a trembling voice.

'So where is he then?' I ask.

The woman looks left and right while making some sort of grunts, until finally she tells me that he went out a little while ago.

'Where did he go?' I ask.

'To give a peasant extreme unction ...'

'When do you expect him back?'

'Hard to say, very hard to say.' She is more and more flustered. 'Up there, that's where he's sick, the peasant,' she says, pointing to some hills in the distance. 'The road gets bad sometimes, really bad, and Father has to move the rocks and stones all by himself. It's hard work, can take hours, the whole day even ...'

'But up there, woman, where you're pointing, I don't see any village. Men!' I say, turning to my retinue. 'Do any of you who are younger than me, with sharper eyesight – do you see a house in those hills, even some ramshackle hut?' They shake their heads as the woman visibly cringes from her lies and embarrassment.

I tell her we will wait for him.

'What, now?' she asks, alarmed.

'If we had arrived yesterday, we would have waited for him yesterday, but as we are here today, we will wait now,' I reply.

'Inside? ... Or here, outside?'

I had no patience left to communicate with this thick-headed underling, so I ordered my aides to do whatever they could to make us comfortable. There was a fine garden behind the house with some wooden benches, above which a leafy grapevine was growing, filtering the sun's hot rays.

'Why are there so many benches here? Does your master sometimes perform Mass outside? Since he apparently doesn't do it in the church.' I look at the woman.

'There's nothing I can tell you, not a thing,' she says and is so uncomfortable she has almost glued herself to the door. The soldiers start arranging themselves nearby, and I cannot help noticing that three or four of them, leaning against the trees, have their eyes fixed on the presbytery's upstairs windows and are elbowing each other in the ribs.

'We are your guests, and guests should be accorded hospitality, all the more so as we're here on official business,' I tell the woman, who is now nervously swinging her arms back and forth. I basically had to force her to bring me and my immediate retinue something to eat and drink, which I did, not because we were rather hungry but because I am curious about the economic standards of our parishes. She hurried into the house, and I signalled one of my men to follow her. And it was a good thing I did, for he caught the woman at the back window telling some boy to run off somewhere and say such-and-such. My aide interrupted her and sent the boy to us so we could keep an eye on him. As I and my immediate retinue sat in the shade sampling the meat and the different kinds of bread and drinking water and wine – which was actually not bad, a white wine, probably a muscat – four male persons appeared in front of the house; they kept glancing back and forth between us and the upstairs windows of the presbytery.

'So where are the four of you going?' I ask, stopping them.

One of the men answers casually, 'To have one.'

'What kind of "one"?' my aide asks, and another man volunteers that it could be long or short but it had to be a wet one, at which all four look at each other and wink.

'But why come here, to the priest's house?' I ask.

'Because it might be the priest's house, but it's also a winehouse and a whorehouse, too.' Now they all burst out laughing. They are speaking German, and I can tell at once that they are Lutheran riffraff from the north. I signal my soldiers to surround them.

'Why? We haven't done anything wrong,' they protest. 'We're foundrymen from up north, and since it's the Lord's Day we thought we'd unwind a little and maybe have something wet.'

I told the soldiers to seize all four and lock them in the pigsty – on charges of vulgar behaviour, inane blather and disrespect for Church authority. And I again noticed that even more of the soldiers were glancing at the upstairs windows, where heads could be seen moving around.

Eventually, a large cart with a yoke of oxen rumbled into the garden; it was sagging under the weight of heavy oak barrels. A short and stocky middle-aged man jumped off and gave orders to his accomplices to roll the barrels off the cart. When he glanced over at the house and saw us beneath the pergola, and then saw the soldiers interspersed among the fruit trees, beads of sweat broke out on his bloated, well-fed face, which reflected the sun with an oily gleam. Although it was only noon, the day was already mercilessly hot. With his hands on his backside, the newcomer – obviously the parish priest and master – staggered over to us uncertainly and greeted us with 'Praise Jesus!'

'You must have drowned the entire village in extreme unction,' I say, 'considering the size of the barrels you just rolled off that cart.'

The man shifts his feet nervously and gives me a hangdog look. I gesture to my men to open the barrels. No heretical books, just wine – white, semi-dry, good quality, they tell me. The priest keeps looking at the house, where his housekeeper is now lurking behind a window downstairs, while upstairs, braids of black, brown and red can be seen bouncing in the windows.

'When was the last time you served Mass in the church?' I ask, peering intently at the priest.

'Oh, I do it regularly ...' he replies.

'Lying is a very grave sin, priest!' I say sharply. Generally speaking, I have to repeat the same words regularly on my visitations. The priest bores his eyes into the ground, as I rapidly question him. Without prevaricating he confesses that he only gives Mass on feast days and at funerals (no one has been married here recently), that he operates a winehouse in the presbytery, and that there are three or four girls in the upstairs rooms who augment his income. When he has confessed everything, he repents. I prescribe him penance, which is partly of a financial nature, and one of my aides collects that part on the spot.

That very day I had my suffragan write an order for that parish priest to be replaced by a new and well-verified member of the clergy.

We left there in the early afternoon and reached the village of Selo before nightfall, just as the bells were ringing for vespers. As we approached the Church of St Barbara, patron saint of artillerymen, builders, stonemasons and miners, I gave the order to stop so we could examine first-hand how God's word was being proclaimed here. I was worried our resplendent entourage might attract too much attention, but such considerations proved groundless. There were only a few old women sitting motionless in the church, some of them, in the front rows, mumbling out prayers, while from the pulpit their elderly priest was similarly mumbling. He did not even notice us entering, and when we went up to him after the service, he asked, squinting in the direction of St Barbara's statue, if we had come to make an offering for the Mass or wished to purchase indulgences, or perhaps one of us was getting married and wanted the banns announced at next Sunday's service, or would we maybe like to bury someone? ... I could not determine if he was merely old or demented, drunk or stupid, or all of the above. When I told him who I was and explained the nature of our visit, he still understood nothing. In that same order, the one just mentioned, I commanded that he, too, be replaced by a younger man.

We went on to a nearby manor where we had made arrangements to spend the night.

Here resided an old knightly family of the lower nobility, loyal to the prince – so I was briefly informed by the aides who had organized the logistical aspects of my visitations. Their ancestors, as well as those living here now, had distinguished themselves in a number of battles, especially the noble Sir Georg, whose sabre felled two dozen Turks in a single day at the Carinthian Gate in the defence of Vienna in 1529.

When we reached the courtyard of the hunting lodge and the family caught sight of us, they did not know what to do. 'You're here already? How did you get here so soon? We thought you were coming tomorrow!' they cried, as panic spread. The staff bustled nervously past, avoiding our eyes, while we climbed the stairs to the main hall, which was decorated with the horns and antlers of hunting trophies; on one wall, a fat boar's head stared out at us. As we took our seats at a round oak table, I heard tense activity in the courtyard, a swarm of male and female voices, despite the closed windows. When I motioned to my men to spread out in the courtyard and sniff around a bit, the lord of the manor, the noble knight, stood up anxiously; it was obvious he did not know how to prevent them from doing what they had been told.

At first I thought the knight was trying to hide Protestant preachers, but it turned out to be more complicated than that. We had indeed announced our arrival for the following day, explaining that on this leg of the journey there were no decent lodgings to be had – which was not entirely true. We could have stayed at a nearby Carthusian monastery, which, I am told, has degenerated in every respect and will soon be dealt with separately. In any case, we had long had this knightly manor in our sights. But how can a visitation be successful if those we visit are given time to prepare, to conceal all suspicious indicators before we arrive and in a single day transform themselves into honest Catholics? To make a long story short, it turned out that certain apostate madmen – Baptists or Anabaptists, or just plain Leapers – were holding gatherings at the manor. When I pressed our hosts a little, saying it would be better to divulge everything straight away rather than have us discover whatever was happening for ourselves, the knight flared into a rage, and I at once understood that he had very likely himself dispatched at least half the carrion, antlers and wild boar hanging on the walls of his lodge. Glassy-eyed, he started telling me in a high, piping voice about some apocalypse in which the world had recently almost been destroyed by a huge comet, which would have wiped the greater part of sinful mankind off the face of the earth. If this did not happen, it was thanks to them: their prayers and rituals had altered the comet's course so it circumvented the earth.

'Prove it!' I say.

'My faith is my proof,' he replies.

'But yours is not the true faith!' I persist.

'It's truer than yours!' he counters.

'Have you personally jumped through fire and hurled yourself around?'

'All that and much more,' he answers without fear or shame.

What should I do now? I asked myself. I had no idea if these Leapers were violent, if they were capable of breaking into our rooms while we slept and slaughtering us like pigs.

As I was tired, I decided that we should spend the night here anyway and gave orders for the door of the bedroom allotted me to be well guarded and also told my soldiers to position themselves around the bed. Every castle, manor and lodge, after all, is riddled with secret doors and panels, and rooms contain various chests that can be opened by levers invisible to unknowing eyes.

'You can be perfectly at ease,' the knight says, as if reading my thoughts. 'You are safe with us. We condemn violence – unlike you papists, who persecute people whose beliefs are different from yours; you blow up their temples and prayer halls and drive Lutherans from their homes.'

'Oh, interesting. You've taken up with the Lutherans now?' I look at him in surprise. 'From what I know, if the Lutherans had just a little more power, they would accuse you and your sort of witchcraft and, sooner than us, have you roasting on those hot coals of yours, where you leap about and flagellate yourselves and fornicate with each other.

You are naïve if you think you'll find allies in the Protestants! They have their own vicious quarrels as it is. The Lutherans get on the Calvinists' nerves, and those Flacians get on the Lutherans' nerves – in fact, those ignorant Flacian peasants get on everybody's nerves. But you and your sort are just plain deluded pagans – that's something even the Lutherans, Calvinists and Flacians have got right.'

'So you think there's no paganism among you papists?' The knight looks at me with contempt. 'What about that bishop of yours who says Mass and consecrates Capuchin monasteries wearing a scarlet vestment made from the military coat of the Beylerbey of Bosnia, Hasan Pasha Predojević?'

To this charge, I honestly confess I had no answer. I have no explanation for the coat of Bishop Thomas Chroen, which this Flagellant, Leaper, warlock, or whatever he is, served up to me. I know that in distant lands people can go so far as to use the desiccated heads of their enemies in their rituals, or they ride with them in parades, a fate that tragically befell Herbard von Auersperg and Friedrich von Weichselberg, high commanders of the Military Frontier, whose embalmed heads were impaled on long spears and carried alongside Ferhad Pasha when he marched triumphantly into Constantinople after his victory at Budački. But the Ottomans are famous for being arrogant, cruel savages. Thomas Chroen's coat, of course, is not in the same heinous category, but in my view, it is no less pagan than the superstitions of the populace. I mention my humble opinion in this report so that I might receive your clarity as to how I should reply in the future when heretics start waving Chroen's Turkish coat in my face.

Otherwise, there is not much we can do at present to the nobility, a point I wish particularly to underscore in my report. The greater part of the nobility is an obstinate bulwark for the new religion and religious apostates, sheltering preachers so they can go into towns and even into villages, despite such activities being strictly forbidden there. From what I have heard, the political hotheads in our nobility are to be tolerated for some time yet. But let me note that among the voices of those present that evening, who kept glancing at the windows of the Knights' Hall and had quite clearly been preparing some barbarian rite, there were people of various ranks and tongues. It was only our own presence that evening which prevented the sectarian ceremony from taking place. I heard not only German and Slovene being spoken, but I also detected, in the cacophony of voices, echoes of Italian and even Bohemian (unless perhaps it was Croat), which means they are all organized and joined in heretical alliance – consequently, we need a less subtle plan to control them. With heretics of this sort the simplest thing would be to deal with them at a single stroke and accuse them all of treason, even if such types of heresy are rare in our parts. Superstition and witchcraft, on the other hand, are everywhere, and special visitations are required to uncover and combat them. For both the one and the other, I suggest that the quickest way to dispose of them is the tried-and-tested method of inquisition.

We set off the next morning, and at our first stop found a priest who, it turned out, could neither read nor write. At our next stop, we faced what we most often encounter on these visitations: church altars originally dedicated to a saint are now empty, lacking even a statue of the Holy Mother of God, while Mass is offered in not one, but both kinds. Catholic teaching is virtually unknown among the local populace. In all such places, therefore, I announce that I will give a sermon and order everyone who lives there, regardless of estate, age, sex or mental soundness, to present themselves in two days' time at Mass, where God's truth will be waiting for them – and I add that all absences will be individually investigated and penalized. These educational measures are effective. The people assemble for Mass. At first, they look uncertainly at the altar and struggle to keep up during prayers and find the right words, but then I bring out a well-proven recipe: the Virgin Mary, whose cloak is large enough to cover and protect all of sinful mankind. I speak of her miracles and appearances, which I illustrate with an example that never fails. I tell in my sermon how, far, far away, on the other side of the great sea in New Spain, the Virgin Mary once appeared to the Indian peasant Juan Diego – Johann in German, Ivan in Slovene. 'Behold,' I say, 'even to them, to those red-skinned people across the ocean' – colourful adjectives can be used to good effect, as vivid images are the best way for the populace to understand our stories, and the more exaggerated they are the better; playing on feelings brings results, while abstract reasoning, categories and concepts are nuts too hard to crack, given the populace's limited abilities – 'even there, far away in the New World, which is so very different from here, a world where forests are so thick that once you set foot in them you can never find your way out, where animals are so wild and dangerous they make our bears and wolves seem like cats and dogs, where snakes are so venomous and vicious they no sooner see you than attack you from pure beastly malice – yes, even there, where until recently no one had ever heard of Jesus and people worshipped their own vicious and venomous animal gods and offered to them not only crops and farm animals but people, too – yes, yes, living people!' (I underscore the point.) 'Even there the Virgin Mary appeared, to lead those people out of darkness, to pluck them from their savage, bestial kingdom and bring them to the kingdom of the spirit.'

I know that at this moment my proselytes are not thinking very much about the kingdom of the spirit, for they still have hissing snakes and roaring beasts before their eyes, and most of all they are wondering about those cruel Indian sacrifices. So I go on to paint them a wonderfully vivid picture that is based on what I have heard from Dominican missionaries and the Jesuits. 'A young maiden, or several, is dragged by force,' I continue, 'to the top of a high stone pyramid not unlike the wooded hills around here, or children, even infants, are carried up, or adults are herded in droves, regardless of sex, if they are enemy captives, and there may be dozens of them, per-haps hundreds. The chosen victims are stripped of their clothes, their bodies are painted with blue dye and they are placed on the altar. The high priest runs his eyes from north to south and from east to west, invoking his cruel deities, then, turning his gaze to the victim on the altar, who in mortal terror is held in the firm grasp of his assistants, with one hand he plunges his dagger into the victim's breast while with the other he pulls out his heart, which for a time is still alive and beating even after the body is dead. There is so much blood it streams down from the altar in specially made grooves; if there are several victims, the entire pyramid is swimming in blood.'

Whenever I include such Indian adventures in my sermons, whether we are in a church or in the open air, in springtime or winter, I feel the atmosphere thicken. People unwittingly grab at their hearts and cross their arms over their chests, as if trying to protect themselves from my words, which, like the red man's weapons, might do injury to their bodies. The populace never tires of these crude, cruel pictures; they hold a special magnetism for them, so even if their ears are hurting, they want more and more. 'Now do you understand?' I ask, looking at them severely. 'Even to these savages, whose only excuse is that they never heard of Jesus, for they never had the opportunity to hear of him before the Dominicans and Jesuits arrived – even to these savages Mary is ready to appear. Even to them God is merciful, although he could strike them all down in one fell swoop. As they performed their bloody rituals, a volcano could erupt nearby and pour down on the pyramid and the dwellings below it; or in the midst of their slaughter, the earth could shake so horribly that everybody, altars and pyramid, too, would go tumbling in all directions far and wide. But no, Jesus is merciful and sends his mother to open her cloak of infinite mercy wide above them and let these cruel creatures know the sort of wicked delusion they have been living in and to tell them that from this time forth they, too, who have been languishing in the sin of ignorance, will have the opportunity to repent, that Jesus is ready to forgive all their sins if only they begin to live as true Catholics, with salvation and everlasting life awaiting them after death.

'So now do you at last understand,' I say to the populace, 'the infinite mercy of God? And if such is his mercy to Indians, how much more will he be merciful to you, who were once of the true faith but were led astray by lying Lutheran lips. At this very moment, you have the opportunity to repent sincerely of your erring ways and sinful lives and return to the flock, to come home. O people,' – by now they are quite moved by such powerful images – 'do you think all the attacks of plague, not to mention other diseases that have been assailing you for centuries – do you think they are without cause or purpose? Do you think stopping the Turks would truly be so impossible if it were God's will? Are the Turks not perhaps a warning to you, so you realize at last the terrible error of your ways?' At this point, some clever Dick usually pipes up with something like, 'We're not the only ones starving because of the Turks – Catholics are, too!' to which I reply, 'How could it be otherwise? It's not just Lutheranism that is sinful; there are many other heresies, too, lurking among the people. And now do you at last understand why you are afflicted by these terrible misfortunes? So start by walking the Catholic path, and if you are faithful and disciplined in following Jesus and the true doctrine – because it's not so very easy to understand the Gospel! Oh, no! Otherwise, Jesus would not have chosen Peter from among his disciples and said, "Peter, you are the rock on which I build my Church," and he would not have handed him the keys to the Kingdom of Heaven – so if you walk the Catholic path, things will be better for you than before. I know the preachers taught you how to read a little, but for the right understanding of the truth it is not enough to move your finger from letter to letter. As difficult as the Gospels are, the Old Testament is even more confusing, and some of its stories must be interpreted with particular care. Especially Genesis, the First Book of Moses, from the time before God gave Moses the Law. Because I don't want to hear some patriarch tell me again, "What did I do that was so wrong? Lot's daughters, too, had a drink with their dad and then, before the eyes of God, they all got drunk and fooled around, and the two girls gave birth to their own brothers."'

By this point the populace has considerably softened. People are looking at each other, looking around, glancing a little at the altar and then staring at the floor, lifting their eyes again and looking at the side altars, as if checking to see if there might still be a statue or picture of a saint somewhere, if maybe not all of them had been demolished. And then they look at each other again and slowly start nodding their heads, as if to say, you know, he's right. 'Because I admit it,' somebody speaks up, 'the last time the plague was ravaging this area, we never closed the Gospel for a second – I mean the one in our own language, in Slovene. Our eldest son would turn the pages backwards and forwards, and we'd repeat after him what he was reading, all the while caring for our sick and then carrying out their bodies. We also fumigated with sage and juniper, but things kept getting worse, so one of us went into the cellar and pulled out the little statues of St Roch and St Rosalia, and we lit candles to them, fumigated the house with dried herbs and brought gifts to the saints.'

'What? What do you mean, gifts?' Such foolish, superstitious customs always infuriate me.

'Well,' they start squirming, 'so the saints will hear us and grant our prayers.'

'And if you didn't give them these stupid gifts but only the pure prayers of your hearts, you don't think they'd listen to you?'

'The plague takes such a terrible toll. When plague comes, death strikes us down left and right. Sometimes it lays waste to almost an entire village, sometimes, literally, to entire families,' they answer me.

'But what sense does it make that instead of praying humbly before the holy images you perform magic and witchcraft? Things that Leviticus, the Third Book of Moses, strictly forbids!' I scold them.

So sorcery, too, will have to be beaten out of their heads, but only when we have brought order to our priestly ranks and dealt with the Lutherans. Personally, however, I think this step-by-step strategy is too slow and we would do well to consider introducing foreign approaches and have more frequent witch trials. Witchcraft is like the plague. And just like physical plague, plague in the soul cannot be driven out by fine words. It would be easier and more effective to use force. This, as well as the concrete methods of implementation, deserves our careful consideration.

In most cases, my visitations have turned up the following: Catholic parish priests who are poorly educated and often drunkards, many who are vile whoremongers, quite a few who are senile and incapable of the least intellectual thought and, most importantly, none with the passion or fervour needed to kindle the true Catholic faith in believers. For if you want to inflame another, you must yourself be on fire! This sort of passion have I rarely found within the Catholic ranks, so I have ordered the replacement of a number of the Church's representatives. Some parish priests, during my visitations, promised and swore on the Latin Scriptures that henceforth they will more zealously undertake God's service. But sadly, I find that the Protestant clergy are better educated and more fervent in their religion, and so, too, are their sheep, who are regularly sheared by their shepherds and taught not only Lutheran bleating but even some meagre reading skills. The Protestants' sermons, too, are more colourful in comparison with what is mumbled out by our Catholic sluggards. I am, therefore, delighted by the great attention that is being paid to the homiletic training of young Jesuits – and more recently Capuchins – for with the proper rhetorical skills they will easily prevail over the preachers. We must not forget that what the populace loves is drama, not bland parables delivered in drab churches plucked of every adornment. The populace loves chubby cherubs and their supernatural hornèd adversaries; they like being terrified by angels with swords and spears and demons with protruding tongues, and then, if they but slightly shift their gaze, being instantly comforted by the benevolent eyes of a saint with a white lily in his hand – but for every care and misfortune, the best panacea of all is the Virgin Mary.

The populace does not like abstractions; they prefer simple, solid things. And if, by rough estimates, at least half of them turn to superstition and witchery, they are also disposed towards eccentrics, who in these parts present themselves under such names as Founders, Leapers and Ecstatics. From what I have learned, there are not many of this last group in these provinces and they do not arouse the sympathies of the people, who think them too fanatical if not outright deluded, so they are neither popular nor dangerously widespread.

To conclude, allow me to offer yet another example of something we encountered time and again on our visitations. If the parish priest is not very old – by which I mean the forces of nature are still pumping blood to his head, although it often does not get there as it is first trapped in his loins – the presbytery door will be opened by a girl, and not some skin-and-bones waif either, but a wench with ample curves who is suggestively dishevelled. When we ask to see the priest, she almost always becomes flustered and evasions follow, which amount to: 'The master is sleeping'.

'What do you mean he's sleeping? The sun is approaching midday!' I say to her sternly.

At this question, the girls usually say the priest had been out during the night giving someone extreme unction and so was lying in a little.

'Extreme unction or not, it's time he gets himself out of bed!' I persist. 'It may happen that a man stays up all night, but it's only sluggards who rise when the sun is pouring out its light on the earth and, in the summer, its heat, too.' I don't mince my words.

Then we push the girl aside and march into the presbytery. We open all the doors, while she fidgets, probably wondering how to slip away and warn her employer about the intruders. 'What! Isn't this where he sleeps?' I ask when we open the door to a room with a bed that is completely untouched. By then, almost all the girls are blushing, but some are still spinning lies in their heads, hoping to cover up the priest's shame.

'Didn't you say, girl, that the priest is asleep? So where is he sleeping?' I give her a merciless stare.

Then the stories vary: there was such an infestation of fleas in his bed that she had to do a total disinfection, or the bed needed a thorough cleaning after the cat crapped on it, or the priest's willy got leaky from a bloating in his belly so, again, everything needed washing.

'How's that? A bloating in his belly? You foolish woman, are you sure the bloating wasn't below his belly?' I am unsparing with her. And all the while we're tramping through the presbytery opening doors. But not to overplay it, I should say that, in fact, there are not very many doors to open and only two or three rooms, and in the smallest one, the attic, a modest, quite ordinary little room, we find a modest little bed and, in it, the parish priest, who is either snoring deeply in his drunkenness from the night before or our noise has wakened him enough for him to be wondering, underneath the goose feathers, how he can escape from this embarrassing position: whether he should slip out of the window (which is not a good idea, since our soldiers are waiting for him below) or hide in a chest (which in a room of this size is either non-existent or too small for his portly parochial body).

'Whose room is this?' I ask the girl.

'The priest's,' she mumbles.

'The priest's? Does he have two bodies so he needs two beds?'

'Well, everything here is the priest's,' many of them will say, now with an adorable sniffle. As the priest is pulling on his shirt and trousers, you can see something bouncing beneath his big belly (nearly all the whorish priests are thickset, while the older, more senile ones are gaunt), the very thing that, according to the girl's testimony, gets bloated at night.

'This is a vile and wicked sin, priest, especially for one who is wed to Holy Church!'

And now the excuses start – 'Really, you've got the wrong idea!' – which are soon followed by begging for forgiveness. At my relentless gaze, every one of them is ready to confess and repent, after which come promises to be different from now on and explanations that he has nothing to do with the Lutherans, whom he truly despises, and if you don't count this one sin, of which he is profoundly ashamed, he has no other blemishes on his conscience, and that he serves Mass regularly, on Sundays and feast days, and no longer preaches in Latin but, as is recommended, in the vernacular, that is, in Slovene, which everyone can understand. Finally, he ends by begging me to let him stay here, in this area, in this village, in this house, and not to send him away.

'Fine,' I tell him, 'but under one condition: get rid of your maid-servant and hire a new one, a woman at least twenty or thirty years older. So what do you say?' I look him up and down, and he assures me, promises me, that he will, and then we say farewell and leave. It's best not to look back. I know very well that as soon as our carriage and retinue and soldiers disappear on the horizon, the priest will wipe his sweaty brow, take a few deep breaths and then call for the maid and everything will be the same as before. Harder! We must be harder with the populace! And I do not mean just the peasants – they are the easiest; they have nothing to bargain with. No, the Provincial Estates are the problem. The towns, too, are a major problem, but the biggest obstacle is the nobility, who are blackmailing the prince with their Lutheranism and making the right to their religion a condition for collecting and transferring taxes and special tribute payments for the defence against the Turks. We must be harsh! Harsher measures are needed with them, otherwise the provinces of Inner Austria will splinter away from us and the Patriarchate of Aquileia will crumble before our eyes. Disunity brings neither order nor strong defence. And only order ensures prosperity and peace. So harder, harsher!

*

Georg Stobaeus von Palmburg, Counsellor and Bishop of Lavant, in a memorandum dated August 20 1598, to the Prince of the Provinces of Inner Austria, Archduke Ferdinand II:

Neither hard nor harsh – everything may be arranged without an inquisition. The war with the Turks means that Catholic reform must begin without delay. Among the many in Styria, Carinthia and Carniola who have publicly and freely declared themselves Lutherans are those who hold some of the most critical posts in the army and administration. When it comes to religion, nothing is more harmful than armed force. The archduke should decree that all his vassals must be Catholic. Whoever does not submit to this command must leave the provinces. To achieve this more easily, the archduke should, if necessary, win his subjects' devotion and filial love with cheap food. Let the reform begin in the capital of the Inner Austrian provinces – in Graz. Protestant preachers should be forbidden to preach and banished from Graz under penalty of death, and the town should be guarded by Catholic soldiers.

Fears that the reform might trigger violent resistance are baseless. We must not forget that most of our Lutherans are real cowards. A sermon or two, threats of banishment and the forced sale of property at below cost, and they will soon admit the error of their ways. Let us proceed slowly and persistently, and the populace will gradually see the light. Not many will be willing to stake their lives on God and their world views and even fewer to renounce their comforts. This is where they live, this is their home; anywhere else they would be foreigners. And being a foreigner takes courage – courage most of them do not have. So let us be neither hard nor harsh, but slow, persistent and gradual, and we will succeed.

The Miraculous Fount

For generations, the ice-cold water that welled up among the birch trees behind the church had been considered to have healing powers. In that very spot, Mary had supposedly appeared to a certain maid-servant a few decades ago and told her that the liege lady, whose loins had remained inexplicably closed, would be swaddling a child the very next spring. Those were her exact words: next spring your mistress will be swaddling a child. As this seemed an even greater miracle than Mary's appearance, the maids and servant girls who were more closely acquainted with the situation in the fiefdom quickly spread the news around. The more coarse-minded girls wondered if the lady of the castle might not miraculously see someone whose seed she would deem suitable, which would be worth carrying for nine months, along with the sufferings of pregnancy, an ordeal that, given her position, was unconditionally expected of her. Just as builders build, wood-workers work wood and lutenists lutenize, so castle ladies give birth to feudal heirs. What's more, Mary was said to have pointed at the fount and told the maidservant that her lady should go there to bathe, as the water was healing and therefore holy as well.

'Go there alone?' the other maids asked the witness.

'Alone. That's what Mary said.'

'So the count doesn't need to go, too?'

'Mary never mentioned him.'

If Mary mentioned only the lady and not the lord, it follows that the child would not necessarily be his, the other maids said, with meaningful smirks and lewd glances at the stable boys and young farmhands, two of whom turned red from embarrassment. Mary must know, they gossiped, since musicians were on the road again, and in these parts they always stopped at the castle. Whenever singers and instrumentalists stayed at the castle, many dames and damsels, and maids and servant girls, too, would start to glow and, regardless of station or age, even blossom, including the lady of the castle, who adored the lute, the queen of all entertainment. From late spring to early autumn lutenists and singers would gather at the castle. Some of them were quite awful, others superb. And the best of them, fully conscious of their talent, were able to create a certain magnetism around themselves, which was irresistible to the majority of people, who lacked such noble, elevated gifts. More than a few ladies, in a state of aural abandonment, were prepared, for a single ricercar, to throw away everything they valued as women, their dignity in particular, as well as other, similar attributes, whose worth, in extreme situations, could vanish in a flash.

As the lutenists plucked the strings with their elegant, slender fingers, they would gaze into the eyes of a chosen lady, or gentleman, in the audience. Then they would look away and glue their eyes on the instrument, with subtle feeling massaging the strings strung tautly across its softly rounded pear-shaped core; then all at once they would again gaze at their victim, whose eyes would mist with excitement and whose vision would soften and blur, and a thick liquid would course down the spine from head to solar plexus and, on its way to the heart, spill into the abdominal cavity. There was no joking with these lutenists, who were known in feudal courts as masters of ceremony and masseurs of souls. When sorrow needed to be kneaded from a soul, when a heart wanted soothing or the black bile that makes a person prey to melancholy, if not madness, had to be staunched, the lutenist would press just the right string, and its sound would flow through the diseased point or organ, reverberate with it and bring the listener relief.

The noble countess, a great admirer and patroness of music and of those who composed and played it, would also organize a less selective programme for the populace, who elicited a less refined and more uninhibited music from the performers. These were not first-rank musicians, but second-class entertainers. At times they were not even lutenists but strummers, accompanied by various percussionists and singers (female ones, too) as well as pipes and horns – all things that could be carried in the same cart in which the musicians travelled from place to place.

These musicians (in the view of many, plain vagrants) would play an evening or two for the populace, who took the precaution of stocking their bellies with food and drink, the latter distilled in their own cellars. And when music combines with the reverberations of brandy, when the spirit is awash with spirits, good sense can soon break free of its bonds and people start howling and baying with frothing mouths, muddled and maddened, and in glassy-eyed, saliva-soaked lust have their way with each other. Since the musicians appeared in the greatest numbers on Midsummer's Night, after the first hay was gathered, the largest demographic increase in the populace would occur the following year at Eastertide – increases not uncommonly marked by a colourful range of physiognomies and complexions and somewhat unusual foreign features.

Something similar happened to the noble lord, who on Maundy Thursday acquired his long-awaited heir. Or, to be precise, heiress, of whom, as the years passed, rumours spread that, even before she took her first steps, her little fingers were reaching for the strings and she would rather cradle a lute in her arms than her rag dolls; that by the time she was really walking she could already strum a few chords and was singing before she was talking; and at the age of ten, it was said, she had even composed a few melodies. It was also strangely suspicious that, in a manner unnatural to her sex, the young Lady Agnes Hypatia was extremely fond of the fine arts and abstruse sciences, and when it came time for her to marry, she made it clear that she herself would choose her husband. Her father, the noble Count Friedrich, was pulling his hair out. Not only could he not hit the nail on the head in bed, he was none too successful at bringing up his daughter either – so said women who knew about such matters, at which remarks his noble lady would always smile enigmatically. It was curious that the daughter, like the noble lord, had green eyes and brown hair, while her mother's hair still gleamed with a warm honeyed radiance, and something of the count's features, too, might have been discerned in the daughter's face were it not that the young lady was unusually temperamental and bold-spirited – this more than anything else raised doubts as to whether she was truly the fruit of the master's loins.

But to shorten the story a little (which will not be difficult as it was, to be sure, not long), of the candidates for marriage, the young lady selected the man she thought least irksome, temperamentally most amusing and not at all ugly. Her father concluded that she had chosen a man who would neither impede nor restrain her passion for the fine arts, the humanities, natural science and spiritual beauty, whose priceless value lies in the fact that it serves no end and whose sole purpose is to offer an elevated spiritual pleasure to whoever can recognize it. But is it possible to divide the spirit from the body as if splitting firewood? This question only a very few considered in those days.

The bridegroom came from the knightly family of the noble Katzensteiners, known widely as 'the noble Cats', who operated as a harmonious clowder. The sons were famous for their fencing skills and nimble duels with bladed weapons. At chivalric tournaments the victories went as a matter of course to the noble Cats, who were also gallant, if not to an equal extent educated. As they were known to behave properly with women, the daughter's decision eased her mother's worries, but no one doubted that the young wife, in her husband's presence, would be the one who sharpened thoughts, tormented wits and, indeed, sparkled with wit herself.

The young lady, looking to foreign examples, had the idea of creating her own circle of talents and sages, starting, reasonably enough, with local scholars; she would have gone on to acquire better-known and more widely influential minds as well if her life had not fallen victim to that banality we call death. It came to her not in military garb, nor was there any epidemiological dimension to it: it did not lodge itself in her body, blacken her armpits and groin or produce oozing boils.

Hers was a lofty death. A pure death. One warm summer's day, the young lady, book in hand, was strolling by herself in the garden among the rose blossoms, which she loved above all other flowers. She was also fond of lilies, hydrangeas and oleanders, which, however, she knew were poisonous and so, perhaps, was also slightly repulsed by them. As she had done countless times, she walked along the garden paths lost in thought, this time with a book by the Renaissance philosopher Marsilio Ficino (or perhaps it was an ancient author); her brow was pressed into three furrows, as it always was when she was thinking at full power. In vain did the female members of the castle staff urge her not to frown, and generally to think as little as possible, so her face would not be prematurely etched in wrinkles or her soul filled with melancholy, as happened with men who thought too much about useless matters, things relating to various philosophies and alchemies, astronomies and mathematics. 'They are men, after all, while you are a lady,' they tried to persuade her, to no avail. But the wrinkles never formed, and she never succumbed to Saturn's gloomy influence, for on that warm morning, between breakfast and the midday meal, while engrossed in the study of life's fundamental questions, she suddenly fainted on the little path; perhaps she lay in the sand too long without help, or perhaps it would not have mattered if somebody had been walking alongside her and offered immediate assistance. There was no blood, no visible injury. The young lady had simply collapsed, and that same afternoon she expired in her bed.

Her mother did not consent to the physician's entreaty to let him examine her late daughter's body so he might discover the reason for her tragically abrupt and untimely death. 'Let's call it the will of God,' she told him. 'Nothing will bring my little girl back to life.' It did not seem very likely that someone could have poisoned her in malice, for, despite her intellectual caprices, everyone respected the young lady and loved her without reservation. Just as unlikely was the idea that she might have poisoned herself by accident, for she had met with the physician every week and, among other topics, they had discussed plants and toxins; she was also very careful and never attempted even the simplest alchemical experiments on her own. There had been no sign of illness before her death, nothing on which to pin any explanation for her sudden demise. Well, almost nothing. For something, indeed, had not escaped the notice of the noble populace: the young lady of the castle was much, was far too much, inclined to thinking. And it was very likely that the constant pressure in her head caused by the great quantity of her thoughts had burst her brain. Nor must it be forgotten that she was a woman, and the female brain, which is smaller and lighter than the male one and of a more rarefied substance, is not made for heavy thoughts; it is made for understanding the instructions of one's parents and, later, one's husband, for bringing up children and managing the household, for social obligations and dances; space might be found in the female brain for embroidery and some, too, for light music-making and one, or at most two, foreign languages (including Latin). But heavy thoughts about the origins of the world, physics, ethics, mathematics, the arts and other masculine studies will overburden the female brain until it simply cracks. An excessive amount of thought, therefore, had very likely dug the young woman's grave. Proponents of this theory blamed the mother, who throughout her daughter's life had never given her proper direction or discouraged her involvement in matters unbefitting the female nature. They did not, however, blame her father, for it was well known that Count Friedrich, the lord of the castle, had had no particular influence over the girl.

Spring Dialogues:

Tuning Up

The syncopated rattle of the carriage at last grew still in the sandy courtyard of a castle. To the neighing of the horses and the metallic sounds of military trappings, the soldiers dismounted and the castle staff bustled around the vehicle, from which an ample-sized body lumbered out awkwardly, its right hand holding on to its tall, young companion for support.

The visitor had barely stepped out when the count's wide-open arms seized him in a tight embrace. 'To what do I owe the honour of Your Grace's unexpected visit? Had we known sooner, we would have made preparations worthy of your status. As it is, after receiving news late last night of your most esteemed imminent arrival, I at once ordered the necks of a few old hens wrung for soup, and early this morning my huntsman came back with quail and pheasants, and the kitchen staff have been cooking and baking all night ...'

'You've gone to far too much trouble for my brief stay. But first, gracious Count Friedrich, allow me to introduce my devoted secretary, Julian, who these last three years has accompanied me on all my travels. Anything intended for my ears is for his as well. My obligations make my visit shorter than I would have wished. But my heart would not allow me not to stop and visit with my very dear friend on my way to Spitzenberg's castle.'

'Ah, Spitzenberg! What an immense tragedy! And no indication that anyone was even plotting such a hideous crime. I am told that the funeral arrangements are still being made,' Count Friedrich says, looking concerned.

'But the little orphans, his children, need their guardian now, to ensure that their inheritance and fragile lives will be safely managed and protected, as justice and law demand,' the prince-bishop replies.

'So you've been appointed the children's guardian?'

'Spitzenberg's noble widow sent for me right after the tragic events and begged me to be their official guardian. How could I refuse? Their father and I have known each other since childhood, and besides, I am godfather to the two sons.'

'But how could this ever have happened?' the count asks.

'Dear friend, I, too, am deeply saddened. But first, let me sit down and get comfortable. Travelling is an ever greater chore for me. My legs swell, my gout acts up, my joints ache – not to mention other problems. And when I see steps in front of me, like these beautiful marble steps in your splendid castle, I always think of the Via Dolorosa, along which our beloved Saviour so painfully bore his cross through the midst of Jerusalem. Why haven't you done what those Katzensteiners did and devised some mechanism that allows the weak and weary to sit comfortably in a chair attached to a railing, which a servant then hoists up and down on a pulley?'

'I'm familiar with the Cats' curious innovation and I've even tried it myself at their place, but here we're still quite able to get around on our own,' Count Friedrich replies as he goes up the steps, with the corpulent prince-bishop, assisted by Julian, wheezing behind him.

'But Her Ladyship might soon be glad to have a pulley. It's said the gracious countess will again be making the pilgrimage – that she's expecting – which sounds like a surprise of sorts, a miracle almost,' the prince-bishop says mischievously.

'A surprise, yes, but hardly a miracle. This time there was no precursory appearance by virgin or saint. Apart from a crazy Leaper, nobody made any predictions,' Count Friedrich responds with a little smile.

'But I suppose that at least an approximate guess might be made as to who did appear to Her Ladyship?' Prince-Bishop Wolfgang enquires meaningfully.

'As it was more than one, I expect that even the gracious countess may be surprised when the child appears – in about six months, the physician predicts. As for that Leaper prophet I mentioned, along with forecasts of plague, floods, locusts and more Turkish raids, he also ranted about her having a son in a year, although he said nothing about me siring the brat.' The count gives the prince-bishop a wink.

'Hahahaha!' the prince-bishop breaks into laughter. 'A good one! But didn't the Virgin Mary say something similar to a maidservant of yours before the birth of your, sadly, much too soon departed daughter, Hypatia? The Virgin, it seems, is determined to slander you, if not to serving girls, then to madmen.'

'That may be true, but you'd think the Virgin would be the last person to know about such things,' Friedrich counters, and the prince-bishop lewdly seconds him; Julian and the count's steward, meanwhile, remain cautiously reserved in the background.

'Do you still have that prophet locked up in your dungeon?' the prince-bishop asks.

'How should I know? It's been a long time since we got him out of the courtyard where he just kept ranting and refused to clear off. So we put him in the dungeon and, oopsie!' – Friedrich puts a hand to his lips – 'I'm afraid that after a while we just forgot about him.'

'Why don't you have him brought up here – after, of course, a good brushing and defleaing – and we'll interrogate him a little, to have some fun while the servants bring us something to eat and drink? It's been a long journey and my stomach, like some ravenous beast, is demanding its own,' Prince-Bishop Wolfgang suggests.

'What's going on with that madman? Is he even still alive?' Friedrich asks the castle steward, who has been following behind the count and his guests, almost unnoticed, since their arrival, and then, in the dining hall, when the prince-bishop and the count were taking their seats, he and Julian sat down at the less distinguished end of the table.

'Gracious Count, I find it difficult to reply,' the steward says guardedly, 'for we must first agree on the notion of life …'

'Stop philosophizing. Is he alive or not?' The count glares at him.

'Considering that even rats must feed their young, and as we know, they multiply quickly and in large numbers, and considering that down there, apart from the occasional stray mouse, they have no other food and are therefore very likely forced to devour each other, I would conclude that he is more not alive than is,' the steward replies.

'Well, forget it. If such was God's plan, there's nothing we can do,' Count Friedrich shrugs.

'God's plan?' The prince-bishop gives Friedrich a cynical look. 'Why, gracious Count, what about man's free will?'

'Will there is, but as it often turns out, it is rarely as free as one might wish,' Friedrich replies.

'My apologies,' a servant says, knocking and entering. 'Her Ladyship wishes to express her regret that she will not be present at supper, for such things give her headaches.'

'Does the countess often suffer from headache?' the prince-bishop turns to his host.

'Fairly often ...' Friedrich replies.

'But for you, gracious Count, I expect that is no great inconvenience?

'I don't complain, but even so it worries me.'

'And how can it not? A baby at her age ... Her Ladyship is now in her forties ...' The prince-bishop thinks for a moment as if worried.

'My noble wife still feels an inconsolable void after the death of her angel,' Friedrich says.

'That is understandable. Hypatia was an exceptional creature, a blend of virtues and talents and filled to overflowing with certain exotic elements ...'

'My noble prince-bishop, I am weary of insinuations that Hypatia resembled me only in appearance. Even a patient man can tire of disagreeable remarks. As close as the countess was to her late daughter, she is as distant from her son. She long ago despaired over his upbringing. And with good reason. The boy is stupid, and lazy to boot. He is the very opposite of Hypatia, whose decision to have me marry her into the family of the noble Cats I had no trouble accepting. Even if the Katzensteiners had me twisting around their claws, her they would have treated well, and her offspring would have been the sum of her brilliance, her mother's cunning and elusiveness and the noble Cats' chivalrous warrior spirit. Agnes was such a marvellous and clever being, and so much braver and more gifted than myself, that I somehow always knew that it wasn't my blood flowing in her veins. There's little doubt, however, that it flows in the veins of that clumsy dunderhead, and sadly, certain facts at my disposal support this theory. I only hope we'll be able to find him a wife who is prepared to endure a few obligatory conjugal nights and then, if she likes, she can follow in his mother's footsteps.'

'And what about you, Friedrich?' the prince-bishop asks.

'Me? Well, I am a man; I am a feudal lord.'

'We are all men and feudal lords, but it's appearances that matter. What's true is what's on the surface; the things we hide and cover up don't exist, and after a while we start believing they never did exist.'

'But what about secrets, gracious prince-bishop?'

'Secrets are for the half-blind and hard of hearing,' the prince-bishop replies. 'And if things are as you say, then let's pray to God that the hue of the new arrival's complexion will not differ too obviously from that of your own lineage, and there will be nothing savage or barbarian in the child's features.'

'Just to be safe, I have two family portraits in readiness,' the count says. 'One is from my side of the family, the other from the countess's. Great-Uncle Maximilian, although born in this very castle, looks as though he might hail from Alexandria, while my wife's grandfather could easily be from Granada or Cartagena. They're both of a sooty shade. Perhaps in those days people hired painters who mixed such dark colours, or maybe they used pigments of poor quality that darkened over the decades.'

'In any case, the new child will not be able to fill your wife's emptiness, although it will certainly divert her attention, at least in its early years. May God grant that it be as gifted as Hypatia was, or nearly so. A good mother will never recover from such a loss, although a bad one may even be glad of it, for such a brilliant gift from her body can easily stir envy and jealousy in her. But tell me, why did you give the girl such an inauspicious name as Hypatia? Why name her after that pagan astronomer, the doyenne of the Alexandrine Neoplatonists, who, like your daughter, suffered a very tragic end because of her intensive thought, slaughtered as a heretic by Christians? I'm superstitious when it comes to names; they must be chosen with great care.'

'You think I wasn't aware of that when she was born?' Count Friedrich replies in a mournful voice. 'But the countess insisted on Hypatia. The most I could do was demand we add the Christian name Agnes. For me, she was always my little Nessie, my Nežica.'

The Apparition in the Pasture

Not long after the visitations, and the sermons that incorporated not only the Indian story but others, too, with all sorts of apparitions, a shepherd knocked on the door of the nearby Dominican monastery. He told the doorkeeper that Mary had appeared to him, just as she had to that heathen Indian, Ivan, only he was no heathen but a deeply devout Catholic.

'I was sitting quietly on a tree stump in the pasture, grazing my cows and goats and little sheep, when amid the tinkling of the cowbells a woman in a light-blue robe stepped out of the evening mists of late spring,' he explained to the Dominican brother through the half-opened door – the monastery only opened wide its door to visitors when there was a serious reason, something more than petty fabrications and delusions.

'I was very frightened and sat on that stump frozen, as if buried up to my waist in it. She stood in front of me, gazing at me with benevolent eyes, as if I had never done anything bad in my entire life.' (Which could not have been further from the truth, for whenever the shepherd got the feeling that his wife was talking too much or didn't know how to turn around the way he liked, he would give her a couple of smacks to convince her to hurry up and put some effort into satisfying his desires and needs. In addition, there were a few thefts on his conscience, such as stealing horses, which he then sold on to fences. And once, in a drunken delirium, which happened more regularly than not, he was thought to have even killed a man, but as there were no witnesses and the victim was a foreigner, the incident was soon forgotten.)

'There, standing in the midst of the cows and goats and sheep,' the shepherd continued, 'as I sat on the tree stump, Mary looked at me with infinite forgiveness, and her eyes seemed to tell me, "The past is the past, and now, shepherd, all is forgiven you." I fell to my knees in amazement and, through the cowpats and small, hard turds of goat and sheep dung scattered all around, I crawled to the apparition and humbly lifted my eyes. Mary looked at me kindly, her hands clasped together, and she stroked my head with her merciful hand. Then she said to me something like what the Mexican Mary said to the Indian peasant Ivan: "Here, shepherd, in this pasture, on this grass, on which the sheep, goats and cows are munching at this very moment – right here, shepherd, build me a church. And not a little chapel either, but a basilica, with room enough for all who come to me on pilgrimage from near and far, who need my help and comfort. Every year in the month of May I expect to see fresh lilies of the valley – which you also know as St Mary's flower – adorning my altar every day. But don't let the priest pour that vinegary St Mary's wine into the chalice, which causes you all to do so much evil; instead, he should pour the white, semi-dry wine which you will all be pressing from the local vineyards, specifically from the vine I now present to you, O shepherd. Plant this vine secretly in your own vineyard; I have imbued it with such incredible power that its wine will be famous far and wide. Because I have breathed miraculous power into your seedling," – that's exactly what she said to me: *your seedling* – "make sure the brothers at the monastery pay you a fair price for it, for as the feudal lords it is they who will receive the greatest benefit from the business. In addition, every May on the feast day of Mary Help of Christians, I would like there to be yet one more great procession, and with it a great fair, so that you can all get back on your feet, economically speaking, and have an easier life. After all, if you don't help yourselves, how can I help you? For I am first and foremost your consoler. That's all for today, shepherd; now go up the mountain to the Dominicans and tell them my demands."

'When she finished speaking, I nodded humbly and glanced up to see if Mary was still there or if her voice had been coming from heaven. Then I ran as fast as I could to the monastery door, and here I am now.'

This is how the doorkeeper retold the shepherd's story to his brothers – a more sophisticated, connected and coherent approximation of what the shepherd had been grinding out through his nearly toothless mouth.

The doorkeeper had inspected the visitor carefully as he told his tale and, since even monks enjoy a laugh now and then, was looking forward to the man entertaining the brothers over supper; Dominicans, after all, are not as reserved or silent as Carthusians. But the prior would not receive just any village drunkard who saw visions and heard voices in his delirium. So, before the shepherd could recount his story, the monks let him wait a few days, and then, after conferring among themselves, they sent for him and had him repeat the tale a few times to test its veracity. Each time it was a little different. The colour of Mary's robe kept changing – it was not always light blue but sometimes other shades of blue and once even pink. The narrator, in response to his listeners' cautions, was constantly correcting himself, and he also added a few things, for Mary had had other demands as well, namely that the naked hills in the area, near and far, must be planted exclusively with vineyards, and the same was true for the wooded hills, which would first have to be cleared, and that every Sunday morning after Mass, wine from the monastery's lands must be made available to all the villagers for free, and the monastery must see to everything.

'But how do we know that you, shepherd, who have not been sober since you were six years old (and now you're well past thirty), did not see all of this in one of your alcoholic fits?' the Dominicans asked, eyeing the witness with suspicion.

'But I didn't,' the shepherd said and swore on the health of himself, his father and his wife – whom, as has been noted, he would beat on a regular basis. He also swore on the lives of his children, whom he also beat, usually to stop them from developing bad habits and to teach them obedience, but more often because, when he was drunk, his arm would, all on its own, start to twitch and strike out in every direction.

'Fine, fine,' the brothers said, 'so leave now and go back to that pasture. Maybe Mary will appear again in the same spot. Sit there, or better, kneel there as you graze your cows and sheep and pray to her, asking her on your knees to appear at least once more to you because you'd like to talk to her about the details. Ask her to give you at least one easily verifiable sign that what you have told us is true and that these are her words, the words of Mary Help of Christians, and not, perhaps, somebody else's. By the way, you must have counted your cows, and maybe your sheep, too, at least roughly, but what about the goats? It wouldn't be a bad idea if you counted the goats, too, the exact number, and then see if there isn't maybe a horned billy goat that turned up recently, who changes, in those mists of yours, into a soft feminine form dressed in more or less light-blue women's clothing and speaks to simpletons like yourself.'

'But he would never demand such things of me,' the shepherd defended himself, feeling insulted and a bit wounded.

'So what would he demand?' the Dominicans enquired, laying a trap for the drunkard, more for their own amusement than with any serious intent.

'I don't know. I don't have that sort of imagination,' the shepherd replied, lowering his eyes cautiously.

'Well, the idea of people planting vineyards everywhere is splendid!' The Dominicans now set about critiquing Mary's demands. 'But the idea that you should somehow be paid for your supposedly miracle-working vine, which she said would flourish as the mother plant? Or the other thing you were going on about, that after Sunday Mass and on the great feast days our brotherhood should dispense wine to all the parishioners for free? No, that's not a good idea; it's a bad one. Because if we did what you say, we wouldn't sell very much. It's true that the populace is content with their spirits, which corrode their stomachs and brains, and what they buy from us on the great feast days is less poisonous, and we produce it with the help of you, our dear vassals, who thus fulfil your vassalage through quit-rents and tribute payments. But we keep this wine in the finest oak casks and do not distribute it for free. Our monastery is known throughout the Holy Roman Empire for its superb wine. But as we do not wish to seem slaves of prejudice, we will plant your little vine and see what it bears and how well it does. But we're not paying you anything for it. First, let it prove reliable, and then we'll talk business. Is it even a little bit miraculous? Well, let's wait and see what grows from it. But again – and think good and hard before you answer – how do you know that everything you're telling us came from Mary and not, perhaps, from some other supernatural being?'

'But why should this be so strange? I mean, wine is a kind of food, isn't it?'

'But that's the problem: alcohol is the basis of your diet, from morning to night.'

'But I can't eat what we don't have. Sad to say, but we live a very modest life. All those stories about me and drinking – it's wicked people who spread them around,' the shepherd replied.

'You mean people who know you all too well, you worthless drunkard, people who have known you for years.'

'Everything I told you about my visions is the honest truth!' the shepherd persisted.

'We'll see. Go back to that pasture and kneel down and pray, and keep praying until Mary appears to you again. Ask her what we told you to ask – one or two signs would be helpful.' The Dominicans were feeling inquisitive. 'Because what if that grapevine of yours isn't from God, and someone with less than noble intentions wants us to plant it? What if we plant it and something crawls out that blights all our vineyards?'

And now for the truth of the matter: the Dominicans, of course, did not believe the inebriated shepherd. Miracles don't happen every day. As a rule, divine grace like that touches only those who are purer in soul – and who are usually much younger, if not childlike, for such people are still, at least to some degree, pure. All the same, one should not rule out the possibility of a miracle happening even to someone who, having wandered the byways for years, comes to a crossroads where he experiences a supernatural event that completely changes him. But if that had been the case here, Mary's packet of gifts would surely have included yet one more miracle, perhaps the greatest: the shepherd would have finally stopped getting drunk and beating up his loved ones. Which did not happen. His arm continued to unleash itself spontaneously on his wife and children.

The commission at the monastery decided to sharpen their evidence-collecting methods so the fool would realize the gravity of his words and stop churning out drunken tales about miracles. 'Good,' the brothers decided. 'This story may prove rather useful. If there's no change at all in that little tippler's life, we can turn his story to our advantage, along with those so-called demands from Mary, and then that shepherd will experience one more phenomenon, for him the ultimate phenomenon: one fine day, sitting on that stump, his soul will grow wings in his delirium and fly away – not upwards, of course, but horizontally, to purgatory, where it will be obliged to do penance for the sins its owner committed in his earthly life. Indeed, the apparition of Mary might, in God's eyes, win him a lesser punishment than if death had come before the vision – in that case, certainly, his ragged soul would have been seized by a sharp-clawed paw, or one of those flaming tongues would have coiled, serpent-like, around his soul as it lay in the cowpats and dragged it, drunken and covered in dung, into the netherworld to be tortured forever with no hope of seeing the Saviour's face – we'll have no trouble coming up with effective images, ones that will be most educational, which is to say, terrifying, for the populace.' This was just the story they needed, the Dominicans concluded, and washed their hands of the drunkard. But not for long.

Two days later the man was again knocking at the monastery door and mumbling something about how when he was kneeling in that pasture the Virgin appeared to him a second time, took his head in her hands and said, 'Here is proof that I have truly appeared to you: shepherd, my dear little lamb, you will receive from the brothers a small patch of hillside land, where, from the miraculous vine I gave you, you will produce the finest wine in all the land, better even than the wine the brothers make, and I, Mary, Queen of May, will see to it myself. And it is my wish and demand that Mass in my basilica be served using wine produced from your vine, but, of course, I have already told you that.'

'She said *that* to you?' The brothers exchanged puzzled glances after their midday meal and, determined to rest and relax a bit before tackling the afternoon chores, began nodding to each other, as if to say, 'So that's the sort of the miracle she promised you, is it?'

'That's what she told me, word for word. She also said that the wine from my vine would cure dysentery and plague, and then she thought a moment, as if troubled by something, and said that, unfortunately, there is a very long war ahead of us, and not with any territorial enemy either, but a war between Christian brothers,' the shepherd said.

'Now listen, shepherd. People are endowed with free will and can do good things or bad things. We monks have pledged ourselves to God, and we perform only deeds that are pleasing to God and to Mary. If we were suddenly to hand over a patch of our most fertile land to a worthless drunkard, so you could produce the finest wine from some supposedly miraculous vine, well, that would mean we were possessed by an evil spirit. So clear off this minute, and take your stories with you, and we'll wait to see if Mary shows up again, maybe to a more trustworthy person, someone she doesn't chat with about alcoholic drinks. Everything you've been spinning us – well, it's not a joke any more. But last time we gave you some well-meaning advice: to count the horns on the goats in your flock.'

The Dominicans, of course, did not believe that the devil would appear in the guise of some bearded fellow with a long tail and horns, but striking images are the best way to educate the simple folk. So in Mary's basilica, too, which in the future would be erected on the basis of a vision by a more trustworthy witness, they would hire artists to cover the ceiling and walls with pictures that clearly showed the differences between the three realms of the afterworld geography, which people would attain according to how much of a mess they made of their lives on earth. They let the shepherd know that lying was one of the worst deadly sins. 'And so is gluttony,' they stressed, 'which in your case, shepherd, occurs in liquefied form in your rancid spirits and vinegary wines. And need we mention sloth? For otherwise you would be occupying yourself more usefully and not idling away the hours in the pasture, where it's mainly your right hand that works, tipping back the flask you take with you every day, filled to the brim, when you go off to do a job any seven-year-old boy is capable of doing. And while you're there hallucinating among the livestock, your family is out in the field doing real work – sowing, ploughing, weeding and all the other chores – and when you drive the cows home in the evening, you are so well rested that, brain-damaged as you are, you lash out at your family.'

'So, did you count the livestock?' the brothers asked the shepherd.

'I did,' the shepherd replied.

'And how many cows are there?'

'Three cows, one calf and a bull in the pen at home.'

'And sheep?'

'Seven ewes, three lambs and only one ram.'

'And billy goats?'

'Nothing but nanny goats, five of them.'

'Not a single billy goat?'

'Nope. I have arrangements with a neighbour for propagation.'

'Ho there, shepherd, just what are you saying? Who is this neighbour of yours? What sort of villain is he? Not so fast, shepherd, not so fast – such things the Book of Leviticus strictly forbids, as does the *Constitutio Criminalis Carolina*, and on pain of death!'

'No, no! I didn't mean it like that!' the shepherd, alarmed, hastened to explain. 'My neighbour simply hires out his billy goat for propagating.'

'Oh, sure, now you're making excuses and want to deceive us.' The brothers were now fully immersed in their rustic playlet.

'No, you're wrong! I'm an honest man, and I'm telling you the truth!'

'Well, shepherd, God doesn't like boasting either; that's the very opposite of humility, not to mention that your lies are like yeast and make your self-regard rise beyond all measure.'

'No! Oh, no! You've got it all wrong!' the shepherd answered, now feeling quite desperate.

'Wrong again are we? Well, if that's so, then prove it!'

'I swear it, by God, Jesus and Mary!'

'Considering your reputation, shepherd, your oath carries but scant weight. God, who sees into your worm-infested soul, is the best judge of whether you're telling the truth. And while we are constantly with God in our thoughts, we are not omnipotent and, on occasion, can be mistaken in our judgement, and as we have no wish to be mistaken here, you must present us with stronger evidence.'

'What sort of evidence?'

'The sort about which we will have no doubt. As you yourself know, you have a lot of things confused in your head. And we warn you in all seriousness: this story of yours, in which you've implicated the Virgin

Mary, is very likely false and therefore terribly sinful, and terrible sins are punished with terrible punishments. With a single stroke of the pen we can send you to the stake.'

'No, please! Anything but that! Because ...'

'Because?'

'Because all that stuff about the vineyard maybe I didn't understand so good.'

'What do you mean, not so good? You swore that you clearly and distinctly heard what Mary said.'

'It seemed like I did ...' the shepherd tried to defend himself.

'Seemed? But it doesn't do to rely on seeming, does it? All sorts of things can seem, but then it turns out there's no truth in them whatsoever.'

'I don't know. Maybe I did miss something, or didn't hear something, or heard it wrong, what with all the bells ringing around me, the cows with their big bells and the sheep and goats with their little ones. And there might have been an echo, too ...'

'An echo? From where? Our hills aren't great mountains, with mountain walls and boulders that sounds and voices can bounce off and return in some distorted form. Nothing bounces off our little round hills! So, shepherd, do you see how important it is to pay attention and listen closely when somebody tells you something? Because very possibly it was not Mary talking to you on your stump, no matter how much it seemed that it was. With such delicate matters, particular care is needed in the interpretation to make sure that the message, no matter how gentle and kind the form that delivers it might seem, does not contain a hidden trap.'

'How should I know? This was the first time anything like this has ever happened to me! A person doesn't talk with Mary every day, you know.'

'But nevertheless, many do – in their prayers, of course, every night before they go to sleep, and they bring her their supplications during the day, too, and they understand her and listen to her without her ever appearing before their eyes, for they feel her presence in their hearts.'

'Well, maybe the whole thing was just a dream, and also I'm very sensitive to changes in the weather, so ...'

'So what you told us, there's not much truth to it?'

'Maybe none of it was true,' the shepherd stammered, hanging his head.

'And you lied about everything?'

'Oh no! I didn't lie. I just … how should I … ummm …'

'How should you express yourself?'

'Yes, I have trouble expressing myself …'

'Maybe that's because, just as you've been from your dewy youth, you were …'

'Sure, I was probably a little tipsy, too, and fell asleep on that tree stump and merely dreamed it all,' the shepherd mumbled, exhausted from the interrogation.

'Dreams are misleading,' the brothers continued. 'They can show us things in a way that seems like we're awake and experiencing them with our senses when they're not actually there. And Mary just doesn't pop in and out of our waking life.'

'It probably was just a dream,' the shepherd volunteered.

'Well, we're glad we could shed some light on this mystery and clear up the problem,' the Dominicans replied.

'And,' they added, 'you should be glad, too – extremely happy, in fact – that it all ended well for you.'

'I am thankful. Very thankful …' the shepherd nodded.

'For there was more than a slight chance it would come to a bad end, even a literal end.'

'I know, and in all humility I am sorry …' the shepherd said, relieved.

'Well, now you really do have something to thank Mary for …' The brothers said, and started completing each other's thoughts.

'And the Holy Spirit, too …'

' … for inspiring us and illuminating our hearts …'

' … so that right in the middle of the village …'

' … or here in front of the monastery …'

' … we didn't pile logs into a lovely pyramid …'

' … and drench them with hot oil …'

' … and set them alight …'

' … having first placed you on top of them …'

'… so that you and your drunken stories would burn to a crisp …'

'… just as your soul will burn in hell! For we're afraid that, when it comes to your life in the afterworld, there is no other possibility.'

'Oh no!' the shepherd yelped. 'I repent! I sincerely repent!'

'Well, maybe there's a way out even for you. For the love of Our Lord Jesus is without end and extends even to drunken idiots like you.' The brothers were conciliatory.

'Thank you, thank you! A million times, thank you!' the shepherd kept repeating as he crawled backwards on his knees out of the room.

'Ho now! Hold it right there! You're not getting off so easily and not without punishment. For this little piece of theatre, you'll be working in our vineyards all summer and well into autumn. And while you work in the scorching heat (at least that's what the astrologers have calculated) with the hot sun frying your brain – a rather negligible part of your body, admittedly, but still indispensable for lifting and lowering the hoe – you will have the opportunity to reflect on truth and falsehood, sin and eternal damnation, mercy and forgiveness. Perhaps your penance will persuade St Peter to turn a blind eye and send you to purgatory rather than hell. A possibility that becomes all the more likely if, once you complete your punitive servitude, you decide upon reflection to do something for us voluntarily. Our well-tended land offers no lack of work. You have never been as close to God as you will be during your servitude with us. No matter what work we do, we pray at the same time, so you will be ceaselessly immersed in an ocean of prayer. And we will, of course, pay you some small amount …'

'But what about my gardens, my fields, my vines?' the shepherd asked in a broken voice.

'Your family will take care of them, as they have always done.'

'And my cows, goats, sheep?'

'Your two youngest sons will do a better job of it than you ever did. In any case, the work you do with us will be so exhausting that, after your fourteen-hour day, all you'll want to do at home is collapse on your bed. Tomorrow, before dawn, and even before those colourful Styrian cocks open their beaks to proclaim to all creation that the Creator has given us yet another beautiful day on earth, which must be spent as usefully and devoutly as possible, you shall rise from your bed so you can be at our door sober and washed before the sun kisses the land, and then your penance shall begin.'

'I am so sorry ...' the shepherd cried out again.

'And so you may be ... Mysterious are the paths of the Lord. When his path intersects with that of a lost sinner lying in filth, he does not kick the man or trample over him: he leaves him to us, who pick him up and wash him clean ... Now, get lost!'

SPRING DIALOGUES:

FIRST WARNING

'And yet, most esteemed prince-bishop, I get the feeling that you did not come here merely on a friendly visit,' Count Friedrich tells his guest over lunch.

'My gracious Friedrich,' the prince-bishop replies, 'I am also here to give you a friendly warning.'

Friedrich takes a quick, shallow breath. His sweaty palms stick to the oak table on which he is nervously tapping his fingers. 'Noble prince-bishop, I hear you have been travelling around looking for heresy and frightening people. But I myself have nothing to hide. There are no devils here, the Lutherans have recently been thinning out on their own accord, and not so long ago the populace took care of the witches ...'

'Oh, but my dear friend, you do have somebody here,' the prince-bishop smirks. 'There is a fat preacher living in your castle. And from what I hear, his sermons delight even the peasants, who usually find Lutheranism bland. I'm told he teaches children how to read and write and that even people from the neighbouring town come to hear his sermons, at which he serves communion in both kinds. People say he's affable, colourful, even witty. And at the mention of the Immaculate Virgin, they say, he contorts his face and lewdly licks his lips, and then clicks his tongue, swings his hips and makes a few forward thrusts ...'

'He's packing up,' Friedrich interrupts. 'His trunks are ready, his books crated, and off he goes to Germany. In a few days, he'll be gone.'

'But the preacher isn't the only one, I hear. You also keep your own *Hofjude* in the castle and feed him very well, people say, after his own customs, and they say he enjoys a fine life here with you ...' the prince-bishop continues.

'I have him here to observe the stars between earth and heaven and warn me of anything that might go wrong, so I can be prepared instead of stupidly staring into the uncertain future and whatever troubles might arise,' Friedrich counters.

'Well, then, did your whatever-he-is foretell a visit? A friendly visit?' Prince-Bishop Wolfgang examines the count carefully.

'Hmm. In fact, he did tell me something.' Friedrich reflects for a moment. 'He said I should expect a guest to arrive before the new moon in Taurus; he would be alone at first but others would arrive after him ... Yes, I remember now. He kept staring and gazing at those strange books of his, running his finger from right to left and peering into a glass ball, which was producing a steamy mist, and all the while he kept grimacing. "You should be afraid, gracious Count! Be afraid!" he said, and kept blinking at me and checking the Old Testament, where, he claims, is written everything that ever happened, everything that is happening now and everything that will happen. Then, I remember, he raised his right hand and started scratching his head. "Oy vey, oy vey," he whimpered from behind his desk. "It looks bad, looks bad," he said, as his left hand milked his thin grey beard. "A visit," he said to me and made a face, "from a friend?" And again he starts leafing through the book backwards and forwards. "It's not good ... oh no ... it's bad ... very bad," he kept bleating at the sphere in front of him and squinting into that book of his.' Friedrich gazes for a moment at his guest, then looks down at the octagons in the oak flooring.

'So he did predict a visit?' the prince-bishop asks again.

'Yes, Wolfgang, a very bad visit. And here you are with your assistant and probably others will come later?' Friedrich asks uncertainly.

'Oh, yes, others will definitely come later. I tell you this as a friend. So you must do all that I advise – it's the only way to appease the authorities. There's no alternative,' the prince-bishop says firmly.

'I'm getting a very bad feeling, Wolfgang. For as long as I've known you, your advice has always meant violence. Is that really necessary?' Count Friedrich asks softly.

'Only destruction can make room for what could and will transpire. And it could be a lot worse, too, but Archduke Ferdinand II, on the advice of the noble Bishop Stobaeus of Lavant, has given us directives to handle everything with kid gloves; still, it's a good idea to take them off now and then and exercise one's fingers a bit. The archduke wishes to establish order in the provinces of Inner Austria. This is the only way to oppose our hereditary enemy, who with his turbans and sabres is whittling away our eastern frontier; meanwhile, inside the empire, even in our beloved Inner Austrian provinces, the flames of Protestantism are fanned. And then there are those colourful folk customs, including irrational superstitions and occult beliefs, although these we can use to good effect to bring an end to the current religious chaos. But we have to take time and carefully inspect the domains and towns and fiefdoms for any such breeding grounds and utterly exterminate them. Only then will the empire be united. And with all these external and internal enemies and, for Inner Austria especially, with our hereditary enemy to the east and the south, as well as the unrest that's being fomented on our western frontiers, the strength which our empire so vitally needs can only be found in unity,' the prince-bishop explains.

'But many have been living under the Augsburg Confession for decades. The Provincial Estates support the right of religious choice, and the nobility is predominantly Lutheran. And then there are the towns, like the one near us, which was given by our gracious Emperor Maximilian to the Provincial Estates and is not under the jurisdiction of the prince.' Count Friedrich says heatedly.

'But there's nothing to choose! Choosing Catholicism is choosing religion and is, therefore, the only right choice. Everything else is heresy!' the prince-bishop curtly replies.

'But what about religious freedom and the Pacification of Bruck? In 1578 Archduke Charles assured us in writing that he would not act against anyone in the Inner Austrian provinces who declares himself a Lutheran,' the count persists.

'The Bruck Peace was extorted from Archduke Charles by the Provincial Estates when he was collecting tribute payments for the defence against the Turks. And not long afterwards the Lutheran lords began using their patronage rights to appoint Protestant preachers for their churches and impose their religion on their vassals (not very successfully, thank God). But Archduke Charles (may God grant him eternal rest and peace) is dead. His successor, Archduke Ferdinand II, interprets the document differently, in the spirit of the Peace of Augsburg, as agreed in 1555 between Emperor Charles V, the German King Ferdinand I and the Provincial Estates, by which vassals must follow the religion of their feudal lord: *Cuius regio, eius religio* – "Whose realm it is, his religion it is." And as our beloved father, Archduke Ferdinand II, the Prince of Inner Austria, is a deeply devout Catholic, so, too, his sons must follow his religion.'

'But Wolfgang, people have become accustomed to their religion. They have built churches and prayer halls where they pray and perform their rituals; families and communities have adopted its customs and celebrate its holidays. And when times are hard, they take refuge in their religion. None of this is going to be easy ...'

'Which is why it must be quick,' Wolfgang replies, 'with faith commissions going with soldiers into homes and inspecting bookshelves, cabinets and chests, cellars and attics, collecting sectarian books and burning them in front of town halls and market-town churches. Well, maybe not into every illiterate, louse-ridden cottage, of course.'

'I myself am clean. In our Church, along with Jesus, God and the Holy Spirit, we also venerate his mother, who stands at the main altar. And she is surrounded, in the side altars, by a crowd of saints, whom we also revere. And if we lose something or there's something we can't remember, we turn to St Anthony for help, and we're always appealing to St Lucy, too, since our eyesight gets worse and worse with every passing year,' Friedrich says.

'Well, it would be a good idea for you to ask St Anthony – and on a regular basis – to help you not to forget your obligation to obey the instructions of the emperor and the prince. And St Lucy can help you sharpen your eyesight so you can detect any anomalies before it's too late,' the prince-bishop says.

'The Provincial Estates will not easily consent to such encroachment on their religious freedoms. The Estates of Styria, Carinthia and Carniola have delivered a memorandum to the archduke, requesting that he call off his measures against the Lutherans ...'

'A request the archduke has rejected ...' the prince-bishop interrupts him.

'But, from what I've heard, new preparations are being made for disobedience in the Hereditary Lands of Inner Austria,' the count continues. 'The Provincial Diets are writing complaints. They are talking about employing the weapons of the past and denying the archduke his war contributions, as well as halting payments on debts and refusing to introduce any new taxes. I hear that deputies from Styria, Carinthia and Carniola are planning to meet as a joint committee from all three Provincial Estates with the aim of negotiating an agreement on religious freedom with Archduke Ferdinand. The Styrian Estates, it's said, are even preparing to kneel down ...'

'You are very well informed, Friedrich. But let me give you some additional information. All these preparations are pointless. In a few months the archduke will ban all assemblies and congresses that do not have his permission. The town councils that are predominantly Lutheran will be dissolved, and new ones made up entirely of Catholics will be installed. Town judges, mayors and town and market-town councillors will be dismissed and their places taken by Catholic representatives. First, the preachers will be run out of Graz, followed by every last Lutheran who does not wish to convert to Catholicism.'

'But the Lutheran nobility will seek alliances with the Protestant courts and princes in other parts of the Holy Roman Empire – in Saxony and, probably, in the Palatinate and Württemberg, too, and they may even turn to Emperor Rudolf II himself, humbly requesting that he intercede with the archduke and persuade him to take softer measures with the Lutherans.'

'All pointless.' The prince-bishop shakes his head. 'For if our efforts to reach the soul are not effective, then we will reach the body and through it touch the soul. Not everybody at once, but with forethought, carefully, one person at a time. As we did with that rebellious ...'

'Spitzenberg?' the host gasps and covers his mouth with his hand.

'Shhhhh ...' The guest looks around and casts sharp glances at everyone in the room. 'The man chose his own fate.'

'But was there no other way?' Friedrich whispers, his hand still over his mouth.

'Possibly, if Spitzenberg had decided differently ...'

'Wolfi!'

'Now don't be so sentimental and dramatic, Friedrich! It's power and politics we're talking about.'

THE PREACHER'S SERMON

'My dear Slovenes, all of you here who speak Slovene or Carniolan, Styrian or Carinthian, and maybe there are some of you here who speak Croatian, all of you who speak Slovene poorly or who have come here out of curiosity or boredom, and you, too, papist spies, who when this sermon is over will run off and report to your bishops, or the Jesuits or Capuchins, or to some provincial office – you stay, too, for today may be the day your ears are opened and some truth gets through, things you may well have heard about but only poorly understood, or not understood at all. And as for you who do understand everything I am now proclaiming but don't understand Slovene, well, come to the Lutheran prayer hall this afternoon, where I will be proclaiming the very same things in German. *Also, am Nachmittag alle deutschsprachigen Menschen herzlich willkommen in der lutherischen Kirche in der Nähe. Aber jetzt,* what I am proclaiming to you here and now – *und auch am Nachmittag* – is the Gospel. I doubt that the papist priests have told you much about this word, which was not coined by Our Lord Jesus, who spoke Aramaic – since, of course, they've been feeding you Latin masses, processions and all kinds of silly rituals … Well, so as not to drag this out …' The preacher picked up the pace; he could see that the populace had no ear for linguistics and were already counting the mildew stains on the walls, looking for spiders and watching the angle of the sunlight as it fell into the church. 'Well, so those priests kept you in darkness and fear …' ('That's true enough!' – the believers now perk up and start listening again) ' …in a darkness that can be lifted by the Gospel alone. The pure Gospel! *Sola scriptura*, my dear Slovenes! You don't need any mediators massaging your ears and milking your purses for all kinds of indulgences, for this day I bring you glad tidings, which I want you to remember word for word, and that is: Jesus has saved you! He has saved every one of you through his death on the Cross, so you don't need to untie your purse strings and buy your way into heaven. You don't need to financially support the afterlife of your loved ones. And you absolutely do not need to do business with the papists, who take your money and build themselves palaces and mansions with it, and who go around dolled up like noble whores in their scarlet robes of velvet, and more than a few of them jingle with so much precious metal that I'd be afraid to share a carriage with them in a thunderstorm. Once lightning starts, you can bet that every last person in that carriage, packed with so much fine plate, will be dead and fried.

'And just as lightning is attracted to metal, so God is repulsed by arrogance and pride! I understand you, dear people, I really do; I understand why you feel so at home with Catholicism. I know that many of you still secretly worship the old goddesses and gods, but this is a very great sin! Witchery is something near to you, and your priests are near to witchery! I know that many of you perform double rituals: whenever you present a gift to Mary, you also bribe one of your own goddesses, and when you celebrate the birth of Jesus, you burn that wooden stump or log, or whatever you call it. And this is hardly surprising when the representatives of your church are decked out like wizards and warlocks, even though a modest garment, like the long brown robe we preachers wear, would be entirely sufficient. And let me remind you of something else, too: the papists hate women! The only woman they respect they've turned into something bizarre. They took an ordinary Jewish girl and created a divine being of her, squeezing out all her womanliness and human passion. But you, my dear Slovenes, know that a man can be healthy only if he has a healthy body. And there are lots of healthy men among you – I just have to look at all the little children here watching me, eager for knowledge; well, some of them are bored and have started crying. Wait just a little, children; I'll soon be done. A healthy body is a gift from God, and it's made to have various abilities and needs. How are we ordinary people supposed to be fruitful and multiply if not with our bodies? We are not angels; angels have such matters arranged differently, in ways that are beyond our comprehension. But a healthy man is, well, healthy, and he's only a man in the real sense of the word when there's a woman by his side, a woman who is also his wife. Only then is his body no longer territory for the Tempter. Only then can a man devote himself to tilling the fields, trade and commerce, educating the people, ruling or, as in my case, proclaiming the pure Gospel. Only then is a man at peace in his soul and able to think with a sober head and make decisions that are pleasing to God. In the opposite situation, if a man does not have a wife or, even worse, if he is forbidden to have a wife, ideas start forming in his head and they soon run foul of the Word of God. Very few of the papist clergy are reconciled to their celibate condition, which is why most of them give their housekeepers indulgences on a regular basis, and some even compel married women to compensate them for the sins they have committed.

'Meanwhile, those clergy who hole up in monasteries and episcopal palaces – they don't even need women, and they satisfy many of their cravings with each other, between themselves. And this, my dear Slovenes, is an abomination to God! It is a most wicked sin! And the terrible plague, and the swarm of locusts that came before it, are but mild punishments for such vileness. The Turks, too, are a punishment for this sin. But another grievous sin, perhaps the worst of all, is that the papist priests have left you captive in a pen of stupidity. But Jesus does not like stupid people! For how can a person do what is right if he is foolish and untaught? Evil, my dear Slovenes (and all you others, too, but I won't list you separately), great evil comes from ignorance, because a person cannot know wrong from right if he cannot avail himself of the Word of God, not only when some preacher happens to come around but every day. The grace of God has given man the printing press, and it is not chance but divine providence that placed it in our hands, in our Lutheran hands. Well, we, too, the proclaimers of the pure Gospel, have our differences, which I don't intend to go into right now. But I implore you, listen to us Lutherans who are travelling around these parts and never confuse us with those Leapers, or Rebaptizers, or Founders, for we have nothing in common with them! Our feet are planted firmly on the ground, and here we stand, while those others babble nonsense and hear strange voices, and it makes them jump up and down, hurl themselves around, shake and quake and I don't know what else.

But the voices they hear are not from God. I'm told that they have been coming here to you, too, under various names. So, dear people, remember this: you must run away from them! They are madmen, nothing but madmen! Everything that is the Word of God you will find in the Gospel; anything else is a sign of illness!

'I also hear that there are Jews circulating among you under certain peculiar titles. Keep away from them, too! And not just because they killed Our Lord Jesus ...'

'But he rose from the dead, didn't he?' the populace interrupts him.

'If Jesus was not God but an ordinary prophet he would have died on that cross. Besides, I want to warn you,' the preacher continues, 'there are many sorcerers among the Jews, people who are capable of wicked magic. Some of them even know how to make a creature out of water and clay who looks like a person but is not one in truth.'

'So what is he then, if he looks like a person but isn't one in truth?' the populace asks with obvious curiosity.

'A creature of the devil, what else? These man-made monsters of theirs, which they call *golems*, the Jews send everywhere to wring the necks of hens, strangle sheep and goats, drink the blood of cattle and, for their occult rituals, to steal innocent Christian babes. But let's put the Jews aside for now. I mention them only to tell you to avoid them, too ...'

'Hold on a minute! Of all the tales you've been spinning us, these monsters are the most interesting thing by far. So how do they make them? Clay and water, you said? Well, we have clay and there's plenty of water, too. Is there a recipe for how you bring these creatures to life?'

'I know nothing about that. I tell you this only so you will stay away from them. But forget about the Jews. There aren't many of them here anyway, so they're hardly worth mentioning ...'

'But you're the one who mentioned them!' the populace said, refusing to give up.

'Yes, I did, and I'm almost sorry for it. I lay these words on your heart: forsake magic and superstition, whether it's from the Jews or it's your own, and all will be well and good. Read the Gospel! Some of you, and especially your children, we have been teaching, so now you can read a few things on your own and not be like sheep, stupidly bleating away as the papists fleece you. And, my dear Slovenes, let me fill your ears with something else: never let anybody belittle you! Nobody! Remember what I am about to tell you: every once in a while someone will leave your ranks and ascend to the pulpit – or to some other high place, it doesn't have to be a pulpit in the House of God, and the pulpiteer doesn't have to be a priest – and he'll start slandering you and insulting you. There is no reason – none whatsoever! – to let anybody call you names! So the next time someone says to you, "You Slovenes, you're nothing but plain old serfs, serfs born and bred," then, my dear Slovenes, I want you to pick up the Bible with both of your hands, pick up that big Slovene Bible bound in wooden boards and pig's leather and smash him on the noggin with it so hard he never gets up again! All those Slovene words, all those words you can understand, for which you must thank your countryman Jurij Dalmatin – you have never had so many words in all your history. So make good use of them! The count has promised to put aside a little money for purchasing the Word of God in the language you understand, so every house and every cottage, every gentleman's house and every burgher's house, every castle and every court will have its own copy of God's Truth. And, later, we'll print other things, too – yearly almanacs, so you will know, from the stars and the moon, when to sow and plant and hoe, when to avoid getting your teeth pulled, when to expect plague or vermin and under which planets it's best to wash the linens.'

'But …' A question can be heard from the populace.

'I see a hand sticking up on the left. Go ahead, peasant, ask your question,' the preacher says, gesturing.

'You mentioned serfs, about being serfs born and bred. Well, does that mean you want us to rebel against the lords and the prince?'

'Oh, no, no! I'm not telling you to rebel against the lords or the prince. But you should rebel against the papist priests who milk you dry and leave you with nothing but kreutzers. But rebellion against the authorities? Oh, no, I'm not saying that,' the preacher replies.

'But …'

'Go on, ask, so there's no misunderstanding …'

'But our prince, the Archduke of our Inner Austrian provinces, well, he's a deeply devout Catholic and hates Lutheranism. So why should we embrace the new religion when the highest authority is persecuting it?'

'You don't have to worry about that. The prince is a reasonable ruler. And besides, it's written in black and white that everybody has the right to pray in their own way and to take communion in one or both kinds. We will very politely remind the prince of all of this and work everything out.'

'But ...'

'Come on, out with it ...'

'Not far from here there are religious commissions going around villages and market towns and putting explosives beneath the prayer halls and blowing them to bits. In the towns they go from house to house looking for heretical books, which they gather up and burn in front of the Town Hall ...'

'All of this will stop. As I said, our representatives are going to Graz to negotiate a fair agreement with the prince,' the preacher answers.

'But why should we give up our saints and the Holy Mother of God? Who among us is brave enough to live without the altars to St Roch, St Sebastian and St Rosalia, who keep the plague from taking us all and make sure that at least some of us stay alive? Who is brave enough to live without the altar dedicated to the Virgin Mary? When everything goes wrong and nobody hears us, when everyone turns their back on us, Mary's gaze of infinite mercy remains before our eyes, comforting us here on earth and, if worse comes to worst, leading us to the other side, whether that means heaven or, for a time, purgatory ...'

'Purgatory!' the preacher explodes. 'Nowhere in the Bible is there a single word about purgatory! Was my sermon a complete waste of time? We will need to meet again, and I will repeat it, and I will keep on repeating it until every one of you understands. And now, dear people, I will give you communion, and later I'll repeat the lesson in the German language, and in between I'll have a little lunch. Some sort of soup perhaps? Maybe some fatty pork ribs swimming in barley and a piece or two of bread, maybe sausage and horseradish with some minced bacon? What do you say? Preaching is also work and no less strenuous than tilling the fields or mining for lead and iron ore. Tomorrow, you know, I'm going to visit the ironworks near here …'

'Oh, maybe it's best you don't,' the populace smiles knowingly. 'They don't like preachers there any more, and those fellows are even stronger than we are. So it's better to skirt around the ironworks and head west or north instead, out of these Catholic lands of ours, since we hear that the commissions are getting closer and they're using some harsh methods …'

'He who has faith is not afraid,' the preacher says.

'Well, preacher from Württemberg, when you see those visitators and their retinue of soldiers, your faith will be put to a terrible test …'

'I have the protection of the feudal lords – the nobility is more familiar with progressive ideas than you are …'

'The nobles will look out for their own arses, just like they've always done – always and everywhere, saving their arses they put ahead of saving your life. What you've been telling us – it's not so bad. And you've got a nice strong voice. If we weren't aware of the circum-stances we might even fall for it. But we're not so completely naïve. It's nice that you preachers have taught us to read and write a little. But that we might all of a sudden stand up to our masters – to our real masters, who have soldiers and power, who send judges around the province and decide if we live or die – and then there's plague, typhus, murrain, dysentery, Turks, earthquakes, floods … No, we'll stay with what we've got, and you do what you think is best for you. And good luck, too, but you're not going to have much of it in these parts. For people like you, there's more luck the further north you go from Graz and Vienna, and even north and west of Prague, or so they say …'

THE ARRIVAL OF
THE SEVEN ODDITIES

The preacher's sermon fell on fertile ground, even if the plants that most vigorously sprouted from its seeds were the ones least likely to delight the proclaimer of the pure Gospel. Soon after his departure, news spread about the arrival of seven individuals on the Kostanšek estate. They appeared to be male, but appearances can be deceiving, and not because they hide something but because they are so blatantly obvious that observers start honing and sharpening their perspectives and drilling into the phenomenon until some hidden truth gushes out of it. Unlike animals, people see what they want to see, whether it's something they dread and fear or something that's to their liking. And the populace started seeing all sorts of things on the Kostanšek estate. And were asking themselves all sorts of questions. And grew more suspicious by the day.

The seven individuals arrived one afternoon in late spring, or maybe it was evening and not quite spring but, actually, the end of winter, on an old cart driven by someone in a black cloak with a broad-brimmed hat. People began talking about their arrival and stories started spreading, although, apparently, only three people from the village had seen the newcomers. 'So what are foreigners doing hanging around here?' the hard-working populace wondered, for that is how they thought of themselves, as hard-working, even if they were always ready to take the time to comment on peculiar manifestations.

Soon all distinction was blurred between the eye-witnesses and most of the rest of the populace, who were able to imagine the things they heard so precisely and clearly that before long many believed that they, too, had been among those who observed the cart and saw a crooked hooked nose and long beard protruding from beneath its canvas cover. Two pairs of horses had been slowly pulling the cart. And no wonder. For when it came to a halt in the Kostanšek courtyard, stopping at an angle that was obviously meant to make it hard to see who was getting out, it was none the less possible to observe that the newcomers were of an enormous size. They were unusually huge. Nobody like that lived in the village or in the nearby town either. People like that didn't come to these parts. Nobody had ever seen anyone like that before.

'They were enormous?'

'Truly enormous.'

'And odd?'

'Very odd.'

'Dangerous?'

'They looked dangerous.'

'Hostile?'

'If they looked dangerous, they're probably hostile, too, right? Or maybe the logic of causes and consequences is backwards here, which is not insignificant, for these two notions leap back and forth, one into the other, and leaping should be mentioned here, too, since that's what a certain type of heretic does, at night in the woods, in remote clearings – leaping through fire and walking over coals, things that an honest person, a person with normal human abilities, is incapable of doing.'

'But how is it that when these supposedly fire-resistant types get caught, they go up in flames?'

'That's because, before we toss them on the fire we use well-tested methods to bend and break the evil spirit inside them, and when the evil spirit has no power their bodies can smoulder just as well as anyone's.'

'But what if they don't confess?'

'So far, anyone who has ever been guilty, whether or not they've confessed, has been utterly consumed by the flames. And anyway, no one is without sin. People are born into the world sinful.'

'But baptism washes away original sin, and besides, the Saviour has saved us from sin by his death …'

'Which, if we're honest, involved a bit of play-acting. After all, Jesus is God, and God is immortal.'

'But Jesus was also a man and died as a man, but as God he overcame death.'

'Still ...'

'Still ... but ... even so ... Doubt, doubt and more doubt! No matter how much our Saviour tried, no matter how many torments he suffered for our sake, the human soul is infested with doubt like the plague. No matter how much the saints, through their lives and the inevitable suffering connected with their lives, provide us with living examples of how to live and, especially, how to believe in a way that is right and pleasing to God; no matter how much the Virgin Mary appears to certain chosen ones; no matter how much painters paint the afterlife geography of purgatory, hell and heaven ... despite everything, there remains, incessantly, that accursed doubt.'

The populace doubts and is afraid and sees things that may or may not be real, sees things that are little more than ghosts, which they also see from time to time – including ghosts who come back from purgatory or stop on their way to the other world to visit a relative or neighbour with whom they never managed to settle accounts, so they go around haunting debtors and collecting debts, which for those who are very sensitive is sometimes fatal.

In general, when it comes to the truth, the populace relies on their eyes, but this does not mean that sight is their favourite sense. When it comes to pleasure, most prefer to shut their eyes and surrender to the sensations on their taste buds and breathe in what is right next to their skin. But when it comes to the truth, the sense of sight is first and foremost, whether it's sharp or hazy, sober or drunken, bold or bashful, hurried, terrified or delusional. And the populace is able to see all sorts of things. And so, much later, it turned out that the hooked nose was not even hooked and many things were not what they seemed to the eye. Things that, for a long time to come, would be spread around and talked about and repeated over and over ...

THE DAY WILL BE HOT AND EVERYTHING SEEMS OPEN

The early morning promised a very warm day, a hot day even. And it got him out of bed, which was unusual, as he tended to be of a slumberous nature. On late-autumn and early-winter mornings especially, he would peek out from beneath the thick layers of blankets and weigh the reasons and motivations for folding back the covers and exposing his body to the sharp tongues of cold damp. More than once, on such occasions, it occurred to him that, given his knowledge of languages and his clerical expertise, he would do well to apply for a position with a trading company in Asia or across the ocean and organize documents in the tropics somewhere, at a temperature to which he was better suited. At least that is how he imagined India and the New World, where it would surely be beneficial to keep inventories of cotton, silk, cane-sugar, coffee, cocoa, tea, spices, indigo, opium and other exotic goods, as well as saltpetre for making military explosives, for which there was a growing demand in the region, not least because the faith commissions were travelling around blowing up Lutheran prayer halls.

The warm morning glowed with an orangish yellow light. He pulled off his nightshirt and hopped naked from the window, through which he cast a glance to see what was happening in the main square below, over to the water pitcher and poured water into the basin. After washing his face, armpits and pubic area, he went to the big brass cage, reached into the linen satchel next to it, carefully opened the little cage door and sprinkled birdseed inside. The bird in the cage eagerly attacked its breakfast while the scrivener looked on, waiting for it to finish eating and start singing, for the bird sang only if it was contented and full. When it was hungry, it had no desire to sing and could even get tetchy, pecking at the fittings on its cage or in some other way making irksome noises.

Loud voices were coming in through the closed window from the square below, and he could not tell if it was a brawl or if someone had brought news that was making people excited.

'Look, Spiritus,' he said, bending towards his feathered pet, who was nervously pecking at the seeds, 'you might feel bad sometimes because you're locked in a brass cage. Being a bird, you probably get a craving to spread your wings and fly through the window, out of the room to freedom, and, like a town bird, sit wherever you wish and do whatever you want. But, my dear little bird' – he looked at Spiritus gobbling up his food in the big, softly rounded cage – 'if I let you out after you've eaten your fill here with me, you have no idea of the danger I'd be sending you into. You, who are a bird, do not understand (and it's debatable if you even know how to think, I mean, think at all like a man) – you don't understand that your unfreedom contains more freedom than if I released you and left you to your own devices. You just need to understand the notion of space a bit differently, and it will somehow be all right. I am protecting you from the violence of freedom; my love protects you, and so does your cage from which you can look through the window and watch everything that happens in the square below, everything you have been spared in your captivity, including the cats that stalk your near and distant relations, who, in moments of inattention, meet their fate in feline paws. Yes, Spiritus, actual experience isn't everything. A living creature can miss out on all sorts of experiences, and that might even keep him alive. Look at everything the common folk experience, and yet, apart from a few banal and threadbare remarks, they're unable to talk about it. That's because they don't know how to think, not really, but are instead trapped by what they see, what they can touch, what they smell, what they taste with their tongues and especially what they grasp through some folk sensibility as the only thing that's believable, and they won't hear any objections. Spiritus, my friend, for as long as I live, you will have your birdseed and even live worms, and you won't have to worry about a thing; you are spared most of the problems that beset your little cousins in their deceptive freedom. You can eat, drink, sleep and, when you feel the urge, you can sing, which will make me very happy. But today it will be hot, and that is reason enough to be happy. Most people will be surly and sulky. The Town Councillors will be nodding and dozing during the session; the whole thing will be drawn out and they probably won't reach any agreement, or maybe because it's so hot, they'll want to rush through everything. It looks like the heat means to stay for a while, and not just for today. So sing me something, little bird. Oh, what I'd give to have a small orchestra here that could sing and play me anything I wished whenever I wished it. Maybe in the future it will be possible to have your own orchestra, right in your home, which you could listen to in your own room whenever you felt like it!'

'Oh, Nikolai, there you go, daydreaming again, wasting time!' most people told him to shut him up whenever he mentioned such fancies. 'How can you imagine things like this, things that, when you think about it, are impossible? All those people living in your house would have to be fed, and no one has that kind of money, other than princely courts and wealthy burghers. It will never be possible; it takes money. And besides, first-rate musicians are hard to come by around here.'

'But maybe one day we'll be able to freeze sound,' Nikolai would protest. 'Maybe we'll freeze the things we see and hear, and later, whenever we wish, unfreeze them. I've read, and some Moors told me, too, that it's possible to make an impression of a human body on cloth so it can never be washed out …'

'Oh, you and your Moors and Jews and who knows who else! Indians, Chinese! Why do you bring up these foreigners, as if they were smarter than us? No, Nikolai, man is the crown of creation, and we are the precious gems in that crown – the educated men of the peoples of Europe, of our people, who draw knowledge and skills from the fountains of the Bible and antiquity. You are a dreamer, dear Nikolai, and you dream of nothing but fairy tales and fables …'

'Sure, sure, but maybe automatons could compress the sound for us …'

'What do you mean, automatons?'

'They would stand in for living people and sing so it's just like listening to singers in the flesh …'

'What an idea! This is total insanity! Every moment you spend thinking about this is a waste of time. So do you imagine people flying through the air, too? Driving carriages on the moon?'

'Why not? Think of everything we have today that in the distant past only the boldest minds could imagine, and most people doubted their visions.'

'Yes, of course, but they had reasons for their visions. Today when we look back at the past, such progress makes sense. It was there in embryo even in ancient times; we just had to wait for things to develop in the right direction.'

'It might seem like that today,' Nikolai answers, 'but, in fact, progress didn't develop smoothly all by itself. It happened through individuals, while the majority not only did not encourage these individuals, they mocked them, just as you're mocking me. They called them madmen and buffoons. And, like today, many of them were even killed because of their ideas. Visionaries have always been rare; they have always been a minority ...'

'Nikolai, Nikolai, that's all well and good, but you're not one of them. You're a smart, well-educated young man, but to count yourself among the great minds of the day is sheer arrogance and pride. You'd do better to perform your official duties faithfully as town scrivener, a profession that provides you with a living and not a bad salary either, rather than grubbing and poking around in things you only imagine or dream but don't really have a clue about ...'

Apart from Spiritus, nobody listens to me. I often feel quite alone, terribly lonely. But if they won't listen to me, maybe they'll read me, and maybe a few will understand me. So, from now on I will write. I will write what I am experiencing and what I am thinking. I'll write down the stories I think up. And soon I'll start writing about fundamental things: about what is and what it is that is.

AT THE TRIESTINE
MERCHANT-WOMAN'S HOUSE

I am writing about how I was struck by a remarkable smell the moment I stepped into the house of the Triestine merchant-woman. The door was opened by a maidservant with fair hair and a pinkish complexion; she was not pretty. Her face was a bit scrunched, her girlish nose stubby, the turned-down corners of her lips displayed annoyance and her beady, hamsterish eyes were watchful. She seemed aloof and slightly devious. She spoke in a nasal voice, the kind I can hardly stand. I've listened to more than my share of such voices, in various tonalities, at judicial proceedings. People talking through their noses, lying, slandering, calling each other names. The nasally ones I've never believed. They may or may not be telling the truth, but it always feels like they're lying, and in women I find it all the more repugnant. She led me to a room with a long walnut table in the middle. The smell of lilac was coming in through the wide open windows. And I thought of travellers who had passed through these parts from different places, and I remembered a woman who had once held a tincture to my nose. 'This is *jorgovan*,' she had said, 'the fragrance of the gardens – our *bašte* – which we left behind.'

When the lady entered the room, I bowed and introduced myself. 'My esteemed lady, I am Nikolai Miklavž Paulin, town scrivener and personal secretary to Mayor Volk Falke.'

'I have prepared the esteemed mayor samples of cloth in various shades. Take them to him, and then he may come here personally himself, or I can go to him, and I will help him choose and match the right combinations,' the Triestine merchant-woman said, slightly embarrassed.

I ran my eyes quickly over the fabrics she had arranged on the table and thought to myself that if I were the town messenger, as soon as I left the house of the Triestine merchant-woman, I would be telling everyone I passed along the way all the things I had seen in her eyes, and especially about the trace of disappointment when she found in the room not the shape she had been expecting and desired but only his envoy. Perhaps she had imagined that she would be the one setting the rules of the game, but the mayor is skilful and wolfishly cunning.

'Nikolai,' the mayor whispers to me before every such mission, 'please be discreet,' and I always nod my head. 'In these sweet yet dangerous battles, one must be cautious,' he instructs me. 'One must preserve the lady's honour and deflect the jealousy of the deceived husband.'

Now she will probably sit down and write a letter for me to take to the mayor, I thought.

'If you would only wait a moment ...' the merchant-woman says, then sits down, opens a drawer and takes out paper and a pen. I watch her as she leans over the table. She has mature features, not so much beautiful as dignified. Her skin is darker than the skin of the women here – olive – that's what you call such a complexion, I remember. Shades of chestnut and black pine mingle in her hair, her eyes are dark grey with tints of brown, her lips ... her hands ... Her figure is not full but seems rather solid, I am thinking when I suddenly realize that I have been holding her sealed letter in my hand for several seconds and am looking directly into her eyes. How strange, it occurs to me. When I was thinking about her, I was not really looking at her at all, but rather connecting her various features as if on some inner canvas.

'Scrivener, forgive me, but what is your name again?' the merchant-woman asks.

'Nikolai, gracious lady. Nikolai Miklavž Paulin,' I repeat, and the thought races through me, wouldn't it be wonderful if for some reason I started coming here regularly? Does she seem old to me? Rather old. Does she seem too old? Most definitely. Do I like her? I do indeed. I do like her. But more than the way she looks, I like the melody and dark colour of her voice.

*

'Nikolai, could you wait a moment?' The mayor had stopped me that hot day after a session of the Town Council. The melody of his voice told me the subject of his question. I am a careful observer. I can tell which matters people think are important and which matters they overlook, even when they are crucial.

'Would you happen to know who that elegant lady was who crossed our path in front of the Town Hall? I noticed that you greeted her. Was that simple courtesy or do you actually know her?' the mayor asked.

'I am not sure which lady you mean,' I dissembled, pleased that on this occasion, too, my expectations had not been wrong. Without this talent, would I be able to write or even to feel the desire to write stories, daily reflections or the philosophical meditations I will soon be attempting? And isn't my desire to return to the Triestine merchant-woman's house related in some obscure way to writing?

'Just because a woman doesn't look at a man,' the mayor continued, 'it doesn't mean she didn't notice him. Perhaps she doesn't look at him precisely because she knows he is watching her, that he is wondering how to get her attention, how to get her to turn her head so their eyes meet. While the man thinks about chance and fate, the woman plays a game of weaving a web of appearances. Women are better than men at this game; they are allotted only a modest space in public life and so have perfected alternative forms of communication.'

I thought a moment. It would not be so easy this time; the Triestine merchant-woman was arousing elevated feelings in the mayor, was leading him into reflection and rumination.

'Are you even listening to me?' The mayor's surprised voice brought me back to myself.

'Yes, sir, I'm listening,' I said.

'So who was that beautiful woman in the pickerel-grey dress, with the dark, slightly reddish hair, who walked by us earlier?'

'If I'm thinking of the right one, you're talking about a merchant-woman from Trieste.'

'So, a Triestine merchant-woman …' The mayor considers this as he twists his moustache, which he does whenever he's plotting something. He looks satisfied.

'Married? A widow?'

'I know nothing about that,' I say. 'She comes here alone, with two assistants. She is said to be a very able businesswoman.'

The muscles in the mayor's face relax, but his lips remain taut. 'So, a Triestine merchant-woman? And without a man? All the same, one must be cautious.'

Since then, their dance has followed the rhythm of Venetian cloth. Mayor Falke orders the cloth, she supplies it, the tailor and his assistants make the clothes, sew curtains, sew tablecloths, sew all sorts of things. And I go from one to the other, bringing samples and messages, and every time they open a letter I watch them and read in their faces what it says. When the clothes are made, other goods follow: olive oil, salt, coffee, southern fruit, almonds. That's what they are: the Triestine merchant-woman has almond eyes. Sometimes I stay for an hour, sometimes longer, and we talk about all sorts of things: the habits and customs of her people, how they worship their God. She tells me stories, sometimes very unusual stories, from different parts of the world, from Prague and Venice and even from Jerusalem and Tsfat, or Safed, the home of the Jewish mystics known as Kabbalists. She lays books in Hebrew on the table in front of me; one of them is the *Terumat ha-Deshen* by Rabbi Israel Isserlein, who lived in our part of the world. And, with particular reverence, she gently evens out a line of books on a silk cloth – the Kabbalistic writings known as the *Zohar*. As with the *Terumat*, I can do nothing but look at them; I know not a word of Hebrew or Aramaic. 'That's all right,' the merchant-woman assures me. 'One day I'll translate something for you, tell you about it, explain it.' Sometimes she lends me a book in German, Latin or Italian. And sometimes she even gives me one as a present.

There are several Triestine merchants who live in our town. They are not here permanently. They arrive, stay a few days, maybe weeks, even months, and then, when someone starts asking if those Triestine merchants have moved here for good, they disappear. They are not all crammed together at one end of town but live in houses distributed discreetly through one of the more prestigious districts; after all, none of them is poor. Some of them, perhaps, are not from Trieste but Gorizia, or from a town in the Gorizia area. They come here, stay for a time, leave and come back.

'But do they speak Slovene?' the townspeople wonder, as they watch them from a distance.

'Sure, they speak Slovene,' say those who do business with them. 'They speak Italian, and some of them speak German, too, and they also know another language, one that hasn't been spoken around here in a long time; it sounds a little like German, but it's not German, and it also has a few words we Slovenes understand.'

'Like what, for instance?'

'Well, for instance, there's a word that contains *grom* – "thunder".'

'You mean *pogrom*? We hear this word from the people who travel through our lands from Poland. And wasn't this word the reason merchants like them left our towns and villages a long time ago?'

'That's right. They had to leave our lands nearly a century ago by the decree of Emperor Maximilian.'

'So if these Triestine merchants are the ones we're thinking of, then should they even be living here?'

'No, they shouldn't. But some of their descendants have started coming back. And, in general, these Triestine merchants sometimes act as though they're not from Trieste or Gorizia but from here!'

'And that's not right, is it?' the people ask and answer their own question, 'Oh, no! No, it isn't, not at all …'

TRULY ODD

Kostanšek, people said, grew money on trees, and it was not just a saying. Part of his money he made from fruit – early-season cherries and apricots to late-season apples, pears and plums – which he would cart to the town to sell. His rye and buckwheat fields produced excellent yields, and his vegetables also did well, while his cows had udders the size of bulls' heads. (Such descriptions, of course, are colourful folk hyperbole and go much further than the usual documentary reports. But who wants to hear boring reports or read them – which is all the harder when reading is a skill rarely mastered? Only boring minds want that. And *mind* is itself a somewhat abstruse term for the boredom which reason, and even common sense, sometimes produces.)

But, whatever success he was having with farming, in years past, possibly because of the witch who was now being nibbled by chub and trout, his fields, like those of others, had been damaged by storms and floods, and the hoofs of his cattle and sheep had rotted, so that in the course of a few months most of his livestock perished. But that wasn't the worst of it: in those terrible times a few years ago, dysentery had completely disinterred the bowels of one of his sons and plague had taken the other and, although his daughter survived, a foul-smelling pus had started oozing from her eyes, so that even now she could barely see. That witch might have saved her, Kostanšek thought; he had not supported the persecution of the poor widow, but nor had he publicly opposed it. The populace, when agitated, can easily spot anyone who assists the scapegoat, so sometimes it's best to keep a low profile and say nothing.

One day when he was taking his produce into town, Kostanšek summoned his nerve and drove his cart, laden with wooden crates, into an area where some Triestine merchants were living, or temporarily residing, in three houses. Just as before the banishment, they dealt in commerce, small business and banking, but they were also known to be skilled at certain forms of healing and in spells unfamiliar to Christians. Kostanšek decided he would introduce his truly woeful springtime produce to the neighbouring culture and even, if necessary, lower his prices to something beneath human dignity, if only he might find somebody in their community who was able to help his daughter, whose poor health was scaring off suitors.

He did not want to offer them meat products, since they were generally known to make things complicated when it came to food, so when he appeared in their neighbourhood he brought only fruit and vegetables as well as some grain left over from the previous year. The women in their headscarves eyed him suspiciously; they had never seen him before. 'Why is he coming here?' they wondered. 'We buy our fruit and vegetables at the market.' But all the same, they sampled his produce. The cherries they spat on the ground half-chewed, saying they weren't even ripe but already had worms; they berated his onions as soft and half-rotten and his peas were puny. If he was hoping to unload his third-rate goods and get money for them, they suggested he bring his prices down as far as they would go, since if there hadn't been such a bad harvest all around after such a wretched spring, they wouldn't even be glancing at his merchandise.

Kostanšek swallowed the insults to his produce and told the women everything was negotiable, while they made faces and stuffed their baskets as if they were doing him a great favour. These people are a bit different from us, Kostanšek consoled himself, with habits and customs that are foreign to us; they're more abrupt, too, and maybe they have such a quick, hot temperament because they're from the coast, from the south. I only hope they don't charge me too much for information about a doctor who might cure the oozing from my daughter's eyes, but if I have to, I'll pay that, too, he thought resignedly.

'Why do we have the feeling that the produce you are pushing on us is simply a ruse?' The women examined him mistrustfully. 'Why didn't you take your wares to the market like others do? Why have you come to our community, which you people never like to do? What is it you really want from us?'

'I am interested in something you might be able to tell me,' Kostanšek replied.

'What makes you think we'd be crazy enough to tell you anything? We know all too well what your kind is like. We could end up like that poor woman you burned the year before last. But actually, we're not all that different from you; we even go to Mass on feast days.'

'You only show yourselves in church when there's a visitation commission in the area. And people who stand near you say you always make mistakes during the prayers; you hunt for the right words and don't really pray with us at all. Everyone knows about that little synagogue of yours, and we know whose house it's in …'

'Sure, if you want, it's all true,' the women said curtly. 'When the visitators show up with their military escorts, we go to your church, and we mumble a little as we pray our own prayers or think about what we'll make for Shabbos. So that's why you're here, to do a little spying, and then you'll accuse us of something, take everything we've got and drive us from our homes. Again.'

'Your homes? But aren't you here just temporarily?' Kostanšek asked.

'Well, aren't we all on this earth just temporarily? We, who by force of circumstance have been dispersed for thousands of years, we are always and everywhere just temporarily,' the women responded.

'You've got the wrong idea,' Kostanšek protested. 'I have nothing at all against you.'

'If you're persecuting those Lutherans and those Founders and Leapers, too, you'll get rid of us even faster …'

'I'm not persecuting anybody. If it were up to me, the world would be run differently. We wouldn't persecute women or other races,' Kostanšek said.

'Who are you to say how the world should be run? You should worry about that Christ of yours and his resurrection! The fact that the world even exists, all of you – Catholics, Lutherans and Turks alike – you have our Jewish God to thank, since he's the one who created it. There wouldn't be anything without our God! Not the market, and not you either, peasant! Not even us Jews! And certainly not your sour cherries, puny peas and rotten vegetables …'

'Who knows what would or wouldn't be. But right now I'm interested in something I think you women might be able to help me with …'

'If it's money or business, go talk to our husbands …'

'But I expect it's you who can tell me more about doctors. My daughter has a foul-smelling pus seeping from her eyes, and she can barely see. And sometimes her back hurts so much that all of a sudden she collapses, and then we go out looking for her, from the sawmill to the barn, and carry her back to the house,' Kostanšek explained.

'It's obvious what the problem is. The girl has been struck by the evil eye. Somebody's put a spell on her, and if you don't act fast it will kill her. You see over there, peasant?' They pointed at one of the houses. 'That's where you need to go, but it won't be cheap. They know what to do against evil magic, and they also know about potions and plants. But now let's settle the bill for the produce, although, in fact, it's you who should pay us for taking it off your hands, and our advice isn't free, you know …'

Without protesting, Kostanšek nodded his head and soon came to an agreement with the women, who paid him enough to at least cover the cost of the trip. 'But what's your physician called?' he asked before leaving them.

'That would depend on whether he or she even has a name,' the women answered, as they laughed and patted their baskets, so Kostanšek wasn't sure if they hadn't maybe pulled a fast one on him and for the next few days would be amusing themselves at his expense.

Not long afterwards, someone with a long black beard started visiting the Kostanšek farm. The clouds in the daughter's eyes cleared and her back pain subsided. Soon everything was getting better or, rather, getting very suspicious, especially after that evening when the sky was no longer bright, but nor was it yet dark, and one could still discern the shadowy shapes that climbed stiffly out of the cart. There were seven of them. Kostanšek seemed minuscule by comparison as he helped the shadows down, assisted by two farmhands, both strapping lads, whose size, however, likewise dwindled in their presence. The last to leave the cart was the same tall, thin person with a long beard and a nose like a candle-snuffer who only weeks before had been poking around Kostanšek's property.

'So what sort are they then? They're not from around here,' the populace asked themselves about the newcomers. The human spirit, it is said, has no boundaries, and a person can travel on the wings of the imagination, but the imagination doesn't always fly; sometimes, as here, it walks with halting steps and trudges along, shod in boots of superstition and the fear of whatever seems different and strange.

Kostanšek was probably lodging them above the pigsty and had laid a little straw down for them there, the populace speculated, becoming evermore preoccupied with them.

Each morning, before dawn, the seven giants, led by Kostanšek, would set off with their tools to the fields and, regardless of sun or rain, work without a break until late evening, ploughing, digging, sowing, hoeing. 'What on earth will he pay them with?' people wondered. 'They can't be working just for room and board, and even if they were, such goliaths must eat more than they produce!'

The giants ploughed, and when they finished the ploughing they sowed, and then in summer they reaped the harvest and mowed and baled the hay. But on Sundays, not one of these lumbering male figures of indeterminate age, who walked like bears (but unlike bears they had not a single hair on their arms or faces, nor even eyebrows, the women noticed) was anywhere to be seen. Now and then, out of curiosity, a woman might bring them a loaf of bread and water, but Kostanšek always sent her on her way, saying tersely that he'd see to his workers, thank you, and she'd do better to feed her children if she couldn't sate her curiosity!

'That puffed-up Kostanšek is hiding something,' the women decided, exchanging glances, and launched into a group interrogation.

'So what sort are those workers of yours? Where'd you find them, Kostanšek? Do they even speak our language?' the women asked, leaning on the fence and surveying from a distance the workers' big round heads and shovel-like hands. 'We had no idea the world contained such tall, enormous … *people!*'

Even when they were measuring them up with their eyes, the strange labourers paid no attention to them. So the women resorted to an ancient fact-finding strategy and sent their daughters over with that importunate loaf in their hands. Men who have spent so many weeks alone, they reasoned, surely wouldn't turn their backs on a young girl. And even if they don't speak her language, they'd have something nice (or more likely, something lewd) to say to her in their own tongue.

But they didn't. They didn't say anything. And when the girls were hanging about nearby, they didn't even turn around.

'So why don't they ever talk?' the women asked Kostanšek.

'They're mutes,' he shot back without thinking.

'What, all of them?' the women persisted.

'Most of them. From the day they were born,' he replied.

'But where are they from?'

'From far away.'

'How far away?' The women would not let up.

'Very far away.'

'From up north?'

'No.'

'So they're southerners.'

'No, they're not,' Kostanšek replied calmly, since he didn't dare tell them to get lost.

'From the east, then?'

'That's right.'

'But where, exactly? They're not from China, or Coromandia either …'

'They're from the Caucasus!' Kostanšek blurted out.

'The Caw-Caws? What's that?' They looked at each other sceptically. 'What kind of a cocked-up name is Caw-Caws? … Caw-Caws! Common sense tells us a place with a name like that, like something crows coughed up, can't exist, and you, Kostanšek, made this caca up just to get rid of us!' And they nudged each other with their elbows, saying, 'Don't they have weird eyes! It's like they're not alive. They're lifeless, like the eyes of a slaughtered calf, completely dead.'

'Why don't they ever come to church? Why do they neglect their religious duties?' The priest had tugged Kostanšek's sleeve one day after Mass, as he and his daughter were climbing on to their cart.

'They're not Christians. They're from far away, from the Caucasus, where they worship different gods,' Kostanšek replied.

'The Caucasus?' The priest thought for a moment. 'But how can they worship other gods when there are no other gods, only *our* God?'

'Well, they have a different opinion. They were raised differently and have different customs and habits, but they're good people.'

The priest thought he had laid suspicious stress on the word *people*, but a moment later Kostanšek pressed five silver coins into his hand. 'For the church, it'll be needing repairs.'

'It certainly will. And will those workers of yours be able to help?' the priest enquired.

'Not very likely,' Kostanšek said. 'They have so much to do at my place. They're good, hard-working fellows.'

'I'm sure they're hard-working, but are they good? How do you know they're good, if they're mutes?' the priest asked.

'Well, they're probably good partly because they're mutes,' Kostanšek replied. 'They don't swear, they don't lie, they don't insult you, they don't gossip, and what's more, they don't stick their noses into other people's business.'

The priest weighed the coins in his palm, glanced down at them and gave Kostanšek a meaningful look. 'I'm not sure it's a good idea for your daughter to be living with seven hard-working musclemen. Seven giants, who've spent so many months away from home, alone, without women ... Who will protect her when you're not there? Your two farmhands? Your elderly maidservants?'

'Nothing's going to happen. They're obedient and meek – they have that in their blood. They belong to a hard-working people who aren't malicious, whose language, I'm told, doesn't even have a word for "kill" or "murder". They don't even know what lying is,' Kostanšek lied.

'Interesting, very interesting ... Did they tell you that themselves?' the priest asked, setting a transparent trap for him.

'No, their agent told me.'

'Their agent!' The priest was amazed. 'I had no idea there were agents going around the area offering farmers mute labourers with foreign manners. So how do they communicate? How do they know what you want from them or what work they should do?'

'I show them,' Kostanšek answered.

'Uh-huh ... You show them ... you show them ...' The priest was thinking. 'But it's not possible to show them everything.'

'Or say everything either,' Kostanšek added. 'But, as a matter of fact, they're not completely mute.'

'They're not? But a moment ago you said they all were.' The priest would not give up.

'Well, they so rarely say anything it's like they're almost always silent. And in general, they'd much rather show you something than say it. And, besides, they use signs to communicate with each other,' Kostanšek said.

'Signs? What sort of signs?'

'Their own signs. Like I told you, they have different habits, a different language; they even write differently.'

'Oh, they know how to write, do they?' the priest asks, surprised. 'How do they do it, from right to left?'

'No, in a circle. They start at a certain point, then keep circling out until they run out of room,' Kostanšek explained.

'Really? What a crazy world this is! But do they know any of our words?' the priest asked.

'They understand a few words, the basic ones. But if a person wants to, and makes an effort, he can communicate not only with people from other places who have different customs, but even with animals. And the opposite is also true. If a person doesn't want to communicate, he won't understand even his own language. Everyone around him will be a foreigner, and he'll be the biggest foreigner of all, to himself ...'

'You sure know how to talk, Kostanšek, and you spin a good tale, but let me tell you right now that this talk of yours is not very convincing. You can sell your fairy stories to me, because I know that when that bony finger points at you, you'll send your daughter for me, and you'll confess your lies about mutes and the Caucasus. And, as you know, you'll get absolution and all will be forgiven you, because Our Lord is infinitely merciful. But our other lords, the populace, are much less merciful. And the populace, as you know yourself, has no idea what mercy means. So, peasant, be very careful and watch what you do with those workers of yours. I can shut my right eye if they come and fix the roof for me, and I can squint my left a little if they bring me some of your produce when they come, and flour, too, but if you think I'll shut both eyes at the same time, well, that's not going to happen.'

'I don't see anything wrong with that,' said Kostanšek.

'And I don't see anything right with what you've been telling me. Lying is a terrible sin, and God may forgive it, but the Church and the secular authorities are far less likely to. Neither you nor I had ever heard of the Caucasus before that Turkish fellow, Zoltan Kotz, came to these parts. He was captured during one of the Turkish raids, but they let him live because he showed the desire and intention to learn another one of our languages (he already knew Croatian) and to settle in the area and translate when translation was needed. And that's what he's done. He has no lack of little anecdotes from the empire of Suleiman the Magnificent – if only because he makes them up as he tells them. And a few weeks ago in the tavern, I noticed that people were all ears when Kotz, speaking in what is by now a rather fluent Slovene (you've got to give him credit for that), was telling his Caucasian fairy tales.'

'All right, fine. Tell me what needs to be done on the church and I'll send them over to you and they'll work for the good of the community,' Kostanšek offered.

'For starters, the roof needs patching. And the damp is seeping into the walls of the presbytery and gnawing at my bones, and I'm sure other things will turn up. But let me give you a friendly, well-meant piece of advice: stop telling these little tales of yours and find some other story. We live in sensitive times: the authorities are watchful and the populace is easily aroused ...'

'Was it ever any different?' Kostanšek looked at the priest.

'Probably not, but these days patience is extremely rare, and caution is a principle we would do well to heed.

'I'll send them over to you; just let me know when,' Kostanšek said and snapped the whip above the horses' heads.

'You do that, and don't forget, the populace has eyes that can see even from behind shut eyelids, and the authorities have ears that can listen even to unspoken thoughts. But go now, peasant, pray and work, and it's best if you do them together. And remember, all sorts of things can happen to a living human being.'

WITH A COLD, PIERCING MIND

'So how are you managing things, noble Count?' Prince-Bishop Wolf-gang, peeling an orange, asks Count Friedrich after supper.

'It's difficult. There's never enough money,' Friedrich replies.

'Money must be collected. Introduce some special tribute payments or an extra quit-rent; the provincial authorities are also planning to raise the standard taxes and introduce some special ones.'

'But what will it all lead to?' Friedrich says, frustrated. 'The populace will rise up against me, just like they did with Spitzenberg. First they set fire to his castle and then those primitive devils ambushed him and impaled his head on a stake, like Turks, and his body they tore apart with horses in all four directions.'

'The story is a bit more complicated ...' the prince-bishop says.

'His vassals rebelled ... It was a peasant uprising.' Count Friedrich looks at him in doubt, but also with fear.

'Yes, it was, but they didn't do it by themselves or on their own initiative.'

'So it was your people who killed him?' Count Friedrich gasps, dumbfounded.

'We never laid a finger on him,' Prince-Bishop Wolfgang replies.

'But what have you done with his family?'

'There is order now. As I said, I've assumed guardianship of the orphans. Our educational goal is that the daughters (whom the Poor Clares have already taken under their supervision) will pledge their lives to God, so the family wealth won't be needlessly whittled away in dowries – unless, of course, we find them strategically important suitors. The sons, meanwhile, we'll divide between the Church and secular service. They're not stupid, you know, despite their tender age, and their father's example has taught them that obstinacy only leads to ruin. The noble Countess Spitzenberg – who even more than the children understands that it's best not to cause trouble – will pledge herself to widowhood. She is profoundly grateful to us for rescuing her and her children from the destruction and slaughter that the rabble intended for them …'

'But Wolfgang, you knew him!' the count breaks in.

'We warned him. I personally warned him several times. "Spitzi," I said, "stop screwing around! You used to be one of us, but more and more you're not. Give up this Protestantism of yours, which is getting out of hand, because if you don't, it'll end badly for you." But he was stubborn and said he was a free man with a free mind and that there were new minds on the horizon that weren't musty like ours, and although we could still be friends he had no intention of submitting to us, to the pope or to the prince, and he added that he read the Bible himself, directly, without interpreters or guides. "*Sola scriptura! Sola scriptura!*" he kept repeating like a madman.'

'But Oswald was our friend!' Count Friedrich interjects with a lump in his throat.

'Our friend made a fatal mistake,' Prince-Bishop Wolfgang responds. 'Given the choice between his fiefdom and his life, he chose both: to live on his own land; he started ordering weapons from armourers and entrenched himself in his castle with a few years' worth of provisions. Oh yes, he knew we weren't joking. But what good are cannon and muskets against a rapacious mob and irrational, greedy human nature? Like us, he realized that the friction between the Habsburg authorities and the Provincial Estates was not about God, it was about power. Even so, why did he have to invite every possible Protestant heretic, domestic and foreign, to join his ranks? Why did he have to fall for his own delusions, believing that there on his fiefdom, in the middle of the increasingly Catholic Inner Austrian provinces, he could set up some autonomous Lutheran entity, citing and relying on past imperial promises about the right to religious choice?

'One evening when I visited his castle unannounced, he got so agitated he was positively sweating. He couldn't give a damn about the prince or the provincial army or the mercenaries, he shouted. "But Spitzi, it's not so simple," I tried to tell him. "There's an entire network of power connecting the emperor, the prince and your fiefdom;

some of its branches are more visible and others are unseen, but it's not wise to circumvent any of them. You can't just split off and black-mail the prince by threatening disobedience and refusing to pay the special taxes. Even if we've been close friends since our early youth, we're mature individuals today. So be careful," I warned him, "not everything is in my hands – the same hands in which, in days long past, your lively cock once made its nest. These are serious matters – political and economic matters. And anyway, what do you see in this heretical Protestantism, which has significantly less spirit, less intellect, than the papal religion and, with the possible exception of music, no feeling whatsoever for beauty? And which makes such a sanctimonious show of despising luxury while, in fact, it's close-fisted and calculating in the most vulgar way? The Lutherans criticize us for selling indul-gences, but they themselves are no better than third-rate pedlars. And need I mention all the fanaticism among their rank and file, which surpasses even the religious manias in ours? As if there's any more spirituality in Protestantism than you could find in a young man's sack or arse!'" The prince-bishop clicked his tongue, giving the count just enough time to cover his face with his hand. 'But Spitzenberg insisted that he had nothing more to say and what would be would be. "Oh, it will be, you can be certain of that. It will be, but it won't be good. No, it will be very bad," I replied, and felt genuinely sorry for him then. "For heaven's sake, Oswald, this is no simple matter," I said. "I'm telling you as a friend: if you don't want to be on our side, then you need leave everything behind and go, because with your beliefs and convictions, if you stay here, you'll lose everything you have." But he just shook his head stubbornly as I looked away and wiped a tear from my eye with my handkerchief. Then I looked at him again and tried one last time. "So, my dear Ožbej" – I used his Slovene name – "there's only one thing to do: hightail it out of here as fast as you can! Go to some place in northern Europe where our long arm won't reach. Get on a boat with those Anabaptists and on the way to the New World pray that God doesn't destroy it as a punishment. And if you do manage to cross the ocean with those fanatics, then put on sackcloth, pick up a shovel and start digging in the foreign soil, and, while you're at it, try not to get an arrow in your neck." Because they say that there across the ocean people don't know much about Jesus, if they know anything at all, and that the locals wear maize around their necks and hop in a circle around the fire, howling with the wolves at the full moon – and that they're extremely peculiar and, mainly, very different from us. Even in appearance. They're not white, like Christians, or blue-blooded like us noblemen (even if those social-climbing burghers like to spread the calumny that if we're blue-blooded it's only because the silver from our silverware seeps into our blood during our banquets and turns our skin blue). No, the people over there aren't even black, like the Moors of Africa, or greyish brown, like their New World potatoes, or yellow, like maize or like the Chinese with their slanted eyes. The people over there are red-skinned like turkeys, and they don't believe, or, rather, don't have a clue, that Christ is the saviour of all mankind, that he suffered and died on the Cross and that through his Resurrection he redeemed even their own little souls from original sin. I doubt they even know their red-hued bodies contain souls. They're more interested in talking with bears and eagles, whom they worship as gods, and they're not unlike the ones our own populace still secretly blathers on about today, with all their sorceries to boot, which smoulder unnoticed like hot coals badly covered by sand, right until somebody pokes them about, blows a spell into them and the populace goes wild. That's why our emissaries of God have been meticulously informing those godless redskins, to whom Jesus had not yet been revealed, of the great error in which they live – among other things, how wrong their couplings have been, no better than the mating of dogs or sheep. But since they don't how to read or write (because, being primitives, they have no script), it is proper that we forgive their ignorance, delusions and errors and announce to them that 'knowing', in the biblical sense of the word, must have one, and only one, purpose: to bring yet one more Christian into the world, that is to say, one more Catholic, who is immersed in holy water right after he is born.'

'You have the gall to say that, Wolfi!' Count Friedrich interrupts him. 'You, who pursue knowledge (in the biblical sense of the word) without the least intention of enlarging the number of God's people! You, who are like the stiff-cocked men of Sodom and Gomorrah, or the prettified *eromenoi* of ancient times ...'

'*Erastai*, darling,' the prince-bishop corrects him. 'The *eromenos* phase, and the firm, milky-white buttocks that go with it, we outgrew long ago. You've confused two essential Socratic ideas. Clearly, you haven't been reading a thing or thinking much either. But then, you never did understand Plato's *Symposium*. You timid dicks, who are the majority, settle for Aristotle's boring middle measure, while Socrates and Plato are meant for elevated minds and noble natures.'

'But as Plato tells us, Socrates was dialoguing with the lads, unlike you, Wolfgang, who wrench the arms and stretch the mouths of children ...' Count Friedrich looks at him reprovingly.

'Such is my fate, dear friend. On the road towards a glimpse of the Beautiful and the Good, divine Eros constantly detains me. I am weak and simply unable to break through to the stage when I no longer see Beauty in bodies but only and exclusively in souls. Still, I persist and, albeit slowly, am moving towards the time when I will see beauty nowhere but in the soul, in Christian rites and, at the very end, in God,' the prince-bishop says, becoming animated.

'Nothing you say has anything to do with Christianity,' Friedrich responds.

'It's not an easy road we poets and philosophers travel. And it's more complex than the calculations the majority makes for their comfort. But let's return to those primitive redskins,' the prince-bishop continues. 'There are places in the New World that could be duplicates of the *eidos* of Paradise itself. I am talking about the Caribbean Islands, Fritzi, where the lovely sugar on our tables comes from, and, if we're very lucky enough to have it, that glorious nectar, chocolate; pumpkins, too, are from those climes and maize has its home there. These are gorgeous places – rich in flora, fauna and such sweet little angels, it's as if the Creator made them just for himself. And while it's true that the people on those islands are not fair in complexion, neither are they red or yellow, but the colour of rich cacao, nicely roasted, and they're as benighted as the darkest lunar eclipse – and let me tell you, Fritzi, the nights are dark there; such darkness we in our part of the world can hardly imagine. Also, the moon there waxes and wanes differently. Not vertically like here, but horizontally. People who have been there say the full moon is like a big red orange and, as it wanes, it empties like a teacup, until at the new moon there is such blackness you can't tell the sea from the sky ...'

'But what does any of this have to do with Spitzenberg?' Friedrich interrupts him.

'Nothing more or less than that he did not take my advice and sail off to those heavenly oases, or go to India, Japan, Africa or even China, but instead entrenched himself in his castle and had the delusion to believe that he'd be able to defend his property, his principles and his person. If he is lucky and such is God's will, all is forgiven him on the other side, and by now quite possibly (we both remember what he was like) he has booted the Baby Jesus out of the Father's lap and is sitting on God's knee rubbing himself up and down ...'

'Wolfgang!'

'The vivid beauty of a landscape, Fritzi, is but a pale shadow in comparison with the vividness of the mind – a rare quality in man. People are lazy, foolish creatures, more foolish even than animals, which are driven by the instinct for survival and have no mind or soul – well, heresy or not, we could say that even certain animals have souls. Unlike the populace, who crave a master and, if they don't have one, invent him, invent somebody who will tell them what to do and what not to do, the right way to copulate and when not to copulate, what is pleasing to God and what God finds wicked. Without guidance, instructions, prohibitions and commands, the poor ignorant populace is lost.'

'But all this is the very opposite of what you were saying a few moments ago ...'

'*Quod licet Iovi, non licet bovi.* Jove may do what cattle may not. What applies to the multitudes does not apply to the select few – to us. The only way to maintain order is to keep the instincts of the majority in check and under firm control. When the populace breaks free of its chains, we both know how hard it is to catch it and put it back in the pens. But none of that applies, of course, to the few of us who are beings of the mind. And, besides, some of us, a rare few, are above reproduction: we don't replicate ourselves and extend our line endlessly through a posterity that will most likely deteriorate over time. The good qualities of a man can't be threshed out from the bad ones through the body, but only by giving the mind a good thrashing.'

'You and I, Wolfi, had the good luck to be born in starched white sheets. This was fate, or intention, or whatever …' Friedrich says.

'So what? Do you think the populace, given the chance, would be willing to wriggle out of those starched sheets and into the bonds of thought? Do you think they'd find it worth getting out of bed in the morning to devote themselves to reflections on God, the soul, being and nothingness, the Logos? No, they'd be content with copulating, eating and shitting. And if one day in the future someone gives them the opportunity to truly learn how to read and write and educate themselves a little, they'll do it only so long as they believe the skills are useful. And who will tell them what is useful if not their masters?'

'But Wolfgang, again we've strayed from the subject. I still do not understand why you didn't let Spitzenberg live. The nobility – the feudal lords – we have been given the right to choose our own religion …'

'Oh, come on, Fritzi! You still don't get it? That bull-headed man refused to do business with us! So we got rid of him. And we did it the way he used to like – from behind, ramming him up the bum. But we left his castle intact; after all, Ožbej always had exquisite taste. When our plans reached his ears, as fast as he could he started ordering weapons from his arms dealer, Mayor Volk Falke, including, for himself, a superbly engraved suit of armour and swords from the Innsbruck masters. He equipped his vassals with weapons, entered into Protestant alliances and was negotiating with his Hungarian and German allies. If he had not been the commander of the forces in the Slavonian and Croatian Military Frontiers, matters could have been handled quite easily. He might have lost his footing somewhere, or fallen off his horse, or accidentally drowned in one of the ponds where he liked to take a dip with the girls. His rebellion might have been cut short by some random personal tragedy, an ordinary mishap, perhaps, or an alleged jealousy killing. No one can say that Spitzi lacked charm. Stubbornness and passion can combine in an irresistible attraction that's difficult to withstand but that can also provoke intense loathing – from envy, of course. It's envy that makes those pallid shadows who languish in a semblance of being alive pounce on such rare, full-blooded individuals, people who think themselves larger than life and whose exalted ideas and obstinate opinions both enchant and repulse the majority. The same thing can happen with passionate lovers who, because of their intense mutual affliction – all right, affection, but love is a kind of affliction, too, is it not? – are ready to gamble away everything, and especially their lives, since they tell themselves: What's life without the person I love? That's no life at all! But because Spitzenberg was the military commander of the Military Frontier, his story needed to be educational, a lesson to deter similar stiff-necked attempts, but also we didn't want to overplay it: we didn't want his story to be blown up into some sort of heroism and infect other fiefdoms.

'As Spitzenberg was making preparations to oppose the prince's forces, we deftly divided the peasantry he had armed. The populace, who were burning with the desire to exchange blows with the provincial army and its mercenaries, were infiltrated by our own people – and for the right price anybody, apart from those of Spitzi's ilk, can be one of our people. And so, from time to time, one of them would start thinking out loud, "Hold on a minute, just hold on," they'd say. "Do we really need to be doing all of this? Why should we fight for our lord, who is resisting the prince, if that only causes more problems for us? Is the count really worth sacrificing our lives for, and our families' lives and our property (regardless of how much it really belongs to us)? And, last but not least, why should we care about Lutheranism? We simple folk have never felt close to this dreary religion, even if some of its preachers are colourful speakers. But we hear that Catholic priests, too, are starting to use colourful images in their sermons and in a language we understand. The so-called Bruck rights to free religious choice? That has nothing to do with us – as if we ordinary people could choose between Catholicism and Lutheranism. That's the privilege of the aristocracy. True, our count isn't exactly forcing us to accept his religion, and he lets us keep our Catholic faith and even turns a blind eye when he goes out hunting and rides past that temple, or prayer hall, or whatever it is those Leapers have set up in his hunting grounds. But, even so, he's made it clear enough that he'd like to see our colourful churches turned into cold, dreary prayer halls, and as soon as possible, too, so his fiefdom will eventually be entirely free of papist pressure. Because it's not just the pope, who lives far away in Rome, there are also patriarchs, archdeacons, suffragans, vicars, provosts, bishops, prince-bishops, canons, priors, prelates, legates … a whole host of papist leeches sucking on the nobility and the populace, sucking on us all the way from Rome to Aquileia and Salzburg – or so the count tells us. But are we really prepared to give up our shrines and side altars just like that? Our religion gives us a saint for every illness, every problem, someone we can turn to and talk to; we press a kreutzer in his hand and do a little bargaining. The idea that we should give up St Florian, whose shrine stands in the middle of our village – we wouldn't think of it for a moment. We don't dare live without the saint who shields us from fires. There have been far too many fires here in the past – whether natural misfortunes or something beyond nature and human power, who can say? But we know it would have been a whole lot worse if we didn't have St Florian protecting us with his bucket of water; without him the whole village would have burned to the ground. And the idea that we'd remove St Roch from the main altar of our church – we'd have to be crazy to do that. The plague visits our village on a regular basis, and each time it does, a part of the population dances off with it in the Dance of Death. Without St Roch or St Rosalia on the side altar or the plague columns and roadside shrines, first one village, then another and eventually every village in the entire area would be dancing that same dance. But saints aren't enough when it comes to the Turks, who have been besieging us for centuries. For them, we need a strong defence, much stronger than anything our liege lord can muster, and that's why unity among the Hereditary Provinces, which guarantees us a common defence, is so extremely important and makes so much sense. Who else will protect us from the Turks? Certainly not the Germans up north, whose nostrils have never had a whiff of Turkish cannon fire. Will the Hungarians protect us? They have their own problems with the Turks. The Bohemians? Don't count on it. They'll wait for us to deal with them first – or for the Turks to deal with us. Because it's easy getting tangled in the briar patch when it's somebody else's dick, but it's our dicks that have to tangle with Turkish sabres to defend Inner Austria – and not just Inner Austria, but like we did at Sisak a few years ago, the entire Holy Roman Empire! It's us, not them, who get captured by the Turks and carried off into their dark empire. And, finally, can we really be so very happy with our count? He may be no worse, but he's also no better than any other lord. Just like the others, he milks us dry with chimney taxes and head taxes; he sends his men to count the tails in our barns and inspect our granaries to make sure we're not holding out on him. And now he's giving us the burden of defending him and his religion. We'll squeeze this in, too, he assures us, just until we get rid of the papists, and then things will be better. Really? Better? When one day soon we see the mercenaries in the distance, those well-trained butchers with the finest helmets and professional weapons, who don't give a damn about us, about our country, our fief-dom or our province but only about the weight of their purses and the denomination of the coins inside them, so that if they survive the battle they'll be richer when they go back to their homes or on to the next field of combat – when we see them coming, there's no way things will be better for us! Just the opposite, things will be bad, very bad, and common sense tells us that we should avoid this. Are we really so crazy as to risk everything for the sake of one lord's feudal arse, especially when we know we're going to lose, and not just lose the battle but our lives as well?"

"'You know, what he's saying, it's not stupid," voices now echo from the populace, at first individual, impersonal voices, then others, still impersonal but louder and increasingly connected, until eventually they merge into one powerful voice, one thought, one conviction, one people, united against their feudal lord.

"'But our count, he's not going to like us deciding not to support his whims," sneers can be heard.

"'Oh, for sure, he's not going to agree." The laughs are getting louder and louder until they are full-throated guffaws. "Only why didn't we realize it before, the enormous power we have – we, the people, against the count and his soldiers, who are well-fed at our expense and protected behind strong walls? Why didn't it hit us until now, just how many more of us there are and how much stronger we are than the count, stronger than his soldiers and those dolled-up sluts of his? Yes, yes, those sluts!" And already mouths are stretched wide, because, naturally, you start by insulting the frailest people connected to the person who is now being transformed from master into enemy. It's not enough to kill the enemy. No, first you have to humiliate him, and do so in a way that causes him pain. And not just physical pain. Because if the body hurts too much, a man will float up into his thoughts and drift away, but if he feels the pain of humiliation, oh, then he might start to think, and only then does it really hurt. So it's good to go after the enemy's loved ones. The women first (that goes without saying), and you start by raping them in front of their master – the enemy. This is not to make *them* suffer, or make his children and his nearest and dearest suffer, because when we attack them, we'll be glancing over at him and checking to see if he's really suffering, if he's afraid, if he's on his knees – to see if that bastard is finally scared of *us*!

'After that, all we needed was to work out the logistics of our plan and its implementation. When the rabble had done their job, believing that their rebellion had broken out spontaneously from within their ranks, that is, that a crowd of ordinary simpletons had carried out an apparent peasant uprising against a tyrannical overlord – Friedrich, you have no idea how easy it is to manipulate the masses; you just need a few sparks to catch fire, and right away the crowd identifies with these eruptions, convincing themselves that they had long felt the need and necessity for change – well, when the poor, stupid wretches with their overheated brains and aching testicles ambushed the count in the courtyard and were already climbing the stairs into the castle, our men stopped them in their tracks. We didn't want them to trample the Turkish carpets, smash those beautiful Chinese vases, crush those fascinating dried Indian heads, break the folding screens with the carved traceries, muck up the chiffon garments and help themselves to the gold and precious gems from God-knows-what country, not to mention the collection of erotic art from distant India, which was carefully stored away in a secret cabinet in Spitzi's bedchamber – you know, those people with their turbans and elephants are experts at nobly transcending mere animal copulation; they do something more than just sow and reap with this godly gift, they create erotic art.'

'But Wolfgang, you, me and Spitzenberg – we've known each other since we were little. We had such wonderful times as children; we used to play together …' Friedrich again interrupts the prince-bishop.

'Yes, we knew each other and had wonderful times playing together when we were little noblemen being sent to all the courts of Europe, including that spring when we were sent to Granada, with the rich fragrance of jasmine blossoms carried on the wind through the gardens of Alhambra and the unfinished palace of Charles V. There, at night, we'd play hide-and-seek and then, disguised as locals, sneak off to Sacromonte, to the gypsies in the hollow, and from there, I don't know how many times we'd run off to some villa and loll about in its aromatic gardens. Do you remember those old Moorish houses, Fritzi? It was there, that spring in Granada, where we lost our innocence – in every respect. From then on, life was no longer child's play but a very dangerous game. Do you remember, Fritzi?'

'Shut up, Wolfgang. Just stop talking.'

'I'll stop talking about this – for now ...' the prince-bishop says.

'Wolfgang, we took an oath that we would support each other no matter what, that we wouldn't let anyone come between us, that nothing would impinge on our friendship ...' Friedrich says, his voice cracking.

'We took an oath, and then we changed. Repetition, Fritzi; it squeezes out all pathos and emotion. That's simply how it is. I need to finish this work of cleansing the lands of Inner Austria, and then my mission in this part of the world is done. And soon that beautiful day will arrive – beautiful for me, but, in fact, it will be a dismal, dingy autumn day, when the cold damp will gnaw at the bones of men and animals, and a thin, cold slime will drip from the roofs and trees, when your feet will sink into muddy snow and everywhere will reek of rot and decay, and the rabble will stink even worse than they do in the summer, when the stream is warm and close enough for them to wash away their foul odours. On that day, all prinked up, in armoured boots of Prussian leather and with all my dearest possessions, as well as fresh meat (indispensable for an ocean crossing), and with my music and books and whatever of the spirit can be compressed into material form, I will set off in a carriage to the sea, board a three-masted ship and sail away to that paradise I was telling you about. Not to the northern part of the New World, where those stiff-necked Protestant heretics are planning to run off to, but farther south, to the Gulf of New Spain, where the only peril an honest man faces is a coconut falling from a palm tree and cracking open on his head. There, on those beaches of fine-grained sand, all other dangers are non-existent, they say, not even out in the sea, as far as the coral reef that guards the beauty of this virginal paradise. But beyond the reef, oh yes, there you will find waiting the sharp and merciless fangs of Satan's maritime spawn ...'

'Spawn? Satan's maritime spawn? Oh, Wolfgang, how quickly your stylistic bravura descends into mawkish bombast!'

'Fritzi, stop interrupting me! I had just caught a wave that was carrying me from this present wilderness all the way to eternity and a well-deserved paradise.'

'A paradise woven from a spiderweb of illusion ...'

'Spiderweb, Friedrich, is the strongest thread in the world – oh, if only our friendships could be woven out of spiderweb ...'

'But not with you, Wolfgang, not for a long time ...' Friedrich shakes his head.

'I speak of what I know, and I sing of what I hope. But you, Friedrich, I see, have not been pumping enough blood to your brain. You've been neglecting yourself. In the lazy comfort of your castle, you've let yourself go, like warm melted butter. You don't read any more, you don't write – except when you sign your name to some document you haven't even carefully read, which is why your fiefdom is in such a mess. You stopped playing music a long time ago and don't even tap a stretched skin – not even that, you've got so lazy! You've become insensible to charm, insensible to the moments life is made of, the here and now, which, like the majority of people, you don't even notice because you take life for granted – until, that is, the rhythm of day and night suddenly starts to falter and, for a brief second, comes to a halt, and who knows if it will keep going forward or not? You've become lazy from fear, like many people who let their bodily juices dry up, who let their passion wither. You're a traitor, Fritzi! A traitor to the dreams the three of us were weaving when we weren't really dreaming but lolling about with each other in a moment of absolute here and now, with the endless open sky above us. Ah, yes ... It's right and proper that man is mortal. The majority don't deserve to reach old age; for most people, it's better they depart no later than when their youthful madness passes, for that's when they become utterly and irrevocably dull. Youth, however, is luscious and thrillingly charming in its vast and profound naïveté, its impulsiveness and total lack of prudence. For it is alive! Later most people become empty, barren furrows, which would be best to fill in as soon as possible – although we mustn't forget that these fallow furrows produce the mandatory taxes for you and me and all of us. As far as I'm concerned, the best thing for this most beautiful land, speaking aesthetically, would be for it to regularly cleanse itself and self-compost the excess waste.

'Just think, Friedrich, what would it be like if a billion people lived on the earth – or two, maybe three, even five billion? Such fecundity, I'm sure, would have to be contained. All those humans, all that organic filth, reproducing and eating and then, without leaving a single trace of the mind behind them, disappearing in organic decomposition … Can you imagine it? That mass of humankind would poison us – us, who alone understand the difference between man and the animals. All that superfluous mass would have to be fenced off in pens and given no chance to maintain their health and multiply. This is not unlike the view of our most prudent teacher from ancient Greece: we must separate the wheat from the chaff. So it wouldn't be a bad idea to come up with some myth, such as our teacher borrowed from the Phoenicians – and the sillier and more improbable the fiction is, the more convincing it will seem. It's amazing what the populace is prepared to believe, what utterly foolish ideas, which need only to be connected in some reasonable way and then endlessly repeated, and soon the appearance is created that a mind is at work and the whole thing is logical and therefore sensible and orderly. Like the myth of the state of Callipolis, whose inhabitants believe they descended from one of three races: bronze, silver or gold. The philosophers and their assistants made sure that people intermixed in a way that favoured only the best people in each individual race – only the most physically and mentally superior men were allowed access to first-rate women, while the weaklings, as if by the luck of the draw, in a lottery overseen by the philosophers, were given weak and ugly women. Thus posterity was partially filtered even before conception, and then at birth completely: measures were taken so the good seeds sprouted and the young shoots were well cared for, while anything bad was hidden away or destroyed. Who knows, maybe one day beautiful Callipolis will flourish again, and propagation will no longer be a matter of chance but, instead, prudent selection.

'Not long ago yet another splendid idea occurred to me: we could devise another myth, about a certain food, say, which the populace would ravenously gobble up, but we'd put something in it that made people sterile. Or we could add something to the corn so those gluttons died sooner, but not immediately. No, first they'd have to seem healthy and even put on some pounds, but later they'd contract a disease, and then another one, and then more and more diseases. The physicians – and we'd be wise to make some investments in medicine and the apothecary's trade – would go around examining people and, as it were, try to help them by prescribing certain decoctions, which people would be obliged to purchase. At first, the decoction would seem to be working, but then it would need to be changed and a new decoction bought, which wasn't all that different from the first one, and, before long, the meaning of life would be that a person gets sick as soon as he's born and then, for the rest of his life, he takes medicine, and in the meantime he does his service, works and pays taxes, and when he is no longer useful, he dies as soon as possible. Whoever is born must die, but it's possible to live a very good life in between, and we, too, on the basis of the aforementioned supply and demand, would be living life at its best – comfortably, with the fewest possible worries. So, Fritzi, do you not think that the author of these words, which at this very moment are making their way through your ears, is, to put it modestly, nothing less than ingenious?'

'What do I think, Most Reverend Prince-Bishop? I think your prattle is odious. What about love? What about the Gospels you have vowed to serve? Have you no sense of guilt? No feeling of sin? None whatsoever?'

'Oh, sure, feelings – sin and guilt, love and other things, too. Well, Fritzi, just try tossing the populace some of that love: here you go, populace, take it, here's some love for you – go ahead, have a nibble, live off it! And if you can, preserve your compassion, so you're not eaten by guilt later. Just try it, Fritzi. Go to the populace and tell them, "Dear populace, from now on, instead of my whip I give you my gentle hand filled with infinite compassion. You will have everything you need to live. We will divide up everything fairly and equally. We will all have enough and no one will lack for anything, which means we will have lots of time to love each other, be kind to each other and help each other." Go on, try it. But let me warn you, gentle soul, that when you have made your announcement, the faces you see in front of you will be animal faces. They will start charging around, grabbing whatever they think they need with their putrid stumps. The crush of the cruellest and most brutal beasts will be extraordinary, made worse by the victims writhing in their paws and beneath their bodies. And when they have grabbed what they can, in all that pushing and shoving, when they have trampled the weaker ones, when they have gorged themselves on their plunder, then they'll take another look around and think, "Now it's time for love!" And they'll set off after the first innocent creature who has not yet realized, not until that very moment, that she'd better make a run for it and hide in the most hidden hole she can find.

'In many ways, man is not so different from the animals. Even if it's not good form to abandon a sick family member who's about to croak, many people are left to die alone like animals. When the blackest of black plagues strikes, the infected are cordoned off, people keep clear of them and they're fumigated with sage and thyme. And while some die in isolation, others survive, whether they believe that luck was on their side, that they were touched by God's hand or that this was simply their fate. And although you can't, with impunity, do away with somebody who, for whatever reason, annoys you to no end, there are situations where this is not only possible but even mandatory and justified, because it is lawful. What else does one do in war if not erase and eliminate the enemy in the name of the emperor, the prince and some sort of fatherland.'

'But Wolfgang ...'

'I need a little break, esteemed host. Have your servants bring up more wine, only this time not Gewürztraminer or Riesling but that dark-red, pungently thick wine from the dry plateau above the sea where the Lipizzaner horses are bred.'

'You mean Teran, Most Reverend Prince-Bishop. Its colour will certainly complement your words, which are making my skin crawl ...'

ON THE DECEPTIVENESS OF THE
SENSES AND OUR PERCEPTIONS

For a long while now I have felt the need to take time and reflect carefully on fundamental things – on fundamental concepts and philosophical truths – which I found so extraordinarily stimulating during my studies in Graz and then in Vienna. To reflect carefully on what is and how it is. But in order to avoid carelessness, and also so I do not merely repeat what others have said before me, I will begin by attempting to free myself of any ideas that I have heretofore taken as self-evident.

A few days ago, when I was looking through the window, I saw black hats moving around somewhat nervously in the square below; they were bowing to each other, moving away and then approaching again. 'What business do these men have with each other?' I wondered, and at the very same moment it struck me: how do I know they are men? Well, they are probably not women, but what leads me to conclude from their hats alone, which concealed their faces, that there are men beneath them? And, even more – that the beings beneath them are, in fact, people? Because I could be wrong and the beings hiding beneath the hats are in reality automatons of a kind. I am aware that some people may think that my reflections are a little confused, but I am not confused. I have the courage and the passion for thinking and, I am sure, even a certain talent for it. Many would say I have far too much time on my hands if I am indulging myself in reflections that, to most, would seem fanciful or delusional, which is why I will not share my thoughts all around but rather, from now on, will examine, alone and in peace, certain questions that the majority views as a needless waste of time, while the few who see some sense in them offer answers that fail to satisfy me.

So on what basis, then, do I conclude that the beings concealed beneath the hats on the square below are not artificially created beings that imitate human movement? The only answer that comes to me at the moment is the following: experience. After all, I have never yet encountered an automaton that walks around dressed in the clothes of a man. The only automatons I have seen were in Graz, during my studies, at the house of a noble family whose son, my classmate at the Jesuit college, had made them to amuse himself and others. But is my visual experience sufficient for me to claim with certainty that if one of the hatted beings looked up at me and I saw his face, the creature would in all truth be human? I can hardly recognize everyone I see out my window. Not until I had run down to the square and examined the creature up close would I be able to determine precisely if it was a man or a man-made monster. And even then I might be wrong. The figure might appear exactly as humans appear, and I might even think I know this man personally, when, in fact, it is not the person I know but a mere replica. For how can I be sure that there is not some master craftsman capable of making human-like replicas of such superb quality that they resemble people in almost every detail? And last but not least, even if this being was a person, would I be able to conclude by appearances alone, without him speaking to me, that he was truly my acquaintance and not somebody who looked exactly like him? Not his double?

I am becoming more and more aware that in my life I behave through an automatism based on experience, and here I use the term *automatism* deliberately, not merely for effect. For in the decisions I make, do I myself not behave rather often like an automaton, or at the very least like an animal? When the housekeeper calls Mitzi, she comes running because she knows there is probably a treat waiting for her, and when she does this, she is obviously not thinking – to the degree that animals are able to think; our religion does not even ascribe them souls, but as the Jesuits report, in Japan people believe that not only man but everything, animals, plants and even stones, has a kind of soul – so Mitzi obviously does not think that the house-keeper might be calling her with the intention of grabbing her, stuffing her in a bag and throwing her in the water, as some people do with animals (which to me is utterly incomprehensible and wrong). As Mitzi has not had any bad experiences with the housekeeper, she usually responds to her calls and runs to her. But if, a little while before, Mitzi has managed to pilfer a piece of meat from the kitchen, she will hide out of sight somewhere, no matter how sweetly the housekeeper calls.

I, too, when it comes to the future, rely on my past and my experience. When I am summoned by the mayor, there is nothing I need to fear, but if soldiers or provincial officials turned up at my door, I would be worried, regardless of whether I had any reason to worry. Situations that are new to me, which I am unable to relate to past experience, present a great quandary, but even these I can connect with things I have seen or heard or read about.

Sometimes, however, I fall into melancholy and, with no reason at all, connect the future with bad things, even horrible, monstrous things. Recently, when the mayor was dictating a letter to me, I broke out in a cold sweat and could not make sense of his words. He noticed my confusion and asked if I was all right. It was becoming harder and harder to breathe, and my heart was pounding as if it was going to jump out of my chest. What had happened was that at that moment it had occurred to me that I might have inadvertently forgotten to shut the door of the birdcage, and I had most probably left the window open in the room. So I was frightened that if the cage was open, Spiritus might fly away to freedom. Whenever I leave the room, I always check a few times to make sure that the cage really is shut and also that Mitzi isn't hanging about in the room, since she would probably take advantage of my absence and attack Spiritus.

Mayor Falke has advised me to have the housekeeper prepare an infusion of valerian and lemon balm for me. I know I am more sensitive than most, but I take consolation from the fact that this is also why I am able to devote myself to fundamental questions, questions that most people view as unimportant. But these attacks are becoming more and more difficult, and when I think of all the horrible things that could happen, to me or to others, I am terrified. It is a fact that cats kill birds. They have not, however, destroyed any bird of mine, for Spiritus is, apart from the housekeeper's Mitzi, the only animal I live with. But still, more and more, I am overcome by a dark foreboding that something terrible will happen to me, or to someone close to me, or to someone I know. And at such times neither lemon balm nor valerian can help. But there is a dark-coloured resin that might be able to help me; I hear that merchants from the Orient sell it here.

From this day forward, if time allows, I will sit here every evening by the fireplace, near which I have placed a table and chair, and I will reflect on fundamental issues and try to determine who and what I am, how to understand myself and the world in the truest and most accurate way and how to avoid the errors that have up to now ensnared me. As for the methodology of my investigations, I am convinced (again this conviction, on which I base such a judgement, for I have not yet done this in any calm and consistent way) that when I devote myself to fundamental questions about the nature of the structure of the world, it is best to do it in peace and total solitude. And everything I think about, I will write as I think it. So I do not forget. And the next time I deliver the mayor's order to the Triestine merchant-woman, I will buy paper and ink, so my thoughts will not be accidentally interrupted. My thoughts – more and more it seems to me that I will be giving a great deal of thought to thought itself, to the capacity for thought. But that's for next time. Right now I am going to go to bed and fall asleep.

Spring Dialogues:
Recipes for Power

'You're right, Friedrich. Teran tastes like life – it's tart, a little harsh, with a hint of blood, but when the different flavours mingle together, there's a velvety, warm, homey feeling that washes over the drinker.' Prince-Bishop Wolfgang expertly rolls the wine they had just been served around in his mouth. 'Pure wine – if I may use such a trite expression – that is what you will have to give the populace, and soon. And they will not object to wine. They won't be happy with just bread and water; you need to give them something else, too.'

'But what can I give them? I don't have anything,' Friedrich says. 'When I enter my treasury, a gust of cold wind strikes my face from the empty corners, where the spiders are skilfully weaving their enormous cathedrals. I have the feeling that the silver's a few pieces short, a gilt candlestick is missing – it's a good thing my most valuable pieces are carefully catalogued in my head. I don't know how many times I've had to badger the steward to draw up the accounts and present a report, but I never get it, and more than once I've wondered if somebody might not be cheating me.'

The prince-bishop, who had been trimming the cuticle on his middle finger with a little knife, now extends the finger in Friedrich's direction and leans towards him confidentially. 'That's because you've been badgering and not beating him,' he says, at the same moment glancing over at the steward, who is sitting next to Julian at the far end of the table. 'I'll send you one of our men. They receive an excellent education at our universities and some practical training as well. The Jesuits are particularly skilled in such matters. They have trained a team of young confessors, who slowly and tenaciously massage rich widows, and when the widow is sufficiently stimulated and believes that her womanly charms have defeated her rival, the Holy Roman Catholic Church, the cleric puts a pen and deed of gift in front of her nose. And as soon as she has signed her property over to the Society of Jesus and pen and deed have both been stored away, the young Jesuit clasps his hands in prayer, turns his eyes heavenwards in thanksgiving and vanishes for ever and ever, amen. So I'll send you a Jesuit – they're highly skilled in both liturgy and finances – and I'll make sure he's young and handsome.' The prince-bishop indecently sticks out his tongue and clicks it revoltingly on his gold front teeth as foul-smelling spittle sprays across the table.

'Do you mean to say,' the count's offended steward pipes up from the other end of the table, 'that I am not doing my job well?'

'How should I know what you're doing?' the count replies with a sharp look. 'For weeks I've been asking you and the secretary to draw up the accounts ...'

'Asking, Fritzi? Tsk, tsk!' The prince-bishop shakes his head.

'But when there have been such terrible storms, and dysentery before that, and plague before that ...' the steward says, making excuses.

'Say another word and you'll think typhus is a sponge bath compared with what I'm going to give you.' Count Friedrich's harsh tone is not entirely convincing.

'Well, well!' the prince-bishop says as he picks up the napkin and starts polishing the amethyst in his massive gold ring. 'Let's start by addressing the current situation, moving in orderly fashion from more abstract matters of principle to concrete issues. First, your economic affairs must be put in order, the accounts examined with a fine-tooth comb, your property inventoried and taxes audited: is a tenth part truly one-tenth and not perhaps one-fiftieth? As a popular revolt is a likely outcome of these procedures, it must be thwarted in advance. Raising taxes and introducing special contributions for the defence against the Turks will not find favour among the populace, but such measures are necessary for the common good. And who if not we are the ones who understand what the common good means? And, besides, in the very near future there will be Lutherans coming through your fiefdom to escape the faith commissions. God only knows if things will really be managed without violence, as the Graz doctrine recommends. So the populace has to be prepared. You need to offer them spiritual food that will make them think about the fundamental questions of existence and the forms of existence that might await them in the afterlife. And the only way to prepare the populace to think about such things, and, indeed, to think at all, is to give them powerful experiences, ones that trigger powerful images, shake people up and provoke an arsenal of strong emotions, which lead them to reflection and to voluntary, devoted obedience,' the prince-bishop says by way of introducing his scheme.

'So should I have St Mary's Church – for which I hold the patronage – repainted with scenes of purgatory and hell?' Friedrich asks.

'I'd strongly advise against it,' the prince-bishop replies. 'Unless you hound the painters, it will take forever …'

'Should I commission an oratorio, then?'

'But who will write it? Do you have people who can produce oratorios at the snap of your fingers? Be serious! And even if you found some foreigner to write it for you, who will sing it? You would have to hire singers, and that entails costs; you have to give them food and a place to sleep, and some will even want to be paid. You'd do better to give the people a show,' the prince-bishop proposes.

'What sort of show? And where do I get the money to pay the actors? And besides, actors like to make merry with the populace, and soon they'll be mating like rabbits.'

'You don't need to hire foreigners; you've got plenty of burlesquers right here, enough to fill all the parts …'

'So a passion play, then?' the count asks.

'The populace can put on their own passion play if they want, and those blackrobe Jesuits will pay for it, and organize it for them, too. No, I'm thinking of a different sort of theatre, which I myself call the theatre of martyrdom.' The prince-bishop glances at Julian at the far end of the long table, and now for the first time since their arrival, the young man speaks.

'Ah, what an excellent idea! I will personally scour the domain for our leading lady,' he says, clenching his hands enthusiastically into tight little fists and whirling them a few times in the air.

'You've trained him well,' says Friedrich, turning back to the prince-bishop. 'But I'd expect nothing less of you!'

Wolfgang gives him a lewd grin and continues, 'Only make sure she's not some crooked crone or emaciated scar-faced tart. The woman has to appear healthy and strong. There has to be a certain existential tension created during the proceedings. She needs to be fighting for her life; her flesh must seem a convincing instrument of the devil's work, his terrain. There has be tragedy unfolding, not death flicking her away with his bony finger.'

'But why?' Friedrich asks, frowning.

'Because it's easier that way,' Wolfgang replies. 'And mainly because that's what the provincial authorities are expecting of you. Just as Spitzenberg was a model example of foolish obstinacy against the prince, so your fiefdom will be a lesson to all who embrace Lutheranism and superstition. As I said, in our counter-reformation we will, in principle, avoid violence. But for this to work, exceptions have to be made in certain sensitive, more infected places.'

'I do not intend to hold any witch trials in my domain. I don't believe in witches, and neither do you!' the count objects.

'Are we talking about belief here, Friedrich? No. We're talking about power and its methods,' the prince-bishop replies calmly.

'But why a woman? Why do you always go after these unfortunate women?' Friedrich looks at him reprovingly.

'Because the evil of women is theologically established in the *Malleus Maleficarum*, and it's not hard to prove in a trial. And you know how I dislike attacking men, although I much prefer youths, and male youngsters most of all. Besides, we must accommodate the tastes of the majority. Women are entirely content with just a single tortured male body – one that has, moreover, redeemed their souls – and those "unfortunate women" will be glad to see our chosen victim suffer, especially if she's the least bit good-looking – both out of female spite and from relief that it's not them standing in her place, which could easily happen, and therefore also out of fear that, by this logic, their little village would soon be empty, and an empty village is no longer a village but just a group of ramshackle buildings. Most men, meanwhile, never tire of seeing a naked woman, so long as our victim isn't all skin and bones. So, Julian, find us a wench who looks like a woman, and the investigative commission will do the rest,' Wolfgang says.

'And who will lead it? You?' Friedrich asks.

'I would never conceive of listening to the screams of naked females. Besides, I'm not talking about serious heresy, just your average witch trial, which, according to imperial law, must be conducted by a criminal judge and his team,' the prince-bishop explains.

'Not only does this sound abhorrent, it's expensive. Fiefdoms and towns are obliged to cover the costs of such trials, and some lords have nearly gone broke from these cruel ceremonies,' the count says.

'Fritzi, have another glass and calm down. I will choose the judge myself and send him to you. He'll be fast and efficient, and we'll make sure his team includes a Dominican or Jesuit who is well versed in such matters. The trial must be inexpensive, but not too quick. Our man will prepare an estimate of costs. If any witness tries to prolong the show by stirring things up, we'll make sure that suspicions and accusations are cast on them, too, and place them on the fire next to the wench. I will see to it personally that you're sent a reliable, well-tested man, one of our own, to conduct the proceedings.

'Our arms are both long and strong. When we get our hands on someone, when he's still a child, he believes that the Church is his mother and we are his fathers. We send him to school and later, if he is very bright, to university. Even the most spirited colts we break sooner or later. Only a very few escape their bridles, and when they do, we keep careful track of them. How we do this, what tools we use, depends on the field the defector has wandered into. If he tries his hand at lay power, we put people in place to be his advisers. Our agents work overtime, with no days off. If he assumes some other public function, we watch him closely and, whenever we wish, we put the squeeze on. Everyone has some little thing in their past for which they'd give anything to keep it from coming to light. It doesn't even have to be patently scandalous; even the tiniest smudge can muck up a life. So we tell the person, "It is not just about what you have been so carefully hiding from others, and from yourself, too, to the point where you don't even believe it exists and think it didn't happen. Yes, we know that, too: we know what you are thinking. Well, if you don't want anyone else to find out about this, we need to agree on certain matters of which we are now going to inform you." And all of them, well, almost all of them, give in. But some can't take the pressure and pull their necks out, using a rope tied to beam. Those who absolutely refuse, we deal with ourselves, in a similar manner. But if they are artists or scientists, we never have a problem. And, in fact, both types can be useful; we just need to be careful about the astronomers and cosmologists – they start poking around in things and mixing up ideas that go far beyond human nature and their own mental capacities.

'If any of these scientists makes some radical claim, we remind him of the Campo de' Fiori, in the middle of Rome, which earlier this year, on February seventeenth, was filled, not with a floral fragrance, but with the smell of the burning flesh of Giordano Bruno, and we also mention the smell of burning books, which will soon fill the main squares of Graz and Judenburg, and then of other towns throughout the provinces of Inner Austria. We have the fewest problems with artists. If they want to create their mental fictions, fanciful images and sweet-sounding melodies, they need their fountain, where they swim in order to survive. If their support comes from the apostate aristocracy or the boorish, free-thinking burgherhood and they are too bold or even brazen, we arrange some terrible incident for them, perhaps involving their sexual proclivities, or we expose them as traitors to their country. But normally it's very easy with artists. Cowards are more the rule than the exception with them. Painters are terrified of dying, no matter how much it might seem that, because they paint cherubs, hell and saints, they should be more comfortable with metaphysics than ordinary people. When we give artists a commission, they are sincerely delighted; they set to work and paint what's expected of them, and we praise them now and then as if they were children, and so we have no trouble with them. It always surprises me, the childish way their eyes light up when you praise them. Even if they themselves suspect that their work isn't worth a broken penny, the moment you compliment an artist, he forgets all his doubts and gladly basks in the adulation. A bit of money, some flattery, and he's eating out of your hand, or kissing your feet if that's what you prefer, and, if you continue, he's licking your balls. With the right methods and tactics, the sky's the limit. Still, some artists refuse to bend, and, in fact, they're the only interesting ones, although, sadly, they're useless ... But now I'm feeling a bit tired from all this chit-chat. Friedrich, I hear you have connections with some merchants from Trieste. I do hope you've managed to procure coffee beans from them. After this excellent meal, coffee is exactly what I need. Perhaps we could have it with a few cardamom seeds, the way we used to drink it from each other's mouths in Granada? Remember, Fritzi?' The prince-bishop glances at Friedrich.

'Don't talk about that!' the count winces.

'I won't, darling,' the prince-bishop smiles indulgently. 'But do you see now how very easy it is to govern? If the right man is sitting in the seat of power, everything runs like clockwork.'

'Please forgive me, most esteemed lords,' the steward speaks up, bowing slightly with his hand across his chest. 'But the costs of this trial will have to be borne entirely by our estate, in consequence of which our annual expenditures will be much higher than the yearly average ...'

The prince-bishop, massaging a finger, rolls his eyes and whispers to the count, 'Not only is he lazy and stupid, his views are gloomy and unimaginative. It wouldn't be a bad idea to send the occasional dim-witted steward, scribbler or what-have-you to the stake as well. Educating this man of yours would be a complete waste of time. And moreover, Fritzi, does not your sensitive nose, which spent a part of its youth lolling about in lush Mediterranean meadows – does it not detect a stale stench issuing from his anger, frustration and hatred for us? Some people, no matter how much they powder themselves, are beyond the help of even expensive perfumes, which in any case are inappropriate for their status. Send him packing to the nearest stream so he can wash off that rancid stench of dullards and idlers.

'But let's forget about that for now,' the prince-bishop continues in a louder voice, 'and instead, in our ripe autumn, gather up succulent fruit to fortify ourselves against the coming cold, dark winter that goes by the name of death. With every step I take into the future, death moves a step towards me. It is she who leads the dance of life; I can but humbly follow her. If I try to resist, to turn away even slightly, she tugs at me, pulls me along and spins me in whatever direction she likes. And just as we're about to forget her, she reminds us she's there, blowing her icy breath on our necks, whispering, "My darlings, there is less and less sand at the top of your hourglass and more and more at the bottom, where a little pile is forming that looks very much like a burial mound."

'So there's no time to waste. Our sweetly sourish breath unambiguously proclaims that life is trapped in the processes of putrefaction, which will slowly nibble away, remould and liquefy our once solid and evermore wilting bodies and decompose them into minerals ... Ah, minerals! They are spared such painful transformations! In life, you are either a gatherer or you get gathered. When you're young, it's rather fine to be one of the gathered. But when the juiciness and ripeness within you develops, it's high time to move from the gathered to the gatherers, before the fate of ripened fruit happens to you and you rot – and nobody likes rotten fruit, even if some are forced by their modest circumstances to consume it. But if, at just the right moment, you jump from the gathered to the gatherers, you can still examine the fruit with all your senses. The berries that are still budding you leave on the vine, or maybe not and you pluck the buds anyway; the tender ones you inspect, feeling them, weighing them – should you leave them a while longer or pluck them now, when they are small and green? – and, meanwhile, you wait to finally sample those other berries, just before their sweetness acquires a hint of rot. But you must keep your hands off some of them, so you don't dirty your fingers, for these berries are cankerous and wormy, teeming with all sorts of slimy creatures, which, to be sure, are there by the laws of nature – because nature very often doesn't give a damn about man's criteria for beauty and creates many things that are nothing less than vile ... Ah, nature, a cold, pale mother, who gives birth only to kill later what she has borne, and if the child succeeds in reproducing itself before its own bitter end, so much the better for her, serial killer and mass murderer that she is, who now has even more material for her slaughter. But not even nature can destroy our institution. Why is that, you ask? ... But Friedrich! You're not even listening, and here I am, doing my best to reflect on fundamental matters!'

Friedrich stirs from his daze at the raised voice, and looks at the prince-bishop. 'Wolfgang, you and your fine words are becoming tiresome. I have neither the patience nor the attention of mind to follow everything you ramble on about.'

'But it wouldn't hurt you to try. So, what do you think? Why is it that not even nature can destroy our Holy Roman Catholic Church? Aren't you curious? Are you mulling it over? Well, of course, it's because we fight nature with the only weapon that can defeat that sneaky bitch – the sword of the mind, which alone is a match for nature. Nature might crush us individually, speaking in the particular, but she cannot destroy our institution. For we do not reproduce ourselves like sheep; rather, we sow our seed in the hearts of men, and it brings forth faith and allegiance to the Church. If nothing sprouts from the seed, or if the sprout withers before it grows or wilts before it ripens, we rip it out or trample it down ... Friedrich, are you all right? You look pale, as if there's not a drop of blood in your lips.' The prince-bishop looks at him with concern.

'Wolfgang, everything you say makes me feel queasy ...'

'That's not a bad sign, Friedrich. As long as you feel something, feel anything, it means at the very least that the worms are not yet burrowing inside you and you're still alive. And that's something, when life is so fragile and short. In my hours of pain, when I am tortured by gout and my prostate is hurting, every particle of life seems endlessly long. But when an angelic creature, smelling of vanilla, spreads his wings in my lap, then I wish for an eternity with my little white angels. You say I'm boring you. But let me tell you, Friedrich, as a friend: you've become more and more dangerously naïve over the years. Right here, in your own little castle, your secretaries and stewards are turning you on the spit like a lamb, and while your fat is dripping on the coals, they're carving you into thin slices, so you don't even feel it, while your charming wife, without the least discretion, turns you into a ... I don't know what metaphor to use, at least not here in front of your lackeys, who can barely wait to fill their ears with words they don't even understand very well, so that later, when they're among their own, they can hold it over them, saying, "We have access to our masters and know all their secrets, big and small, beautiful and shameful; we know their filth and their stench, so in our view, the masters are not gentlefolk but the same as us, and maybe even worse." This, at the very least, is reason enough to take the servants firmly in hand and make sure they understand and do not forget that witnessing our human foibles does not lift them above their fellows, nor does it place in their hands any trump card by which they might somehow get the better of us; on the contrary, their service places them in an even worse position than the others. If they are present or in any way involved in a situation that could be embarrassing for their master, their height will inevitably need to be reduced by a head, except in the rare case where someone has previously demonstrated unwavering loyalty. It goes without saying that, with me, the first warning is also the last, with no mercy for second blunders. They think they can wear the livery, that if they can only make it to the livery, they will, at least from a distance, look the same as us, but they are mistaken. Not only can they not hide their bumpkin looks beneath brocade; mainly, they will never shake off their bumpkin simplicity, no matter how much they primp and preen. Fritzi, you're too lenient with them, just as you are far too gentle with Her Ladyship, who to put it mildly, lacks style. There are certain simple and elegant methods for establishing order in your home life and restoring harmony to your fiefdom. Chaos is violence, so the only way to get the world back on track is through force. And once you've done that, everything is lovely again, clean and orderly, and people understand and accept that the collateral victims who lost their lives in the cleansing process, whether they were guilty or innocent, did not die in vain.'

'What are you talking about, Wolfgang?'

'About the good, Friedrich. About the idea of the good and how to implement it ...'

'I don't understand what ...'

'What or who, it's all a matter of taste, but how – now that is a matter of mental methodology. But clearly you have not yet fully grasped the fact that I am here on a mission, and I'm not at this table nibbling at pheasant bones for no purpose. Say what you want, but I hear that your fiefdom, too, is infested with vermin, which we must eradicate completely as soon as possible. Right here, some of these vermin are skulking all around you, and you don't even notice, but we have been carefully monitoring them a long time. You are much too indulgent with your fiefdom. You say you pray as a Catholic, and yet you've been playing host to a preacher and keep a wizard in your home. You cultivate cordial ties with Volk Falke, the mayor of the neighbouring town, which is almost entirely Lutheran. And I hear you have promised the town printer a little money so he can print up some Lutheran reading materials, not only for the townspeople but for your own vassals as well. Oh, my dear friend, there is a well-tested and highly effective method for disciplining both individuals and the populace, and that method is to activate primarily one emotion: fear, Friedrich. The dark, shrill melodies of fear, which are neither melodious nor tuneful but chromatic, like a Gesualdo madrigal.

'Fear may be effectively combined with other emotions, too – envy, for example, or the fear of losing something you never actually had. Oh, the wonderful world of illusions, that gauze of fantasy, which glues itself over human eyes and creates truly incredible optic deceptions. Fear is the crown before which even the boldest kneel; you just have to touch the right spot. And you don't have to touch it hard, either, a single light pat is enough, and the whole body starts to tremble, starts to vibrate, to the melody of fear. One rules by fear, and it's all the more effective when you mix in guilt, so the person feels guilt for his own fear, because the God-fearing man, after all, should trust the Creator completely and surrender to his infinite forgiveness and divine mercy. But most people lack the courage to believe that the Almighty God is able and willing to forgive them. Those who do believe in forgiveness, meanwhile, are normally the greatest frauds and connivers, telling themselves, "Our dear Lord will surely forgive us, and if he forgives us this sin, he will also be able to forgive the villainy we haven't yet done but are only now planning." But even they can be squeezed, for they are the ones who most fear the loss of their mortal lives. If a person has lived an honest life, or is at least free of mortal sin, there isn't much they have to fear. Physical pain, yes, but the pains of the body pass, no matter how much the time they are wrenched by pain stretches beyond all endurance. But the soul is eternal and, if it hasn't wasted its everlasting life, it has nothing to fear; it will rise effortlessly into the sky and hover there forever. In the opposite situation, when a sinful life has plucked the soul's wings bare, the weight of the sin will drag the soul down into the nether geography of the afterlife, which will be no life at all, for the only thing alive will be the endless, eternal pain in which the depraved soul is roasting and frying with other depraved souls. They say that … it's said that … I hear …' As if weary of his own chatter, Wolfgang starts humming a Gesualdo melody. 'We know there is a prayer hall on your property that is frequented by some of the wealthier peasants and occasionally even people from the nearby town. We know that the town is a breeding ground for Lutherans, who will be harder to tackle because the town belongs not to the prince but to the Provincial Estates. We know that, although you may be more or less a Catholic, you confide in the town's Lutheran mayor, Volk Falke. He, too, cannot be faulted for any lack of charm, or for his nice, firm buttocks, although his shoulders are too triangular in shape. Your wife, too, I hear, is close to him. Would you be surprised, Friedrich, if the countess bore a son who, as the years passed, developed a certain triangular droop in his shoulders?'

'Not in the least. I might even be glad of it,' Friedrich says.

'But if you want to avoid the calamities threatening your fiefdom,' the prince-bishop continues, 'I advise you, Friedrich, be well prepared for the faith commission; it will be merciless, and it will be here in a couple of months. I hear there's a special plan being prepared for the town, but not even I have been told of it yet. I'm sure it will present a sufficiently convincing threat to make the town fall on its knees and swear allegiance to Catholicism in front of Bishop Thomas Chroen.'

'What will happen to me, to my wife and children and to the castle and its staff?' Count Friedrich asks uncertainly.

'If you follow my instructions all will be well with you and your loved ones. Given the heretical spawn of various kinds that have infested your fiefdom, not to mention the town, you must hold this witch trial; it will show the populace that the authorities mean business, and at the same time you'll give them a chance to go a little wild, get drunk on blood and cleanse themselves. Then, after the visitation arrives, order will be restored and everything will be almost the way it used to be, if not better. Tomorrow we'll talk about the spectacle that will hasten these procedures along. But now is not the time to wrack your brain over strategies; it's better you do your duties as host and see about our entertainment. Well, actually, I've taken care of that myself, since over the past few years you've become such a terrible moralizer! I've had them deliver some tender flesh from an orphanage to which our archdiocese gives magnanimous financial support. Julian,' he gestures to his assistant at the far end of the table, 'go fetch that flock of lads in angelic attire – I do hope they've been done up as I ordered: with lyres in their hands and goosefeather wings on their backs.'

'Wolfi, you once told me that our friendship would be a blessing to me, but I haven't believed that for a very long time,' Friedrich shakes his head.

'Fritzi, you once purred that knowing me was paradise and there were only two things you feared – that this earthly paradise must one day end and that the heavenly paradise would never attain the same bliss,' the prince-bishop smiles suggestively.

'A person changes. We have both changed; you even more than me …' Friedrich says.

'Everything changes except our eternal God, who observes all these changes and never bats an eyelid. So we must find our own way, such as we are, endowed with free will, created with it, but only a very few know how to use it, while the herds in their ignorance chew whatever we toss into their troughs and pens. Now, where are those little angels?' The prince-bishop glances over at the door.

'They've flown back to where they came from,' Friedrich replies. 'When they arrived this morning, I had them sent back.'

'What! Sent back? What sort of hospitality is this?' the prince-bishop is upset.

'In my home at least, Wolfgang, you might try to restrain yourself.' Friedrich looks at him with disapproval. 'If the gracious countess had found out she'd have strangled you with her bare hands, and me, too. And, besides, the very thought of your predilections and what you do with them makes my stomach turn.'

'But the gracious countess has a headache and would have never found out. I am surprised and a little saddened, esteemed Count, by your opposition to me. I should be furious at you, but instead I will be merciful and understanding, given that your noble spouse is expecting and you are worried about whether what she is expecting will, in appearance, resemble you at least enough to keep malicious tongues from wagging about miracles again.'

'Get some rest, Most Reverend Prince-Bishop. You have another long journey awaiting you tomorrow,' Friedrich replies. And as they rise from the table, he ends by adding, 'After all the bad news you have brought me today, I, too, am in desperate need of rest – although I'll be surprised if I even shut my eyes.'

WHERE DOES THE CAPACITY FOR THOUGHT COME FROM?

In my first meditation I expressed doubt about the reliability of my senses, which, for as long as I can remember, have presented me with many errors. Of course, I do not doubt that I am now sitting here in front of the fireplace, wrapped in a blanket, thinking and writing. Nor do I doubt that the hand that moves the goose quill across the paper is mine, or that these are my feet being warmed by the heat of the fireplace. If I doubted all of this, that would probably indicate madness. But I am not mad. I am thinking in a disciplined manner, and in the future, too, I will proceed carefully from idea to idea so I do not stray into phantasmagoria and daydreaming.

Last time I ended my meditation with the idea of thought, which of all my properties and capacities seems to me to be what most defines me. Animals do not have this ability, and it is only through their behaviour and vocalizations that they communicate to us their desires and needs, which we humans try to interpret through our thought. I do not know how animals understand us, but surely it is different from how people understand. Animals are defined primarily by their senses, which help them to survive. And maybe they have more than just the five we humans have, for it is possible they perceive the world through other senses, too, ones for which human language has no names.

Human relationships are embedded in words. And even if we speak the same language, it can happen that the listener imagines and understands the aural or written message in a different way than the speaker intended. But there are also other means of communication involved in human relations. A blow means an attack, although it might not necessarily be intentional but only the result of an excess of black bile, so that later the attacker does not understand his own action and even regrets it.

The way a woman looks at you – and recently I have been thinking about this more and more – is harder to understand. A friendly look is not necessarily an expression of favour, for it may be nothing more than mischievous deception; it could be for mercenary reasons, which is hardly relevant as regards me, who makes my living as the town scrivener and secretary to the mayor. But, no matter what happens to a person, if the incident is sensual, emotional and mentally intense, he will seek to explain it in his mind. Whatever I do or whatever occurs in my life, it is only by harnessing my thoughts that I am able to create some idea of it.

I have already determined that I have increasing doubts about the senses, which are sometimes misleading. If I look out of the window, I will see all sorts of things outside. The sounds from below are clearer and more distinct if I have the window open, but when the window is closed they are difficult to understand, and I hear only a swarm of sounds. From where, then, comes my capacity to understand the world through my senses? This capacity must certainly come from my body, but, as I have noted, my senses alone, in themselves, do not present me with accurate truths and can mislead me. When I do not harness my thoughts, it seems I behave no differently from an automaton. When I walk, I do not consider each step separately, where I must put my foot or which foot to put in front of the other. When I take the pitcher and fill it with water, I do not normally think about what I am doing. I do most of my small daily chores without actually thinking about them. And then there is memory, which can be similarly deceptive, as it proves to be on those occasions when I am attacked by melancholic apprehensions and fears and, no matter how I try, I cannot remember if I performed a certain action or not.

If the source of my senses is the body, then where does my capacity for thought come from? Can I be satisfied with so simple an answer as: I am the way I am because this is how I was born? I am unable to imagine my life without my body. But can I imagine my life without the capacity for imagining? No, even less. I can conceive of losing my reason completely and withering away in some asylum like a plant, but even for such an idea I need to possess the capacity for ideas and thoughts. And if I were indeed languishing somewhere like a plant, I can say with certainty that this would no longer be me, at least not me as I know myself; it would be me only to other people but no longer to myself. Without the capacity for ideas and thoughts, I would disappear and all that remained would be a dull-witted body performing the basic life functions, but I as I am would not exist.

Where, then, does my capacity for thought come from, a capacity that in certain states of being, such as sleep, vanishes, even if the body remains and is still alive? Where does the capacity come from for thinking about things that transcend me, things that are much greater than myself?

For instance, I am able to think of myself flying. Not necessarily the way Spiritus flies – although, in fact, he cannot fly because I keep him in a cage, which I sometimes think is not very fair to a bird, whose essence, probably, is as much to fly as mine is to think. Sometimes I ask myself whether it might not be possible to make some sort of contrivance that a person would drape around his body and fly with. Sometimes I wonder if it would be possible to make some device like a carriage or cart, which a person could sit in, and it would convey him through the sky, or even farther – to the sun, the stars and the moon. My thoughts contain ideas that go beyond the capacities of my body and my experience. I do not doubt that in the past, too, people had ideas that went beyond the capacities of their bodies and the discoveries of their time. The idea of travelling by cart must have seemed a total delusion a long time ago before any carts existed, although nowadays it seems that the invention and making of the cart followed a course of development that would have inevitably happened sooner or later.

The same is true of the printing press. Many a monk in a monastery scriptorium must have wondered if the day would ever come when texts could be duplicated in a less time-consuming way, and if his labour would ever be replaced by some device. And I have many other ideas in my thoughts as well. I am able to imagine beings that do not exist in reality, such beings as chimeras, whose bodies are composed of different animal and human parts. I am also able to imagine beings that, in fact, have no shape at all but only a kind of changing form, which is neither round nor triangular nor polygonal. But here the question is, do I actually imagine this or is it not more the case that I merely think it? I am able to think of a formless being that is infinitely bigger than a human being and infinitely more powerful than humans. I am able to think of an infinite being, but I am not also able to imagine it. I am able to think of God, who has always existed and will never cease to exist, and who is infinitely good, all-powerful and perfect, and about whom I will never be able to know everything, for his nature transcends the capacity of my thought.

How, then, can I think about things, or actually about concepts, that transcend me, who am a finite being? If such abilities do not reside within my physical nature, they can originate only in something that is infinitely more perfect than me. If I am mentally and, to an even greater degree, physically limited, then the source of my thought can only be a being that is more perfect than me. And this is God, who of all beings is the most perfect.

God, then, is what I will be thinking about next time.

Did Something Somewhere Go Bang?

The unusual seven, who slogged away from morning to night and were never weary, even if they always gave an impression of fatigue, were preoccupying the populace more and more. Especially because, after the lean years, Kostanšek, with such a strong workforce, was having a bumper crop, which could be seen as well in his property and image. There was a new pair of horses, harnessed to a brand-new cart like the ones people drove in town. His daughter, whose eyes, not long before, had been diseased and sealed shut and whose face had been puffy and swollen with rashes, was, since the start of summer, strutting around with a healthy, peaches-and-cream complexion, such as fine young townswomen had. And if she was still coming to church in modest clothes in muted, unpretentious colours (although the material was clearly of high quality), she had gone beyond the limit at the biggest fair of the summer when she appeared in a brocade dress decked out in such jewels as the village had never seen – the sort of get-up that not only peasants but even many townsfolk were forbidden to wear by police ordinance. As if she herself was not of peasant stock, resigned to remaining a peasant to the end of her days, but was instead stubbornly determined to see that peasants and peasant work would soon be ancient history for this future tradesman's – or even merchant's – wife.

Things were going well for Kostanšek, very well after all the dysentery, plague and murrain that had devastated his family, the populace thought, mulling things over, trying to find the reason for the farmer's sudden change in fortune. If, from time to time, something bad happens to a person, the reason lies in natural phenomena or divine punishment, common sense told them. But when a person's conditions improve so unexpectedly, the turnaround is very likely the result of other, indisputably dark, forces. And when the person has, overnight as it were, brought foreigners into the village who not only did not speak their language but didn't speak any language at all and, what's more, worshipped a different God, or even gods, there could be no question that bizarre and dangerous things were happening on the Kostanšek farm, things that might again call some disaster down on the people's heads, just as that witch had done, who had been justly tried and justly punished.

As Kostanšek and his daughter took their places on the back seat of the cart in which the farmhands and maidservants were already seated, the populace was wondering how they might discover, before it was too late, exactly what was happening on his farm. It was not just that every Sunday the seven vanished from the face of the village; they were not to be seen in Kostanšek's yard either. They did not even take part in village fairs, where they might have done a good job spending some of the money they earned at Kostanšek's. Such disregard of local customs was deeply offensive to the populace. If they're living here, even for a short time, they might make a little more effort to partici-pate in village life, at least on feast days. Not that we would ever accept them. On the contrary, we would very likely push them away, or at least let them know that between us and them, between locals and foreigners, there was an unbridgeable difference.

But how could the populace feel like locals without somebody living in the vicinity who had not been here forever? Well, *forever* does not mean from time immemorial, as was evident from those foreign tombstones washed up by the river. Besides, there were certain ideas spreading around which, although only a few people dealt with them, were none the less dangerous because they contradicted everything that was held to be true and righteous.

Not long ago the astronomer Johannes Kepler had been in the area; he had been teaching at the Protestant seminary in Graz, at the Paradeishof next to the Mura River below the Schlossberg, and had dis-covered that the planets do not move around the sun evenly in their ellipses, but, rather, they move faster when they are closer to the sun. Kepler had spent some time in the Trans-Mura region, and maybe Lower Styria, too, before the seminary was shut down, but later he went north and ended up in Prague with the astronomer and astrologist Tycho

Brahe. After Brahe's unexplained death, which was probably caused by lead poisoning, he took his place in the court of Emperor Rudolf II, who, more than his other Habsburg relations, was receptive to the frontier fields of science and financially supported such aberrant research.

But let there be no mistake: science without God did not exist in those days. But there were among the scientists some of a very delicate nature, highly strung and fragile, who sometimes got a little light-headed and simply deviated from the established orbit, which then, after intense thought or personal tragedy, started tilting. And when a person slips to the edge and a little beyond it, there, on the other side, a surprise awaits the deviant: there may be something there, in the beyond, or maybe not.

Because it is possible that the planets do not revolve each in its own orbit in some disciplined order, whether this is around the earth or around the sun (not the most desirable theory back then). It may be that the celestial bodies are not aligned in some mathematical choreography with movements that produce the divine music of the spheres. Possibly, on the other side, the planets do not revolve in the same direction as on this side; possibly, there is, yawning somewhere in between them, a thick black whirlwind that devours celestial bodies.

What if there is no other side, but only the perspective changes, with a big jolt, so that everything looks entirely different? And maybe you can't see anything at all because there ... on the other side ... there isn't anything?

And how and why are all these celestial bodies fixed in their orbits? Is it because this is what the Creator wanted, or did the world originate in the absence of any desire, from pure and indifferent divine mathematics? Maybe from a certain number, from zero? Or maybe from one? Or from the oscillation between zero and one, between non-being and being? And when the oscillation reached the right wavelength, something resonated, and from that point on, there was existence; from that point on, the world existed and with it – maybe, or maybe not – God?

But what was there before nature, before God, before everything that is? What set off this movement? Was there maybe a bang, and the superlunary and sublunary worlds originated from this bang?

(Do you feel how such thoughts pull you into eternity, so there are no more boundaries, edges, sides, no past and no future, while the now folds into something that both is and is not at the same time? Do you sense the dilemma, how to be finite with the idea of eternity in your head, when, without you willing or wanting it, eternity begins to expand, so it becomes harder and harder to think?)

What if everything – the world and, with it, nature and god, space and time, past, future, present – originated from a single crack?

'A crack? A crack in what? What sort of crack are we talking about? Did something crack? Was there a bang? Did anybody hear anything?'

'No, no, it's all right, populace. No need to tire yourselves out worrying about this; you can live perfectly good lives without ever thinking about such cracks and bangs …'

'So something did crack? And if it did, what was it?'

'Yes, there was a crack, a bang, but it was far away, very far away, just before the time when time itself twisted out of something, with one end facing the past and the other shooting into the future. And from then on, that accursed time has been continuously glued to us.'

'But this is such rubbish! A complete waste of time! Some things are simply beyond us, things we will never know and never understand! Because what could have existed before that banging, or cracking, or whatever it was? Come on, tell us – what?'

'It wasn't. It's impossible to say. It's all beyond words … There are no words outside of time. And it won't be any easier for those who come after you four centuries from now, when, above Lake Geneva, where the Calvinists are burning heretics, there will be something buried in the earth, in a circle, and it will be known as CERN. Just as today you think this sort of thinking is complete rubbish, so, too, in the future the populace will think CERN is a senseless waste of money and time, especially because you don't need such things to have a perfectly good life, roasting chestnuts over coals, mowing meadows, slaughtering chickens and calves, selling wool and wine, siring descendants, handing out Church indulgences, taking communion in one or two kinds – it makes no difference, no difference at all …'

'So even in the future people will be handing out indulgences and other such things?'

'How could they not? Now, populace, you have entered something called the reign of capital, which is when the feudal lords begin losing their power. At the moment you can hardly imagine this, but more will be clearer in the future – a few radical strokes still need to be drawn, including some revolutions …'

'Including what?'

'We're talking about certain processes where blood flows and other substances, too, don't just trickle out …'

'And that's when things will be better?'

'No, they won't be better. Things will be very good for some, but for the majority, no. So do you get it now? Do at least some of you under-stand? But where were we exactly? We got carried away and knocked off our axis, although we held on with all our might while the spinning was happening. But now the spinning is slowing down, and we'll try to get back on track, slowly … because when you turn around too fast it can cause painful throbbing and odd sensations in the head … easy now … Well, then, we left off … Now where did we leave off?'

The populace was interested in knowing who in town was buying Kostanšek's produce, which by the end of that summer nature was bestowing on him with great generosity. Maybe those seven oddities knew about more effective methods of cultivation than they them-selves did? If that was true, it was selfish of Kostanšek not to share them with his fellow villagers but instead keep a tight lid on such secrets. But ever since he acquired his new work force, Kostanšek would always say he had too much to do whenever somebody from the village tried to invite himself over.

So the mothers plotted a new strategy and sent their sons into the fire as suitors for Kostanšek's daughter, who in recent months had become well off and therefore interesting and good-looking. Wealth creates the appearance of beauty; it improves the looks of almost any female and makes even plain girls striking. So Kostanšek's daughter was now undoubtedly good-looking, despite the scars on her face, which could be seen from close up but not from a distance.

'Now that things are going well for Kostanšek, the girl's put on airs and graces. What if she gets married and brings a stranger into our village?'

'If he was rich, would that be such a bad thing?'

'If he was rich, maybe not. But there are already those seven oddities living there, and then in the town we have those Triestine merchants, and some of them have been hanging around here, too, lately, or at least it seems that way. And since Kostanšek's daughter is his only surviving child, when he dies the property will have to go to a man. Rich or not, it's all the same to us who we have as a neighbour. But wouldn't it be best if Kostanšek gave his daughter to someone from the village?'

One day the men started grilling Kostanšek after Mass.

'Your daughter's not young any more, Kostanšek – she's already twenty-four ...'

'So she is,' he replied.

'And time is passing ...'

'So it is,' he replied.

'What if she's stays an old maid?'

'One day she'll be old, God willing, but a maid, I don't know about that ...' Kostanšek said.

'Well, who's going to take over the farm when you die?'

'I have no idea ...'

'We don't like your answers, Kostanšek. We expect you, as a responsible farmer, to put things in order before we lay you to rest.'

'I've still got time ...'

'We're not so sure. There are a lot of things wrong on your farm.'

'No, there aren't.'

'Yes, there are. Everything! You've been doing some deal-making, but we don't know who with. And you've got those seven oddities living with you, but we don't know who they are. And while it's mainly weeds growing in our fields, at your place everything that comes out of the ground is big and fat.'

'No, it's not. I've had miserable crops, too,' Kostanšek replied.

'That's true. Until this spring. But when summer came your hay started growing so fast you could barely keep up with the mowing, and your trees are bending from the weight of their plump fruit … So it's no surprise you're showing off your nice new cart. But isn't it a little suspicious the way everything's going so very well for you?'

'I don't think so.'

'Maybe you don't, but you're in the minority, Kostanšek. So tell us, who are you going to marry your daughter to?'

'Whoever she wants.'

'But it's your decision.'

'After being so ill, she's putting it off a while until she's completely recovered …'

'She looks healthy to us,' the populace would not let up.

'But she's still not feeling well,' Kostanšek replies.

'Kostanšek, rumour has it that her prospective husband is not from our village …'

'Well, rumour is wrong.' And without a word of farewell, he started the horses home, while the men put their heads together and stared after him with serious, worried faces.

SHE IS EXTRAORDINARY

No matter how much I have tried these past few evenings to reflect on the nature of thought or on God, my attention is constantly being drawn elsewhere: to her. I do not know how to explain this, but does not the mystery of love lie precisely in the fact that we cannot entirely explain it? What is it in the other that stimulates our senses, stirs our imagination, plucks us from our everyday existence and hurls us outwards and upwards and makes life exciting? So that life is suddenly transformed from a boring, even disgusting caterpillar into something marvellous, something extraordinary?

I can't say exactly when I fell so unreservedly in love with her. It did not happen at first sight. I don't even remember when I first saw her. I would see her from time to time at the mayor's, but the fact that she was married possibly impeded my emotional-sensual system and I unintentionally kept my distance. But even before her husband's death, something must have been simmering there. I remember clearly that when I learned that he had died, I felt a pleasant excitement. And I was not alone in this but merely one of many, including my employer, the mayor, who was similarly unable to fully suppress his delight at the news, even though he and the deceased were second cousins. It's not that her late husband was such a very bad man – well, he wasn't very good either. He had been nearly three decades older, and their marriage was the usual feudal transaction. At the age of seventeen she was married off by her family to a member of the lower nobility who had the reputation of being an exceptionally skilful merchant and one of the wealthiest men in town. People who did business with him said he was a stern man who was unmoved by any human misfortune other than his own. He was also a great miser, and for a person with such talents and traits of character it is not difficult to become rich. People said he was also stern towards her and that it was not hard to understand why his first wife had vanished overnight. As the story went, it took several days for him to even notice that she was gone, although others had observed a suspicious glow about her before she left. What, or rather who, was the source of her glow became clear when news arrived that she was somewhere in Istria, blossoming among the lavender. Not alone, of course, but with someone her own age who had been supplying her husband with sea salt, olive oil and other Mediterranean goods. The townsfolk needed some time to untangle the knots of the story. While there had been no Adriatic merchant coming here to sell oil and wine, there had been, from time to time, a merchant-woman, with thick, curly hair and a bronze complexion, whose laughter had been loud and conspicuous – as conspicuous as the fact that her marital status was unknown and she never responded to the advances of even the most notorious womanizers.

'What? Impossible! But does that mean she didn't leave her husband for another man?'

'Yes, it means' – and here both Lutherans and Catholics agreed – 'that when her life in the hot Adriatic sun is over there will be an even worse heat, a truly hellish heat, waiting for her!'

Her husband pretended to know nothing about the new life of his runaway wife – until her lawyers paid him a visit and they worked out the legal arrangements of the divorce. After her flight, he became even more set in his ways and honed his miserliness to perfection. The ungrateful woman he had given everything to – everything he felt she needed – had humiliated him, so it was essential that as soon as possible he hide his shame behind a new marriage, only this time he would have to be more careful and choose not another degenerate but a young girl from a family with no reputation for extravagance, and, most importantly, he would have to bear down hard on her, starting with the wedding night.

But a miser is repellent and miserly even in bed. It is, indeed, the biggest spendthrifts who make the best seducers, for they understand the transience of things and so value the moment all the more, investing in it everything they at that moment possess, even if, in fact, they have nothing. Such a carefree approach to existence women find alluring. It makes no difference that the squanderers are known to be wastrels, undependables, easy-talkers and schemers; women see strength in their light-hearted attitude towards time, which says, 'The past is the past and the future, well, who knows if there will even be a future?' – they see victory over time, which means victory over transience, victory over the fear of death and extinction. And this is a rare, a very rare, talent. More than a few such talents may be found among the travelling musicians to whom more than a few women are prepared to surrender themselves, regardless of the consequences. Misers, meanwhile, pile up a future wrapped in illusory haze and constricted by uncertainty and fear: 'What if the future never happens, which means you must meticulously protect it? Or, worse, what if the future does happen, for then it will bring us only more troubles and worries?'

'But life is lost before it begins,' these merry men grin, 'but while we have it, oh, for as long as life has us, we'll harvest it, press it and suck and squeeze out every last drop of it!'

Her husband was not only of the miserly sort, but, as is often the case with such people, he neglected his own person. While his business dealings flourished, he himself, in his living body, was slowly rotting away. The idea that he should have his teeth seen to – this was, in his view, simply throwing away money. That he was corpulent or that the jagged stubs in his mouth made him repugnant to his wife, all the more so because he possessed not an ounce of humour and the only vibrant thing about him was his body odour – this he never considered. Some of this can be attributed to his years, but certainly not all of it. Mayor Volk Falke, who is the same age he was, is considered to be an extremely charming person. And, as one might expect of a trustworthy and dignified man, he is sometimes surprisingly merciful and generous, as only the self-confident can be, who hand out alms, punishments, forgiveness and awards on the basis of their own judgements. Mayor Volk Falke – whose very name effuses the boldness of the wolf and the sharp-wittedness of the falcon – is well liked by women. They feel safe in his company, and he respects his wife, no matter what people say about her, that she is sometimes unbearable, sometimes pleasant, more and more seldom amusing and more and more often mad. His wife is lucky, people gossip, that God, or maybe fate, sent her a husband who is able to put up with a woman like that and, apparently, even loves her. Our mayor is a good man, who, as befits a man of his type, has a widespread network of relationships with many ladies. Our mayor is an honourable man in every respect ... Yes, but what about women who have similar ideas, and some of them are even bold enough to live like that? Well, nobody calls them anything other than sluts, whores, courtesans, concubines and the like, and if the women so characterized happen to be married, they do not, usually, live very long. Such is the order of the world, and that this order is right and good, most people in our town, and far and wide, regardless of their sex, do not doubt.

Except for one or two of his business partners, nobody was saddened by the merchant's death. Many, indeed, have welcomed it and, of these, not a few have welcomed it because it has liberated a woman of physically attractive yet emotionally still undeveloped attributes. The young widow is wealthy. And illness has accomplished what these men had themselves considered doing, or hoped that nature, or God, or at least somebody would do.

At last, she will be able to spend the evenings and nights as she desires. Well, almost as she desires, for if she wants to live at all differently from how people imagine she should live, she will have to do it discreetly. At last, she will be able to breathe deeply; at last, she will truly start to live. If only she can ... and for as long as she can ... so long as somebody doesn't show up with the intention of shoving her into a new cage ... or maybe a dungeon ... for she is, after all, a woman ... But how will she manage her property on her own? Where will she find advisers, people she can fully trust? Her late husband's family is even somewhat worse than he himself was and even more miserly. And then there are those men in black robes, who pay visits to rich widows with Jesus Christ between their teeth. Oh, my beautiful lady – for that's how I think of you, ever since you became a widow – cling to Mayor Volk, for he alone can protect you, and he will stand by your side, and not only him personally but his people, too, among whom I count my own insignificant self, who am endlessly devoted to you. And if, despite everything, you begin to think that you might perhaps, this time independently and deliberately, desire out of love to ... oh, I fear to say it even to myself ... let's wait a little ... let everything calm down ... and then we'll see ... and then, perhaps, something really will happen ...

FINANCIAL PLANNING

'The spectacle I proposed to you last night – and my proposal, dear Friedrich, should be understood as pure inspiration – needs to include the entire populace. They must feel that they are part of the whole, and the whole is the sum of them, of insignificant parts which when joined together form an organism that, because of its mass, is no longer negligible,' the prince-bishop explains the next day to his host, Count Friedrich, over breakfast. 'The populace must be made to understand that they are like grains of corn, ground one by one into flour, from which the bread is made. And the bread does not make itself but can only be made by someone who knows about bread-making, who knows how to add the water, salt and yeast in the proper amounts – in other words, the bakers, which is to say, us. And this should not be taken simply as a metaphor. You know, this year's yield in buckwheat and rye has not been meagre – although, of course, we won't admit that and we'll nevertheless grumble that even if the yield is better than previous ones, we need to be careful and build up reserves; times are hard and it's even harder to say they won't be worse in the coming future. So the spectacle must be done as a community gathering. Choose millers and bakers, who, for this special occasion, will make buns out of rye flour (and offer them what seems like a favourable price for the flour, although later you can tax them heavily and get it back), and these buns will be shaped like women, and, in the spirit of the event, we can call them – now listen to this, Fritzi – baked witches! And later you can charge them additional taxes for holding public ceremonies, so that what you paid out will be returned to you twice over.'

'How on earth do you come up with these ideas?' Friedrich asks.

'Awake or asleep, the poet dreams without ceasing, and while the populace dozes and snores, the poet, alone and lonely, keeps watch over beauty, keeps watch over truth …' the prince-bishop rhapsodizes.

'But taxes? New taxes? I have no idea any more what else can I impose on the populace?' The count takes a moment to think.

'You're not very creative, Friedrich. Training the mind is like training the body. If you neglect it, it will atrophy; it will become a bare, dead bone, which not even a starving dog would pick up. And the majority walk around with minds whose only rhythm is a skeletal clatter, the sound of useless dead material that isn't worth a thing! Fritzi, Fritzi, breathe! Take a deep breath and start studying, until your fingers grow stiff from turning the pages of some book of philosophy and your eyes are sore from tireless reading. Then close your eyes, and you will see with your inner sight an endless world opening to you, a world your senses could never encompass but thinking it is easier. Thinking up taxes is like dessert for the mind; it's an exercise in style … Now consider this. Everything that appears around you, all that your eyes can see – who does it belong to?'

'To me, of course,' Friedrich responds.

'Of course it does. It belongs to you. You, however, did not create yourself, but you were created by…? Come on, Friedrich, who created you?'

'Well, I was made the way it's usually done,' answers the count.

'True, but who made the ones who made you?'

'They were made by their forebears – they probably didn't fall from the moon and the stars, now did they?'

'I've heard something about that, too, but it's not important here. So then, everything that exists, somebody made. And who was that?'

'Most probably, God.'

'Well, was it God or not? You're hedging, Friedrich …'

'It was.'

'Good. Now, are there not two people, who were not only made but also chosen by the Creator – two people who, along with God and our archduke, have power over everything around here?'

'Hmmm,' Friedrich thinks for a moment. 'Who might that be? I couldn't say …'

'Come on, Fritzi, tighten the reins; otherwise, that mind of yours, which you've only just saddled, will start bolting again. Let me help you out. I'm talking about the two people who right now are sitting at this table and drilling their minds.'

'But we are the only ones at this table.'

'Yes, the two of us and your bird dog, who's leaning on the edge of the table with drool dripping from his mouth, and there's also that cold stuffed duck, which we will now – hand me the knife, please – slice into nice, thin pieces. After all, isn't everything that exists from the Creator?'

'It is.'

'So let's be precise. If he created everything, beginning with the light; if he delved into matter and set in motion the genesis of the world, then all of this is his, or isn't it?' Wolfgang asks in a rhetorical tone.

'Yes, but …'

'Good. For the spiritual part of his creation, God has chosen individuals who through their birth are entrusted with managing the material world and exercising power. So then, to whom does this table belong or the chairs in this castle? To whom do the horses belong and the pigs, turkeys, fields, forests, deer, quail, pheasants, serfs, squirrels, ants, hills, valleys – everything in the castle grounds and all around?'

'To me. To no one but me – and, lest I forget, to God, and indirectly to the Archduke of the Inner Austrian provinces and to the emperor …' Friedrich replies.

'Yes, that's right, to all of these, and a certain power, too, is wielded by the Patriarchate of Aquileia and the Archdiocese of Salzburg, which have divided the Inner Austrian lands between them, south and north of the Drava River. But now, answer me this, would there be light without the Creator?'

'No, there would not,' the count answers.

'Would there be darkness without the Creator?'

'That question is harder for me to answer …'

'You don't have to, Friedrich, because I'll tell you. There would be nothing without the Creator, neither light nor dark, neither day nor night, neither the sun nor the moon, and not even the two of us or the prince, Archduke Ferdinand. And we who have power also have the duty to manage God's creation carefully so the world keeps turning as it should in accord with the Creator's laws. But for this, will is needed, and will is always above the laws of man. Without will, it is impossible to make the laws reality. Will is a condition for belief and faith. If a person does not have the will to perform God's rituals, there can be no faith either. That is why in cases of religious lethargy, it is worth using the following prescription: if there is no faith, act as if there is; pray, even if you think the words are hard to understand or foolish; crawl on your knees, even if you are not thinking about God when you do it but instead are fighting off the pain; cross yourself a hundred times, a thousand times if necessary, because as you repeat this meaningless movement of the arm, faith will eventually start flickering. The same holds true for other situations, too. When you are feeling glum and miserable, it's good to lift up the corners of your mouth with your fingers every so often, until your face gets used to the position and, with your artificial smile, your mood will gradually lighten and ultimately your misery will be banished. Maybe right now you're thinking that our conversation is taking time away from God, but it's not. The same rules apply to thinking as to prayer: from a multitude of simple words, and even the kind of high-flown phrases you criticize me for, there will, through repetition, eventually be a flash of meaning, and each tiny particle of it will find its proper place in a universe that draws its power from the grace of the mind of God.

'But to return to our topic: light and darkness are in no way something self-evident. As we said, without the Creator they would not exist. But we who have power must be careful that the celestial rhythm and harmony remain in tune. A person should work when it is day and rest when it is night. Most of those who work at night – putting aside such necessary exceptions as night guards, bakers, physicians and midwives – are off-notes and skewed tones, which make the melody of the human universe discordant. But that is why we are here, the singers and instrumentalists who lead the orchestra, so it stays in key and the melody does not fall apart. And we must be rewarded for our work. The purpose of the time God has given us is to make sure that the world does not run off course. This is the aim of our knowledge and skills, which we have developed from greater or lesser talents. But to get my point – the light outside, which is just now thickening into darkness, is a gift from God, and everything that is outside we control, we, who have been chosen by God. So then, just as we impose a chimney tax on the populace, so it would be possible to introduce a new tax, a tax on sunlight.'

'A tax on what?' The count is utterly astonished.

'On sunlight, Friedrich. Let's assume that what people have in their flea-bitten burrows is more or less theirs, keeping in mind, of course, that many of these people, along with their property, belong to the feudal estate, not to mention to God and the prince. Well, the candles they burn in their cottages, which they themselves purchased, are indisputably theirs. If they buy a candle or burn some sort of fat, then it will be bright inside their cottage; if not, it will be dark. Darkness is the original condition – man is born from darkness and into darkness he dies. But to live life on earth man needs light, and light must not be taken for granted. While the inside of a house or cottage may be categorized as private life – putting aside whether the house actually belongs to the people who live inside it or to us, who are their masters – everything that comes into the living space from the outside belongs to the feudal lord or to the town. So then, what comes in from the outside, except when the people themselves have made, bought or created it, does not belong to them and, therefore, it cannot be for free. Just as hunting wild game is forbidden on your feudal land without your permission, so, too, people have access to sunlight because they live in your fiefdom.'

'But they would also have sunlight if they lived anywhere else,' Friedrich says.

'Not necessarily. If they lived in a dungeon they wouldn't; at the very least, for every ray of light that comes from the sun they should be grateful to our emperor or, if they live somewhere else, to the French king, etc.'

'So you want me to put out and light the sun for them?' the count smiles in disbelief.

'No, just charge a fair price for it …'

'And how do I do that?'

'It's easy, Friedrich. You base it on the amount of window space. Have windows and other openings measured in every house, barn and pigsty, and then, in direct proportion to the size of the surface area, charge the owners, or tenants, or whatever you want to call them, a tax.'

'But they'll think I'm bonkers!' the count breaks into laughter.

'The populace may well think that, among other things, but it won't do them much good,' the prince-bishop continues. 'No matter how crazy even the craziest tax seems at first, people soon get used to it – it's surprising how fast – and before long it seems normal, rational, logical and essential.'

'But how do I explain it to the populace?'

'Friedrich! You are their overlord! You have nothing to explain to the populace! If there's anyone you need to explain something to, it would be a prince of the Church, such as My Excellency, and, of course, the prince, who, by the way, thinks about you not in the singular but, together with the other members of the nobility, in the plural. But if you want to have some fun, you could, in fact, say something to the populace about it, and it wouldn't be a bad idea either, since you can learn a lot from how your subjects respond, and you can predict how they'll react to future measures. But, don't worry, Julian will write you an explanation with reasons for the new levy, and then you'll memorize the text and try to inhabit the role a little, the way comedians do. I'm not saying the whole thing doesn't sound ludicrous or even absurd. People will be angry at first, they'll be furious, but not for long. Soon they will start thinking rationally, and many of them will brick up a window or some other unnecessary opening, but, regardless, money will start flowing into your treasury, whether you need it or not – it doesn't make a damn bit of difference. By taking such action you let the populace know not only that you are a scrupulous master but mainly that you *are* the master. Our branch of power, meanwhile, for the public good, will introduce regular bell-ringing to warn of hailstorms, and not only when heavy clouds are amassing over this beautiful land but once a week, as a precautionary measure. On Friday afternoons, for example, around three o'clock, in memory of our Saviour's death, when the sky darkened above his Cross. Anything, absolutely anything, can be arranged. For where there is will there is power – but the inverse is not true. Many a lord has power, but has not the will to express it in the manner expected of him.'

'But you have forgotten the wind, Wolfgang, and water, and the sunrise and sunset, rainbows and mist,' Friedrich mocks him, appalled by the prince-bishop's ideas.

'You still doubt me. Tsk tsk ... How indecisive you are! What a dithering overlord! A tax on water – both the water in the streams that meander through your domain and the water that rains down from heaven – this is also worth thinking about. As for the wind, well, we'll be generous and give it to them for free, and when we announce the new tax on sunlight, we'll underscore this point and warn the populace that if they give us the least bit of trouble, a whirlwind will come whirling down on their hovels as punishment, tearing up their roofs and flattening everything they've sown and planted. So when they start railing against the new taxes, we offer them the tax-free wind in the same package, and at once they'll understand that, despite our strict measures, the authorities are wise and just. Because we could have taxed the wind, too, as we did the light, but being so merciful we didn't. Everything, truly everything, can be controlled. Well, everything except nature. Her, no; even if there are many who believe differently. The idea that, with Satan's help, witches can pass water and make it rain – what utter nonsense! Superstition! Magic! Witchery!'

'And yet here you are in my castle because of them ...' Friedrich says.

'Because of them, and much else and many others, too, which, however, does not negate what I have just said – that it's complete idiocy to believe that certain obsessed women may think they can cast a spell with the devil's help and make it hail, even if the bumpkin populace, as well as various members of government, believe the same thing.'

'Well, since you've been addressing my finances with such visionary imagination,' Friedrich says with a wry smile, 'perhaps you can give some thought to an issue that really does need resolving. If what you've said so far was merely a mental exercise, now that we're all warmed up, we might tackle a problem that has recently been robbing me of sleep.'

'The purpose of my earlier elaboration was not simply to keep you mentally fit – far from it. And I am sorry you think so, Friedrich. With a little more flexibility you wouldn't be struggling with financial difficulties, and I doubt I'll be far off the mark if I say they include debts.'

'It's true. That is one of the sources of my worries.'

'There is no worry that can't be eliminated. So what's the problem?'

'The Jews,' Friedrich says.

'What? But didn't we expel them in 1515 and cleanse the Inner Austrian lands of this Oriental brood?' the prince-bishop asks in surprise.

'We did, but they've come back ...'

'They shouldn't have. Among the Inner Austrian provinces, an exception was made for Gorizia and Trieste, and that's where they were concentrated.'

'But they have started gradually returning in the guise of Triestine merchants, until one day they approached me and said humbly, "Most esteemed Count Friedrich, we come to you with peace on our lips and money in our hands. May God grant you descendants, as well as happiness and health, no typhus or plague and a long life without Turks or Uskok pirates; may the prince be merciful towards you and allow you to have communion in one or two kinds, and may he impose the lowest possible taxes on you."

'"Fine," I told them. "Peace we have never had here, and money has always been lacking." And I proposed a not very small indemnity for settling here temporarily. They agreed without haggling and started pulling out papers for us to sign. "Oh no, we're not signing anything," I told them with an adamant wave of my arm. "You can stay here under the condition that you pass yourselves off as merchants from Trieste. But when the seven cows in my barns start sweetly lowing because, poor things, they're hungry, or when funds need to be collected, again, because the Turks are at our gates, then, Triestine merchants, I will summon you, and you will pay me back without hesitating. We will tell no one that you have settled among us. And finally, let me ask you, why have you come to us? Why didn't you go to Bohemia? Or even Poland? They'd be more accepting of you there; they'd probably cram you all together in the towns – but here?"

'"It's where we come from; we left here a few generations back. We know wine; we're skilled merchants; money multiplies in our hands all by itself," they said.

'"But why don't you settle in the nearby town, where there are already some Triestine merchants milling around?"

"'Because we have a commercial network with them – and they're more or less related to us since we all come from one of the Twelve Tribes of Israel – and that network extends in all directions, so you, too, will be able to benefit from it,' they tell me.

"'Fine, fine,' I say. "Move into the most inconspicuous market villages and don't do anything to attract attention. Make sure you dress in a way that blends in as much as possible with the majority, and when you start mashing up that strange food of yours in your bowls, I advise you to shut your windows. The populace is sensitive, and unusual foreign smells can agitate them."

"'But, except for pork, we don't eat all that differently from you, basically. What we like most of all, same as you, is boiled beef with horseradish or pea sauce,' they reply.

"'Sure, sure,' I say, "but you also have that Shabbos feast of yours … no need to tell me about it. But in every respect – visual, aural or olfactory – stay in the background, and we'll all get along fine. Even if …"

"'Yes, but it'll be hard for people not to recognize us. No matter where we go, even if we look like everyone else, they still point their fingers at us and stare."

"'That's why I'm telling you to stay in the background and don't stand out in any way. And, when I summon you, don't make excuses and say it's one of your holidays, but leave your work, leave your strange rituals, forget your own troubles and come to me at once, purses in hand." That's what I proposed to them.

'And that's the agreement we made, but soon things got complicated,' Count Friedrich scowls. 'No matter how much you try to anticipate things and make a plan, there's always a reason why you need to go back into your treasury, take a painful look around and decide what can possibly be put up for sale.'

'If I understand correctly,' the prince-bishop grins, 'the reason for your difficulties is exactly what made the emperor banish them by decree from our lands so long ago: they're blackmailing you with high interest rates … Oh dear, oh dear … I implored you not into get into debt with these hyenas, or if you had to, never without Jesuit-trained lawyers. Those usurious misers hike up the interest rates and then buy from us only when they can't get something from their own people.

How many poor Christians have had to leave their homes with only the clothes on their back because they miscalculated when they were paying off their debts and those weasels confiscated their houses. You say they're living here in disguise. Well, the only official taxes that come into play are those on trade, but unofficial contributions – for them to be allowed to live here and, indeed, to be allowed to live at all – could be used as a bargaining chip. The situation, then, is that officially there are no Jews living in your domain; there are only a handful of Triestine merchants, who smuggle in wine, wool, sea salt, olive oil and noble metals, and being so wealthy, they also lend money. I'm sure you're not the only one in your fiefdom who's in debt to them. But even if they have nobody else in their claws, these behemoths, these bestial Old Testament creatures, will never run out of money! Maybe they do know how to conjure it from thin air! But I know a way to wriggle out of this dilemma, too, and elegantly fleece the fleecers! How, you may ask? Simply. The most complicated problems are solved by the simplest methods, the sharp corners trimmed with Occam's razor, because when you tackle complications with complicated approaches, it only gets more complicated.

'First, since they're not of our religion and don't participate in our rituals, the Church authorities are deprived of their offerings at Mass. We'll calculate some average amount each honest Christian brings to the offering on a yearly basis and figure it in as an annual loss with the Triestine merchants. Next, since they don't buy all the food we Christians grow and buy, we'll calculate that, too, as a financial curtailment and add it to the first. And that's not all. Most importantly, we'll levy a tax on them for the coordination of customs and practices; the fact that they live among us with their peculiar traditions and, very often, disgusting habits – this also costs us something, if nothing else our nerves. Absolutely everything can be translated into money,' the prince-bishop puts forward his proposal.

'But recently, it's all become a little more complicated,' the count says. 'There are stories circulating among the populace that defy belief. People are saying there's a certain farm where certain farmhands live who not only are not really farmhands, they're not even people – they're some sort of automatons made out of clay, which were supposedly whipped up by these people, the Triestine merchants, with their abracadabra gibberish. The populace has been coming to me and even offering me money to drive them out.'

'Let's take things one at time, Fritzi. It's clear that the brains of the populace are yet again playing tricks on them and they're experiencing a collective hallucination woven from their own frustrations, fears and wickedness. But how much are they offering you to drive those others out? Because we could easily collect from both sides.'

'They haven't said yet. So far we've been talking more in the abstract. But, in fact, I don't have any real arguments to support banishing them. They are exemplary when it comes to paying the contributions we agreed on and they've blended in quite nicely with the surroundings. They speak and understand our languages and, swots that they are, a couple others, too. But when there's something serious they need to discuss with each other, they switch to their own language, so no one but their own cruel god can understand them. And in a way I even feel sorry for the poor devils, always living in exile ...'

'Pity is a beautiful emotion, Friedrich, a fine and noble feeling, and, what's more, it's arrogantly condescending towards those for whom one hypocritically cultivates it. But you shouldn't feel sorry for these people, not in the least! They even walk differently from the rest of us. The men with their black ringlets stuck behind their ears, which, actually, you don't see around here – they sway back and forth, as if they're making a figure of eight when they walk – or not even an eight, a six! We will cleanse your domain of them, and we'll cleanse the nearby town, too! We'll cleanse all the Habsburg Hereditary Lands and then the Holy Roman Empire and then our continent, Mother Europe! We'll cleanse the whole world!'

'How?' The count gazes at the prince-bishop.

'We'll do it with love ... Hahahaha! Certainly not with love! We'll do it with metal and fire, with swords and spears, with crossbows, bonfires, muskets and cannon; if we have to, we'll strangle them with our bare hands. But that won't be necessary. There are more refined, but no less brutal methods.'

'But, like I said, they pay their contributions regularly,' Friedrich says.

'So, if they're useful, have them offer you a higher price than the bumpkin populace, and then tell them you can protect them and give them everything honest people deserve, but that it won't come cheap, and then impose a tax on them for protection ...'

'Protection from what?'

'From themselves. From their arrogance and miserliness. Of course, you won't tell them that but, if they ask, just say it's a protection tax. They'll know what they need protecting from. Jewish people have an even stronger and more developed sense of guilt than Christians, who to some degree can avoid it by means of confession. You don't need to explain any further. Once the thing is done, various explanations can be devised after the fact; if there's no rationale behind the action, you can always introduce it retrospectively. Every possible foolishness can be explained in syllogisms; in every possible situation, you can pull that tedious Greek out of your sleeve, the one the scholastics never get tired of quoting. There is nothing you have to worry about; even the most idiotic things have been sold as the honest truth and pure gold.

'So summon the Triestine merchants and say this to them, "Our dear Triestine merchants, I am in a terrible predicament." Then tell them, "But you, even more than me, are in a most dire predicament. Look!" Then you wave a sheaf of papers in front of their hooked noses, although they're actually all blank. "Our dear populace is begging me to drive you out of our beautiful, peace-loving land, which also means out of your warm houses, which by now are almost your homes ... They claim you are encroaching on their trade rights, that you fleece them with high interest rates, live at their expense and get rich while they themselves barely scrape by. And, what's more, the populace informs me" – emphasize that – "that you disguise yourselves as Christians and sneak into the sacristy, where you steal the consecrated hosts, spit on them and trample them, and some of them you dip in the innocent blood of Christian babes, which, the populace says, also explains all the missing children you've been abducting for your rituals, whom you slaughter and offer up to your dark god – if not to Satan himself. What I am saying is not my opinion but only summarizes the testimonies of the populace, who are pressing me to expel you and offering me a sizeable amount of money to cover the costs. As a wise master with a gentle and benevolent disposition, my primary concern is the welfare of my fiefdom, so I am not sure what I should do. What is your opinion, dear Triestine merchants? What might be done in such a situation?"

'Of course, they will be writhing in fear and pleading with you, saying something like, "But we've made a life for ourselves here, and our families live honest lives here, in our own houses, which we bought at a fair price, and also in the houses we confiscated because of unpaid debts. We beg you, don't force us into exile again! But ultimately, it was our God who created everything that is here, in front of you and behind you, including this land on which you, apostates from the Jewish faith, have built your lives, so you should be profoundly grateful to us for the very fact that you even have a place to live on this earth of ours." Of course, they won't say this last sentence, but it's what they'll be thinking. And, remember this, if you ever feel like you're being too hard on them, they went after our Saviour, and those Christ-killers should be made to pay for it every once in a while.

'So then, tell them very kindly, with a worried look, that maybe something might somehow be arranged after all, and then pretend that you are deep in thought, trying to figure out the best solution, and wait, wait calmly, until one of them speaks up and offers you a suitable amount, an amount they think is higher than what the populace has offered, even if the populace hasn't offered you anything.'

'What should I tell them? What price should I set?'

'Tell them nothing, nothing whatsoever, and only say the following, "What the populace has been up to – trying to make a deal so I'll expel you from the fiefdom – I couldn't keep it to myself. You live here; this is your home – well, not entirely but almost. And when the need arises, you lend us money, although you charge interest worthy of a Jew and not a Christian, whose New Testament religion is based on love." And if any of them starts asking indirect questions about the kind of money you might be talking about, given the Christians' offer, you just lower your eyes and say something like, "Maybe it would have been better if I hadn't brought it up, but you and I have always done good business together," and so on. They will exchange glances and search each other's eyes for some idea of the amount they should mention, a number as low as possible, of course, but at the same time large enough so they won't have to leave. But, no matter what they offer, don't agree right away. Be evasive, say you don't know how you'd explain it to the populace and that you sincerely do want to protect them but the populace is putting pressure on you. And when those usurers finally quintuple the amount, then you slowly start to relent, so the moment your scrivener sticks a protection contract in front of their noses, along with a goose quill, they'll be ready to sign anything.'

'But what do I tell the populace?' Friedrich asks.

'The populace?' The prince-bishop is astonished. 'What is there to tell the populace? You won't even mention it to them! Fritzi, you forget the things I tell you as soon as I say them. Governing requires at least a modicum of memory, otherwise they'll roast you and turn you on the spit and you won't feel a thing, you won't notice at all. Don't lower yourself by offering explanations, let alone apologies. You're a feudal lord, for God's sake! When you're done with the Triestine merchants, then you talk to those whiners from the populace, not about the Triestine merchants but about the poor astrological forecasts, and here you make the point that if a person isn't prudent and only lives for the moment, he'll have nothing put away for when the bad times come. Tell the populace, "It might seem that things are going pretty well today, but tomorrow some catastrophe could come down on our heads, so it would be wise to agree on a new tax." Do this and, as the saying goes, the wolf will be full and the goat unharmed – and the sheep will still be sheep, and the asses even bigger asses. Well, has that steward of yours, or whatever he is, remembered what I've been saying?'

'I have, Your Grace,' the steward says, bowing humbly and thinking that if he could ever pluck up the courage he would pack his things and take off across the ocean to the New World where, he has heard, there are God-fearing Christian communities who read the Bible even more literally than the Lutherans or Calvinists do, and they live by Gospel, too. The men have long beards and walk around with black hats on their heads, and the women wear white bonnets, and they all till the fields, sow the grain, sow the maize and plant the potatoes, and when there's any dispute between them, they don't pull out weapons but, in the spirit of Christ, they use words, wisely and justly, for they believe that God remembers every sentence they utter, every deed they do, even if he has chosen their destinies in advance. And, because they are devout, and deeply devout, each of them in turn believes that he or she is one of the chosen, and so they live from birth to death, honouring one another and honouring God, and living by their own labour on the land without being parasites on any ecclesiastical or feudal power. But it would not be wise to tell anyone about such life plans, for if the wrong ears happen to be listening, that could cost the planner his life. Silence. In silence you must think, and don't walk around with your mouth open, the steward is thinking as he politely excuses himself to the others at the table and leaves the dining hall.

Prelude

In late August the seven from the Kostanšek farm appeared in front of the church; they had come to do the necessary renovations. This was one of that summer's most interesting social events, the biggest, indeed, since the persecution of the witch a few years earlier. Almost the entire village had gathered for it, and the men, with their arms crossed or resting on their hips, stood beneath the church tower and watched as the giants passed the wooden roof tiles to each other and sealed the holes in the church walls.

'They're strong, I'll give them that,' people were commenting. The women, wrapping their hands in their greasy, stain-spotted aprons, wondered how they were able to work without eating or drinking anything. They did all the work properly, despite their ungainly appearance. In fact, they finished the repairs much sooner than the populace themselves would have done, since they didn't waste any time in chit-chat or seeing to their bodily needs.

Despite months of careful observation, the populace had not yet managed to unravel the mystery of the giants' origin and nature, so now they came up with a new plan.

Kostanšek had three vicious dogs that ran free at night in the fenced area around the house, and these dogs had more than once caused the populace to modify their plan. But that day they had the idea of organizing a small group who would do some sniffing around the farm. The seven giants had never since their arrival on the farm given so much as a wink to any girl or woman, no matter how sweaty she was in the summer or how much her filthy work clothes adhered to her body, which, in most cases, because of poor harvests, was rather bony. 'This could be because those seven giants don't need anybody but themselves,' the populace speculated, 'and that is wicked in the eyes of our God. As we all know, it was because of such vile creatures that God destroyed Sodom and Gomorrah. So we at least need to see if what's going on might be what we think it is, or if it might be the no less wicked abomination that all seven are being serviced by Kostanšek's daughter' – and that, too, would not be very pleasing to God, who for such whorish behaviour might easily strike the area with plague, if not something worse.

Out of eleven volunteers, the populace, after judicious consideration, selected three men to investigate the situation. The plan was as follows: in the evening, when the seven giants were seen returning from the orchards and fields, the three would sneak on to the farm carrying three cow thighs smeared with herbs sautéed in fat, and they would use the raw meat to distract the dogs, who would then fall asleep licking their lips; after that, the three would climb up to the loft over the pigsty – there was a question as to whether there were still any pigs there or only sheep and goats. In general, the number of Kostanšek's livestock was suspiciously on the rise: there had been an unusual increase in cattle as well as, of course, in turkeys, geese and chickens, but as for pigs, honest Christian pigs, all indications were that there was none left on the farm.

The three men should see how the giants were arranged on their beds and what, if anything, they did with each other. 'And then report back to us in detail about everything,' the populace concluded. The trio – one of whom was just over twenty, while the other two were around thirty – stole up to the farm with the cow legs, threw the dogs the bones and waited just long enough for the barking dogs to tear into the feast and grow quiet. Then, from the other end, they climbed over the fence, which (another suspicious fact) Kostanšek had erected only after the arrival of the giants; after that, they climbed up to the loft above the pigsty and waited for the seven to return.

What happened that night in late August on the Kostanšek farm would be the subject, several weeks later, of testimony given by the three men at the first of two trials, which followed the events that, from this point on, unfolded evermore rapidly and irrationally, almost completely out of control.

'The seven lumbered up the wooden stairs with heavy footsteps,' the three began their testimony before the judge. 'Kostanšek came up after them, and, at his command, all seven lay down on the wooden floor – no, there wasn't even any straw spread out for them; they lay down right on the floor. Kostanšek went up to each of them separately, leaned over and took some sort of little disc out of their mouths, which he put into his pouch; then he left the pigsty. The giants were obviously asleep and didn't move a muscle all night. It was like they were dead; they weren't even breathing – in fact, has anyone before this ever noticed them breathing? But they weren't. How could they not be breathing?

'No, we didn't have the courage to see if the giants were really asleep – any one of them could have crushed us with a single wave of his arm. We sat there all night without moving, and the next morning we witnessed the same thing again, only in reverse: Kostanšek came up the steep stairs and fed the giants their discs, and they came back to life, stood up and, without saying good morning, without changing clothes, without breakfast, they went down to the yard, where their tools were ready and waiting for them. One of them picked up a scythe, another a sickle, a third a basket and so on.

'What were those discs? Who are those seven? Why has Kostanšek's farm had such abundant yields while our crops are not only meagre in number but also sour, puny and rancid? And who does he sell his produce to and, more importantly, at what sort of prices? That night we spent above the pigsty we weren't able to find out any of these things,' the trio said, concluding their report.

Of the three eye-witnesses, one was especially talkative; he answered even when the question was addressed to all three of them or to one of the other two specifically. But their narrative started getting tangled. The facts didn't add up. They didn't always tell the same story.

'But weren't the three of you together?' the judge asks.

'Yes, but it was dark and hard to see,' the talkative one answers.

'So how can you talk about something you could barely see?' the judge asks.

'There were three of us. Three pairs of eyes see more than a single pair,' the trio's representative explains.

'Yes, especially when the brains behind the eyeballs are soaked in foul-smelling liquor,' the judge says. 'Don't think anybody believes for an instant that you were sober all night or that you were waiting for the seven to return without some marc brandy on hand.'

'But we *were* sober,' the leader of the three replies.

'Of course you weren't. Brandy fried your brains a long time ago, and you, chatty mouth, are willing to say anything anyone tells you to say, so long as they pay you.'

'That's not true, I swear …' the witness insists.

'This story you've been spinning us, about little discs and man-made creatures – I heard it years ago when I was a student in Prague, and I'm told that not long ago there was a preacher in these parts who was talking about it, who took a crack at the Jews while excoriating the papists. You're too stupid to have come up with the idea yourselves, so what I want to know is, who taught you these fairy tales about golems, which mothers in the ghettos use to terrify their children?'

'But it's true,' replies the chief of the three.

'Fine. I can put your sincerity to the test and charge you in advance with perjury. You assert that everything you said is the honest truth, and meanwhile I'll order the executioner to show you the tools of his trade, and if you keep on asserting the same thing, then the executioner and I will try a few of them out. Well, what do you say?' The judge asks sharply.

The witness, alarmed, now surveys the courtroom, seeking support, but not one of the heads he sees shows any sign of having the slightest connection with the three of them or with the story they had just told.

'So, what will it be? Will you repeat your story and insist on its veracity, or will you withdraw it, saying, for example, that the light wasn't bright enough to dispel the darkness thickening above the pigsty, or rather, thickening in your heads?'

The three look around in fear, casting glances at everyone in the room, but nobody bats an eyelid.

'Summon the executioner,' the judge orders.

A thickset giant of a man with an almost childishly bloated face and liquid-blue eyes now enters the courtroom. The executioner's appearance alone, with the incongruity between his huge, solid body and puffy, naïve face, was enough to provoke a sense of unease – of horror, even. He looked like an enormous burly child who might suddenly, without any provocation, lay into someone out of pure childish cruelty and spite. Only a very few children are born with a kind of marvellous feeling for others, which makes them seem like little angels of a non-human variety, whose innate goodness and sensitivity strike one as extraordinary and unnatural, and a person might even worry that our beloved God will be so greatly enamoured of the child that he will call him to himself right now, when the boy is still small and innocent – please, God, leave him with us, let us have him at least long enough to watch him grow up! Such angels are a blessing to hale and hearty humanity, for whom they might serve as an example, however unattainable. But most children are not like that; sensitivity towards others is something most human offspring need to be taught, beginning with the fact that their tiny hands – which, relative to their size, are disproportionately strong – ought not to pull the tails of dogs or human hair.

The aforementioned executioner had never fully absorbed such childhood lessons. Not a single feature could be detected on him that might betray any capacity for identifying with the feelings of others. Especially with their pain – which is right and proper in the execution profession, even if some executioners, before carrying out the punishment, would secretly, out of empathy, give their victims some herb to chew on, so that even before the executioner positioned their head on the block or right after he began tying them to the stake, they might await their end in a state of near anaesthesia, and even if the victim seemed to the outside observer still somewhat conscious, their soul was already flapping its wings and detaching itself from the material substance which the executioner, in the name of the imperial criminal code, the *Carolina*, was obliged to destroy.

This particular executioner would melt with delight like a child every time he saw on the table before him braised chicken livers or a still steaming roast leg of veal, and, like a child, his eyes would light up when, after completing his assignment, he received a bag of coins in his hand; another bag went to his assistant, who would cheerfully test its weight and, as he did so, let out the shrillest, most repulsive squawk. The executioner was meticulous when he worked. The only things that interested him were the functioning of the execution equipment and the expected degree of responsiveness from the human organism. Why a person had ended up in a position which he, in the name of the authorities, had to finalize – no, this was not something which that honest fellow, a civil servant who always drew up beforehand a detailed estimate of execution costs and afterwards presented a scrupulous expense report, ever speculated about.

'Executioner, will you be kind enough to show these three men your instruments?' the judge asks him.

The executioner smiles and nods, sending a shudder through the trio, and asks, 'Right now?'

'No,' the judge answers, 'tomorrow morning, when they have had some sleep and are well-rested, you will escort them to the rooms in the cellar.'

'Sure, that's good, too,' the executioner responds.

But it was not good, not for everybody. The day that was about to end was not a good day for the judge. Indeed, it was his last.

'What could have happened to him?' most people would be wondering as evening approached on that warm autumn day, only weeks after the three men's night above the pigsty.

'So it happened, then?' a few would say, exchanging glances.

'Is it done? Finished?' a handful would whisper among themselves. 'Is it over?'

Not yet, populace. This trial, which is interrupted by the death of the judge, will be followed by a second trial. And it will not end in just a day or two.

But now the hot summer is drawing to a close. And after it comes autumn. A hot autumn, which will be made hotter by fire.

But until then there are still many things to happen.

WHY, DESPITE MY REASON, AM I SOMETIMES IN ERROR?

As I search for the causes of things, I find I am confronted not only by a real and positive idea of God as the utterly perfect being but also by a negative idea of nothing, or something that is very far from perfection. The reason for my errors lies in the fact that I am positioned in the middle between God and nothing; I am suspended between the highest Being and Non-being. Because I also have the experience of nothing, it is not surprising that I am fairly often wrong and that the capacity for making correct judgements, which is given to me by God, is not infinite in me.

But, in the past few weeks, a strange force has been pulling me towards Non-being, which results not only in errors in judgement but also ever less certainty about things which up to now I have not doubted. Maybe I am not trying hard enough to direct myself towards Being so as to think in a more concentrated way, so my attention is not distracted by the kind of melancholic anxieties that not even I have known before now. There are moments when I have the feeling that this non-beingness, which is the opposite of the perfect beingness of God, is, like a kind of abyss, expanding and contracting beside me.

More and more, I am besieged by the thought that a sudden and unexpected catastrophe will occur. I am beset by indescribable fears, in particular, the fear of death, which, as a Catholic who believes in an elaborate and colourful afterlife, I have never before experienced. People live as though death has nothing to do with them and are constantly forgetting that it exists. Which is good. A life in which you are conscious of your mortality every moment, and not just on the level of abstract ideas but as an evermore concrete conception, is extremely exhausting. If such mental states continue, I don't know what sort of life this will be, for already they are becoming harder and harder to bear.

The idea of life after death, behind which is hope and a new life, is becoming inexplicably porous. Every night I am afraid to fall asleep. Sleep is a state I cannot control. I am afraid of disappearing forever in my dreams. When I am having a nightmare, only rarely does it occur to me that none of these horrible images are real, that this is only a dream, which means that any moment now I will wake up. But at that moment, how can I be sure that I am awake, that I am not actually dreaming and asleep? What if, a little earlier, I started choking and then broke out in a cold sweat and keeled over in a swoon, in an episode of syncope, and now I am lying on the floor, and my consciousness, which is detached from my immobile body, does not know this and is prattling away here all by itself?

I feel myself keeling over; more and more often the floor gives way beneath my feet, and I'm left hovering in a void with nothing for me to hold on to.

In such moments, what happens to my soul? I don't even know any more where to locate the soul. I am not sure if I even have one. Or if I even am. A strange feeling comes over me that, less and less, I am.

SPRING DIALOGUES:

BECAUSE HE DOESN'T HEAR? ...
BECAUSE HE DOESN'T
WANT TO HEAR?

'Fritzi, Fritzi, you've let yourself go to rot in this fiefdom of yours,' the prince-bishop shakes his head as they stroll at midday down a path lined with sweet-smelling linden trees; he supports himself with his left hand on Julian. 'You, Friedrich, you promised me long ago, as my palm ran down your warm back and the southern breeze was drying our hair, still thick and soft and wet with the sea and our own sweat, that you would never waste away in idle boredom, that you would never stop reading or let the ravenous beast in you degenerate into the scraggy creature you've become. How you used to strut and stride when as little aristocrats we were sent off to the castles of Europe, where first we'd pine for our homes and all we'd left behind, but then, after a while, we didn't even want to go back, for we had each other and we realized that we were the centre of the universe.'

'You, too, Wolfgang. You said a lot of things back then that are the complete opposite of what you are today. So we're the centre of the universe, are we? Is that what you think? They say that not even the earth is the centre of the universe and that the planets, the earth included, rotate around the sun,' Friedrich replies.

'Who in the universe rotates around whom and what – only God knows that. But as for how things should properly rotate, that's something we the chosen know. And any idea that seeks to change the direction of the rotation we crush before it sprouts. Here it's not important what's true and what isn't true. What's important is that we are always right, for only thus can we ensure that things run smoothly and correctly and that there's some degree of peace in the world. But there isn't. So, with eccentrics, we knock the dangerous ideas out of their heads. Take that Italian, Galileo, who's been trumpeting the idea that the earth rotates around the sun – we'll soon put the screws on him and make him pull back, and by doing this we'll stopper many other mouths as well. Most clever minds are cautious in their thinking – and Galileo has a clever mind; I hear that only recently he made some contrivance that measures warmth and cold – but is it worth drilling holes into the eternal verities? Giordano Bruno, on the other hand, was stubborn, the way mystics are; he rejected the divine person, fantasized about some all-pervasive infinite substance and made delusional claims about multiple solar systems and parallel worlds, which, when you think about it, isn't at all stupid, but unfortunately it's blasphemous. In the past people believed all kinds of things that today seem incredibly foolish. People used to believe the earth was flat, but then it turned out there's no rim on the earth where you could fall into the void and that there's a force in the earth that binds all earthly creation to itself like a mother so things don't fly off into the sky. Even in ancient Greece, cosmologists knew about forces acting on the world and the wider cosmos which cause things to be mutually attracted or repelled and which have nothing to do with God.

'More than once the thought has occurred to me that maybe the created world is just one big shambles. The very idea that God wants something, wants anything – is not that a sign of his lack of perfection? But God does want something. Oh yes, God wants action, he wants drama and comedy, and perfection would get in the way of all of that. Maybe that's why everything that exists has been created more or less so-so and is more of a botch-up than not. For the world to turn at all, and events to unfold within it, man had to be given free will. But has it ever crossed your mind, Friedrich, that this is exactly what God, bored inside his own perfection, longs to see – blunders, errors, lies, excitement, drama, disaster, cripples, freaks and corpses? A mere seven days is really not enough time for a project as demanding as the creation of the world, no matter how supremely perfect the Creator. And the idea that man was knocked together in a single day – well, that's seems obvious, doesn't it? He's a total cock-up! At first glance, the instrument looks pretty good, but then that tender white body suddenly turns yellow, a black formation swells up in the armpit and what only the day before was a little-boy body, an angel almost, fragrant with vanilla, is now a reeking cadaver. The simple fact that God created the world within time does not bode well for creation. Such linearity, counting down our existence on earth moment by moment, is simply horrifying …

'That's why I can barely wait to shove off to the New World, where, they say, when someone does you a favour it has the authentic semblance of love, and where love, they say, is overflowing. As master, you lie down on a net that's suspended between two palm trees and drink alcohol from a coconut shell – those chocolate cherubs distil it from sugar cane – and then, a little tipsy, you revel in the beauty of God's creation and every once in a while, with a touch of gleeful malice, you might think of your former homeland, where your former compatriots, in carriages or on foot, have to slog through mud and snow, grumpy and full of mites, lice and fleas, as well as boils of every sort, diseased and hungry …'

'I don't know, Wolfgang, I just don't know. I'm not sure you'll manage it. Ever since you arrived, I've been smelling the odour of decay on you. You better hope it's just your teeth …' the count says, giving the prince-bishop a wry look.

'Ugh! I fear that it's not my teeth and these foul vapours are belching up from somewhere deeper inside me.' Wolfgang pauses, covers his mouth with his right hand and lowers his voice. 'I'm increasingly worried that I'll fall apart before I ever step off the boat – just as everything falls apart, and just as some people would love to see our Most Holy Church fall apart and rot away. So it's high time, my dear friend,' the prince-bishop continues, now in a louder voice, 'that I set off as soon as my obligations here are finished – the ones I still have left to do. I've already started packing, thinking about what to take; I'm going there, you know, to be governor, and my task is to save that scum from their delusions and lead them by the hand to the countenance of our Creator.'

'I haven't heard so much grandiloquence and brutality in a very long time,' Friedrich says, shaking his head.

'Well, aren't you cheeky, Fritzi! To say something like that, and in these times, too, right after a sentence that ends with "the countenance of our Creator"! Tsk tsk … As for your criticism of my grandiloquence, you need to remember once and for all: speech and expression must be exercised, just as the stableman exercises the horses to keep them in condition so they don't lose their rhythm and throw the rider from the saddle.'

'So you have said, Wolfgang. We've been over your lesson about the dressage of the mind more than once in the past two days.'

'But you must let my words reverberate inside you ...'

'Wolfgang, *reverberate*? Your flowery words are making me sick to my stomach, as if I've been stuffing myself on the cloying Arabian sweetmeats that are waiting for us in the pavilion.'

'Well, even if my words strike you as mawkish, what I have said is suffused with my sincere and profound faith.'

'Your sincere and profound faith?' Friedrich nearly bursts out laughing. 'Faith? Faith in what, Wolfgang?'

'Faith in what I keep telling you, that in the very near future I will board a three-master and sail across the ocean – really and truly in nothing but this. Faith in the another world, a world I've had painted on the walls of my orangery, where I organize shows for my most valued guests. I have my little angels, a selection of my finest fruits, dressed in costumes so they look like those natives across the sea, that is to say, more naked than not and girded only in frondage from the palm trees that grow in the orangery along with the citruses. And just so it all looks authentically primitive, they sing tunes that the Indians sing, in their own tongues, with the missionaries. And they also dance a little. Oh, I only hope I can board that ship as soon as possible, before I'm ravaged by gout and those strange cramps I keep getting in my abdomen.'

'But what about faith in God, Wolfgang?' Friedrich asks, stopping in front of the pavilion.

'Oh, God definitely exists in my head,' the prince-bishop replies. 'But I fear that his existence has no significant influence on the structure of our lives. And, even more, that after he made the world, God forgot about mankind, saying to himself, "I'll deal with people later, when they're dead. I gave them laws, which they'll have to figure out for themselves as best they can, and I gave them a little intelligence, so they have enough. Because if I interfered too much in their lives, I'd deprive them of free will, which some of them extol as my greatest gift to humanity." But it got mucked up right at the beginning, when those two nudists plundered that tree because they wanted to understand what made the world go round, because they wanted to know what God knows. So is it any wonder that his imperfect creation rebelled against him? Because if God created humans in his own image, it's understandable that his stunted replicas would want to be exactly like the original and so, as children do, rebelled – and God gave them a good hard smack for it, so they'd remember who created whom. Most people simply accept this smack, but I'm not sure that's what God likes. I'd say God prefers people who continue to persevere in their resemblance to him, to their Creator, who keep rebelling against him in the desire that one day they will become exactly like him and then, as in Greek mythology, they will topple him from his throne and finish him off. Because maybe God thinks something like, "That sort, the rebellious types, they're the ones most like me, full of energy, the way I'm described in the Old Testament – the sort who strut around and beat their heads against the wall, who flare up in a second and unleash destruction all around them and only later think about what they've done, or maybe not even bother to think about it. They are my dearest children, unpredictable and passionate, full-blooded and bold, not the bland ones, who are as docile as sheep, mindless animals that, unlike man, I never breathed my spirit into."

'That's why it's important that, as early as possible, we detect those bull-headed rebels – who are, in fact, the only truly interesting, valuable segment of the human mob – and recruit them using the methods I've described. And at the same time, we have to maintain order with a consolidated system so that the world turns in the right direction. Because, Fritzi, if even one of the cogs acts up and slips off its bearings, they will drag us from our beds, from our exquisitely furnished chambers, shake us out of our fine clothes and rip the caps and crowns off our heads, pluck out our fingers one by one and then dismember us, nice and slow, or maybe some big strong men with no imagination will sever us from our heads with a single stroke, so they can be rid of us right away and create for themselves justice on earth. But let me tell you something – as soon as they succeed, only then will they know what cruelty means, for when the beasts lose the leader of the pack, evil spreads its wings, and beneath its wings the poor start baring their teeth and turning on each other, until finally it hits them that they are not all equal; then they let a few of them take power and restore order to the chaos. But, don't worry, there is no chance of this happening. You yourself know – we both know – it's something we all know – we are not here by accident; we are the fruit of a carefully cultivated, ancient seed ... Ah, now where was I?'

'But what about evil, Most Reverend Prince-Bishop?' Friedrich looks intently at the prince-bishop, who, with Julian's help, is seating himself on a cushioned armchair in the garden pavilion.

'Evil? Oh, I know evil! After all, I make a rather excellent living fighting the devil. But, as you know, those hairy Luciferian types with their dark tails have never been my preference; Turks, Arabs, Jews, gypsies and similar filthy demons – I hardly ever touch them. I have always preferred the little angels with the whipped-cream skin, although if those cacao angels over there could be blended with the creamy ones, it would be delicious ...'

'I'm not talking about mythological beings, Wolfgang, I'm talking about human evil, the hatred all your chattering is stuffed with.'

'Paradise! Paradise is my unshakeable faith! I believe in a white heaven, and I am confident that I will experience it a few more times on this earth before I finally close my eyes and there will be nothing more ...'

'Nothing after death, Venerable Prince-Bishop?' Friedrich eyes him mockingly.

'Shhhh ... Not every truth is for every ear. And, in general, I've noticed your people eavesdropping on us, even when we whisper. Send them away, Fritzi; they've been getting on my nerves from the moment I arrived.'

'Would you leave us alone, please?' Friedrich, with a gesture, tells the serving staff, who have been unobtrusively pouring drinks and bringing them plates, utensils, sweets and fruit.

'*Would you leave us alone, please?*' the prince-bishop mimics Friedrich. 'How soft you are with them! Tsk tsk tsk ... That's not good, that's not good at all ...'

'Wolfgang, every time we meet, you are more lacking in compassion, even crueller and more brutal than I remember you!'

'Oh, I stopped believing in compassion a long time ago – ever since that night we found ourselves in that dimly lit room, not yet adults but, from that moment on, no longer children, and our adolescent play degenerated into wilfulness and crime. Do you remember the feeling we had, that everything was beneath our feet and nothing was above us, not the law, not the pope, not the emperor, not even God?' The prince-bishop looks at Friedrich.

'I remember nothing!'

'Oh, but you do, darling … Granada, drowning in the smell of blossoming jasmine, which, ever since, somehow both excites you and turns your stomach. A sharp wind off the Sierra Nevada, still white with the April snows, carried the blossoming fragrance through an open window into that hall, where it mingled with the smells of blood, of freshly opened entrails, of human horror and fear … Fritzi, do you remember the faces on those boys?'

'Shut up, Wolfgang! I beg you, just shut up!'

'I can shut up, but the cries from that dungeon – they will never be silent, will they, Friedrich?' Wolfgang studies the count. 'What happened to compassion then? You tell me that. How was it that we could keep gazing at that abhorrent scene when every day they were feeding us Jesus and a gospel of love?'

'We were drunk, we were gorged with intoxicants of every sort. You and that little Bavarian count took it all in your stride. I hear he's become quite adept at burning women, and the very mention of his name strikes terror in people's hearts. But Emilio, that gentle Tuscan viscount, threw himself off a cliff two days later, or maybe, even likelier, you and your friends pushed him.'

'No, he just slipped and fell. So be careful you don't slip, too, Friedrich. But tell me, where was God then, in those strangely protracted hours? Did he remove himself from that dungeon on a hill in the Alhambra?'

'Maybe not. Maybe it was the Old Testament God there, who reveals himself as clouds and burning bushes and trios of men, as he revealed himself to Sarah in her old age, in front of that desert tent, and told her she would bear a son but later commanded her husband, Abraham, to slay that son on Mount Moriah. Or was it perhaps the Christian God, who begot his son just so he could later sacrifice him? Was it merely coincidence, Wolfgang, that three men appeared to us, too, and incited us to this slaughter? …'

'Many people, Friedrich, were there that evening in the dungeon of the palace of Charles V. Many people … But Jesus? No, he definitely was not there.'

'Oh, but he was. Jesus, too, was in that room, in the image of those local boys who were lying there cut open.'

'You're getting sentimental, Friedrich. As if the slaughter on battle-fields made any more sense! When our armies invade foreign soil, they behave no better than the Turks. They skewer children on their spears, rape women – men, too – and kill everyone around. Whoever believes mankind learns anything from history is exceedingly naïve. The only thing mankind truly learns is to keep idiotically repeating that platitude about history being the teacher of mankind, which is nothing more than the wet dream of the soft-hearted. As if people really wanted to learn! As if the majority received greater pleasure from reflection and learning than they do from their baser barbaric passions. It's not like it is with animals. A person knows when he's inflecting pain on another but does it anyway. History is a series of repetitions of violence, and it won't be any different in the future either, only the means and forms of destruction will be faster and more massive. But for a real killer, nothing can replace the pleasure of killing with your own hands, when you penetrate your victim's body and feel the warmth of his blood on your fingers and smell his guts.'

'Wolfgang, do you really have no regrets at all about this?' the count says, leaping up from the table.

'About what, Friedrich? We had no choice,' Wolfgang replies, as he slowly lowers his hand, signalling to the count to sit back down and calm himself. 'We ended up in that mess because they deliberately pushed us into it. Everything had been prepared in advance, to the precise detail: the place had been chosen, and the time, with all the trappings of ritual everywhere around; the victims had been chosen at random, and we, too, long before, had also been chosen, very carefully.'

'How do you know all this?' Friedrich looks at him.

'Because later, I myself, on several occasions, was one of those who prepared similar rituals and conducted them with different lambs and different young beasts who needed to be trained for power,' Wolfgang calmly explains.

'You are despicable!" Friedrich angrily exclaims.

'Yes, among other things. That night we were born into power. In that repugnant deed, which had no other meaning than to mark us for life with the pleasure of initiation, with point zero and, indeed, with pure murder, outside the law, outside everything we had ever believed or known up to then. Let's put aside the ritual trappings, which were nothing more than ornament meant to fill our imaginations. But later, with each repetition, it became easier. Because if you're able to bring off a massacre with no content, which serves nothing but the pleasure of the moment, then every subsequent murder – in the service of higher ideals, the common good, the state, the Church, power or God – becomes unimaginably easy. Do you remember that strange marquis with the viscous gaze? He was then what I became later. Do you remember the expression in those boys' eyes? They had no idea why this was happening to them …'

'But those boys surely hoped that God, whichever God it was, would answer their prayers,' Friedrich says, now standing in front of the prince-bishop.

'But he didn't. He was silent, just as he would be in similar situations in the future.'

'But why, Most Reverend Prince-Bishop? Because God doesn't hear? Because he doesn't want to hear?' Friedrich asks, outraged.

'Yes. All of that and many other things, too – for instance, because he cannot hear, which is, perhaps, because …' Wolfgang lowers his voice, puts a finger to his lips and leans over to Friedrich, 'God … simply … does not … exist …'

ASSUMPTION DAY

The populace likes simple things and is suspicious of anything that seems complicated. Common sense will tell you that the devil hides in tangled balls of thread and becomes active when you least expect it, especially when there's something you don't understand. And anything that comes from the castle, and, literally, anything the parish priest says to us in Latin from the pulpit, we, of course, do not understand. But since God is all-powerful, it is also within his strength to pour out his spirit on creation at times like the Latin Mass and, by the power of his grace, to sprinkle upon us his saving truth through its opaque sentences.

It was Assumption Day. The muggy heat of August was in full force. Horse-flies, seeking coolness in the packed church, were biting the faithful and drinking their blood. People were tapping at their faces, arms and legs, and if they were quick enough, the horse-fly or flesh-fly would be crushed on their fetid bodies, stewing in the heat and the throng. Pilgrims were there from the neighbouring villages, and some had even come from the nearby town, and, although the church was dedicated not to Mary of the Assumption but to Mary Immaculate, there is only one Virgin Mary, so it is right to celebrate all her feasts.

In the midst of the crowd of believers jostling with the insects for room in the church, one of the women fainted and blood started spreading from beneath her body. Just the day before she had been fine, people said in surprise, and she was not the only one; two others had a similar experience a little later. Some women carried the unfortunate worshippers to the healing fount behind the church, and as they poured the cold water over them, a word was dropped which called forth all the words that followed. Around the fount, an opinion began to form which asserted that it was probably no coincidence that the self-same phenomenon had befallen the women on the same day and on the very day of the Feast of the Assumption of the Holy Mother of God. There must be something wrong with the church – such was the thread the women spun beside the fount, after one of them spoke up and said that during Mass she, too, had started having sharp pains in her stomach. And then someone else added that she had suddenly felt dizzy in church, and it seemed like Mary on the altar wanted to reach her arms out to her but probably didn't because she would have dropped the Baby Jesus, who would have tumbled to the floor. And a third woman said that she had seen a coloured haze begin to rise from behind the pastor during the sermon, and a fifth woman also noticed this, and a sixth confirmed it and a seventh agreed. Who, if not our parish priest, could be the reason for these phenomena, considering that they had all happened in the church?

The priest, when he finished the Latin part of the service, would always start berating the populace in their own language, listing all their sins, from laziness, spitefulness and adultery to skipping church and being stingy, since they were close-hearted when it came to indulgences and preferred to invest their savings in pointless junk. Whenever a pedlar came into the area, both women and men, who would normally be moaning about the bad harvests and how poor they were, would all run up to him at once and buy the worst rubbish – and when the populace came into contact with strangers like these pedlars (who had come there from God knows where), they could easily be infected with foreign diseases, which might then spread throughout the area. But worst of all was the unbridled dancing, the priest would scold the populace every Sunday. First the carnival dancing and then the dancing on St John's Eve, when the devil, who does not even have to try to lead people into sin, cleans his hoofs in his idleness or, being bored, just stares into the distance and doesn't notice people at all – with a kind of *Weltschmerz*, intellectuals might say a few centuries later, but in the sixteenth century this soul sickness was not yet widespread among the educated elite, for whom the fashionable disease was melancholy. It would be another few hundred years before the psychological virus known as *Weltschmerz* became active and attacked the more sensitive segments of the elite, at a time when it seemed that reason had almost triumphed in this part of Europe.

But the populace, shamefaced and conscience-stricken while the sermons were thundering, also have their limits, and their patience is not endless. Besides, they were convinced that sooner or later the truth would shine forth and, in the darkness in which the priest was holding them, every ray of light was a herald of new, better and more agreeable times. 'Sure, we're sinful,' the populace thought, 'but that's the way God created us. If God had made us just a little different, then the first human couple wouldn't have been led into such terrible temptation, and therefore into transgression, by some fast-talking reptile rubbing himself on an apple tree, with the result that all mankind is suffering because of the theft of a single apple, and, what's more, the Creator's son had to give his life for us. Well, maybe he performed that self-sacrifice with a bit of a fig in his pocket – there are plenty of figs in the Holy Land, and who knows if people had pockets back then, but both God the Father and God the Son must have known that it's not possible to kill God and that Jesus would suffer a little and die, but then, no later than Sunday, he'd rise from the dead and go out and be with people ...' This is the sort of thing the populace might speculate about over glasses of spruce brandy while performing their winter chores – threshing flax, weaving baskets and panniers and many other activities that belong in an ethnological treasure house – but they never dared broach such topics when they kept vigil over their dead, who were unequivocal proof that God was extremely serious when it came to disciplining his sinful people.

One of the priest's main criticisms was that the populace only ever heeded God's commandments because they were afraid – intellectuals would say, 'afraid for their own being', but the priest formulated this idea in a way people could understand, as fear for their own behinds. In their heart of hearts, they were all pure ordinary scoundrels, who sinned at every possible opportunity, for they knew that every week had a Sunday when they could crawl into church and barter with God for forgiveness, while for bigger transgressions, indulgences were available for purchase, when God, who is infinite in mercy, dispenses forgiveness to the sinner through his ecclesiastical collection officers, which meant that as soon as the sinner stepped out of the confessional he could start on some new wickedness.

The populace did not like the priest's chastisements. 'Something of what he says about us may be true,' the populace thought, 'but not everything! That's just the way we're made: we're too easily thrown off course or we get carried away by passion or some other strong emotion. God created us like that, with all these senses and feelings, and he made our lives harder because he didn't grab that rebellious angel by his forked tongue and flatten his skull for ever and ever. Because if God had crushed that serpent's snout beneath his infinite foot, he'd have kept the little devils, or whatever you call the Evil One's organized brood, from multiplying, and mankind would be planting turnips and corn in peace and propagating on a regular basis, and the various nations wouldn't be attacking and slaughtering each other, and at home around the hearth it would be homey and peaceful, with the right amount of love, which wouldn't make people do all sorts of crazy things, and the feudal lords and Church dignitaries would be kind to the populace and not the least bit greedy or cruel. What's more, maybe none of these human lords, whether secular or ecclesiastical, would even be necessary, and the populace, free of lordly oppression, would live happy, peaceful lives in harmony with other nations. And then they'd only get into fights with nations who worshipped a different God and with those individuals who had the gall to claim there was no God. 'Because it's possible,' said the ones who were very good at reading, 'that it's written in the Old Testament that some were created by a different god. Adam and Eve's two daughters-in-law, for instance, who obviously came from races that weren't created in Eden.' But only a rare few ever strayed so far in their thinking, and they were careful not to broadcast such deductions and questions, for a single verbal slip or ill-considered remark could serve as proof that the person was consorting with bad company, with company that was neither human nor animal, although the most vivid descriptions of this company did recall a certain type of domestic animal.

The populace has both good and bad qualities. They can be good as bread, which is why the sweeping rebukes which the priest fired from the pulpit contained a lot of lies. He never praised the populace, not even after a bolt of lightning struck the church tower and the very next day they all came without being asked and repaired it with their own hands. When the women would bring the priest baked goods, he would send them on their way with nothing but a cold 'God reward you', as if it was obvious that God was the one who would deal with them; the idea that the priest himself might ever thank them in his own name – oh no, no chance of that.

It was at the fount, then, that the female part of the community reached the consensus that the faintings, the visions and the queasiness were mysteriously connected with the Mass on the Feast of the Assumption itself. And then one of the women exclaimed, 'But we don't even know what the priest is saying to us during Mass! We don't know Latin! What if the priest isn't saying godly prayers at all but fiendish ones, while we in good faith cross ourselves and fall on our knees? What if the priest, with those Latin words we can't understand, has put some spell on us?' The women nodded and looked at each other. 'Don't you think our priest is a little strange? Ever since they sent him to us a few years ago, we can't shake off the feeling that there's something shifty, something shady, about him.'

The populace thus linked up the effects to a cause, and everything matched perfectly; all that was left was to inform the castle gentry. As was expected, it did not go smoothly, so the populace increased the pressure and came up with a few more stories. Count Friedrich, who held the patronage over the Church of Mary Immaculate, at first considered having the situation investigated, but he soon reconsidered as the stories were becoming more and more extreme. He had no doubt that the priest was the victim of a conspiracy by the benighted populace, who blamed him for all the troubles they had created for themselves through their dull-witted and sinful nature. But since lies are like logs thrown on hot coals, which can burst into flame at the slightest breeze, Friedrich replaced the priest with a new one, a man closer to the people, in the hope that the populace would accept him as one of their own with all his garrulous, gossipy traits.

The old priest left without a word of farewell. Three days later the new one appeared, and two days after that said Mass in Latin but preached in Slovene, which made the populace especially happy. What's more, he did not berate them and instead offered them a strategy: they weren't all guilty, not each and every one, but, rather, it was essential to identify in advance not only the guilty ones but also, in every community, the potential perpetrators and so prevent misfortune and disaster. This was a logic easy to understand, and the populace gladly accepted it. And breathed a sigh of relief. Finally, they had a shepherd who went among the sheep without a rod and who, if necessary, would join them in their bleating. And the sheep were not afraid of their shepherd but huddled around his legs whenever they felt fear, and if they sensed a wolf nearby, or a pack of wolves, they told the shepherd right away.

But the truth of the events which had swept away the parish priest lay elsewhere. Nausea in women was not a rare occurrence in mid-August. If not earlier, then it was around Assumption Day that a woman's body would begin to show signs of the impulsive, mis-guided actions she had committed on midsummer night, signs which every midwife knew how to remove through potions and mechanics, although accidents did sometimes occur. So it was important to have stories ready in advance, and culprits, too, on whom one could hang the causes of such phenomena, and who, in line with the people's logic, could be thrown on the altar as an offering, so that peace and order would be restored in the community.

HOPE DIES NEXT TO LAST

In the middle of the meeting room in the Town Hall, in the late-afternoon heat, a fat fly was circling above the heads of the members of the Town Council, and every so often it would fly into the face of a councillor staring pensively at the table in front of him. Nobody was saying a word. There was only the fat fly buzzing around in the sweltering silence, which, with every moment, measured out by the insect's aerobatic stunts and provocations, was becoming heavier, denser and more unbearable. But suddenly, the buzzing of the fly was joined by the sound of scraping on paper. Most of those assembled still had their eyes fixed on the solid oak table when the apothecary, one of the more distinguished members of the council, slammed his hand down – a blow the bothersome fly only just managed to escape – and turned abruptly to the scrivener. 'Scrivener,' he barked, 'what's that scribbling you're doing now? You're obviously not even following the discussion!'

'I am following it, very carefully, too, and writing everything down, only nobody has said anything for some time now,' Nikolai replies.

'Then explain to me what those illegible symbols are all about! They're not Christian, and I find it suspicious the way they're coiled like turbans. So are they Turkish?' the apothecary persists.

'No, they're not,' says Nikolai.

'Scrivener, from the moment I first saw you, you seemed suspicious to me ...'

'Leave him alone,' Volk Falke, the mayor, interrupts the apothecary. 'The scrivener can be trusted. You have my word on that.'

'Your word, esteemed mayor and judge, not to list all your titles' – the apothecary darts a mocking glance at the other councillors – 'your word stands on increasingly shaky ground.'

The mayor, visibly uncertain and confused, looks at the clock-maker, who is sitting in front of him. 'Are you convinced that what you have told us here is not mere rumour?'

'Everything I said came to my ear from entirely reliable sources. Our town, too, will definitely share the fate of Graz and Judenburg. It's only a matter of weeks,' the clockmaker says, nodding.

'I can confirm this from my own reliable sources,' the apothecary says, as he triumphantly surveys the room. 'What has been will be no more, most greeecious Mayor Voook,' he adds, intentionally distorting the words. 'The deck will soon be reshuffled, and some people will get an extremely bad hand.'

'I am a Lutheran, as are most people in this town. As you were yourself, until very recently.' Trying to maintain a calm appearance, the mayor darts a look at the apothecary. 'But, in any case, our town is open to both groups ...'

'And clearly, many more besides!' the apothecary breaks in.

'I see you have joined the provincial government's anti-Lutheran campaign and seek to sow hatred among us so we'll be at each other's throats even before they attempt to subjugate us by force,' the mayor counters.

'Oh no, it's not that simple,' the apothecary continues. 'Many a thing, esteemed mayor, has leaked out of rooms you thought were closed. And, believe it or not, many of your private conversations may be found in written form ...'

'All these malicious insinuations are being spread by you and your friends with a very specific goal. But we're not here to talk about me but about the welfare of our town, and to reach an agreement regarding an audience with the archduke in Graz,' the mayor continues.

'Too late for that ...' the apothecary interjects.

'That's not true! There are documents signed by the prince and the Provincial Estates,' the mayor says.

'The new prince, Archduke Ferdinand II, interprets them differently,' the apothecary replies.

'The written statement by the prince and the Estates remains in force regardless of the new representatives of either institution,' Mayor Falke insists.

'If the eye of man has not perused them and his mind appraised them, documents are nothing but dead letters. It's too late ... Too late, esteemed mayor,' the apothecary, smiling cynically, shakes his head.

'It's clear we have very different interests here,' the mayor responds.

'It's even clearer that not all of us can distinguish good interests from bad ones,' says the apothecary.

'And you are here to point your finger at such distinctions?' the mayor asks.

'I point ... I tell ... I explain ...' the apothecary smirks.

'What have they promised you?' the mayor looks at him sharply. 'For a few weeks now I've been watching your growing confidence. I hear about your increasingly intimate contacts with the Jesuits, who have found a reliable confederate in you. So are you planning to help the Jesuits drive out that handful of Franciscans so they can turn their monastery into a Jesuit college?'

'No one is driving out the Franciscans,' the apothecary replies. 'They themselves decided to leave, and they'll be handing the monastery over to the Jesuits, who will see to it that the cream of society gets a good education, at the highest level and much more thorough than they would get at Protestant seminaries. Even in Graz, the Protestants didn't like the Protestant schools and preferred to send their sons to the Jesuit College, which offered them a better education.'

'Some people did. But since those blackrobes took over in Graz a few weeks ago, all the Lutherans have been driven out of the town,' the mayor says.

'The ones who converted and took the Catholic oath were allowed to stay and are still living peaceful lives in Graz,' the apothecary replies.

'Many of Graz's finest minds left with the Lutherans, including Kepler,' the mayor says. 'Right after they disbanded the Protestant seminary there, I offered him refuge in our town.'

'A foolish idea. He would have barely had time to unpack his heretical astronomical scribblings before he'd have to crate them up again and run somewhere else,' the apothecary replies disdainfully.

'So what is it you want?' Now it's the mayor who strikes the table.

'Nothing. Everything is developing of its own accord, guided by Divine Providence, as is best for the Habsburg lands,' the apothecary replies obsequiously.

'Best only for some …' the mayor says.

'But they – I mean, we – have the power, and we are becoming many, and in time we will be the majority,' the apothecary replies and suddenly looks over at Nikolai. 'Scrivener, stop making those awful magical symbols this instant! If you have nothing better to do, draw circles, squares, triangles, pyramids – geometrical forms filled with harmonies that reverberate with the order of the cosmos. In those scratchings of yours all I hear is an evil-sounding wind.'

'But turn the first letter of *wind* upside down and you get *mind*,' Nikolai smiles to himself.

'And if I knock the wind out of you, scrivener, what do you get then?' the apothecary cries in a shrill voice.

'I think we're finished for the day,' the mayor says and adjourns the meeting.

'It's all finished, and not just for the day. So get ready, Volk Falke. Tell the town to festoon the streets for the arrival of a faith commission, which will be led by the Most Reverend Bishop Chroen. And all of you, prepare yourselves for the proclamation of the true faith …' the apothecary says confidently.

'When will that be?' The mayor can barely contain his fury.

'Very soon. Oh, and by the way, let me give you some well-meaning advice: don't go dressing up in helmets and armour and strutting around with weapons; do not plan any resistance at all. Wouldn't you agree, esteemed colleague?' The apothecary turns to one of the councillors. 'And you, as well?' he adds, looking at another and then a third and a fourth. All four council members simply stare at the table. The mayor watches in amazement, expecting some explanation, but the four men do not even blink.

'You weren't able to so much as wait for the real pressure to come before you converted …' says the mayor, looking at them reprovingly.

'Why should they have waited? Besides, they have relatives, friends and acquaintances who would be glad to occupy some well-paying position in the local or provincial government – among others, that of town scrivener.' He looks at Nikolai. 'It's over, mayor. It's over ...'

'Oh, it's not over yet, and there is still a lot to happen before it is. And it won't necessarily end the way you think it will.' The mayor is struggling to preserve an air of determination.

'Ah yes, hope, which dies last, or so say mediocre minds.' The apothecary rolls his eyes. 'No, hope dies next to last, for after hope there is still the hoper who must die. And when hope dies, and the now-former hoper beholds its dead corpse, this is one of the most tragic scenes mankind is capable of producing.'

'It will not be easy,' the mayor says.

'But it will be quick and thorough,' the apothecary says, ending the discussion.

Paved with Good Intentions

'Can you imagine a state, Fritzi, which, in organizational terms, would transcend the unreliability of reproduction, so that noble gentlemen of a somewhat special sort, a group to which you yourself belong, would have no need to marry just so their power and wealth can be siphoned into their hereditary progeny?' Wolfgang, frowning slightly, is sitting in the pavilion and stroking his distended belly. 'Can you conceive of sexual propagation being taken out of the picture altogether, so it's done not by natural means the way animals do it, but that man carries it off in some godlike fashion, by hand, using a *techne* not yet known to us? Otherwise, why should our beloved earth, which has endured more suffering, more bitter salt than could be extracted from all the oceans and seas, why should it be overcrowded by mankind? Our earth, so green and round, moist and dry – oh, yes, I've read about deserts in Herodotus, and I've also been told about them, the deserts the Tuaregs, tall and lithe, cross on camels like desert cats; they wrap themselves in dark-blue fabric through which they flash their viscous almond eyes. Fritzi, do you have any thoughts about this? Do you desire it for yourself? Where's that old fire of yours, so incredibly naïve, tempestuous and blind to fear and doubt? Because without fire there's only coldness and death! Where is that fervour of yours, which made you want to dash into the unknown with no fear of the future, even if the next moment it took you into eternity? Fritzi! You're not listening to me! You're dozing again – you've fallen asleep!'

'Wolfgang,' Friedrich opens his eyes and stares at the prince-bishop. 'It's been years since I've heard so much empty blather – to be precise, not since our last encounter. And your verbal diarrhoea has only got worse since then. Over these past two days the rhythm of your voice and the way you pile on words has more than once almost lulled me into a doze, but then, every time, some brutal witticism of yours wakes me up. After you leave, I'm not sure I'll ever be able to sleep again ...'

'I only hope that some of my words have found their way past your ears and into your brain and cleared a path through the gate of understanding into your soul – the soul, now isn't that a lovely idea? Oh, if only, after leaving the Greek priests, poets and rulers we had stopped with Plato, with Greek beauty, and not taken that next step, marching into the promised land of Palestine. Oh, if only that little Jewish girl had encountered, not the angelic rhetoric of a winged messenger but her regular monthly flow – then, Fritzi, God knows what things would be like today. But I believe there would be more exalted beauty and virtue in the world, with wisdom and righteousness at the helm and less foolishness such as guilt, sin and contrition, and the desire for forgiveness, for renunciation or, rather, re-duncification, which is what that celebrated Christian asceticism is really about. As I said, when I've done what I have to do here I will leave for a world that I hope has not yet been infected with those re-duncifying germs, a world where our missionaries' words have not yet fully reshaped the heathens' brains and where Christian swords have not yet damaged their bodies ...'

'Enough, Wolfgang! Just shut up! Not another word!' Friedrich cries, and, springing to his feet, he places himself directly in front of the prince-bishop. 'Wolfgang, you cling to the Holy Roman Empire like a tick, but otherwise you're just a broken-down old pederast with rotten teeth, swollen legs and aching, inflamed joints, whose "little angels" pluck the stiff little hairs out of your ears and nose! You're not inspired by youth; on the contrary, you're so powerless yourself that you despise youth, because you despise life, which breathes in all its fullness around you. You're as cold as that filthy stream you plan to cross on that dingy November day, when you'll be leaving destruction everywhere in your wake and setting off for a place where you will do just what you've always done: destroy. You're a destroyer, Wolfgang! As ruthless and deadly as the teeth of those sea creatures you weave into your pretentious poetry. So, Wolfi, what do you say? How about dispensing a few more drops of poison before you and your fine words leave these shores forever? Do you really believe you'll get there, that you'll make it across the ocean? I admit, for many long years I've been like a mouse, frozen in terror before your gaping jaws while you kept hissing all around me. But, although I might not be as erudite as you or as clever as you, still, I am better than you, because I know that while good can produce both good and evil, evil produces only evil and nothing else.

'They'll see through you on that ship sooner or later. Those men, yes, the very people you constantly ridicule, those rough-hewn men who have nothing at all but who also have everything, since from the day they were born they've had nothing to lose but their lives. Maybe they won't even hate you – well, they might be afraid of you, but they won't be afraid of you for long. In the middle of the sea, nature is sovereign, and blathering about God won't get you very far. What these men worship are good winds and peaceful waves; with every stroke of the oars, despotic realms and lords are pushed deeper into the past, while the future, uncertain though it is, promises a better life, without the masters who ruled over them in an evermore distant homeland, in what is less and less their home. They set sail across the ocean so they can forget and start life over – like you, who believe that on the other side of the earth you'll wield power afresh. But it won't go smoothly, if you even do reach the opposite shore. Because sooner or later you'll start to disgust them, which easily happens in confined spaces. And when something goes wrong, when all at once the seas get rough, when the ship inexplicably loses its bearings and instead of heading west to the New World it's carried south down the coast of Africa, when the food spoils and disease breaks out and rats start coming up from below decks – then it's time to find the cause of the problems. Then the only question will be who should they put on the altar and offer up to the divinities of nature so the gods will be appeased by the offering and so they'll survive. So most of them will survive, or at least some of them, and, most importantly, that they themselves survive. You know how it goes, you know that very well. And there, in the middle of the saltwater wasteland, it might well happen that they will see in you what you have seen and persecuted in others, not because you truly believed their guilt but because the altar of sacrifice had to be preserved in order to maintain the appearance that everything has a purpose and that sacrifice can bring peace and restore order to the world – so long as it's the kind of order where you're in a good position, which is to say, in a position that is incomparably better than it would be otherwise.

'I'm repeating things that were said by many others before me, and that will be said by many who come after me. I am talking about something that lies at the very core of mankind, even if you call it the God-given Christian community, but I expect things aren't all that different in Indian societies. Nothing I'm saying is new, although if I hadn't been crippled by fear all my life and, I admit it, by laziness, too, to some degree, I might possibly be able to add a thought or two of my own. But while I do have the occasional spark of light, when it comes to repeating a truth that stretches from our rectum back through time, the person who says it can even be a little bit stupid.

'One morning with their heads aching from bad alcohol, or having been up all night fighting the rough waves, your shipmates will open their eyes, miserable and out of sorts, and they'll ask themselves, "Why did we ever get on this boat? Sure, things were bad at home, and our poor feet were slipping deeper into destitution, but the ground was firm." They'll rub their crapulent eyes, look all around until at last their gaze settles on your cabin. "Look over there," they'll say as it dawns on them. "While we held the ropes and trimmed the sails to keep the wind from shredding them and shattering the ship or carrying her off to Africa, while we bailed out the deck with buckets in our bare, salt-ravaged feet, pouring the sea back from whence it was flooding us, and while we struggled with our last strength, raining obscenities on God, Mary and the saints, while we risked our lives so the waves wouldn't crush us, wouldn't pull us down to be eaten by the fishes, all that time we were also saving his fat arse as he waited behind closed doors for the tempest to pass. Is that fair and just? No, it's not. Is it fine and good? No, not that either. Do we have to put up with this in the future, too? No, of course not. Is there still any need, any need at all, to be meek and obedient, while some people strut around behind closed doors with legs of veal in their hands, their fat bums knocking aside tiny little bodies that will surely never reach land? Not on your life! Land is still far away, and our homeland even farther away, and the laws that governed life there don't apply here, in this salty wilderness, not any more … So there's only one thing left to us, because it's possible that not even God wants to see such things, and anyway it's good to rely on God, since he helped us during this last storm, too. But if we don't help ourselves, and if we let people like this noble churchly lard-arse remain among us, we could face the wrath of God. And even if God doesn't get angry, some devil could fuck things up and take advantage of the confusion just as we're trying to keep the ship from going down. So what do you say?" And then they all look at each other – "Let's do it!" – and pounce on you.

'Neither of us, Wolfgang, was given much of a chance to choose in our lives. We were both pushed into roles that were assigned us at birth.' Count Friedrich pauses a moment and drops into a cushioned wicker armchair. 'But I am convinced that a person can decide freely between good and evil, and if through no fault of his own he gets caught up in evil, he'll later regret it. Apart from Granada, what I most regret in my life is that I've never been able to free myself of the cowardice that has crippled me for as long as I can remember. But I believe that a person must strive for the good, without consideration of threats of punishment in this world or the next.'

'Not bad, Friedrich. You've surprised me, and I was almost enchanted by your style – if only you hadn't ruined your performance at the end by bringing up the idea of the good. Most evil has, from time immemorial, been done with good intentions, because it's good for both the powers that be and the God-fearing populace – most wars and massacres, and the burning of heretics, too. Pure evil, Friedrich, is extremely rare in this world. Most people are incapable of it, which is why evil is decked out in the most diverse ideas and aims. And this is true, too, of the witch trial you'll be holding here …'

'I have told you firmly, I have no intention of holding any witch trial on my land …' Friedrich loudly interrupts him.

But the prince-bishop nonchalantly waves his arm and continues, 'I'd be delighted to comment on another disquisition of yours, but for now I think I need to retire, rest a little and, God willing, sleep an hour or two. Ever since dinner I've had such terrible indigestion I can hardly stay seated – well, at least I forget the pain a little when I'm talking.

And after that I'll be off to do what I have to do. Finish what I have to finish. And then, on the other side of the world, I'll reinvent myself. The astrologers are predicting a hot summer, but according to my theological predictions, there will be an even hotter autumn, which will drag on deep into winter, if not all the way to next spring. But I won't have to see any of it. Before the year's out, I'll be on my way to paradise, but I'll let you know before I leave, so you can decide if you want to stay or, maybe, go with me. Hanging around with those preachers, you may have forgotten that it's not all up to God's whim to decide who's saved and who's doomed and that you can, through your own works and deeds, win heaven for yourself, not only in the great beyond but here on earth, too. As ridiculous as it might sound, Friedrich, you're a free man.'

Julian helps the prince-bishop to his feet, and as the two of them move slowly down the linden allée, Friedrich watches them and thinks he'll try again before the prince-bishop leaves. If there is no way around this accursed trial, then at least the alleged suspect might be acquitted in the end. So it won't be the way it was a few years ago, when the populace went after that widow and goaded the provincial powers into sending a judge to his fiefdom, who sealed the fate of that innocent woman. And recently, those truly incredible rumours have been spreading about foreigners living on one of the farms, only fewer and fewer people believe they are actually living. And then there's a very young girl hanging about the local church who points her finger first at the sky and then at her own belly. It's only a matter of time before she starts pointing it at others, too.

He must do whatever he can to keep the trial from spreading like the plague. Otherwise, his entire domain and maybe even the neighbouring town can expect killings … pogroms … a bloodbath …

Just One Big Euphoria

Yesterday at the mayor's, when our eyes met, she first turned away, but then she looked at me again and smiled, as no one has ever smiled at me before. Such immense happiness washed over me that my head was spinning a little all morning and, as I was leaving, I slipped and fell down the stairs. And when I landed on my side and felt a sharp pain in my hip, I burst out laughing instead of screaming in pain. I have never before experienced such indescribable happiness. I am careful that the people around me do not notice my changeable moods. I watch myself, I contain myself, so my excitement does not become annoying; I control the expression on my face, so my smile does not stretch into the foolish grin of an idiot. I am afraid of nothing – oh, what immense relief! No more racing heart, no more tremors, no more shortness of breath, dry lips or all those ridiculous thoughts: will it or won't it, will it happen or not, will there or won't there be some disaster? Life and death seem like pure comedy to me. Do I exist or don't I, who gives a damn! There's only this, the here and now, and, even as I say this, I know I am saying it in hindsight, that I can't capture the moment itself in words, which annoys me a little, but it also amuses me. It's like when I was a child and my mother would move the mirror around and conjure up little bunnies of light, which I'd leap after and try to catch but never could. Oh, how I'd cry, 'The bunnies, Mama! Let me catch at least one of them!'

'Come on, come on,' she would encourage me, 'try a little harder, Miklavžek.'

'But why should I try harder when I know I can't catch them?'

'Because you can't know until you try,' she'd tease me. 'And I believe that if you try, Miklavžek, you will succeed. Maybe not the first time, but one day for sure.'

I am careful, but maybe not careful enough to keep people from giving me strange and worried looks. Or at least that's how it seems. Is it important? Never before have I felt such immensely stimulating restlessness. When I think of my beloved, it's like a swarm of ants are crawling with tiny feet throughout my body; it's like they've nested in the pit of my stomach and are running from there to my head along the fibres of my nerves; I feel them in my fingers and my feet, they're dancing in my heart, jumping up and down, hop-hop-hop …

But now there is no more fear. Now there is just one big fat euphoria. Should I be worried? At least a little? The tiniest bit? But I'm not so crazy as to worry about conditions and feelings that most people don't even know exist! Every so often something flows through me that I have no words for. Please let it last. Please, God, or nature, or whatever it is that controls my conditions and feelings, let it last, please let it last … No matter what happens, whether life or death or something in between, let it happen, or not – what's important is only what is here and now. And that something happens.

APRICOTTERS

And something does happen when a carriage rolls into the inner courtyard of the mayor's mansion and a tall man, the prince's provincial commissioner, steps out accompanied by his aides. As the military escort is dismounting from their horses, a cry is heard, perhaps from someone who happened to be looking up at the mansion's Renaissance façade. Everyone flinches. The provincial commissioner, by chance or possibly fate, steps a little to the left, and a fraction of a second later a statue comes crashing down at his feet from a window in the mansion.

'Whose room is that up there?' the commissioner asks, pointing to an open third-storey window.

The mayor's footman hesitates, and when the new arrival repeats the question, he answers in a low voice, 'The rooms of the honourable mayor's esteemed wife.'

The commissioner's face darkens. He gives his entourage a knowing look, and at the sound of the mayor's approaching footsteps, he makes a point of not turning around.

'Welcome to our home,' Mayor Volk Falke greets his guests; he is still pale from the incident, which he saw as he was coming down the steps. The provincial commissioner turns to him with a rapid motion and, without returning his greeting, asks the mayor sharply, 'Did you see it? I was nearly killed! Is that … Was that the famous statue?' He is looking at the sculpture that is now in pieces on the ground.

'I am profoundly sorry, esteemed commissioner. I have no idea how the wind could have knocked it over and blown it out of the window …' the mayor says, abashed.

'The wind?' the commissioner responds gruffly, making a face, and darts a glance at his entourage. 'The wind! Don't be ridiculous, Falke!'

The mayor nervously follows his guests inside, as thoughts are sparking in his mind: the prince and his officials are running out of patience. Apart from the fiefdoms, the towns are the last bastion of Lutheranism. The nobility has for some time now been allowed to profess the Lutheran faith, but this is no longer true for the towns, even those directly under the Provincial Estates. The faith commissions are getting closer and closer. But still, an unannounced visit to our town by one of the prince's commissioners? Could this be connected to that rich young widow, the old merchant's wife, who so infuriated the Jesuits when they were unable to wrest her houses and lands from her?

'First they sent an elderly Jesuit to talk to the widow, thinking, she's used to old men who dole out platitudes as advice,' the provincial commissioner, in a monotone voice, was explaining a little later in an apricot-coloured room. 'She would surely give in after a few allusions to matrimonial faithfulness to the grave, everlasting life and meeting her late husband in the world beyond. And, of course, to the guilt she would feel if she ever got ideas in her head about remarrying, for what God has joined together remains joined even after death. But the widow didn't respond to the Jesuit's advice; she obviously viewed her husband's death as the mercy of God, who had rescued her from an uncaring and miserly old man.'

'Well, she wasn't the one who decided on the marriage,' the mayor interrupts the commissioner.

'Of course not. It was the will of God, who sealed the marriage between a young girl and a wealthy, respected merchant before the community of the Holy Church – and I don't want to hear any talk about reverence for youth! What are women for if not to obey Holy Scripture and the scripturally approved desires and commands of her earthly lord and master, who gives her a position in society, takes care of her and gives her sustenance as the potentially full womb for his seed,' adds the commissioner, who is now imperiously leaning back on a tall chair with his legs spread out in front of him.

'I can't entirely agree,' the mayor objects.

'Well, from now on, you'll just have to try harder. Your position, esteemed mayor, is no longer as unshakeable as you perhaps still imagine it to be. We are in possession of information that your town is infected with the kind of ideas which will not be tolerated by the provincial authorities, who intend to address them thoroughly, to the very core. And then there's this episode with the widow. When she proved immune to the old man, we sent her a reliable and well-tested member of the order, whose passion is channelled nobly into liturgical and financial expertise and who is distinguished by one invaluable quality in particular: he is able to ignite sparks in another while remaining cool and uninflammable himself. She was expecting the tedious old man, whose murmuring voice after dinner would lull her into a little doze so she could enjoy her ungodly yet pleasurable daydreams, but it was he who appeared, standing like a sharpened stone on the threshold to her rooms. Instead of a crooked body and wizened face, the widow saw in her doorway a tall Jesuit with slicked-back hair and a body as chiselled as David's, the very embodiment, sadly, of women's too-frequent dreams. For we know that, at the sight of such a perfect specimen of material creation, women will, with wobbly knees and a swarm of bees in their stomachs, kneel down and, without a second thought, commit a mortal sin or two. When it comes to sinning, women her age can be insatiable, simply ravenous.

'The young widow initially behaved as we expected. She bashfully lowered her eyes in front of our emissary, and at the mention of anything that might suggest she was thinking about remarrying at the end of the mourning period, she strategically blushed. She shifted her Bible from hand to hand, laid aside her embroidery only to pick it up again, in apparent embarrassment, and started jabbing the needle hysterically into the floral motif. Then, as she listened to the Jesuit brother, she kept stitching and stitching until, by repeating these idiotic motions, she gradually misled our emissary. Together they prayed through I don't know how many feet of rosary beads, with countless Hail Marys for her departed husband, and when our man suggested that she might finally sign the deed of gift, which he laid on the table in front of her, when it was nearly a done deal that she would endow the Society of Jesus with the mansion and its grounds, which would be the ideal location for the Jesuit college dormitories, and when her slender white fingers had clasped the ink-dipped goose quill proffered by the young Jesuit and she was leaning over the papers and had nearly touched the tip of the quill to the document we had so eagerly been waiting for – while our emissary, now relaxed, was already somewhere else in his thoughts, focusing on his next target, after this nearly finished and rather easy assignment, for all that was needed was one last act and his mission would be done – she slowly moved the hand holding the quill away from the papers, turned to our emissary and pierced him with a Satanic gaze. The emissary, a man accustomed to all sorts of tricks, recoiled in surprise. In self-defence, he grabbed her right hand and was trying to bend it over the document, to make it submit and move in the proper direction, when the widow, with superhuman strength, resisted his effort and, still peering into his eyes, unfurled her face into such a wicked grin that he let go of her hand, gasped for air and fell back powerless into the upholstered armchair. God only knows how long he would have sat there in that half-numb, vanquished state, splayed in that chair with the apricot-coloured upholstery – the very shade, in fact, in which this room of yours is furnished – but then the door handle turned and those apricotters came bounding into the room.'

'Apricotters?' The mayor looks at him in surprise.

'Two vicious *Aprikosen*, with curly hair and little pink bows on their heads, their bodies sheared almost to the skin and their tails teased into bushy balls and similarly decorated with apricot-coloured ribbons,' the commissioner replies.

'I don't understand … I have no idea what you're talking about,' the mayor is confused.

'When those apricot behemoths barged into the room – only later did our Jesuit realize that the beasts must have been trained to open doors with their paws – they immediately went after him. While the first one, assuming the hunting position, was barking at him, the other lunged at his leg and bit him so hard there was blood. Our emissary screamed and tried to kick the attacker but missed; then, leaping from the chair, he plastered himself against the bookcase, rigid with fear. Oh, what endless apologies followed from the lady, who arranged the beasts behind her legs, where they crouched and snarled as she summoned her staff and told them to fetch bandages as fast as possible. It was only the pain that cleared our man's powers of perception, allowing him to see the true nature of the situation. Although copies of the Bible were strategically distributed throughout the lady's rooms, her bookcases were, in fact, stocked with such questionable works as *In Praise of Folly* by Erasmus and Montaigne's *Essais*. Earlier, he had noticed none of this, but then, he had not expected to find any reading matter at all in her home, other than, perhaps, the writings of the saints, an occasional adventurous tale of chivalry, weepy wives' handbooks or maybe travel writings. He had seen nothing but the open prayer books, arranged with seeming nonchalance at every step – one on the low table, another on the sideboard – to give the impression that the crafty woman was reading them everywhere. What a mistake! What an irreparable disaster! But very likely it could not have been prevented. The young lady had been superbly tutored and must have thought herself quite the comedienne when later she replayed her adventures with our Jesuits for that female league of hers. I can only imagine the triumph they felt as she described how she dealt the final blow to the Jesuits, the way she set her fanged beasts on that young man.'

'Forgive me, Your Grace, but I'm afraid I don't understand what you've been saying,' the mayor says.

'But I could not have been clearer – apricotters!' the commissioner emphatically repeats.

'Who? This is the first I've heard of them.'

'So much the worse for you! If you're not playing dumb, then, obviously, some very dangerous things are being knitted together right in front of your eyes and you don't even notice,' the provincial commissioner says.

'Dangerous for whom?'

'Dangerous for everything our Holy Church proclaims and St Paul writes about in his Epistles to the Romans and the Corinthians. Dangerous for you and for everyone who respects the laws of society and the Church, and the laws of nature, too. I think you get my meaning with this last point ...'

'I haven't the foggiest idea ...'

'Then I seriously advise you to clarify your ideas and wake up at once! Otherwise, you will suffer nightmares – nightmares dangerous to the Hereditary Lands of Austria, every last inch of which must be cleansed. She will regret every garden path up which she led the

Society of Jesus – and misled the provinces of Inner Austria. She will regret every inhuman trick she employed to do this. She will burn! Most certainly she will burn, and not alone either! Many other women in your town will burn with her, just as soon as we prepare the documents, collect the evidence and procure the witnesses.'

'I sincerely beg your pardon, but I have heard nothing about this apricotter phenomenon.'

'They're impossible to see at first. Some of them operate in disguise, and instead of apricot curls they have grey, brown, white or black ones, and their number also includes those who keep company with other types of dogs, from lapdogs to gigantic hounds, the latter being used also for the satisfaction of certain needs, for which the *Carolina* prescribes burning at the stake. The wiliest of them disguise themselves by not having any animal beasts at all near their persons, or by surrounding themselves with cats or birds or any other manifestation of God's creation that possesses neither soul nor spirit, which they can control for the execution of their sordid operations – just as *he* controls them …'

'*He*?' Mayor Falke asks in wonder.

'You're not being naïve – you're being flippant!' the provincial commissioner says sharply. 'You obviously do not realize that all that separates your name from my list of accused heretics are a few strokes of the pen by my right hand.'

'But please, this connection between apricot poodles and some underground organization that supposedly presents a threat to the Habsburg lands – it's rather far-fetched, don't you think?' the mayor says with a slight smirk.

'We won't have to go far to fetch these suspects, and, when we do, we'll chop off their hair, shave their heads, crush their bones and set them alight!' the commissioner answers gruffly.

'I can understand such theories as a means of discipline, but don't tell me you actually believe any of this,' the mayor replies.

'They warned me it would be impossible to reach any agreement with you. Besides, I see what great pleasure you're taking in your dismissive insinuations and cynical dissembling …'

'Fine. So what do you propose I do in the given situation? What measures should I take?' the mayor asks.

'As a matter of fact, there's not much you need to do. From what I've observed, you're mostly a lot of air on the inside, not counting your digestive tract, and I have my doubts about the existence of your heart, too, for if there is no love for God within the heart, there is no heart. And if I go a little higher, up to your skull, I'd say there's no solid matter there either, nor has the Holy Spirit made his nest in your head, for otherwise you would restrain yourself from making foolish comments and questions about something you will never understand until that pack of apricots tears you to bits. And they will, too, piece by piece, unless you're already one of their dogs. From what I've heard you have a curly-haired pup trotting around your living quarters; it belongs to your esteemed wife, I believe ...'

'Yes, she's fond of animals, and I myself have three bird dogs,' the mayor replies.

'A man with a bird dog is something entirely different from those beribboned killers that loll around on upholstered chairs and on the bed of the very room from which the mother of Our Lord Jesus, the Blessed Virgin Mary, came flying down at me and nearly bashed my head in ...'

'Well, let's be precise,' the mayor interrupts him. 'What came flying down was not Immaculate Mary herself, who, as you Catholics believe, was taken by her son into heaven on Assumption Day; it was just a piece of carved stone.'

'Don't talk to me about stones and statues!' the commissioner shouts, almost shooting out of his chair; then, as he speaks, he starts pacing up and down the apricot room and from time to time flaps his arms. 'This particular *stone*,' he says, pointing at the window, 'is none other than the statue of Mary Immaculate, which the Poor Clares guarded with their purity and humbly venerated. When one morning bloody tears began trickling down the Immaculate's cheek, none but God could say why she was weeping blood, although it was possible to guess, for the tears never ceased until the Poor Clares, out of pity, magnanimously gave the Virgin as a gift to your esteemed wife so that Mary might cure her of hysteria and melancholy, if not madness as well! If the Virgin's tears dried up in the company of your esteemed wife, perhaps it was from an even deeper sorrow. And now, at a single brutal stroke, the ungrateful lady has dried Mary's tears for all time.'

'Nobody asked the Poor Clares for that statue. My esteemed wife is of the Lutheran faith, as are her parents and as I myself am. The Poor Clares sent it to her because they were ordered to do so. And by the way, some pilgrims have said that the heavy acrid taste of Mary's tears, which they applied to the ailing parts of their bodies, reminded them, surprisingly, of beet juice.'

'What? Falke, you are insane!' The commissioner clutches his head in his hands. 'You have no idea of how serious a position you are in – you and your town and your esteemed wife. Only, why did she do it, I ask myself. Who persuaded her to hurl the mother of Our Lord down on my head?'

'Nobody persuaded her. There are days in the month when she becomes irrational, and even my bird dogs, with their tails between their legs and flattened ears, keep as far away from her as possible,' the mayor answers.

'But still, that curly haired demon, sprawled out on the bed, stays with her while she throws a sacred statue out of the window? And let me remind you, rumour has it that your attitude, too, has never been very respectful towards the sculpture and that on one merry occasion you told the people you were with it wasn't bloody tears this now, sadly, former statue of Mary Immaculate was shedding, but rather, it was her Virginal blood seeping from a different and still fully intact orifice in her immaculate corporeality!' The territorial commissioner is almost screaming.

'What? I never said anything like that!' the astonished mayor protests.

'Oh, but you did! We have witnesses who will confirm it in court, and they'll remember many other things, too! So do you finally understand what I'm trying to tell you? Because there are even worse things! We hear that you are not even a Lutheran or a Calvinist, or even one of those Leapers or Ecstatics. We hear that as far as you're concerned, God doesn't exist, that you live in a world without God, which is why you so thoughtlessly wag your sarcastic tongue about all that is holy and sacrosanct. And that you and your blasphemous coterie would like first to torture God in some dungeon, put him on the rack and stretch him in all directions, and then, in the end, hang him on the gallows.'

'Not a word of that is true!' the mayor says firmly. 'And, in any case, if we're now at the level of ontology and the issue of God's existence, how would it be possible to even plan such a fate for the Almighty, one that is limited to lasting torment followed by murder?'

'In your thoughts, in your thoughts ... Our God has already been killed once, but he rose from the dead. And ever since, people have been killing him in their thoughts. And if we don't stop you and your kind right now, then others will come after you who proclaim that God is completely dead. The way you parade around, it's as if you're not aware that my righteous right hand is an extension of divine judgement. Did someone perhaps suggest to you that our time is past, that it's fading into oblivion? The action committed by your esteemed wife is by no means a simple matter, especially since I am informed of the nature of her associations with persons of the female sex, who meet not for the purpose of coming together in contrite prayer or embroidering tapestries with pious and floral motifs – on the contrary, I hear that their gatherings include discussions unsuitable for women, on topics the female mind is not even capable of understanding ...'

'Let's be clear. God created human beings, that is, man and woman, in his own image,' the mayor counters.

'God created man in his own image; woman he made from the rib of man – and ribs are the only bones in the human body that have no marrow!' the commissioner growls.

'Perhaps not all things in the Bible should be taken literally but rather as vivid metaphor, so that the simple folk can more easily understand the meaning ...'

'You dare suggest to me how I should interpret the Holy Scriptures? To me' – the commissioner directs a forefinger at himself – 'who after years of arduous study has been inspired by the Holy Spirit to rightly interpret the Word of God?'

'Considering that the Holy Spirit himself is present in the Holy Scriptures, a believer is capable of understanding the Word of God on his own,' the mayor says.

'So you think someone like you is capable of distinguishing literal from metaphorical meaning? Damn it, I'm not sure if you're being stupid for real, or if you have maybe just enough intelligence to pretend that you're stupid, or if you are so utterly and thoroughly stupid that there's no chance of you choosing, by your own volition, either to pretend to be intelligent or to act like an idiotic moron,' the provincial commissioner responds in a rage.

'Rather than beating around the bush with unlikely hypotheses, I propose we get to the point of your visit,' the mayor says, trying to calm the situation. 'Our town, which Emperor Maximilian graciously bestowed on the Estates, is a Lutheran town. We know that visitators and faith commissions are travelling around the province demanding under threat of force that Lutherans renounce their faith and accept Catholicism. But we will not surrender easily. Freedom of religion is our right, and we are prepared to defend it with arms.'

'A foolish idea. For months, our agents have been sending us information which indicates that the weaker sex of your town, from both noble and burgher families, has been meeting in secret over glasses of apricot liqueur and brandy – not perry, mind you, or blueberry or spruce schnapps, but apricot brandy! – and are forging plans contrary to the Word of God. Not only are women teaching each other and exchanging different tricks and stratagems – including how to hoodwink a papal emissary – but they have even organized some sort of reading circles and are holding discussions where they talk about such blasphemous topics as the earth not being the centre of the universe, when it is clear and indisputable that it could be nothing else. What's more, they exchange all sorts of recipes and instructions – and not about how a woman should humbly serve her husband, the head of the family, or how she should serve God! Instead, while they're passing around litters of those tarted-up apricot brutes, they perform magic rituals. They are witches! Witches have infested your town, and at the highest levels of society! Witches! This danger is no longer confined only to the unwashed plebeians; it now includes educated, wealthy witches, who know how to read and write and are as depraved and elusive as cats. But they will not elude us. We will track them down, get the truth out of them and send them to the stake!'

'I am the mayor, and as the leading citizen of the town I can assure you we have no witches here. Where is your evidence?' the mayor says.

'Woman is a malleable creature, and with the right methods she can be induced to do all sorts of things. Our methods are tested and true – a kreutzer here, a threat there, and the little birds open their wings and, like sparrows, infiltrate the flock. And when they return, we seize them by the neck and make them sing out whatever they've seen and heard.'

'The poor girls are probably so intimidated by you they make things up …'

'We will interrogate them, and before the Cross and the Holy Virgin they will swear on their own lives and the lives of their children that what they say is the pure and honest truth,' the commissioner insists.

'If it's as you say, I'll order an investigation, and if anything of the sort is happening here, which I strongly doubt, I will personally put a stop to it,' the mayor says.

'You won't do anything. You had your chance, but you weren't even aware of it,' the provincial commissioner replies in a calm voice. 'From this point on, you will abide by our instructions. This is not some ordinary heterodoxy or heresy. We are dealing with Sabbat witchcraft. And you know what the *Carolina* says about that. In precisely one month, we will return to your town and declare a week of grace. During this week, we will set up a chancellery in your offices, where anyone can come who has heresy on their conscience or who has committed some other villainy in thought, word or deed. If they tell us the truth, we will be lenient, if only by giving them as quick and painless a death as possible. After one week we will, with their help, unearth everyone who stayed away and missed their opportunity, and we will bring them in by force and initiate proceedings. If anyone tries to keep something from us, we will press them until they squeal out whatever they may have forgotten to mention. But, even before this, you should prepare for the arrival of the faith commission. As a preliminary measure, I advise you to go personally, yourself, from house to house and collect all heretical books, and then, before the commission arrives, place them on a pyre in front of the Town Hall, so that His Grace, Bishop Thomas Chroen, need only start the fire.'

And What Now?

'You look very worried,' the Triestine merchant-woman presses against Mayor Falke after the departure of the provincial commissioner. They are in her bedroom.

'I don't know what to do, dear friend,' says the mayor as he snuggles up to her.

'You've always found some solution ...' His lover wants to be encouraging.

'But now I am powerless.'

'O Volki, my little wolf, don't be a pessimist. They're just trying to scare you. Lay your head in my lap and I'll brush your fur. I'll be gentle ...'

'They have a strategy worked out to the last detail. Their plan is to go after women – to accuse them of witchcraft. In a month, they will proclaim a week of grace in our town, but first they will procure people, buy them with money, who will later play the role of reliable witnesses in the trial.'

'A month is a long time, time enough to ...'

'I'm afraid not. They're going to bring the town to its knees with some truly crazy story about apricotters.'

'You mean the dogs? The apricots? I'm not sure I understand ...' the Triestine merchant-woman says, baffled.

'Apparently, the apricot poodles are the secret sign of some sisterhood,' the mayor explains.

'Well, we've been exchanging a few litters ...'

'The more improbable the story, the greater the chance that not only those who hear it will believe it but that eventually so will the ones who invented it. And then there's the incident involving my wife ...'

'It's one of the more amusing stories I've heard recently. I'm only sorry I wasn't there to see it with my own eyes ...' the merchant-woman laughs.

'I'd be smiling, too, if I didn't know they might use this foolish blunder against her and the town. And, by the way, I've been meaning to advise you, several times already, to be a little firmer with your Petey or Paulie or whatever it is you call that beastie of yours. The very fact that you give your dog a human name, and an important Christian name at that …'

'Oh, come on, Volki, calm down and stop growling. Petey, who will be Peter when he grows up, guards the door to my house,' the merchant-woman smiles.

'He's too afraid to go any farther than the door on his own, but otherwise he's constantly hanging about your feet. Clearly, the entire litter have a talent in their blood for opening doors, and I'm just waiting any moment for that handle to start turning and your beast to run in and jump on the bed,' the mayor says.

'No, he won't. He had a big meal before you got here, and now he'll be dozing until morning. But I see you haven't yet forgiven him for that shoe he chewed up a while back.' She looks at him playfully.

'A chain – a gold one, of course – would not be a bad idea for that dog, given his volatile temperament. But it's not just the town I'm worried about. More and more, I'm concerned about my wife. She's getting worse. She shuts herself in her bedroom, closes the curtains and lies on the bed and cries. When I try to approach her, she leaps off the bed and attacks me, screaming and hitting me, and then she collapses again for a few days. I don't know what to do. There's so much madness spreading around me – the town is becoming more submissive, the count's domains next door are becoming more and more aggressive, at home my wife is going crazy, in the office my scrivener is getting delusional and recently he's been giving me this glassy-eyed stare …'

'Send her away. Her and the children. And the scrivener, too. Send them to the convent, to the Benedictine nuns.'

'They also have the Benedictine sisters in the crosshairs. They suspect that the nuns are being told in advance about the visitations and are merely putting on a show of humility. On the most recent visitation, they went through the sisters' bookcases and inspected their cellars, and when they didn't find anything, someone remembered their *medicina naturalis*. So they're going after the herbs the sisters use to prepare medicines for people who can't afford a physician. They're leaving them for last, but it's only a matter of time before they interrogate the nuns, too.'

'In that case, send your family and the scrivener out of the Inner Austrian provinces altogether,' the Triestine merchant-woman suggests. 'To Germany or, even better, to the Venetian Republic – I have some close acquaintances there. But, Volki,' his lover makes a frown, 'I hear that you, too, have forged some very close ties in Venice, in particular with a certain famous, if not to say, notorious, lady. And what will you do with that snooty young widow who is breaking your scrivener's heart? She says such horrible things about Nikolai. After her husband's death and her triumph over the Jesuits, she's turned from a defenceless victim into a conceited, coquettish bitch ...'

'A little jealous are you?' The mayor looks at her with satisfaction, with love even. 'I'll send her away, too, to somewhere safe. For some time now my scrivener has been warning me that the Jesuits are plotting their revenge against her, but he's been in such a fraught state recently, I didn't believe him – not until the provincial commissioner showed up today. But let's try to forget all this madness, at least for a while, and devote ourselves to each other. The fragrance, the softness of your skin will soothe my nerves, my darling, my very special love ...'

'Shhh ... no more words, only kisses, dear mayor, only caresses, no more words ...' the Triestine merchant-woman whispers.

(A LETTER TO THE NOBLE WIDOW)

Gracious lady,

I do not know how to tell you of the terrible plan that is being prepared for you behind your back. You will not believe me. You will ascribe the news, which someone whispered in my ear, to my confused and overly sensitive condition. How, then, can I convince you to leave this place as soon as possible? I am prepared to do anything, I am even prepared to weave you some lie, if only so you believe me and escape the fate that has been sealed for you.

That black-haired Jesuit who was coming to see you for months and whom you so humiliated, after which he was supposedly attacked by your dogs, had told his brothers that you are of only modest intelligence, that it would be easy to handle you and that your property was, so to speak, already in the hands of the Society of Jesus. Just a few more formalities, he boasted, and then we'll move her without delay into the side wing of one of her soon-to-be-former houses, where she'll live out her life in poverty.

They have accused you of heresy, my beloved lady. Of blasphemy, witchcraft and even sodomy. And they are planning to link you to a few other respected noblewomen. They have decided to subdue the men in this Estate-governed Lutheran town by attacking their wives, daughters, mothers, sisters and other close female relatives.

Oh, how you have enraged them! I know that young Jesuit. I met him once when he was part of a visitation commission, and he looked at me differently from the way men look at men. The look he gave me, my beloved lady, was like the look you would see in my eyes if I did not turn them away from you in shame. When he was leaving, he intentionally placed himself right next to me, and when he touched me with his tense body, it trembled, the way a man's body trembles at the touch of a woman.

After his last and utterly disappointing visit to your home, he suddenly took ill. Festering blisters appeared around his mouth. They say that you put a hex on him with your eye. They say many other things, too, things I cannot repeat even when I am by myself and imagine that I am speaking with you.

I also hear that recently some people in town noticed that when you came out of church in your mourning clothes with a black veil over your face, you suddenly stopped in the middle of the steps and looked up at the stone griffin on the church façade. They say you pointed at it with your black-gloved right hand and extended your forefinger and little finger in a way that made your hand look like a head with horns, and then the griffin stuck its tongue out at you and opened its mouth, and there was growling sound which froze the blood of the witnesses. When your footman offered you his arm and you were climbing into your carriage, the growling turned into wailing, as if a pack of wolves were saluting their mistress. The bodies of those who were present were shaking in horror, until at last you made some mysterious sign, which silenced the stone monsters and the growling ceased.

'What was the expression on her face at the time?' the townspeople have been asking themselves ever since. After the incident with the Jesuit, they were initially on your side, but now, because of fears triggered by rumours about the fate of the town, hatred for you has flared up inside them.

'How should we know? Her face was hidden in black tulle,' the witnesses answer. 'Maybe in those few moments she did not even have a face. Maybe it wasn't even her behind that veil ...'

'But then how can people say it was her in front of the church, that she was the one whose eyes and gestures commanded the griffin, with the sound of growling and wailing echoing all around, when nobody could see her veiled face?'

'Oh, it was her all right. It was her,' more and more people are saying in the town. 'It was her carriage and her footman. Also, it was her way of walking, whether it was she herself who was there or evil disguised in her image.'

More and More Signs,
Bad Signs

The populace was evermore suspicious of the Kostanšek girl. It seemed clear that she had no intention of marrying any boy from the fiefdom. And then there were those seven workers, and a young woman with seven mute giants of unusual and, most importantly, very foreign pedigree – no, that cannot be good; on the contrary, it's very bad for all of us, the populace believed.

Their suspicions were reinforced when one of the women saw the following scene in her dreams one night. She (the dreamer) was sitting in the garden in front of her house when the sky suddenly grew dark and nature became still. This is a sign of some awful catastrophe, the woman thought. Will there be a storm, terrible hail, plague, maybe the Turks? The Turks were the least suspicious possibility; with them, at least, you know what to expect: pillage, rape, abduction and slaughter. Storms, hail, plague – this is the ordinary work of nature, and they don't necessarily involve forces that are abusing nature. 'And then, all at once,' the dreamer continued her account, 'there was a great noise from somewhere, and a goat came flying over the houses, and a girl, a young woman, was holding on to its horns and clenching the animal's body with her thighs. And it smelled disgusting! I could smell it even in the dream.'

'She was riding a goat? A girl is not such a small thing, and a goat could hardly carry one on land, let alone fly with her on its back,' her sceptical listeners observed.

'Well, if it was flying with her on its back, then it could carry her on land, too, couldn't it?' the dreamer said to bolster her vision.

'But it was flying with her? … So you're saying the goat was flying?' the populace had their doubts.

'Of course it's strange that the goat was flying,' said the dreamer, feeling almost offended. 'Just like it's strange that it was carrying such a big, well-fed girl. But the goat was much bigger than the goats in our pens, and it had a coat as black as soot, the kind you don't find around here. And if you put everything together, common sense will tell you that the big black goat wasn't a goat at all, that it could only be the devil himself, which is proven by the goat's ability to fly with a naked wench on its back, and when it was flying, just above the ground, along the main road in the village, it steered far clear of St Rosalia's Chapel.'

'But a dream can't be proof...' said the sceptical populace.

'But it can be a warning. Do you remember last year, when I had a dream about a great windstorm that uprooted trees and about hail that left so many holes in the rooftops they looked like beehives, and then the wind and hail really happened.'

'Sure, but disasters like that aren't so unusual in these parts – they happened before your dream and they happened after it. And, besides, the time frame wasn't right.'

'But it happened that same year, and it was exactly the way I predicted it, the way I described it.'

'Well, that's true,' the populace agreed. 'So what did the woman look like, the one on the goat's back? Did she seem at all familiar to you?'

'Oh yes, she was familiar. Very familiar,' the dreamer said with a big smile on her face. 'I don't have the least doubt who it was.'

'I don't either,' a second person then confirmed her dream with his own variation of it, for Kostanšek's daughter had found her way into one of his dreams as well. He was married, young, well-built, but, sadly, he was childless. His young wife would go regularly to the holy fount by St Mary's Chapel and dip herself in the water, but it was of no help. It made no difference if she bathed herself or him in the water, there was still no child. The husband was healthy, so how could his scythe not be whetted enough to fell a young woman like ears of grain? There had to be a reason behind it, he thought. And ever since that time when he was coupling with his wife and cried out the name of Kostanšek's daughter, it was clear that the young man was the victim of a spell, for he could only fulfil his conjugal obligation through some strange connection to that little tart.

There were also a few other accusations and suspicions. Just before the lightning bolt struck the church tower and left it scorched (as two random eyewitnesses recounted), who should be running past but that Kostanšek girl, looking completely dishevelled.

The castle lord, Count Friedrich – delegates from the populace had gone straight to him to lodge their complaint – listened to the accusations and decided that he had had enough of these stories. He made it clear to the populace that such fictions were causing them to neglect their work, and the farming season wasn't even over yet; dealing with this sort of thing would have to wait until late autumn.

'No! We won't wait,' the populace told him. 'If we don't act now, she and her witchcraft will destroy all our crops – and yours, too, gracious Count!'

'No, she won't,' the lord answered, 'because you will be praying more. The days are long now, and we'll start holding another Mass in the middle of the week, so that when you have finished your work for the day, you will go to the church and get on your knees and afterwards go straight home to bed, and the next day, hale and well-rested, you will go before sunrise to my fields and then to your own, and you will do everything you have not yet had time to do because you've been more concerned about some foolish nonsense that benefits neither yourselves nor me. And I will also order the sexton to ring the church bell a couple of times a week as a preventive measure against hailstorms. Do we understand each other?' Count Friedrich looked at his vassals sternly.

The populace shook their heads and rolled their eyes. 'What if none of these things has any effect?'

'Then you have only yourselves to blame, for neither God nor I like sluggards. I'll tell the parish priest – who, I hear, you're very happy with – to read out at Mass some suitable parables from the Old and New Testaments, so you'll more clearly understand your obligations as vassals,' said the count.

'When Mary appeared to that shepherd in the pasture, it was another sign that not all is well and good in the region,' the people's delegates tried again.

'From what I've been told, Mary's apparition talked about building and wine-growing,' Count Friedrich responded.

'But there has to be a big reason to build the kind of big church that Mary wants. In less sinful places than ours, a chapel would probably be enough …' the populace persisted.

'We'll deal with these reasons when you finish your work and the season is over.'

'So you'll arrest the Kostanšek girl?' the populace asked.

'If your suspicions are well-founded, she'll be arrested,' the count replied.

'We want to be present at the trial.'

'I will decide what is right and lawful.'

'The best thing would be to do it the way we, the people, want it done; otherwise, we won't be so meek and submissive any more …'

'Now, now, people, take it easy. No threats, no acting up, or else there will be punishment and some new taxes, too,' Friedrich says with a lump in his throat as he dismisses his vassals' delegates.

The mechanism has been started. The victim chosen. The circumstances are becoming clearer with each new development. A dangerous seed has fallen among the populace and is already sprouting.

A single victim would be enough, Prince-Bishop Wolfgang had suggested in May, during his two-day visit. The populace would then more easily accept new taxes and reject the Protestant preachers, and the obstinate town next door, seeing in the fiefdom a fate that could possibly be its own, would renounce Lutheranism.

'If that's true, then the woman under suspicion could ultimately be acquitted,' Friedrich had argued, trying to find a compromise; this was right before the prince-bishop's departure, as he was seating himself in the carriage with Julian's assistance.

'You really don't get it, do you, Friedrich?' Prince-Bishop Wolfgang had looked him directly in the eye there in the courtyard. 'The whole point of having a suspect is for her to be accused and then burned!'

'But whoever it is, she'll be innocent! And besides, a witchcraft epidemic can quickly spread,' Friedrich persisted.

'So you must see to it that things do not get out of hand,' the prince-bishop replied.

'Wolfgang, I'm telling you one more time, and I mean it – I have no intention of holding a witch trial here! I find the idea disgusting!'

'Hmm, Friedrich …' The prince-bishop gives him a meaningful look through the carriage window. 'So the idea of a witch trial disgusts you, does it? Well, darling, the Habsburg authorities might find certain inclinations and actions of yours even more disgusting, were they to learn of them.'

'What the hell are you talking about?' Count Friedrich is astonished.

'There have recently been whispers in circles close to Archduke Ferdinand regarding your intimacy with a certain stableman, and also about your love for music, for the viola da gamba in particular, and even more for a particular dark-haired gambist …' says the prince-bishop, pursing his lips.

'Who is saying this?' Count Friedrich recoils, as everything around him begins to shake before his eyes and his legs become heavy and limp, as if they didn't contain single bone.

'It's a rumour, and rumours have no names. Just as I warned Spitzenberg, I am warning you now, Friedrich: hold this witch trial. If you don't, information will come to the archduke's ear that will cost you your life. Birds of our feather the *Carolina* tosses on the fire. I myself am protected by sturdy armour, but you are soft and vulnerable. And if they come after you, there will be consequences for your loved ones, too.'

'And you would be willing to do this to me, Wolfgang?' Friedrich feels the sandy ground giving way beneath his feet.

'No, not me. But I can't prevent the rumours from reaching the archduke. Now, as I'm about to leave, I see you have finally understood the nature of my visit. For some time, the archducal court in Graz has been wondering how to subjugate that stubborn town next to you, which is controlled by the Provincial Estates. So they came up with the idea – God knows how – of clamping down on the town from inside and out. From the inside, they will put pressure on the towns-women, and from outside they will squeeze you. So have this trial; it will serve as a warning to both the town and your fiefdom. After all, Friedrich, you really do not have a choice,' the prince-bishop had said with a wave of his arm through the window of the carriage, which, surrounded by his military escort, rolled out of the castle courtyard.

It was too late. And it was not just about Kostanšek's daughter; a few other suspected names were also being whispered around, Friedrich remembered when the delegates of the populace had left. Violence always breeds violence and nothing else. But, Friedrich wondered, was it really too late? Was there still a chance to bring this madness to a halt? Would Mayor Volk Falke, perhaps, be able to stop it?

'Esteemed mayor, have you heard what is happening in my domain? We are both of us in their grip,' Friedrich anxiously explains to Mayor Falke.

'Of course I've heard. Ever since you had that visit in spring from that high Church dignitary, there have been a number of strange and very dangerous stories going around, even in our town,' the mayor replies.

'That preacher of yours, too, in his sermon – he didn't stint on that crazy story about Jewish golems, which made such an impression on the people that now they're talking nonsense about some seven creatures on the Kostanšek farm and witchcraft,' Friedrich counters, becoming more and more agitated.

'I agree. It was a foolish thing for him to say. And the papists, I hear, have taken that story and blown it up to their own advantage. I've also heard that there's a very young and very pregnant girl who is shuffling on her knees around Mary's altar and repeating certain names under her breath …'

'Esteemed Mayor Falke, I am being forced to hold a witch trial. The provincial powers are blackmailing me, and I am also getting pressure from the populace, who become more aggressive by the day. Do you have any ideas about how I might avoid this trial?' the worried count asks.

'I'm afraid I don't, not even for myself. I can try to prevent them from sending you the criminal judge they've selected, so instead you get someone who thinks accusations and trials of this sort are delusional. And I can try to arrange it so that, contrary to established practice, the trial is open to the people, who then might realize their mistake.'

'So you think it's possible there won't be any victims?' the count asks.

'Not unless things get out of hand,' the mayor replies.

'But you, Volk, how are you going to free yourself from the papists' grip? How will you defend your Lutheranism? Your town?' the count asks.

'Honestly, ever since that visit from the prince's commissioner, I don't have any answers.'

'I have a very bad feeling about all this ...'

'It's not feelings we need to rely on, gracious Count, but reason.'

'Reason, esteemed mayor, is not exactly abundant in our region. Feelings, sensations, mad passions – these are what drive the world,' Friedrich responds.

THE DISAPPEARANCE OF
THE SEVEN ODDITIES

'Where are those workers of yours?' the populace stopped Kostanšek one day in late September as he was returning home in his cart.

'They've gone home,' he replied.

'Gone home?' the populace repeated, disappointed. 'You mean back to the Caw-Caws?'

'Back to their own country. They have families there. Their relatives can't wait to see them – or their money.'

'That makes sense … So they have families, do they?' the populace asks.

'Yes, they do. They have children, wives, as well as mothers, fathers, sisters, brothers, uncles, cousins – large families, and they're all very close to each other,' Kostanšek says.

'So who works on their farms when they're away from home for months at a time?'

'Theirs is a nation of big, strong people, and everyone works in the fields, from five-year-old children, who are as big as our fifteen-year-olds, right up to sturdy hundred-year-olds, and all of them plough and mow and plant,' Kostanšek tells them.

But the populace was not happy with his answer and wanted to know if they would be back next spring.

'Maybe they will, maybe they won't,' Kostanšek replied, now not as sure of himself as he used to be, now rather cautious. Frightened, even.

A Cold Hand on
the Back of the Neck

The shepherd to whom Mary appeared in the pasture in late spring had, at the brothers' order, transformed himself into a farmer who worked from the early hours of the morning until late at night, but secretly, so the monks wouldn't notice, he took sips of wine and spirits as he laboured, and when he came home he would pour into himself whatever his exhausted arm was still able to lift. The hot summer passed, interspersed by huge downpours, which, however, did not alleviate the heat, and was followed by a rather cool autumn. At the beginning of October, the man approached the brothers and explained, in some distress and fear, that there was a saint who wanted to speak to him.

'A saint? Which saint?' the brothers asked him.

'It's hard to say because maybe it's not just one; it might be a whole community of them. When I was in the vineyard, I reached out my hand to pick a bunch of grapes and what I felt in my fingers, behind the yellowed and reddened leaves, wasn't grapes but a cold, withered hand,' the shepherd told them.

'A cold hand, you say? Not a cloven hoof?'

'No, no! There are bony arms hiding in the vines. Sometimes I hear something rustling behind my back, but it's not the leaves or the autumn wind in those trellises. And when I turn around, I see eyes looking back at me with no faces. It doesn't come from nature. I'm scared … I'm really scared. And before I fall asleep at night, I see figures coming out of the corners; whether they're saints or someone else, I don't know. Holy fathers, what should I do?'

'You must pray, peasant. There's nothing you can do but pray.'

'But I can't take these horrors any more. I'm even afraid to go into the vineyard. I'm afraid to fall asleep at night. What if these figures attack me when I close my eyes and then in the morning I don't wake up again?'

'If you don't wake up in your cottage, then at some point in the future you will awaken into eternal life. Pray, shepherd. Where there is prayer there is God, and where there is God there is no fear.'

The peasant prayed and worked, right up until the morning when he did not appear at the monastery. The brothers were not overly concerned about his absence; we can forgive him this one day, they thought, since for the first time in his life he's really been made to work. But the shepherd did not show up the next day either. Then, as evening approached, the monks received the news that the shepherd's work in the monastery vineyards was over forever. Two nights earlier he had begun to feel a pain beneath a rib on his right side, where his body was hard and swollen. If that's the case, said the medical experts among the brothers, then we are certainly not dealing with something supernatural here, but a natural phenomenon arising from long years of guzzling alcohol: the shepherd's liver became swollen and eventually stopped working. The Dominicans allocated money so the penitent shepherd would have a dignified burial and gave his family a lump sum for his four months' labour in their penal colony. They also discovered that, of the shepherd's five children, the eleven-year-old was surprisingly good for his age at adding, dividing and subtracting, and he could draw so well it was as though he had been trained not among the sheep and the goats but at a carved table in the home of a nobleman, burgher or, at least, a tradesman.

'If you agree, we will take him and look after his needs,' the brothers told the widow. 'We'll give him a good upbringing and educate him, and then we'll send him to the Jesuit college in Ljubljana, and if he does well, maybe afterwards he can go to the university in Vienna or in Padua.'

The shepherd's widow bowed her head in gratitude. Without a twinge of guilt, the widow realized that even bad things can have a good side. And her husband's death was good in several respects. From now on there would be nobody beating them, nobody shoving her on to the bed at night.

'What about the little ones?' the widow asked.

'Let's wait a year or so. Maybe the other two boys will also show some promise. But your daughters are just daughters; you'll have to take care of them yourself,' the brothers replied.

'What will happen to him? He was cruel and a boor, but, even so, he was my husband,' the shepherd's wife asks.

'The Lord will decide.'

'But what do you think? You're holy men, after all. Do you think he's been able to avoid hell? What should I tell his son when I send him away from home and place him in your hands? Should I tell him that while he's going into the arms of the Church, his father is roasting in hell?'

'Forget your husband. You are still young enough to find a new husband and have a few more children, too. We believe your husband did enough penance over the summer so that he's now paying off his sins in purgatory. Not hell. No, he's not in hell,' the brothers reply.

'Holy fathers, before the summer, maybe you thought he made up those visions in the pasture. Who knows if he did or not? But I know that he believed in his visions, and me, too, I started believing him. It was a good sign, I thought, Mary talking to him. And whenever he talked about her, he was the way he used to be when I first married him. Not rough at all, almost gentle and sweet. And he wasn't lying either about the bony fingers or the eyes that were following him in the vineyard and frightening him from the corners of the room. He was genuinely afraid of these things …'

'Woman, the only certain connection he had to Mary was that St Mary's wine. How such toxic piss got named after the mother of Our Lord, we'll never know. But when you mix it with wormwood schnapps, strange things can happen …'

'But will there be a church, that big basilica?'

'Oh yes, there will definitely be a church. Not long ago, we had a visit from a young girl with a bloated belly, and she told us a story that was similar to the shepherd's, only it didn't involve alcohol. But it did contain some terrible things that would have consequences. Before there can be a church, a lot of other things will have to happen first. There will be some very bad times, but then it will get better. When the church is built, there will be a big fair, perhaps the biggest any-where around. Perhaps your daughters will decorate the church with flowers, and your sons, if they don't take after their father and ruin their lives, may one day even say Mass in it.'

'So a few years from now, will my husband become a saint, like that Indian peasant Ivan?'

'Oh no, there's no chance of that. A saint he never was and never will be. But now go and find yourself a husband and raise your children. As for the oldest, bring him to us in three days' time.'

'But my boy will be all right, won't he, if I hand him over to you?'

'What could possibly happen to him in our hands?'

'It's said that some priests take in peasant children and promise to send them to school, but then a few weeks later their little bodies are found mutilated behind some churchyard wall.'

'The Protestant preachers say that to make you afraid of us. None of it's true. We take very good care of these chosen children. Go now, woman, your time of suffering is over and a new life awaits you. An uncertain life, perhaps, but that's how life is.'

(A LETTER TO THE NOBLE WIDOW)

Most gracious lady,

You breathe meaning into my day simply by casting a glance at me, for then I distract myself for hours, trying to interpret the message in your eyes. My body quivers when I think of everything I would do with you, and at the same moment I am overcome with shame and trembling, which is like what happens before one of my attacks, and sometimes an attack might even spring forth from this. I have never in my life experienced such great excitement; I did not even know it existed. I truly must keep a hold on myself so I don't explode in ecstasy like some Lutheran prayer hall! How marvellous life is! Everything is open – here I am, standing at this point, and at another, almost in my immediate proximity, you are standing, with a line drawn between us which connects us. Let nothing worry you, my dear love: here, in your proximity, am I, who protect you and save you from all that is bad. But something unfathomable now troubles me: what if the moment here and now is stronger than the moment when – and, of course, if – I manage to reach that desired point at the other end of the line? Would it not be better if this moment were extended in a repeated series of euphorias and then, at the climax of my life, I simply crack? Oh, let this openness, this warm, quivering tremor expand into infinity. May it last, may it fill me completely, and then ... and then it doesn't matter if I lose consciousness and disappear for all time ... For a while now I haven't been able to reflect philosophically on fundamental matters, for my thoughts play leap-frog with each other, all out of order. In such a state, how can I reflect on things philosophically? How can I sleep?

Before the First
Special Assignment

It is difficult, but towards morning he finally falls asleep in the autumn damp. But only a few hours later he is awoken by shouts and pounding on his door, after which three town bailiffs burst into his room.

'Ooooh, so we're sleeping in today like some frail old lady or spoiled young miss? It's almost noon! Not only has the cock crowed his morning tune – which you usually sleep through anyway – but more than a few cocks have been killed and cooked and right now their soup is being poured into tin bowls,' the chief bailiff says derisively.

'Scrivener Nikolai has been working all night …' the housekeeper defends him, feeling guilty that she had not able to keep out the intruders.

'So Scrivener Nikolai has been working all night?' the bailiff mocks her. 'Blah-blah-blah! But what was he doing … awwwll night? So scribbling of any sort is scrivener's work now, is it? Well, why do we have working hours, then? And rooms meant for working in?' the chief bailiff asks.

'I am an educated man, and I also do things for which I receive no salary,' the scrivener replies.

'And what I'm here to take you away to doesn't exactly fall under your job description either,' the bailiff says and clicks his tongue. 'So get ready! People like you – all your sort – I'd just as soon run out of town! Why should we have to get up before the crack of dawn and run around the whole day, at the most ungodly hours, too, sometimes, just to drag you sluggards out of bed! So get dressed! You're coming with us!'

'Coming where? Why?'

'You'll see when we take you to where you belong.'

'But I haven't done anything wrong!'

'It's not our job to explain anything to you.'

'Mayor Volk has told me nothing.'

'Yes, the mayor, your protector – he'll tell you all about it!' the chief bailiff breaks into laughter. 'Get dressed at once! Where we're taking you,' he says with a menacing chuckle, 'they'll supply you with everything they think you need. Fucking lazy-arse scribbler!'

'Did they tell you you're going on a trip?' Mayor Volk asks the scrivener at the Town Hall.

'That's all they told me; nothing about where or why,' Nikolai replies.

'Something rather awkward has happened in Count Friedrich's domain,' the mayor explains. 'The day after the judge arrived, his scrivener came down with dysentery, and it's possible that something was put in his and the judge's food, only the judge managed to avoid it. The scrivener was taken to hospital early this morning, and he'll be out of commission for a while, if he ever does recover. But the trial cannot be postponed, and you, Nikolai, are the closest judicial scrivener in the area. On such short notice, there was nobody else we could think of for this special assignment.'

'Please, anything but this!' Nikolai cries out and pleads with the mayor. 'I beg you, esteemed mayor! I'm not the man for such trials. Accusations about crooked grocer's scales, thefts and similar foolishness I can still put up with, but when it's a question of life or death – I just can't …'

'Compose yourself, Nikolai. This particular judge is a fine, cultivated man; we chose him ourselves. There's nothing to worry about; he's on our side.'

'I'm sorry, what do you mean?'

'I'll explain it to you another time,' the mayor says calmly. 'I took advantage of some connections to make sure they didn't send that notorious judicial butcher to oversee the trial in the count's fiefdom – don't ask me who I mean; it's better you don't know. But this judge will conduct the trial quickly and intelligently, and in front of the people, too, so they are publicly confronted with the absurdity of such accusations. While it's a fact that some people are involved with spells and sorcery, the whole thing is just irrational superstition. And I'm not going to waste words talking about the devil.'

'But what if something goes wrong?' the scrivener asks.

'Nothing will go wrong. We've taken care of everything. You'll saddle up a horse, and by evening you'll be at the count's castle, where they're expecting you and have everything prepared. You'll be paid at the provincial rate for such assignments, and, when you're done, you'll come back and keep doing what you've always done.'

THE FIRST TRIAL

'We begin the second day of judicial proceedings against those accused of witchcraft in the domains of the Count Friedrich von Lamberg,' the provincial criminal judge addresses the public in the courtroom. 'Present are the criminal judge and the members of the judicial council. As my scrivener suddenly took ill late last night, the proceedings will be recorded by the town scrivener, Nikolai Miklavž Paulin. Members of the populace are attending the trial. Besides the populace, also present in the courtroom are witnesses, who will swear on the Holy Scriptures that they will speak rationally and will not weave any lies into their testimonies or in any way whatsoever misrepresent the facts. If the commission finds that the witness is not of sound mind, whether because physical illness is impairing his reason or because his mind is darkened due to troubles relating to the soul, the witness will be excluded, as he also will be if he is drunk or in any other way intoxicated when he takes part in the trial.

'I will begin by reading the accusation that has been brought against the accused L. M., female, age sixty-one, single. "This individual was allegedly discovered in the field of her neighbour, who noticed a woman taking something out of a bag and scattering it around, and while doing this she whistled a little, hummed a little and every so often would hawk up some sort of green phlegm and spit it out on the field. This occurred at the beginning of the summer, when the wheat was still young, tender and green, but after this happened, it stopped growing and one week later had withered. The farmer who makes the accusation suspects that this woman is the reason for the damage in his field and that she allegedly put a spell on the wheat with her spittle so that it would completely fail."

'Let the accused now stand and comment on the accusations,' the judge says.

The woman does not stand and remains sitting on the chair, hunched over with her head resting on her chest.

'Accused, you must stand up!' he repeats.

'She can't,' explains the bailiff standing next to her. 'She's got broken bones.'

'How did they get broken?' the judge asks in surprise.

'The same way it happens to anyone who resists arrest,' the bailiff explains.

The judge leans over the bench, looks first at the accused, then at the bailiff, and again at the accused, and turns to the bailiff. 'How can I question people who are accused if, before they even get here, you mangle their bodies so much they can neither stand nor speak?'

'If they resist we put a little pressure on them. Those are our methods,' the bailiff answers.

'Who gave you permission to torture the accused before I questioned her?'

'She was giving us a lot of trouble in that cage and attacking the guards, so we had no choice but to discipline her,' the bailiff answers.

'You broke her bones ...' the judge says.

'Yeah, but she had old bones that broke easy,' the bailiff says indifferently.

The judge signals to the physician in attendance that he should examine her.

The doctor goes over to the accused and lifts her head. Her eyelids are half-shut; he determines that her eyes are not moving. Then he raises her head and lets go, and it drops back on to her chest. The doctor examines her legs and checks the pulse on her arm. He pauses a moment with a wry smile that shows that he is thinking. He pulls a little mirror out of his pocket, holds it in front of the accused's slightly open mouth and then turns it towards himself. He twirls his right moustache, looks at the commission and states his conclusion, 'The person in question is no longer among the living. She is dead.'

'Are you certain?' the judge asks.

'Completely,' the physician answers.

The judge runs his right hand over his bald head, which shines with an oily gleam; then he turns to the scrivener.

'Write: "The accused does not answer questions because she is no longer alive." Carry her out of the courtroom. Have the next accused brought before the commission.

'A woman, twenty-one years of age, unmarried with one child,' the judge continues. '"It is not known who the father is, but it is suspicious" – so states the indictment – "as the mother has a fair complexion and reddish hair, while her child, a four-year-old boy, has curly black hair and a complexion that is unusually dark for our area." On the basis of rumours, the indictment alleges that "the father of the woman's child is no one from her village nor from the neighbouring village, and that the child's father is from no village of any sort and is not even to be found among men ..." What in the world is this indictment talking about?' the judge frowns. '"For his home lies beneath the earth's surface, where his father is the king of hell. And like father, like son – dark hair, hairy, dark skin ..." This can't be serious!' The judge darts an angry look at the members of the commission. 'What's written here is utter nonsense.' And he continues reading: '"The woman is accused of the following deeds: A villager, male, blacksmith, thirty-four years of age, the father of five children – it would have been seven, only two died, one at birth, the other in its third year, which is mentioned because the accused person in question may have been guilty of the two children's deaths – the blacksmith, who is known as an honest man, goes regularly to Catholic Mass on Sunday, and, when his health and time allow, he also likes to help out around the church. In the past few weeks, however, his health has made it impossible for him to participate regularly in worship, and his work, too, has become harder for him to do. For reasons he himself does not understand, his hands have started to shake – and this is a blacksmith, a man accustomed to fire and heavy, hard work. The ironwork he forges is not the same as it was before; the horses brought to him by their owners for shoeing are said to look at him strangely, and they resist when he tries to take their hoof in his hands. Even the horses can sense" – the indictment stresses the point – "that something is not right with him. And something isn't right. The past few months he has been sleeping poorly and wakes up in the middle of the night in unusual and ungodly positions." What positions these might be is not stated,' the judge says, casting a glance over the courtroom. '"His sleeplessness forces the blacksmith to attempt more often to unite with his wife, who lies next to him, but instead of his wife's face, the face that appears to him is that of the accused, whom he has never known in the biblical sense of the word. No matter how hard he tries or how much he begs forgiveness and does penance before God, the white face and reddish hair of the accused, as well as certain other parts of her body, appear to him during the unsuccessful performance of his conjugal duties. When he is sitting on the wooden stool in his workshop and holding the hoof of a horse in his hands, he has the sudden impression that it is not a horse's leg he is holding but a woman's." The indictment concludes as follows: "If the blacksmith, an honest man and faithful husband, is compelled while holding the leg of a horse to think that the leg belongs not to a horse but to a woman and that the hoof is not a hoof but a woman's knee, then such substitution points to a confusion of perception that is neither accidental nor natural in origin, for the man is healthy in body and soul, or at least he was such before the abovementioned disturbances. In consequence of the facts cited, it is possible to conclude that the mixing of impressions is due to incursions from outside human nature, and even outside divine super-nature, for everything that has been cited is caused by a person who is neither human nor God, but the very one with whom the accused has had a child black as coal."

'What does the accused have to say to these charges?' the judge asks.

'I had nothing to do with any of this,' the accused woman replies.

'Write,' the judge turns to Nikolai, '"The accused denies all guilt." How, then, do you explain the charge that it is your image that appears to the blacksmith?'

'I don't know. I hardly know the blacksmith,' she says.

'Write: "The accused does not know why her image is compelled to appear before the blacksmith's eyes." Have you ever spoken with him?'

'Twice, but after that never again because he asked me to do indecent things.'

'You lying bitch!' a woman's voice is heard from the courtroom.

'Bring forward the plaintiff,' the judge orders. 'What do you say, blacksmith, considering that the accused has denied all guilt. Personally, I believe you when you say that the female person in question is the reason for your visions, but I suspect that she herself is not to blame and that the reason for these apparitions lies within you. Very likely you are not the only one to whom the person in question appears,' the judge's face takes on a mocking expression, 'and undoubtedly there are others whose wet thoughts *compel* her image to appear to them. Only yesterday we heard plenty of similar stories about Kostanšek's daughter, who also smuggles herself into the thoughts and dreams of pious villagers – and I won't even mention all those suppositions about the seven inhuman workers on Kostanšek's farm.'

'I am an honest and God-fearing man,' the blacksmith begins to defend himself. 'I have never done anything bad to anyone ...'

'Keep the blandishments short,' the judge interrupts him.

'I am a truthful man ...'

'Don't tell me you never cheated anyone or squeezed money out of them in some underhanded way ...'

'Never! I'm an honest man, as honest as you can get!' the black-smith replies.

The judge looks up at the mural on the ceiling and conspicuously rolls his eyes.

'The statement you just read out about her – it's true,' the black-smith continues. 'That redheaded witch has forced herself into my head so I can't live like I did before. Those weedy red curls, those watery green eyes and all her other parts have taken root in my mind so I'm not the way I used to be. When I'm alone with my wife – you know what I mean, gracious judge – my wife disappears before my eyes, and it doesn't matter if my eyes are open or closed, all I see is that witch, and she's pecking inside my head and everything hurts.'

'Let's take things one at a time. You say everything hurts ... How does it hurt?' the judge asks.

'It hurts a lot!' the blacksmith replies.

'Where, blacksmith? Where in your body does it hurt?'

'Everything hurts. My arms hurt ...'

'I don't doubt that your right hand hurts you,' the judge adds cynically.

'My head and my stomach both hurt when I'm with my wife – you know what I mean – and then, I don't just feel pain, but there's also this smell everywhere ...'

'A smell? What kind of smell?' the judge asks.

'Like rotten eggs ...'

'Like sulphur?'

'You might say it was like sulphur, only I should stress that my wife is a devout woman who prays every night, and in the morning, too ...'

'Do you have meat on your table every day?' the judge interrupts him.

'If only that were true! But sadly enough, we don't. The only time we have meat on our table is on feast days; otherwise, we eat modest meals.'

'Like what, for example?' the judge asks.

'Whatever grows in the field,' the blacksmith answers.

'Kohlrabi?'

'Kohlrabi, carrots ...'

'Cabbage? Beans?' the judge asks.

'Cabbage, yes, and beans, too,' the blacksmith replies.

'Do you have them every day? Both cabbage and beans?'

'Sure, both, but I'd rather be picking meat off bones,' the blacksmith says.

'They say that beans fuel the mind, but that's hardly true in your case. On the other hand, it's common knowledge that cabbage and beans fill the bowels with wind,' the judge says. To quell the excitement that now spreads through the courtroom, he strikes the gavel a few times on the massive wooden bench, trying to silence the audience, which includes people from the town eager for entertainment and a good time, who were thinking, 'We really enjoy the theatre, but since our town isn't big and shows don't come to us very often, we go to watch killers being hanged on the gallows, thieves getting their hands and noses chopped off and now and then somebody's tongue being cut out. Every once in a while we're able to pressure them into giving us a public court trial, which can be even more fun than the burlesque players who arrive in carts and put on plays for us; sometimes we laugh and sometimes we throw things at the actors, all the rotten crap we collected from our larders beforehand. But what we love more than anything else are court trials in which the country folk from the neighbouring fiefdom appear, because the sort of idiocies those boneheaded rustics come up with not even the most talented burlesquers can match. Sometimes we don't really understand what they're saying, sometimes not at all, and we don't know how the judge can understand them either, except that occasionally somebody whispers a translation in his ear. The way the peasants torture the meanings of words, and the words themselves, inexhaustibly and mercilessly – we wouldn't be able to do that, even if we are so infinitely smarter than those yokels.'

'Quiet! Otherwise I'll have you thrown out of the courtroom!' the judge shouts.

'Oh no, not that!' the townsfolk simmer down, and some open up their haversacks and pull out bread, roast chicken legs or some other meat, and then, for the rest of the time, they attentively follow the proceedings while smacking their lips.

'If you eat cabbage and beans every blessed day …' the judge continues, turned towards the plaintiff.

'Yes, that's right,' the plaintiff confirms.

'Then the stink you've been smelling, blacksmith, originates in your own body …'

'No, it doesn't!'

'And therefore, as even ancient medicine recognized, that sulphur and those smells do not come from I don't know where …' the judge continues.

'… but from the blacksmith and his wife – from their own farting bums!' a voice is heard from the courtroom, which starts rumbling with laughter, and it is only with some effort that the judge puts a stop to it.

'Well, I won't say it's not that,' the plaintiff continues, somewhat embarrassed, 'but it never smelled so bad before.'

'Age and the heavy food you eat have stunk up your bowels. And don't say you don't fill up on crackling before you go to bed,' the judge continues.

'What else can I do? If I wake up hungry after the first bout of sleep, I go and see if there are any leftovers from supper; then I have a snack and go back to bed,' the plaintiff answers.

'That's not very good for your digestion ...'

'But we all do it! Only that wench in my dreams has nothing to do with beans!' He points at the accused with disgust. 'And my wife knows it, too!'

'What does she know?' the judge asks.

'Everything I'm going through.'

'I doubt that, but let her come up and tell us what she knows,' the judge orders.

'With pleasure!' says a corpulent woman in her late twenties as she marches to the front; she has dirty, greasy skin and shaggy hair, but her clothes are clean and she has obviously fixed herself up for the occasion, having never been to such an event before.

'Ever since that whore of Satan hexed him, there's nothing to be done with him ...' the witness begins.

'What do you mean?' the judge asks.

'I mean nothing. When I'm with him – you know what I mean, gracious judge – it's all soft ...'

'What is soft? His character? He has a soft soul?' Muffled laughter is heard in the courtroom, but the judge silences it with his wooden gavel.

'Not his soul. His clapper. It's just hanging there like pig gut ...' the witness replies.

'Silence! Silence!' the judge tries to calm down the townspeople, who are slapping their knees with their greasy hands and elbowing each other in the ribs.

'Woman, choose your words more carefully!' the judge snaps at her.

'Do forgive me, gracious judge,' the witness says, and continues in the same fawning tone. 'There is nothing left of my husband. He does his best to prepare, but then, nothing. And it's all because of that whore' – she points her right forefinger at the accused – 'who walks around the yard with her big boobs when she's hanging out the laundry. She never does her blouse up, the bitch; she's half-naked, all rumpled like, with her underskirt hiked up, as if she doesn't want it to get soiled, but everyone knows she'll squeeze anyone who wants it between those tits of hers. That whore!'

'Woman! You are violating civil order! We are not in the farmyard here; we're in a court of law!' the judge warns her.

'But that black thing she spawned from God knows where and with God knows who – his eyes are black as coal, and sometimes they flash with lightning! And her, too, she's got the same fire in her eyes, and she looked at me once, gave me a really weird look with her eyeballs bulging out, so I swore at her there and then – "Who you staring at, whore?" But she just keeps looking at me, and then I get such stomach cramps I'm rolling on the floor in pain, and when I stand up later, all covered in puke, and look out of the window, I see her still standing there by the fence, and she's staring at our house. And later the whore is forcing herself into *my* dreams, too. I dream there's somebody knocking at the door, and when I open it, she steps into the house, goes over to my guy and, before you know it, she's got her tits out and is squeezing my husband's head with them, trying to smother him. My man's kicking like a poisoned dog. And when I grab the pothook and am about to thwack her with it, and hard, too, I wake up. And there's something else I can tell you that wasn't a dream – it was all true: this past winter, around St Valentine's, when it was already dark out, I'm taking the swill out to the hog when this black shadow bolts out from behind the pigsty. Ooh, that's a bad sign, I think, so I cross myself and call on the all the saints to help me. And then I see her, and she's waving some clothes in front of the pigsty. "Hey, what are you doing here, whore?" I yell, and she disappears in a flash. Then when I go to pour the swill into the trough for the hog, I think, what if it wasn't true and it just seemed like it was, but when I'm going back from the pigsty to the house, I see her footprints in the snow and there's a thin line between them, and from that point on I don't have any more doubts about what sort of a creature she is …'

'Maybe she's just got a reeeally long dick?' a voice is heard in the courtroom.

'Nope. She's got a tail! Only she hides it; she's got it tied around her waist. But I found her out, that depraved bitch!'

'Enough! Take the witness away!' the judge orders.

'But wait, there's something else I got to say ...'

'We're not interested!' The judge waves his arm in the direction of the witness and then turns to the scrivener. 'Write: "The testimonies of the husband and wife about phenomena relating to the accused are without rational argument, and therefore, if there is no other witness, the accused is acquitted."

There's fury in the courtroom.

'What?' the blacksmith's wife is screaming. 'You're letting that whore of Satan go free?'

SYNCOPE

How can something be infinitely larger than the thing in which it is located? How can an idea like the idea of an infinite God lodge itself in my finite mind? What if my assertions that I have perfect ideas because my infinite and perfect Creator has implanted them in my imperfect reason are not precise? Can I really be sure that my limited rational deductions about the infinite are correct? In truth, I am unable to really think the notion of infinity – such a notion appears as a flash, it is dangerous to think it too long – in a single instant a shift can occur that thrusts the thinker ...

'Scrivener! You're not writing anything down! What's wrong with you?' the judge looks at Nikolai.

'I am paying attention, gracious judge. I am writing ...' Nikolai says distractedly.

'Write everything down in precise detail.' The judge leans over to him. 'Mayor Volk Falke personally recommended you to me. With reason and consistency, we can prevent the outcome that's expected from this insane trial. I am not sending anybody to their death. So do your part, and we'll put an end to this madness as quickly as we can.' The judge pulls back from Nikolai and continues the trial.

'Remove the disruptive witness from the courtroom!' he orders.

As the guards seize the blacksmith's wife and are about to lead her away, a little arm sticks out from behind a pillar in a corner of the room, and then the little head of a young girl appears. 'I would ... there's something I would like to say.'

'You, little girl? You have something to add? I find that difficult to believe. You're too young for such matters. I advise you not to get involved,' the judge replies.

'It's too late for that,' the little voice responds. 'And now it is what it is.'

'What is? Well, all right. Come up and tell us what you know. Even so, little girl, I warn you, these are dangerous matters, and once you're involved in them they're not easy to get out of,' the judge tells her.

When the girl stands up and heads towards the judge, the women in the room give her the once over and exchange knowing glances with each other.

'So what are you going to tell us about?' the judge asks.

'About this.' The girl points a finger at her belly.

'Is yours bloated, too?' the judge asks, examining her abdomen.

'Yes, gracious judge, it is, but not from cabbage and beans,' she says.

'No?'

'No. He bloated me up. Don't you see, gracious judge?' She is rubbing her belly.

'Oh, dear Lord!' the judge sighs. 'You're too young – you're much too young for something like this …'

'That's what I thought, too. But he didn't ask me what I thought …' the girl says.

'He forced himself on you?'

'Yes. But not the way it usually happens, not really.'

'How, then?'

'Gracious judge, if I could have, I would have resisted with all my might, but I didn't have the strength. Right up until that night – I shudder to think of it – I worked and lived as is right and proper. I helped a lot around the house – it was me and not my mother who cooked and washed the dishes, who tidied up and scrubbed the floors, and at the same time I was looking after my little brother and sister. Whatever time was left I spent praying and helping the needy, and I also used it to decorate our beautiful church, which is dedicated to Mary Immaculate. But then, gracious judge, then, forces I had no power to resist invaded my young, short life. As young as I was, as innocent as I was,' she began to sob, 'a man took me against my will and got me with child – and I promise to God, I will take care of this child and raise it to be an honest Catholic, and I will do so even if the father denies his fatherhood right here in front of you.'

'Is that man, the father of your child, here in the courtroom?'

'He is sitting over there, but I can't look,' she holds out her right hand and points it at the front door of the room.

'Which one is he? There are quite a few people over there,' the judge says.

'Maybe it's not just one, maybe it's all of them,' a voice can be heard saying in the courtroom.

'That man, the one who's tall and old – well, he's old to me, since I'm still so very young.' The girl is now pointing her finger directly at the blacksmith.

'You mean the blacksmith?'

'That's the one, gracious judge,' she sobs.

'Who does that whore think she is, making false accusations about my husband?' the blacksmith's wife starts shouting.

'Silence!' the judge interrupts the woman. A court officer is holding her tightly to keep her from lunging at the witness. 'Let the girl tell us what happened and how it happened,' the judge continues. 'And you, little girl, don't even think about making anything up, because if you do, it will be very bad for you.'

'It couldn't be worse than what happened to me, gracious judge. Never in my life did I imagine the pain I endured, for which I now feel the consequences, and I expect there'll be consequences for my child, too, who was conceived in such dreadful, almost indescribable circumstances. This is how it happened. In addition to all the chores I mentioned, every morning I would lead our five little cows out to pasture and then every evening I'd go and bring them back. On the way home I would usually be praying, because when it starts getting dark it's not safe for a young girl to be out walking by herself. So one late afternoon, I see a little old woman lying on the grass next to the path. "Old mother, old mother!" I cry, and I run and lean over her, "Did something happen to you? Did you fall? Let me help you. How can I help you?" "Oh, little girl," the little woman says, "here I lie and in all probability I am dying. I had a fall, and it seems I'm completely done in. If you, *angelic creature*" – those are the exact words she used, angelic creature, and so she deceived me even more – "if you would truly be so good as to help me return to my house, I will be grateful to you for the rest of my life, and Jesus will reward you." The very sight of this helpless, broken old woman brought tears to my eyes. Although I knew they were waiting for me anxiously at home – well, not for me so much, actually, but for our five cows – although I knew I would be late getting home, and that my mother would yell at me, and my father would take the whip in his hands and beat me until I was bleeding, and then … and after that … oh, I don't know, sir, esteemed judge, I don't know how to say it, when it's the opposite of everything that we learned in catechism, and it's such a great sin that very likely the Creator has some terrible punishment for it.'

The judge was thinking of interrupting her, to get her to clarify the terribly sinful thing that occurred after the beating, although he did have some idea of what she had in mind, when the witness herself lifted her hand to stop him, as if to say, let me finish my story. The judge nodded and stared in wonder at his own hand, which now gestured to the girl to go on with her narrative. How in the world had this young oratrix, who now continued to be skilfully in charge of her own performance, managed to keep him from getting a word in edgeways?

'Despite the threats waiting for me at home,' the girl was saying, 'despite the horrors, which I never did get used to,' she sniffed, 'I felt awfully sorry for that helpless little woman. I helped her get up; then I put my arm around her and draped her left arm over my shoulders, and we started walking, and as we walked the cowbells were tinkling next to us, and from the leafy branches of the treetops, which were getting darker and darker, came the cries of night birds, and from the undergrowth, the sounds of other nocturnal creatures as well. I won't say I wasn't a little scared, even at the very beginning, but I believed that my guardian angel, to whom I commend myself every evening, was walking beside me, and that Mary Immaculate, whose altar I decorate every eighth of December with pine needles and red Christmas holly, would protect me. And the two of us kept walking and walking, until finally we came to a crossroads and she said to me, "Here, little girl, we turn right."

"'Why do we turn right,' I ask, "when I and my cows have to go left?"

"'You do, maybe,' she answers, "but I live in that direction," and she points to the right, "and I won't be able to get to my modest little house all by myself."

"'But in that direction, on the right,' – and I was sure of this because I know the thicket very well – "there isn't any house, and the path soon disappears in the undergrowth."

"'You are mistaken, little girl,' she tells me. "It just looks like there's no more path. But if you lift a branch or two, the path reappears. Imagine what it'd be like if anyone at all could come to my little house, which is very isolated. Because people – and you should remember this, little girl," the woman tells me, "not all of them are good and trustworthy, you know. Many of them are very bad."

"'Yes, I know,' I said, lowering my eyes. "Unfortunately, I know that all too well," I told her and could barely keep from bursting into tears, but I didn't want to upset the poor woman with my own unhappy life.

"'So what do I do now?' I wondered, standing at the crossroads. "What do I do with the cows? They won't wait for me here. I can only hope they'll find their way home on their own and won't get lost." I petted the lead cow, and then waved goodbye to the cows, and the woman and I took the path on the right. And so we walked and walked, and I would lift up the branches, and we just kept walking, and meanwhile it was almost dark.

"'Is it much farther?' I ask.

"'Oh, no! Not at all!' she replies.

"'So we're almost there?' I repeat.

"'We're very close,' she says.

"'But there's no house anywhere to be seen,' I say.

"'Oh, but there will be, there will be, you'll see!' she tells me, and then suddenly she turns around and straightens up. And, oh, it's so horrible! The little woman vanishes and in her place stands a big strong man – him! He is standing there,' the girl says, pointing to the blacksmith. 'And he's laughing in my face! "Oh, dear heaven!" I cry. "Where has the old mother gone?" I ask the terrible apparition.

"'The old mother? Yes, well, the old mother's gone to the devil!" he tells me, laughing. "And she'll be coming back with him, too, with the devil, and they won't be alone, but they'll have others with them, and then we'll all go to a clearing not very far from here, and we'll dance and have a wild old time!" And as he's saying this, he gives me a quick pinch down there' – she points to the area of her genitals – 'but I'm too ashamed to describe anything else.'

'She's blushing! The little slut is actually blushing,' the townspeople say and look at each other. 'Oh, she's very good! The little girl is excellent! We'll be coming back again to watch her. Oh yes, we'll definitely be back!'

'And then it happened, just as that horrible man said it would,' the witness continues. 'All at once, gracious judge, the sky goes dark, with thunder and rumbling everywhere – I don't remember there ever being such great thunder before, not even last year during that terrible storm, when just above our village, not far from the chapel with the holy miracle water, half the hill was torn away and carried into the valley. And then, in the midst of those dark spruce trees, a bolt of red lightning strikes, chopping the trees in half, and an even greater thunder starts rumbling from the earth. Oh what a sound it was! I look up at the sky and I see men and women on broomsticks, and they're coming down to earth, and when they are all on the ground, they throw the broomsticks into a pile … Oh, and I almost forgot, there was a man in a sort of greenish turban, with enormous gold rings in his ears, and he arrived on a flying carpet, and since the people with broomsticks weren't paying any special attention to him, I figured they must all know each other pretty well.'

'What scoundrels! They're not just friends with the devil but with the Turks, too! Traitors!' Such comments were percolating through the courtroom, but the judge silenced them at once.

'Then all of a sudden, the earth opens up in front of me, and stinky smoke starts coming out, and then the devil himself, the actual living devil, springs out of the crack, and, oh, gracious judge, he is so disgusting and terrifying that I thought I was going to die right there and then, but, as you see, I didn't. The witches arranged themselves in a circle dance in the middle of the clearing, and at the centre of the circle was the devil, who was sticking his tongue out like this, gracious judge' – the girl licks her lips in an obscene manner – 'and like this, with his tongue, he makes a sign to the blacksmith, who grabs me and throws me in front of the devil's hoofs. Oh, what eyes he had! Yellow-green eyes – never in all my life did I see such terrible eyes! And then a strange force knocks me on my back and spreads out my legs, and the blacksmith is already on top of me, and he's as naked as the day he was born, only a lot bigger, of course. And all during the thing that comes next, which was too horrible and shameful to describe, the others are murmuring something as the devil stomps his hoofs to set the rhythm. "Oh, Jesus," I prayed, "please let me lose conscious-ness!" – because I'd gathered from their murmuring that when the blacksmith was done, the others would all take their turn, ending with their hornèd master. But then, gracious judge, a miracle happened. A blue sky starts to shine, piercing that red light, and it sucks up all the red. Then the earth swallows up the devil, while everyone else, and the blacksmith, too, are blown away like leaves. I am completely alone in the clearing, which is glowing with heavenly light, when I hear a strange fluttering overhead. I look up at the sky and right above me I see a great white bird flapping its wings, and it looks at me with eyes that, for a bird, are strangely friendly. "Who are you?" I think, and the bird, who can hear my thoughts, opens its beak and sings, "I am the Holy Spirit, my dear, erstwhile virgin," and he brushes me with his wing, and never did I feel a more gentle touch, not even from my mother, who was always very strict with me, and certainly not from my father, which is something I'd rather not talk about.

'What happened after that, I do not know. I do not even know how I got home. I woke up in the ferns behind our house with our dog licking my face, but I was at peace, for I knew that the Holy Spirit was protecting me and that all would be well. But all was not well. A month and a half later, what happens to women started happening to me. When they found out at home, and I told them everything down to the last detail, just as I have told you here, under oath, my father gave me such a beating that even now I bear its marks. Just let all be well with the baby – I ask the Blessed Virgin every night – and I will accept everything that is meant for me. "It will be, it will be," the Virgin tells me in my dreams. "All will be well with the baby and with you; only you must make sure that an enormous basilica is erected in my honour in this sinful land. But first, you must reveal the truth about the sinners so they may receive the strictest possible punishment from the authorities. Let the flames burn their bodies to a crisp, just as their souls will burn after death."

'And ever since that time I have been praying and doing good deeds, but I avoid our farm like a mangy dog, because nobody at home believes what I am telling you here. Even in my condition, I sleep in barns and beg bread from good people, and in exchange I do some small chore for them, whatever I can, given my condition,' the girl, sniffling, concludes her narrative.

The girl is clever – the judge thinks – cleverer than most of those brats from noble and burgher families who are sent to the Jesuits for an education. If she lived in a different place and was of a different sex, with her oratorical skills – although I expect she's made the whole thing up from beginning to end – she could climb all the way to a bishopric, if not a cardinalship. At the age of fifteen, to chatter on like this and have everyone listening attentively to that fiction of hers and not interrupting, even if they don't believe her, it shows she's got a talent for speech-making. She could easily toss off a few sermons, do some nimble scheming and weave her way from one high position to another. Or she could be a successful Protestant preacher and write a book or two for the common people in their own language. But the world is unjust, and many an agile mind is born in the wrong body with the wrong sex in the wrong place, no matter how right the time might be. The girl and her baby need to be protected, the judge thinks, protected mainly from herself. And the mayhem she's trying to whip up has to be prevented.

So he makes his decision. 'Are the girl's parents here?' he asks. 'They're not? Well, have them brought here tomorrow so I can examine the case thoroughly.'

'Excellent!' The townspeople are satisfied. 'We've just seen a real drama almost, a comedy, actually, and we're promised the continuation tomorrow. Oh, we will be here – tomorrow, the day after, for as long as the play lasts! Because that little minx could be a real actress. She and her kid could join one of those travelling burlesque troupes, and no matter where their cart stopped, she'd guarantee them a big success. She could play victims and villains, virgins and bitches. That little girl has talent, and if the kid takes after her, she'll have no reason to fear poverty in her old age. If the child's a boy, at the very least he could become a merchant, or a crafty thief and flim-flammer, or maybe a lawyer or priest, with sophisticated tricks for wheedling money and favours out of people. And if it's a girl, and she has at least some of her mother's talents, she could easily be a rich man's whore, or make an excellent career for herself as the mother superior of a convent. Blood is thicker than water, and the apple that falls from her, whether it's been implanted in her by Satan, the blacksmith or somebody else, won't fall far from the family tree. Oh, the fun's not over yet!'

SYNCOPE

… how can I, who am imperfect, be certain that the idea of a perfect and good God was not implanted in me by someone who diverges from this idea – who is all-capable but not well meaning, as it had seemed to me before? Someone who in his omnipotence is evil, and who perhaps is not the only such powerful entity, and we humans have the misfortune of being his creation and not the creation of some benevolent being? If the Creator was truly good, he would not allow the kind of scenes that I as a scrivener am being forced to see and hear. He would not allow disease and war and misfortune. Possibly, he would not allow even the suffering I have again been so unbearably enduring recently …

'Female, thirty-two years of age, the mother of six children, accused of practising witchcraft, as a result of which the loins of certain women, who are cited by name in the indictment, have been bound,' the judge announces the next case.

'Accused, do you deal in the magic spells mentioned in the indictment?' the judge asks.

'I do!' the woman replies.

'Do you do them alone, or do you have a helper when you do them?'

'I have a helper.'

'Is it somebody from the village?'

'Humph! I could say he was from the village, since he certainly feels at home there, and I've been keeping company with him for a good while myself.'

'And who is this person?'

'The Deeevilll!' the woman cries in a lascivious tone, and at the same time sticks out her tongue and licks her lips.

'Woman, you are violating the civil order! It is forbidden to use profanities in court,' the judge says sternly.

'But that's his name – the Deeevilll!' The accused again cries out the word. 'But my partner and companion also answers to such names as the Evil One, the Adversary, Satan ... I also call him the Impaler, because I impale myself on him at least five times a day!'

The judge turns to the scrivener and shakes his head. 'And why do you perform spells that, as is written in the indictment, prevent other women from having children?'

'I do it from spite, from pure wickedness!' the accused replies.

'And what do you get out of it?' the judge asks.

'It makes me feel better, and I laugh a lot. And laughter's the best medicine – isn't that what they say?' She looks around the courtroom in triumph.

Half the courtroom audience is shouting for her to be sent to the stake immediately, while the other half objects to this idea, saying, 'Not to the stake! We haven't seen a woman this crazy in ages!'

'Woman, are you aware that if you confess to this, you will not escape the stake?'

'Well, it won't escape me either, because stakes don't have legs ...' she replies, and right away, as if she's a little ashamed of the misfired witticism, throws the audience a sheepish look, as the townsfolk let her know they're not happy with the quip. But then she straightens up and pulls out all the stops. 'I'm looking forward to the stake, because straight from there I go into my lover's home, and he won't be boiling me in some cauldron either, oh no! He'll be all the time, endlessly, having his pleasure with me!'

'Oh, wow!' can be heard from the audience.

'Into the fire with her!' come voices from the opposite side.

'If you don't be quiet, I'll have you all thrown out of the courtroom!' the judge says sharply.

'Oh no, we don't want that!' the people shake their heads, because this one is even more interesting than the Holy Spirit's erstwhile virgin.

'But what about your children?'

'Let God worry about them, or the populace! I couldn't care less about raising brats. The only thing I'm interested in this world, before I finally take up residence in hell, is fucking and fucking and more fucking!'

'That's enough!' the judge shouts.

'You mean doing it with him, your horny hornèd huuusband?' the voice of the people enquires.

'Mostly with him, because he's got a dick hard as flint, harder than any other I've sat on, and you all know there's not a man far or wide I wouldn't let screw me. But, greecious jadge, the fellers we got here ain't got nothin between their legs but little worms,' she says, speaking in a funny voice. 'They talk you up a storm at first, but as soon as I lift me skirt up, they're just start shitting themselves. "Well, what's yer problem, ya mushy clappers," I start yellin. "Is somethin' gonna happen or not? Get your damn cocks out so I can suck the juice out of ya, so there'll be nothin left over for those bitches at home! C'mon! What the hell's your problem?" I'm screamin' at them. "Ain't no one gonna fuck me or do I have to wait for some arse-kickin mercenaries to show up so the whole regiment can screw me?"'

'That is enough!' the judge repeats, more firmly this time, and then looks over at the scrivener, lets out a deep sigh and wipes his greasy face with his handkerchief.

'To the stake! To the stake!" one part of the courtroom is bellowing.

'She's mad! She's mad! But she's so entertaining, you can't send her to the stake!' shouts the more refined segment of the public.

'Is there any witness here who will testify against her? Any of the men the accused has alluded to?' the judge asks. He waits for a moment or two and then repeats the question. 'Any witnesses? Nobody? Maybe one of the women whom the accused has allegedly deprived of descendants?'

Not a single woman raises her hand. The demands coming from the audience are getting louder and louder. 'To the stake with her! Let the she-devil burn!' And, from the other side, 'Keep her talking, judge! Because what's the point of us all being here if not to have a really good time?'

'Scrivener, write this,' the judge says, turning to the scrivener. '"The statements made by the accused are completely irrational, which indicates that the woman is insane. Apart from the alleged spells, she has done nothing that violates the *Carolina* criminal code, and the evil she is said to have done has not been confirmed by any witness. There is, therefore, no evidence to support any of the statements she has made nor anything for which she is being accused. I order that she be sent to hospital, and in the meantime I place her in the custody of the parish priest, who in the next few days shall visit her to see if she is more or less all right, if she needs food or anything else. Her children shall be removed from her at once. They shall be cared for by neighbours until they are sent to the orphanage. All expenses shall be borne by the fiefdom."'

'I knew it,' the count's steward slaps his forehead. 'I warned the count that trials like this produce nothing but expenses. We've already exceeded the budget. The count will have my hide if he doesn't throw me in the dungeon. I told him from the start it was a risky investment, and not even with special taxes would he ever see any return on his money. But that cunning prince-bishop of his ...'

'This isn't right! She's got to go the stake! She's spreading disease!' somebody shouts from the courtroom.

'Disease? What sort of disease? Does any of you have a disease you caught from her?' the judge replies. 'If so, then come up here and tell us.'

Shamefaced, the country folk look around furtively, while the townsfolk watch the peasants and laugh at their embarrassment.

'If no one will come forward, then take the woman away. Let's start by getting all the filth washed off her. And then she should say goodbye to her children so they don't go mad themselves living with a crazy mother or die from hunger and disease because of her neglect. The innocent little children are not to blame if their mother's gone crazy on them. And, as I said, until we can take her to hospital, the parish priest should look after her.'

'Look after Satan's whore?' the audience is crackling with laughter.

'We'll get it all worked out,' the judge says. 'The woman's mind is clouded.'

'You think I'm ill? No sirree, I'm not ill. But I got nothin' against the priest – why, I'll fool around with him, too!'

'Oh, wow! Did you hear that?' the townsfolk cry. 'She's going to screw the priest!'

'Well, we're not taking care of her kids, the spawn of the devil's whore!' the country folk are saying.

'Then the fiefdom shall care for the orphans,' the judge rules.

'Fine with me! I don't give a hoot what happens to 'em,' the now-acquitted defendant starts ranting. 'But when their father comes to fetch 'em, if anybody's standing in his way, he'll grab 'em with his talons and stuff 'em into sacks!'

'So he's got talons now, has he?' one of the townsfolk pipes up. 'But we thought your man was a hoofed creature, like goats or bulls or horses? Gracious judge, the witness's testimony lacks consistency ...'

'That's all for today! Everybody out! Starting tomorrow, these sessions are closed to the public.'

'No! Oh, nooo!' come sounds of disapproval and disgruntlement.

'Out! Everybody out!' the judge repeats, as the bailiffs start pushing people out of the door, although some are doing their best to resist.

'We'll complain to the count! We told him explicitly that we wanted to be present at the trial, and he promised us we would be.'

'We townspeople, too – we don't think it's fair to exclude us from such proceedings!'

'They're all complete idiots, townsfolk and peasants alike!' the exhausted judge hisses to the scrivener, who is seated to his right.

'Take her to the dungeon for now until we can find a suitable place for her. And have a bailiff go with two women to her home and bring the children here. And may God send you some trouble to clear your mind a little,' the judge says and tells the scrivener in a whisper not to include this last remark in the record. Air ... I need fresh air, the judge thinks. And my stomach, too, is making its demands. I only hope they don't stint on dinner and it will at least be good enough for human consumption ... Eleven more months and I retire, but, until then, I'll just grit my teeth and somehow keep going.

... until recently I believed I was most myself in those moments when I forgot everything around me and devoted all my attention to thinking. But now, in my reflections, I become a stranger to myself. In the stream of thought coursing through me, I get strange ideas, ideas I don't know how to, am unable to, resist. I am tormented by unwanted thoughts. By fears – as when I don't know if I shut the birdcage door or not. By worries – that my bird will suddenly get sick ... Or that when I least expect it, officials will knock on my door and send me off to some unpleasant assignment ... or guards will knock on her door and cart her away and what comes next will be what always comes next in such cases.

I've recently become obsessed with the idea that whatever forces itself into my thoughts will happen in reality, too. Bad things ... Horrible things ... I must leave at once, immediately!

But not only did the judge not make it to retirement, he did not make it to the next day. He did, however, get some fresh air and his late dinner was tasty. But one mustn't rely on taste or on the senses in general, which can be deceptive and their deception fatal. The boiled beef was delicious, the succulent roast duck not the least bit dry, the smoked trout with barley mash and horseradish was excellent, the pea sauce melted in the mouth like butter, the salad was fresh and dressed with cider vinegar and even olive oil and sea salt, the latter ingredients having been supplied by Triestine merchants. But the delicious meal, never fully digested, was also the judge's last.

When, after dinner, he went to take a rest and was reclining in a comfortable armchair on the terrace and gazing out at the gentle hills covered in orchards and vineyards, which were glowing with warm autumn hues, he started to bring up wind, which was followed by stomach cramps, and, halfway to the privy, he collapsed in the middle of the room and lay there on the oak parquet. The servants heard the fall and at once came running; they tried to help him vomit, but this only made the digestive problems worse, bringing on convulsions and nausea. The count, still in his hunting garb, rushed in soon after, nervously rubbing his beard with his knuckles. As he watched the judge fight for his life, he begged help from all the saints and at the same time was cursing at the servants, 'But I warned you to be careful and pay special attention to everything the judge put on his plate!' The other members of the judicial council had taken their meals separately, while the executioner and his assistant, whom nobody had wanted to eat with, had used their *per diem* to treat themselves to a feast in the darkest corner of their inn.

'The scrivener – what about the scrivener Nikolai?' the count asked his staff.

'The scrivener did not take part in the dinner. As soon as the court session was over, he got on a horse and left. He was not in the best of moods; we thought he seemed very tense. His eyes, we noticed, were unusually bright. He said nothing about where he was going or if he would be coming back tonight.'

'Did he eat before he left?' the count asks.

'No, sir.'

'So the judge ate alone?'

'Yes, sir, alone, if we don't count your two old greyhounds who had strategically crept up to the table and were begging for bones by the judge's feet.'

'Did the dogs eat anything?'

'The judge must have tossed them a bone or two or a piece of meat. There was enough food on the table for three – we expected you and the scrivener to be dining with the judge; the other members of the council we served separately.'

'Why did you do that?' the count asks angrily.

'We were told to do it,' the servants reply.

'Who told you to do it?'

They look down at the floor.

'Well, are the dogs all right?' the count asks.

'They're dozing contentedly in the corner. There doesn't seem to be anything wrong with them at all.'

'So if the dogs had no problem digesting the meal, then what did the judge have besides the meat, which I'm told was beef?' the count asks.

'Only good things. There was salad ...'

'Forget the salad!' the count interrupts.

'There was barley mash as a side dish, and buckwheat porridge, a bit of boiled turnip and kohlrabi, pea sauce ...'

'What sort of sauce?' the count interrupts again.

'Pea sauce. The judge was most happy with it, as the footmen noticed when they were serving him …'

'With all of these dishes, there are many things that can be mixed into them which might certainly end the eater's life within minutes or days.' This came from the physician, who was standing in the doorway. 'Was any mushroom dish served?'

The cook, who is extremely upset, insists there was not. 'I didn't dare include mushrooms on the menu so there'd be no chance of anything like this happening. Who else but me will be blamed for this tragic mishap? I'm facing a death sentence; I've accepted that. It's a risky profession, cooking for the nobility and people in high places; sooner or later there's some complication, and then it's always the cook's fault, no one else's …'

'Do be quiet!' the count interrupts him. 'I'm sure you're not involved. But something must have been sprinkled or mixed into the food after it was prepared – that I do not doubt,' says the count, who by now is shaking. 'What about the dessert?'

'It makes not the slightest difference whether it was raspberries or cake,' says the physician. 'I find that the judge's pulse is getting weaker and weaker, his complexion is turning a yellowish grey, bubbles are starting to come out of his mouth – another moment or two and he'll be gone … I don't feel a pulse any more, and there's no more condensation on the mirror from the judge's breath, so I declare at this moment that the judge has died under suspicious circumstances. But I am convinced that even if I had arrived just as the judge was starting to feel sick, there is nothing that I, or any of my profession, could have done. We do not yet know what sort of poison was added to his food; to determine this, there will have to be certain examinations.'

'That's all I need,' the count moans. 'The provincial sheriff will be furious! And what about that scrivener from the town? Was he hanging about anywhere near the food?'

'It's as we told you, gracious Count. He ran straight from the courtroom to the stables where he got on his horse, Maron, and rode off God knows where.'

'I demand an examination of the deceased's victuals, which will be your responsibility, physician!'

'Are the funds to cover this guaranteed?' the physician enquires.

'Yes, they are, damn you!' the count replies.

'I am only asking so there won't be any problem later with the payment ...' the physician says, scratching his chin.

'And you,' the count turns to his steward. 'Round up anyone who was hanging around here today. And all of you, prepare your statements. Have the judge carried to the dungeon. You're scoundrels one and all! As if this idiotic trial was my idea! Summon my secretary – he needs to compose two letters for me right away, to Prince-Bishop Wolfgang and Mayor Falke.'

'As you command, my most gracious lord.'

'"My most gracious lord"!' Friedrich repeats. 'I've had it with you sycophantic scoundrels! Any one of you could have done this. Everyone has his price, for a certain fee anyone can be bought ...' he says, cursing under his breath.

'What happened to him?' most people were wondering as the evening of that autumn day approached .

'So it really did happen, then?' some were exchanging glances.

'So it's done? Finished?' a handful whispered among themselves.

It is not finished yet, populace. Very soon, as soon as late October, there will be a second trial. And this one will not be over in just a day or two.

WHAT IF ...? OH, NO!

Ever since I came back from the trial, which was suspended after the death of the judge, I don't sleep any more. I sit in my room. I think. I write. I turn the goose quill in my hand and stare at the log smouldering in the fireplace – the cold autumn damp chills me to the bone and is driving me into a boundless melancholy.

An idea crosses my mind. What if, in fact, it is not me who is thinking, but I only think that I am thinking? What if the one who endowed me with the capacity for thought has given me the wrong idea about my own thinking, and actually I am nothing more than a conduit through which the stream of thought is flowing? And therefore, the one who gives me my capacity for thought is not a good God but a deceptive devil, who misleads me by instilling in me the idea of a benevolent and infinite perfect being? How can I be sure that he is not able to do such a thing? That he does not have evil desires and intentions? The Creator could have made man differently, so he would not be so easily drawn to error and corruption. He might, indeed, have created a free being with a more refined sense of good and evil.

I cannot explain why I was so shaken by the court proceedings that I immediately saddled my horse and rushed home. The judge was right. My thoughts often wandered during the trial. I was thinking about all sorts of things until finally the wall paintings started to move and came to life, and the horses on the walls were restlessly stomping their hoofs, and then the knights donned their helmets and charged at each other with their spears. Nobody forced me to disappear right after the trial. And yet, had I stayed, the judge's fate would very likely have been mine as well. Should I be thankful to God for this escape? Is there even anyone to whom I can be thankful for this?

When I lose consciousness during my syncopal swoons, I am no longer there. My body is alive, but during those moments without consciousness, I know nothing at all about the life processes operating inside it. It is possible that I exist only when the deceiver is thinking through me, and when he stops thinking, I swoon, melt away and disappear, as I disappear in dreams, for the one that is in dreams is not me. Where do I go when I experience an attack? Where does my consciousness go? What does my reason dissolve into? … Where does my self go?

It is possible that the Creator takes pleasure in misleading his creation, that this is his joy, and he plays games with me because I have shown such enthusiasm, passion and willingness for these matters. But isn't the fact that the Creator has any desire at all only proof of his incompleteness, his imperfection? And is free will merely a human illusion? And is the deceiver's thought wrapped in what is allegedly my thinking self, which is nothing more than an empty nothing?

Even worse, what if the Creator, whatever he is, does not actually exist?

And this allegedly free will is merely the effect of certain physical processes and an organic automatism?

I no longer have any solid foundation, nothing that might give me certainty …

The world is fragile, damaged completely …

URGENT

'At last, Friedrich! I've been inviting you for years to visit my episcopal palace, and now you are finally here! Although I'm told it's because of problems in your fiefdom,' Prince-Bishop Wolfgang greets his guest. 'Tonight, in your honour, I've prepared a special performance in the orangery, with my little angels. You'll see how wonderfully they sing, and dance, too ...'

'I'll be going back tonight,' Friedrich responds. 'It's all gone wrong. Things have got out of hand. I should never have listened to you ...'

'It's mainly because you didn't listen to me that the situation in your fiefdom has run into trouble. Why did you and that mayor try to undermine our plans? Why did you prevent the chosen judge from overseeing the trial and instead had him replaced by that super-annuated, dithering milksop? I'm told he was dreadfully lenient and understanding and that he applied certain soul-based doctrines and viewed delusions and madness as extenuating circumstances, and said he was going to exclude the populace from the proceedings, which was, for him, a fatal mistake. And you, I hear, were absent from the trial, purportedly because you were detained at the hunt ... tsk tsk tsk ...'

'If I couldn't bear to pull the legs off frogs when I was a child, how could I be present at such a massacre?' Friedrich says in despair.

'But that's just the problem – there was no massacre. Besides, Friedrich, when the trial is being held in your own castle, you have at least to make an appearance; that's why things have run amok and you're in the present situation. I heard that you've ordered an investigation, which is good. The deceased is not the first or last judge who's been the victim of his own court proceedings. And, indeed, it had nothing to do with him personally, only his wrong-headed methods. Why did you ever let yourself be persuaded by that mayor, who, as you know, moves in rather dubious circles? I advised you not to rush things; the trial needed to develop over time, a few weeks at least. There had to be a certain ceremony. I implored you to let the populace have their fill of blood, for then they'd be more malleable, more willing to accept whatever measures you might impose.'

'The very thought of it turns my stomach. And now the provincial sheriff has sent a team of inspectors to the castle to investigate the judge's death. His officials are all over my castle; they don't even knock before entering a room.'

'But, taken all together, it's really not so terrible,' the prince-bishop says as he makes himself comfortable in a chair.

'How can it not be terrible?'

'I've seen to everything. Your physician will put together a report saying he found no trace of poison in the judge's body, but that he did discover lumpy formations in the stomach, which had burst during ingestion and were entirely cancerous. In addition, I have personally sent you a man of ours from the provincial government – I'm sorry, but politesse is entirely foreign to him – and the results of his investigation will provide expert corroboration of your physician's findings.'

'But my physician is an honest man ...' the count says.

'Who has a particularly honest interest in money. And money is like the plague. At first you think, "Not me, no! I won't get sick. I fumigate the rooms with juniper, I don't touch infected corpses, I don't open my door to anyone who looks suspicious." But it doesn't help. All at once you feel a black lump under your arm and are a little queasy, and a day or two later you're in your bed waiting for death to take you. Only a very few are resistant to plague, and even fewer are able to resist the gleam of gold. So pay your physician for his investigation, and I will take care of the expert with the second opinion, and the provincial authorities will be thoroughly satisfied with their scientifically supported analyses.'

'And after that?' the count asks.

'After that, we will send you a second criminal judge. Someone very different from the first.'

'Who will that be?'

'You've heard of him – Fabjančič.'

'Fabjančič?' The count turns white.

'He will execute the proceedings in the fullest sense of the term.'

Friedrich grabs hold of his chair; nausea washes over him and his eyes fill with fog.

'My gracious Count, why, you are quite pale. Let's have some supper, and then after supper, the angels ...'

'I have lost all appetite, Wolfgang. I must leave at once. Maybe I can still do something; maybe I can prevent ...'

'It's too late, Friedrich. From the very start it was too late. Everything was decided even before I came to see you. But it will pass; all things pass ... And then it will be better. Maybe even good. Very good. Well, no, it will never be very good.'

(A Letter to the Supremely Noble and Beautiful Widow)

My most graciously charming beauty,

Terrible rumours are being spread. But I am filled with the feeling that as long as I can preserve you in the stream of my consciousness you will be safe and nothing bad can happen to you. And that is possible only when I am writing to you. For when I am not writing, it often happens that I merely think that I am thinking, and thoughts without order mill around my head … conjoin into meanings … and are even more ruttish for non-meanings …

Oh, beloved beauty, who, sadly, will never be mine, my wonderful angel, how terribly I am afraid for you! Evil men are lying in wait for you! They have planned a most dreadful fate for you, a fate that has befallen so many women already. Oh, my beloved, why do you not believe me but think that I am feverish and ill? It's true that I am feverish, for I burn and glow, but the fires within me are what give me life – and they are very different from the fires they intend for you, which will destroy you … But not your soul; your most wonderful soul will go straight to heaven – or maybe not, maybe it won't go anywhere – but your, and I am almost afraid to say it, your no less wonderful body … your body … Ah, my dearest! I am appalled by the image of your body disappearing for all eternity with the burning wood … oh, horror … oh, God, in whom I no longer believe … oh, everything … oh, nothing … oh, more and more, nothing …

Yet Another Blow
from the Noble Widow

'My gracious lady, your devoted friend, the scrivener Nikolai Miklavž Paulin, would like a word with you. He has been trying his hardest, sending us messages; his courier brings them to us a dozen a day ...' the servants complain to the noble widow.

'Let Mayor Falke deal with him. I know he sent his physician to him, but the scrivener rudely sent him away,' the widow replies.

'You could ask your friends for help; they might have some powder, or maybe they know somebody. Or you could try the mayor again. Because, gracious lady, conveying all those messages of his, both written and oral, is most exhausting.'

'Don't be so dramatic. There are plenty of people who'd be glad to have your jobs, so stop all your moaning and grumbling. I have no intention of speaking to madmen! I refuse to see him!'

'Most gracious lady,' the housekeeper now speaks up, 'I was told by the scrivener's housekeeper that he's not sleeping any more, or eating. He only writes, and he says peculiar things when he's writing. If you were to receive him, and especially if the doctor and Mayor Falke were present, he might just agree to submit to some therapy, some cure. But I'm not sure, of course. I don't know much about madness and such,' the housekeeper says.

'It's best not to admit you know anything. These days, knowing something can arouse suspicions. But I'm just joking. Things are hardly as serious as certain people think, who go around scaring others.'

'Even so, we fear there might be some truth in his ramblings – some terribly unpleasant truth ...'

'Oh, please! What are you talking about?' the widow says angrily.

'My gracious lady, it has reached my ear as well that something is under way which will be the ruin of all of us, and you most especially,' the chief servant says.

'Do not frighten me! Our mayor is a rational man; he would not let this happen,' the widow replies.

'Not him, no. But what can he do when there are others who are more powerful? And everyone has someone for whose sake they are prepared to give way and let even the most horrible things happen.'

'Not with us. It's not possible ... They have already tried and failed,' the widow says.

'It's because they failed that they will now have their revenge,' the housekeeper makes another attempt.

'I beg you, gracious lady,' her secretary says.

'If not for yourself, think of us, think of our loved ones,' the chief servant continues. 'If they are going after you, they'll put pressure on us, too; they'll try to make us to say the impossible, to speak lies and bear false witness, and with the methods they use, they will succeed. Our souls will be strong at first, but our bodies – the body is weaker than the soul and sooner or later it will give in and the soul will break, and not only the body, but the soul, too, will fail, because of the lies we'll have told, and then it will be forever lost.'

'Don't start getting pious on me! Nothing is going to happen. It will all be fine,' the widow replies in a soothing tone.

'But it won't all be fine. A lot of things are going to happen, and then nothing will be left.'

'I'm so awfully bored with you all! Fine, have it your way. I will write a letter to the mayor and ask him to look after that deluded madman. And then I'm not dealing with this any more!'

'Thank you, gracious lady! A million thanks!'

'What cowards!' she says to herself, and then she sits down and takes a blank sheet of paper and a goose quill from the drawer.'

'But what should we do with the scrivener?' a servant asks. 'Ever since morning, if not all night, he's been standing outside in front of the house motionless, looking up at your window.'

'I've had it with him! I've had it with those importunate looks of his! For months he's been slinking around me like some malnourished dog!' the widow says sharply. Then she walks over to the window, throws open the sash and stares down in fury at the scrivener.

EVERYTHING IS OPEN

Like my bird in his copper cage, I am captive in this body. Is it even mine? I don't think it is. But today I am a little bit better, whatever I am or am not.

Only now, Spiritus, do I understand what a terrible wrong I have done you, keeping you here out of love. What do you have of life here? Food and water, yes, and my increasingly incomprehensible blather – I wouldn't be surprised if by now my vocal musings are terribly annoying to you. But, Spiritus, you don't know much about life. With me you would have a long, safe life, but also a stupid one. So let's settle this matter of captivity and freedom right now. I will open your cage, and I'll open the window, too, so you can smell the scent of freedom, and then *you* decide whether to fly away or stay. But, I warn you, if you leave, your life will be counted not in years, as it might well be if you stay, but, I expect, in hours or seconds. So, Spiritus, who are completely unprepared for the normal life of a bird, you must make the decision, whether it is instinct or some sort of intelligence that guides you. Maybe, indeed, you have understood something of my babbling, and you've probably learned a thing or two from Mitzi as well. Her lessons I am sure you understood. Whenever she would be lingering by the cage, with her bushy red tail and long whiskers, you'd get frightened and pick at your feathers, which would fly all over the room. Look, Spiritus! The cage door is open, and even more open is my heart, which from this moment on sets you free even from the cage called love. You are free! I free you from my love and from this brass structure, which has protected you even as it confined you. So consider your choice carefully: safety or freedom; love or freedom. Choose, my darling. No longer is there anything that can keep you in this worthless cage. And me, too – there is nothing that keeps me in my cage any more. No more strictures, no more structures, no more windows or doors. Not only your cage, dear bird, but mine, too, in which, like you, I've been languishing safe and sound for years, is from this day forth wide open.

I do not know what you will decide, dear bird.

But as for me, regardless of what happens, I am leaving.

The Physician Meets
with Mayor Falke

'So it's melancholy?' Mayor Falke suggests, standing in front of the physician.

'Black bile,' the physician confirms. 'The scrivener is a tender soul. Even to look at him, he seems honest, which only means he's not really cut out for this life. And so he suffers. And he's suffering, too, I hear, from an irrational infatuation with that widow, who, only recently, first refused to see him and then, in front of the servants, shouted at him through the window, calling him a madman and bitterly humiliating him.'

'But he still has another job to do,' the mayor says. 'Criminal judges and their scriveners are dropping like flies around here – or vanishing without a trace. For a day, at most two days, we need him to replace Judge Fabjančič's scrivener for the trial at the castle. Something very strange happened. On their way to Count Friedrich's, the judge and his team stopped at an inn; Fabjančič, the executioner and the executioner's assistant all went to bed, but the judge's scrivener decided to have another beer before turning in. Who can say if it was just one beer or possibly more? In any case, in the morning, the scrivener was nowhere to be found.'

'Falke, I beg you! Your scrivener will go completely mad in such a situation, I'm sure of it! He may go so far as to disrobe in the middle of the trial, which is what people like him do under extreme pressure. And then they will arrest him and add him to the list of the accused. You are his employer, his protector – look after him!'

'But I can't.'

'You can't or you don't dare?'

'Both,' the mayor replies.

'I strongly advise you to remove him from all possible assignments and convince him to submit to treatment. Cold-water showers and baths can sometimes be effective, although usually they aren't. But I know of one medicinal method from ancient times that might be worth trying. But we would need to purchase the tools, since they don't live around here.'

'Tools that live?' the mayor asks, surprised.

'There are in the sublunary world invisible forces that have tremendous effects. We don't know much about how they work, but when a person is afflicted by the kind of severe illness that's attacking your scrivener, it's worth trying something out, even if it's not fully tested.'

'But I don't understand. Are you talking about plants, minerals, some alchemical substance?' the mayor asks.

'No, I'm talking about fish, certain live fish, which have a remarkable property. When they attack their prey, or are themselves attacked by an enemy – which they consider to be anything that pokes at them – they release an unusual jolting force. I'm suggesting the rhomboidal narke fish, which are depicted in the floor mosaic of the basilica in Aquileia. You'll need to have them brought here from the sea. The locals there are familiar with them and know how to catch them. Two of these creatures are then released into a pool. The melancholiac is sent into the pool, and the fish cause him to shake so much it clears his mind,' the physician explains.

'Are you certain? Is it safe?' the mayor looks at him doubtfully.

'In one's travels a person sees and encounters all sorts of things. I haven't heard that anyone has ever been harmed by the fish; on the contrary, they have cured many people of lethargy and over-excitability. I expect your Triestine merchant-woman could procure them for you.'

'But how do we get them through customs?' the mayor asks.

'As fish, esteemed mayor, as very delicate live fish, which you will be importing for your fish ponds.'

'Which, however, are not saltwater ponds ...' the mayor says.

'Well, we can add a little salt.'

'That's all you have?'

'It's more than other physicians could offer you.'

'So what should we do with the scrivener in the meantime?'

'He should be given black resin regularly, in small doses, but care is needed; a person can easily become too fond of it too quickly,' the physician says.

'His housekeeper won't have the skill to do that.'

'And, I'm telling you, keep him out of that trial. Bring him here to your house, lock him in a room until he comes to his senses. If you want what's best for him, don't let him out of your sight. And this, too – collect his writings and hide them somewhere. In these sensitive times, if the wrong eyes see them, it will surely lead to his death.'

I AM FADING

When I stand in front of the mirror, I do not recognize myself. The person in the mirror is not me. The image that is supposedly mine is not the same as the image I have seen here previously. It is distorted. Disfigured.

At first I thought there must be something wrong with the mirror; after all, badly made mirrors start rippling over time. But the same warped me also appears in the mirrors in the mayor's residence, when I see my reflection in the hallway on the way to his office. When I asked my housekeeper if she noticed any change in me, she just looked at me with a strange bug-eyed stare.

I can't hold on to anything any more. I scatter like star dust, which crackles off a star and dissipates in all directions. Into infinity, which, however, is not the eternity you reach, as I once believed, when you enter the afterlife geography you have earned through your deeds and thoughts, as decided at the Last Judgement by our Creator. Our Creator? Whose Creator? Hahahaha!

Every day I drink a tea brewed from St John's wort and camomile, as well as an infusion of hellebore and certain other herbs which my housekeeper gets from the gypsies, but nothing calms me any more. Nothing stops me. I observe the hands on this body, the fingers that hold the quill and are incessantly writing. If I could only for a moment step outside this stranger, if I was able to step outside this body, perhaps I could reassemble myself into an approximation, at least, of what I once was. The way burlesquers remove themselves from the stage and go behind the curtain and then, a little later, return. But here, in this life, there is neither stage nor curtain and no possibility of removing yourself from yourself, at least not a voluntary removal in which you retain awareness and consciousness. Awareness and consciousness? Hahaha! Does anyone still care about such things? I don't, not any longer!

Before Fleeing

Without knocking, Mayor Falke flings open the door and steps boldly into the rooms of the noble widow.

'Esteemed Mayor Falke! How dare you!' she recoils, but the mayor interrupts her.

'Gracious lady, I see you have not heeded my advice and packed bags for a hasty retreat. So, without delay, you must gather up only the most necessary things, put on this black robe and say goodbye to your dogs,' he tells her sharply.

'What are you talking about? I don't understand ... Pack bags? Say goodbye?' The noble widow looks at him in amazement.

'Brother Philip, who is going with you, will explain everything to you during the journey – which will be long enough for you to become convinced of the urgency of your departure and start believing in it.'

'But ...'

'Gracious lady, I have information from reliable sources that an indictment against you has been written and is on its way to our town. People will be here before morning to arrest you on the charge of Sabbat witchcraft and cart you off to the Town Hall. There you will be interrogated by the provincial court. They have prepared some very picturesque forms of pain and suffering for you. So, I tell you, you must this very instant gather up only what is essential for the journey – where you are going you will have everything you need, maybe even more than what you have here.'

'And where, exactly, are you sending me?'

'To a lady I know, a dear friend, in the Venetian Republic.'

'And who would that be? Not, perhaps, that *opera singer* and ...'

'She is one of the most enchanting women in Venice, or anywhere for that matter. In our land, there is not her equal.'

'But this lady, this opera singer – she's not just a singer, is she? Primarily, she's a ...'

'She is a lady of many talents and abilities, and I myself would be hard pressed to say if she is more exquisite in her public or private performances.'

'You are sending me to a courtesan!'

'Gracious young lady, I am turning away so you can disguise yourself in a Jesuit's black robe, and in the meantime let me give you some wise advice: stop resting on the laurels of your victory over the Jesuits – it is getting boring and, for you, perilous. It's high time you take responsibility for your own life. Will you remain single, a widow to the end of your days? That's not a bad social position to have, given your status as a noblewoman, for it offers you more freedom than if you remarry. But, let me warn you, as the years pass, or, to put it another way, as you age, you will start feeling lonely. And you have nothing of what that Venetian lady has, which might offer you satisfaction beyond your intimate relations. You can live out your life in widowhood, or you can remarry, or you can assemble a discreet network of lovers, but – and again let me warn you – they will not remain hidden, for men are even bigger blabbermouths than women and are braggarts most of all. You can enter a convent and devote your life to God, perhaps to the healing sciences, but I doubt that interests you. Only stop playing the part of the rebellious ingénue – for with your social status, age and experience, you haven't been that in a long time. I could have sent you to the Palatinate, Württemberg or Cologne, but I decided to spare you that tight-arsed German Protestantism and instead am sending you to a free country permeated with Catholicism, which has far greater feeling for refined and fleshly, sinful and, indeed, aesthetic pleasures.'

'But you don't expect me to live ...'

'No, you won't be living with Constanza, who owns not only a luxurious palace near the Rialto but also a few smaller houses on the lagoon islands. One of these she has set aside for you, along with a dependable staff of servants and everything else you will need.'

'But what about my good name?' the widow asks.

'There will be nothing at all wrong with your reputation when you get there, but you will still need to earn a good name for yourself.

You'll be arriving in a Jesuit robe as a young widow from the provinces who has escaped mayhem by a whisker. And, don't forget, you're not some helpless beggar-woman but a relatively well-off member of the lower nobility who will be paying her own expenses in Venice. So you will be dependant neither on her nor on me, but solely and exclusively on yourself.'

'But what about my dogs?'

'Do you not think that two Jesuits travelling with two apricot dogs might look suspicious? The dogs stay here, and they will be extremely well cared for. When things calm down, I personally will bring them to you in Venice.'

When the mayor turns his head for a moment to look at her, he is dumbfounded. 'Why, you're not taking me seriously! You haven't even changed …'

'But who could consider me so terribly suspicious? Besides, they have no evidence against me. And the story with that Jesuit is no proof – he more or less made the whole thing up,' the widow objects.

'Young lady, you will put that Jesuit robe on right now, or I will undress you with my own hands and put it on you myself!'

'Esteemed mayor …' she says seductively, lowering her eyes.

'Stop fooling around!' the mayor snaps back. 'I had my fill years ago of women feigning naïveté. You owe a boundless debt of gratitude to Brother Philip of the Jesuits. At the insistence of your admirer, Nikolai – whom, I hear, you have brutally humiliated – Brother Philip has been monitoring events, and when the news reached his ear that they intended to come after you, he informed me at once. This was also recently confirmed to me by the prince's commissioner. The point is not so much to make you suffer, but to force you to give them the names they want. You are a spoiled noblewoman who has no idea what the world is like. It's true you were the victim of your late husband, but now you are a victim of your own illusions. I won't hear another word of lament out of you. The scrivener warned you, and so did your servants, and believe me, both the scrivener and your servants, as well as your friends and acquaintances – they will all be pulled into this trial.'

'But they can't go after everyone …'

'It's never about everyone. It's about a few individuals who can serve as a reminder to everyone, and for that role, you are more than ideal.'

'How long will I have to stay in Venice?' she asks.

'At least until things calm down here. But don't worry about that now and just hope that you and Brother Philip arrive there safely and without incident. Even for two humble Jesuits the road to Venice can be dangerous, but, in fact, you won't be going all the way to Venice on foot and horseback. Once you are out of these parts, more comfortable transportation has been arranged for you.'

'But what am I supposed to do in Venice?' the widow frowns.

'That depends on your imagination. Apart from reading, socializing and cultivating your mind – for which you will have vastly more opportunities in Venice than here in the provinces – I recommend you take up swimming, since you'll be living on one of those wonderful Venetian islands. The sea has an immensely purifying effect. Yes, definitely learn how to swim, so in the future you'll be able to swim out disagreeable situations on your own, or at least be able to keep your head above water.'

'Were you the one who helped my predecessor? When she went to Istria or wherever it was?'

'She was a woman of a different mettle and knew quite well how to help herself.'

'But how will I manage there ... on my own?'

'Stop complaining! Many women would literally kill to have the status of a wealthy young widow. You are in a far more privileged position than you imagine, so pull yourself together this instant! You can, of course, go on playing the role of the beautiful widow who's a little daft, but, let me warn you, as the years pass you will be less and less the slightly daft beautiful widow and more and more just daft.'

'Why are you doing this? Why are you helping me? You don't need to.'

'I could leave you to your own devices and keep my head down like any spineless coward. Why I risk my life and the life of my family, not to mention the town itself, I really don't know. It just seems right to me, full stop. But there's no time to waste words. Get yourself ready. Brother Philip, who is also risking his life doing this, will be here any moment. I advise you to start learning some Italian right away, on your journey. With your solid foundation in Latin, it won't be hard ... Oh, by the way,' the mayor, now standing in the doorway, turns to face her, 'the first word you might want to remember is *frotto-lara*, which, in the Venetian language, is what they call the kind of singer your hostess is ...'

BEFORE THE SECOND TRIAL

Heavy pounding on the scrivener's door. And the same three bailiffs as before the first trial burst into his room.

'Oh, this time I must have made a mistake! Why, it seems we haven't even gone to bed yet, have we? We're still working, writing, scribbling ...' the chief bailiff attacks him, just as before.

'Scrivener Nikolai hasn't slept for days ...' says the housekeeper, out of breath and wheezing, as she enters behind the bailiffs.

'Quiet, woman! Nobody asked you anything! Come on, scribbler, let's go! Get dressed!'

'Where are we going this time?' the scrivener asks.

'It's a big surprise. Now hurry up! Don't keep us waiting like last time. And I'd better not see any shutters opening and someone wriggling out of the window!'

'Leave him alone! Scrivener Nikolai is not feeling well, he's much too exhausted ...' the housekeeper tries to defend him.

'And who are you to judge his feelings and abilities?'

'I'm his housekeeper, and I know him very well ...'

'Shut up, old woman!' the chief bailiff snaps at her.

'Why are you barking at her, you flunkeys? Because you don't have the guts to bark at your masters?'

'Ooooh! This time we're really awake! And we dare to speak so hoity-toity to the provincial authorities' official representatives! If we didn't have orders to deliver you intact, believe me, big mouth, we'd be carrying you there piece by piece. It's going to be hard not to give you a few good kicks on the way.'

'Go ahead! Kick me, bite me, swear at me – I don't care! I'm not going anywhere!' Nikolai says firmly.

'Is this resistance? You're resisting the provincial authorities? You will not escape the gallows! All right, lads, we'll just go and tell the higher-ups that he didn't want to come with us and let them decide the best way to punish a big-mouth layabout who refuses to execute an official provincial decree. This time it's serious, scribbler-boy, not like last time, when you ticked off a day and then got to go home because of a bit of unpleasantness, and with a hefty fee, too, even though you never finished the job. Now you'll be grinding away till the work is done. And this new judge isn't some bought-and-paid-for mama's boy like the old one, who got what was coming to him, thank God. All those accused witches, and he wanted to let them off, just because of some so-called diseases or lack of evidence. Oh yes, Nicky boy, this time you're going to earn your pay. Your courtroom labour won't be over in a day or two. This new criminal judge is not some unknown – he might be new here, but he's got a long and notorious reputation.'

'But why does it have to be me – again?' the scrivener asks.

'Maybe because you've got such gooorgeous handwriting – maybe that's why they always want you … Now, let's go!'

'Esteemed mayor …' With distraught eyes, the scrivener gazes at his employer.

'I am sorry, Nikolai. On this occasion I am completely powerless,' the mayor responds.

'Who is the criminal judge?' Nikolai asks.

'Fabjančič …'

'Fabjančič?'

'His scrivener disappeared last night. At the inn where the judge and his team were staying. Late in the evening, a tall, long-haired man arrived, accompanied by other long-haired men just like him. When he was about to sit down, he suddenly collapsed on the floor and started shaking, right there between the tables. As he was rolling around, he pointed up at the ceiling and, in broken sentences, cried out that the devil was dozing in a room above the inn and that he would soon be opening the doors to hell and flames would consume many innocent people. And a terrible punishment from God would rain down not only on that devil but on everyone in his retinue – the longhair said this as he was writhing on the floor – and that four horsemen were that very night thundering through our land: the first

314

one held a bow in his hand, the second a sword, the third was holding scales and the fourth was as pale as death. Anyone who remained with them – and again the longhair points to the ceiling – would be struck down by plague, war, famine and death! "But whoever comes with us," he said, "will be saved!" So it looks like,' Mayor Volk, with a slight smile, concludes the anecdote, 'the judge's scrivener decided to be saved.'

'I won't be able … I can't any more …' Nikolai says, exhausted.

'Just hold on for these few days, Nikolai, until they can send a new provincial scrivener to the castle. And besides, how can you write about the world if you haven't really experienced it? And the world, as you know, is composed of horrible things as well. Now, hurry. They're waiting for you. When you're done with this, come and stay with me for a while.'

HEATING UP

All is ready for the arrival of the criminal judge and his team. The necessary instruments have been polished, from needles to pincers, and so has the brand-new rack, which the castle gentry ordered from a tradesman in the market town. Kostanšek's daughter is waiting, locked in one of the castle's dungeons. But as for Kostanšek himself, nobody knows where he is. He has simply vanished.

The populace condemns him for this. His daughter is about to be interrogated, they say; the poor girl will be suffering, and he goes off somewhere, probably on some money-making business deals. Where there's an excess of money, the devil's work is much easier than in humbler circumstances, where people in their poverty are constantly turning for help to God, the populace reasoned. Rich people can soon start thinking they don't need God, and where there is no God, evil most easily flourishes. What the populace had really been expecting was that Kostanšek, as a shattered father, would be pleading humbly in front of the castle, begging forgiveness and promising to do whatever was possible. That they would at last see Kostanšek the way they liked him best, as he had once been, in that terrible year not so long ago, when illness had destroyed half of his family. That was the Kostanšek the populace wanted: shattered, humble, humiliated, for only one who is shattered, humble and humiliated can be a good Christian. It would be good if he could at least rage and rail against God, like that Old Testament Job, who was similarly beset by sudden misfortunes. But Kostanšek did nothing. He just vanished, and meanwhile his daughter, poor girl, was counting the moments to her interrogation by the judicial council, who, without compassion and with cold, neutral methods, would get the truth out of the accused with the help of white-hot instruments, searing concoctions and solutions, which leave deep scars that never heal, as well as Spanish boots and devices for breaking bones, all these things and more, right up to the predictable end. Death. 'Poor girl, poor girl!' the populace keeps repeating, but is that what they truly think? No, not at all.

With a different father and in different circumstances, she would have been spared all this misery. But now it is what it is. The girl is in the clutches of the Evil One, and it's her father's fault, because he brought those odd foreigners to his farm. And only death will snatch her from the devil's claws. If the poor girl repents of her sins, maybe she can still avoid hell. But it's in God's hands, and we, the populace, are one of God's fingers – the pointing finger on his right hand.

The interrogation of Kostanšek's daughter had been going on since morning. The populace was waiting in front of the castle, but Kostanšek was still nowhere to be seen. The populace wondered if he might not be afraid of suffering the same fate as his daughter. It's too bad the interrogation is taking place behind the castle's closed doors, because they would like to hear her testimony, and maybe her screams, too. But such interrogations normally happen in dungeons. They are the best places for getting at the truth, for conversations and confessions, which the questioners so brutally pull out of their victims that sometimes after such dialogues not another word will slip from the interrogated's mouth, but only some ant or worm. That's how it was in the past, and that's how it will be in the future, too.

Despite the poor transmission of sound, there was news coming out of the dank dungeon; it was being delivered, for a fee, by bailiffs, who informed the populace, 'The girl has started screaming, but she hasn't confessed to anything yet.'

'She's as stubborn as her father, but they'll make her talk; they'll break her,' the populace commented; they no longer felt sympathy for the girl, and their only worry was whether the news they were paying the castle flunkeys for was true or not. They wanted to know if the witch was writhing on the rack, they wanted to hear her screams, to see all the things they were doing to her ...

'You sure about that?' one of the castle bailiffs asks. 'Because it won't be long now before all the pain and misery make her remember who helped her do what she did.'

'What, she had helpers?' the populace asks in surprise.

'Once they turn the screws a little tighter, she'll squeal out the name of the person who joined her in her witchery,' the bailiffs tell them.

'You mean didn't she do it alone?' they continue to be surprised.

'Pay up, populace, and we'll tell you,' the bailiffs say.

'Hold on now, bailiffs, just you hold on. What sort of helpers? Who are you talking about?'

'Who exactly, they don't know yet, but who else could it be, if not one of you?'

'That's impossible! We had nothing to do with her!' The populace is agitated.

'We'll listen in and let you know. But the information won't be cheap; it'll cost more than what you've paid so far. For the person whose name is uttered, this will be a decisive moment.'

'We're not guilty of anything ...'

'Like we said, we'll listen in, and, in the meantime, you fill up some money bags ...'

People start turning pale and look at each other carefully. They are uneasy; it will be hard to sleep from now on. Because there's a chance that the Kostanšek girl will mention their name, mention his name, her name, the name of someone close to them.

'We could pray,' one of them suggests.

'Pray for what?' another asks.

'Pray that it doesn't hurt her so much that she starts telling lies from the pain.'

'We could pray that it hurts her so terribly that she dies from the pain right away.'

'What if we prayed that the judge finds her innocent and lets her go?'

'Oh, no, but she's not innocent! She's guilty! So let's pray that she says only your name, not mine ...'

'So pray then! Go on and pray!' a person steps out of the crowd and lets out a big laugh.

'Who was that man in the long black coat with a tall hat on his head who laughed and then suddenly disappeared? Wearing the garb of a Black Carniolan, in one of the black guises in which the devil sometimes appears in these parts? He goes around dressed like us, as if he was one of us. So how are we supposed to recognize him? How do we tell who's the devil and who's us?'

I BURN!

SYNCOPE

… I am still unable to free myself from this organic substance. And it is clear that the body in which I am confined is damaged. When it was damaged, how and why, I have no idea. I have nothing to do with this body. I haven't been in control of it for a long time. Who is controlling it, I don't know and I have no intention of finding out. If I was created as a puppet, all right then; I won't try to make myself pull the strings and move the arms and legs, since it's obvious that somebody else is doing all this. Through the eyes of the body I see a cut on the thigh and blood that is not yet dry. I noticed this today, when I was recording the minutes of the trial and my quill fell on the floor. I do not know what the body is doing, if it is awake or asleep. I'm not interested. My only concern is how to be completely free of it. I don't need it. The body only gives me problems. It occupies the mind too much. Mostly with entirely stupid … with useless matters … But now I'm putting the writings about this blasted witch trial in order. I'm writing everything down! Owww, My head is throbbing so much I can't bear it! The whole thing, with all the dialogues – I'm writing it all down! So here's the stupid record for you … Squeezed out of an aching brain … Here you have it … all gone to hell with your devil himself … by the laudato ferdammen and all fucked up … the truth …

The record of a trial the likes of which has never been seen before in our parts and God only knows – or if not God, then the devil himself – if there will ever be anything like it again:

At the end of the investigative process, the judge pronounced the verdict: Kostanšek's daughter is guilty. Beyond any shadow of a doubt! She is a witch! So she will be justly punished. Tomorrow at noon. She will burn!

On the day of the execution three young shepherd boys ran into the village square and, with eyes bulging and arms waving, stammered out that they had seen, had seen something, something they'd never seen before, really never before, and it was enormous, enormous, maybe even taller than the bell tower on the church, and it looked like a woman, but it couldn't have been, could it?

'Come on, boys, what were you doing up there in the meadow? You weren't stuffing yourselves with poisonous berries or picking at those red fly mushrooms, were you?' the populace chided them, trying to get them to calm down, but the shepherd boys wouldn't be calm and kept pointing their little hands in the direction they had just come from. Then one of the populace climbed to the top of the bell tower and started shouting that he could see an odd-looking procession, which was led by – 'but you'll never believe me!' – an actual giant.

The populace didn't know whether to give in to curiosity and run towards where the bizarre procession was reportedly coming from or to scatter and hide. But what the shepherd boys had described and what the young man had seen from the top of the bell tower was true. A procession was coming towards the populace, and Kostanšek was at the head of it; after him, with lumbering steps, came a giantess who was so immense that the seven goliaths marching behind her – 'so they didn't go back to the Caw-Caws, then?' – looked like seven dwarfs.

The populace was dumbstruck as, with a low booming sound, the terrifying parade drew closer, and someone else was part of it, too – the black-bearded man who from time to time had been seen on the Kostanšek farm. The woman was naked, with broad hips and breasts bigger than the bells in the bell tower, and her thighs were as thick as the towers on the castle. The populace raced off to different parts of the village but soon returned armed with pitchforks, sickles, scythes and other sharp-pointed tools, with which they meant to defend themselves and their homes. But the procession did not stop and lumbered on towards the castle. When it reached the populace, Kostanšek moved to the rear, which was brought up by two of the seven goliaths. Every attempt by the populace to stab at the giantess with the farm implements failed, for she simply brushed the attackers off or stepped on them with her gargantuan foot.

'What sort of a monster is this?' the populace shouted in horror, looking at the parish priest, but all such questions were pointless.

As the giantess was going past the church, somebody jabbed her with a pitchfork, and she turned around, kicked the attacker away and crushed him like a bug. But as she was turning, her heavy, immense right breast swung and struck the bell tower, which dangled a bit and then broke off. 'She's going to wreck our church!' screamed the populace, who, as when the Turks attacked, had instinctively sought refuge in the sanctuary, but now they started running after the procession.

The castle gentry had already been informed of what was happening and suspended the execution proceedings. The cannon were filled with gunpowder as the members of the judicial council arranged themselves comfortably near windows that would allow them to view the events in safety. As the procession was approaching, the castle guard fired cannon at it, but the cannonballs missed their target and, instead, destroyed St Mary's Chapel by the healing fount. When the procession was right in front of the entrance to the castle, Kostanšek stepped forward and shouted that he wanted to speak with Their Lordships. But as Their Lordships were unwilling, the black-haired foreigner gestured to the giantess, who came up and kicked three times at the wooden doors, which fell down like bark off a tree. The judicial council, alarmed, now turned towards the castle lord and demanded he take immediate action. He should speak to Kostanšek and consent to any possible compromise, for there was clearly some terrible magic at work here, which not even the Holy Roman Catholic Church was a match for, let alone the law and the army.

'What do you want, Kostanšek?' the castle lord asks, leaning through the window. 'Why are you doing us harm?'

'I've come for my daughter ...' Kostanšek replies.

'She has been charged with witchcraft and will soon be punished,' the castle lord says.

'She is innocent. Release her at once!' Kostanšek demands.

'Peasant, you shall not be giving orders to your liege lords!' one of the members of the judicial council shouts through the window.

'But what is all this? There's wicked magic happening here!' Panic begins to spread through the council members. 'Count, summon that wizard of yours, the one you keep here in your residence and whom we have turned a blind eye to, for people of such professions we normally burn at the stake.'

'I keep him here to mix healing powders and examine the stars for me,' the castle lord says. 'He is able to look into the past, the present and the future, to undress the soul and expose its darkest corners, to look into the heart and the brain and expose evil-minded intentions ...'

'Did your wizard tell you this madness would occur?' one of them asks the castle lord.

'No,' he says, shaking his head.

The man enters, whatever he is – healer, soothsayer, wizard or mage, which is what he calls himself.

'Tell us, wizard, what do you see below in the courtyard?' someone from the judicial council asks.

The wizard leans out of the window and replies, 'I see many different things. Which plane of existence are you curious about?'

'The plane on which a pyre has been made and a stake erected, and around it the terrified populace moves back and forth, and we are here, above everything, observing the scene, and there is an enormous womanish monster walking around in the courtyard and seven sturdy creatures, who are very likely monsters, too, and then there's a filthy peasant and one of your own black-bearded folk ...'

The wizard takes another quick look at the scene below and says, 'All that you are describing is true. True on one plane, to be precise. But what, exactly, would you like to know?'

'What should we do? Because that is wicked magic down there,' one of them says.

'It happens,' the wizard responds almost nonchalantly.

'There is something I'd like to ask you,' another person says. 'What if we are all the victims of some mass hallucination and, for instance, the mushroom sauce that came with the venison and wild boar contained not ceps and chanterelles but blushing, if not spotted, amanita mushrooms, which as a result has rearranged us along different planes of reality?'

'That is also possible,' the wizard replies. 'It would not be the first time that one kind of mushroom has been replaced with another; there has been much vomiting and even tragic death on this account. The two kinds you mention, however, have led many to expand their narrow perspectives on God's creation. So where is the problem in that?'

'To begin with, is what we are seeing actually real, or are all these monsters simply illusions?' one of them asks.

'The world itself, as most people see it, is an illusion,' the wizard replies. 'The essence of creation is hidden to the human senses and can be penetrated only by the spirit, but this ability has been given solely to the select, who know how to use God's greatest gift – creativity. This is also what makes humans similar to God and not, as you Christians think, having beards and moustaches and I don't know what else.'

'Could we try and hurry these debates along?' another person suggests. 'That bearded Jew is walking around with a wand in his hand and doing magic right and left. The giantess is blinking her glowing eyes, the seven sturdies are walking around her with a rigid stride, and most of the populace are on their knees, weeping and wailing and lifting their arms to heaven. Some are cursing, others wagging their fingers at the sky. The executioner – his overfed body is visible from here – has pulled the red hood off his head, and his face is entirely flushed from heat and rage, so he looks like a big angry baby. The parish priest is holding a cross in one hand and with the other seems like he's going to pull out all his hair, while the soldiers would like nothing better than to drop everything, disband and run for cover ...'

'All that you have described is true,' the wizard responds in a calm voice. 'What is happening below is magic. Not everything down there was thrust from human womb. At least eight were in all likelihood made from water and clay, which, for a well-versed mage, is nothing special ...'

'I don't know, but are we all mad or is it only me who thinks time is getting slower?' comes a voice from somewhere.

'Like I told you, we should just close our eyes, because it's possible we're all asleep,' somebody suggests. 'Well, maybe not all of us; maybe it's only me who's asleep, lying at home in my soft canopied bed and dreaming, and when I wake up you'll all be gone and the dark-brown canopy will be above me, and in front of me, slightly open, I will see my green velvet curtains through which a sunbeam is creeping in, and a spider, too, probably. So now I'll start counting from one to ten …'

'It won't be any sun creeping in, it'll be us crippling your body if you don't shut up!' the others say, becoming more and more anxious.

'Why all the panic?' The wizard gazes at everyone present. 'You know what I've never understood about you Christians? That Yehoshua of yours, one of our apostates, whom you consider to be the messiah and who around the year 3800 in our reckoning, or in the first years of your reckoning, was walking around Palestine, that Jesus, as you call him – he was a great wizard, one of the greatest of his day. And, as I know, he was not at all difficult or ill-natured. Most apostates back then were hot-headed schemers, oafs and ruffians. But your Yehoshua was a calm, well-mannered man. The very fact that he renounced propagation lent a certain dignity to his character and raised him above the cattle and sheep and beasts and people. Nor was he a recluse, like those misanthropic groups who lived apart from everyone else in caves by the Dead Sea. Only I don't understand why you haven't included his magic skills in your teaching. He undoubtedly passed them on to his disciples, or at least to his women, like that Magdalene whore and the sisters Mary and Martha. Yehoshua could have pulled such man-made monsters out of his sleeve just for laughs. He didn't only know how to turn water into wine, which, after all, any unscrupulous innkeeper can do. As I know, he is said to have done even stronger magic than making creatures out of clay and water – he summoned back to life the decomposing flesh of those two sisters' brother, whose soul was already waving goodbye. So is it really possible that his disciples, who tramped around with him for years, didn't learn anything from him, or were they just careful to keep this knowledge to themselves?

'There's no special trick to getting rid of those seven goliaths and that gigantic clay scarecrow, even if such knowledge is not for your ears – these secrets belong to the elite ranks of God's chosen people, by which I mean our Jewish nation. But to bring to life a rotting body, as happened with Lazarus, and even more, when you yourself are pierced by Roman spears and bleed out on a cross at the start of the Shabbos and then lie dead for two days in a tomb and on the third day loosen your wrappings, stand straight up and go out for a Sunday stroll – no, gentlemen, this is no joke; only the greatest mages can do this. And even the fact he first showed himself to women – it tells you what an intelligent fellow he was. Because if men had seen him, with no previous warning, it's very possible they would have attacked him out of fear, or maybe from guilt. From what I've heard, his disciples didn't believe at first that their messiah had literally overcome death. Of course not! After all, didn't one of them betray him, and this led to the Romans arresting him? And I suspect that before Jesus was crucified many of them were wondering if their teacher hadn't maybe gone completely mad, since any sane and rational person would have fled when he learned he could be facing death. And maybe after the crucifixion, a couple of the disciples were tormented by a bad conscience, wondering if they could have saved him. Maybe their teacher had been going through a bad time and was hearing more and more divine voices and in all the polyphony had misunderstood God's message. And maybe the voices weren't from God anyway, but only the teacher's madness. If Yehoshua had shown himself first to men, it's likely they would have grabbed him and, in their terrified frenzy, maybe even killed him – which, however, would not have been fatal, since he'd probably just rise from the grave again. But while repeated resurrections like that are fine for those Indian show-offs, who go around bragging about it like burlesquers, and they even drape a brood of venomous snakes around their bodies when they're resurrecting themselves, it's not the kind of thing a serious mystic like Yehoshua would do. Other nations, too, are familiar with the skill of rising from the dead. The mages of Persia and India know how to do it, and so do the ones who live in those faraway Russian climes, with mosquitos in the summer and winters so cold your footsteps freeze behind you. Supposedly there are people who live there who lie down in a grave and keep lying in it for years, decades, maybe even centuries, and they just lie there and never rot. People come to look at them, generation after generation, to see if they have finally decomposed, but they're still there, lying in the grave, not breathing but smelling like a living person; it's as if they are neither dead nor alive. So to die for three days and then get up and walk calmly out of the tomb and proclaim your message and then go east to Baghdad and from there to northern India ...'

'Will nobody shut this wizard up?' someone cries. 'What will we hear next, that Jesus was married and had children?'

'I'd have to say no to that,' the wizard answers. 'Mages of Yehoshua's type are unresponsive to external erotic stimuli. If they are able to die and bring themselves back to life, they can also cause such states of being through the power of their own will without having to get involved in interpersonal relations. They are undoubtedly capable of sexual climaxes that can last for hours, months, years, maybe their entire lives, without any release of seed ...'

'Should I give the warlock a smack myself or do any of you want to clobber him?' somebody asks.

'I can't believe it – there are horrific spectres down there, right in front of us, while up here in the hall, it seems, we're holding a symposium on wizardry!'

'I don't understand. Usually when I have a nightmare, I can wake myself up, but now, no matter how much I keep slapping and pinching myself, I can't do it. I don't even know if I'm dreaming or if I'm actually smacking myself. Quite possibly, I'm dreaming and still asleep ... I'll try going backwards, counting from ten to one ...'

SYNCOPE

'For heaven's sake, Nikolai! You're still sitting at the table writing! In all this time did you even get up to stretch your legs? And you haven't touched your food. It's not just me, even Mitzi is worried about you. When I was washing the stairs, she was scratching and scratching at your door and wouldn't stop – and this time I don't think it's because she wanted to mistreat your bird; I think she's worried about you. Just look at her, she's sitting there on your table and any moment now will start rubbing herself against your face ... Can I bring you anything? Valerian tea? Or maybe a lemon balm or mint infusion?' My housekeeper, at intervals, is babbling behind my back.

Sleeping, dreaming, writing, I speak, and meanwhile the cat rubs herself against my left hand, which is supporting my head so it doesn't drop on the table ... sleeping ... seven ... dreaming ... six ... writing ... three ... two ... one ...

'Now listen up, wizard, there's more than enough wood down there in the courtyard. If you don't come up with a solution at once for how to get this madness under control, I will personally throw you out of the window with my own hands on to that pyre, which the executioner will set ablaze without delay ...'

'Fine, go ahead. But you won't be able to do anything without my help,' the wizard says, unruffled. 'You know nothing about the Kabbalah, and the Gospel won't be of much help to you here. It might give you some consolation, but that's about all. Oh, and by the way, there's something else I never understood. Why does your religion include letters by that Jewish mercenary in the Roman army? There have always been sick people in the world who hear all sorts of voices, which, however, don't usually come from God but from the dark shadows at the bottom of their skull. When that Saul fell off his horse, he shook his brain so badly he started believing he had direct access to divine truth. It's incredible to me that you constructed an entire religious doctrine on the basis of his delusions. And, besides, his knobbly Greek was something only Jews could understand, certainly not Greeks or Romans. But then it's mainly people like that who you've taken your truths from – I mean people who fell on their heads, including that wounded Spanish officer Iñigo López de Loyola, who was stuck by a cannonball in his leg, and while his knee was healing had hallucinations about an organized army of God, and then, after his recovery, he founded the militant Society of Jesus. You're also very fond of taking ideas from madwomen in convents whose only nourishment is light, and from that fat theologian Aquinas, who expanded a little on Aristotle – you know, right before he died he had a craving for herring, and that very same day those fish swam to him, all the way from the cold Atlantic Ocean into the Adriatic, which was recognized as enough of a miracle to get him beatified. They're the traditions you're interested in instead of learning magic from your messiah – well, at least you've had the opportunity to study, while, for your benefit, the populace treads the earth and pulls crops out of it.

'That sorcerer down below is protected by the monsters, who are more devoted to him than dogs. No living creature could ever be so loyal, only an automaton, and nobody can stop such an automaton except the one who made it with his own hands. If you're thinking our Elohim will take pity on you, well, at the moment I wouldn't count on it, since it's you who got yourselves into this mess. I could try going head to head with that sorcerer, but I can't say what the outcome would be since I don't know what his powers are. But there's an easier way, the easiest of all, so let me ask you. Why in the world did that procession of clay dummies show up down there in the first place? What is it their masters want?'

'That's none of your damn business, you miserable warlock!'

'If everybody else knows what's happening, the wizard should know, too; he might be the only one who can get us out of this mare's nest. Standing in front of them all, right next to the man with the black beard, is the father of the witch who is destined to be roasted to her white bones ...'

'You mean that one down there, the woman the bailiffs just brought out, who's been brutally flogged and has had her bones broken?' the wizard asks in disbelief.

'That's her!'

'You can't be serious! Even from a distance you can see she's nothing but a simple peasant with no education,'

'That's not true! She can even write her name!'

'She might know how to make a nice marigold cream or prepare a tincture from sage, but not much more than that,' the wizard replies.

'She is definitely a witch – we have proof!' the others are insisting.

'Hold on a moment, just hold on! Now you're forcing me to defend my profession,' the wizard says, slightly offended. 'If you think it's so easy to do magic, you are mistaken. For such arts you need the right teacher and years of study and practice; it's certainly not something any ordinary peasant can do.'

'You hold on, wizard! Doesn't it say in Leviticus that people like you should be set alight? We suggest you just go down those steps of your own free will and make yourself comfortable on the pyre down there …'

'Well, here's my advice: let the woman go, and that parade of monsters will clear out,' the wizard says.

'Utter nonsense! We'll catch every one of them, set fire to them and kill them!' the others insist.

'Fine, but it will end very badly,' the wizard warns.

'Make haste, your graces and worthy lords!' a servant dashes into the room without knocking. 'The populace are pulling their hair out! They're getting intoxicated, drunk, using whatever means they can get their hands on. Some of them are convinced that the last days are here and they're trying to squeeze out the final pleasures of life, so they're copulating down there right in front of everyone, screwing the way dogs do and grunting like pigs. And that gigantic female thing is looking around and every once in while, when somebody tries to stick her with a pitchfork or halberd or points a musket at her, she grabs him, lifts him up to her eyes and crushes him in her fist, and brownish trickles run down her arm …'

SYNCOPE

Silence … all at once silence from the inside, which is different from the silence from the outside. Voices and noises have thickened into a swarm of sound, which has spiralled away through circles of blue, red and yellow into blackness, the black spot into which the surrounding world has shrunk. Everything is becoming unrecognizable, incomprehensible; everything is shrinking and thickening into a buzzing noise and dark-tinged pounding, into the rhythms, perhaps, of bodily fluids and the beating of the heart. A moment later with your body drenched in a hot cold sweat, the darkness sucks you in. Your body is lying on the floor, your consciousness yanked out of it. Time is for others now, not for you who have slipped out of time – not any more. And later, when you come to, you find yourself again in this immensely anxious silence. Who are these people around you? Why are they checking your pulse, listening to your heart, wetting your face and chest with damp cloths? What happened while you were gone? You are lying on the floor and nothing hurts any more as the silence creeps slowly outward into the unbearable buzzing in your head and the syncopated pounding of your blood. Your entire body is vibrating at a strange rhythm. Were you close to death? Close to nothing? Because during this time you were absent from life ...

'What do you want from us, you damn peasant?' the castle lord asks, leaning out of the window.

'I demand you let my daughter go,' Kostanšek repeats. 'And then I will leave, and she will leave, and all of these with me will leave.'

'Not a chance! We'll grab you, too, peasant, and burn the whole lot of you!' the castle lord rejects Kostanšek's proposal.

'Your graces and gracious lords!' Another servant now runs into the room. 'Now that huge female thing is stomping up to the pyre and she's kicking out the big logs, which are flying like firewood, and those goliaths are grabbing people, and everyone is running around screaming ...'

'Release the wench, so the populace doesn't go completely wild on us!' the members of the judicial council are demanding.

'No, I won't!' the castle lord replies obstinately.

'Your graces and gracious lords! Quick! Look out of the window!' A third servant has run in. 'That sorcerer, the one who's been waving his arms around and making weird gestures by which he's been conducting this madness – all of a sudden his beard fell off!'

'His beard fell off? What does that mean, wizard?' Everyone looks at the wizard.

'Many things,' he answers. 'At the very least, it means the beard was not a real beard, that the sorcerer was not a sorcerer and the man was not a man ...'

'Your graces and gracious lords! There's something else, too ...' Now a fourth servant rushes in.

The room ... my room ... every moment it's more crammed with people, with things ...

'What is it now? Spit it out!' the castle lord snarls.

'There's been a very embarrassing revelation,' the servant says. 'It turns out that the bakers did not abstain, even on this occasion, from their notorious dishonesty and made those so-called baked witches using third-rate ingredients, which isn't the worst part. But they also used rye flour they had swept up from the floor and obviously rye mould had got into it, and it's making the populace shake with St Vitus dance, and they're seeing things and acting crazy ...'

'Well, didn't I say that these were all just illusions?' the supposed dreamer glances at the others.

'Let's take things one by one, analytically, and start by answering the question, did any of us by chance not eat the rye bread? You, wizard, I expect you didn't touch the pork?' one of them asks.

'Certainly not. But I used rye bread to sop up the venison goulash,' the wizard answers.

'So does this mean we're having some sort of group delirium?'

'And the question is, are we even here?'

'Do we even exist?'

'Oh, Jesus Christ!'

'Jesus? Is Jesus here? Did you conjure him up for us, wizard?'

SYNCOPE

The chance you might in an instant slip out of life is constantly here. It watches you ceaselessly, listens to what you say and understands what you are thinking. It is here when you are experiencing important things, when you are happy and joyful, when you are exuberant and know you can do anything and are afraid of nothing, for fear will only get in your way. It is here when in despair you think about ending your life, but you don't because you dread disappearing. It is here when you're not thinking about her; it is here when you do think about her; it is here when you are suffused with euphoria; it is here when you feel a cold hand stroke the back of your neck. So you're not sure any more which is worse, to live or to die. You are a stranger in the world. A stranger in your own life. A stranger in your body. And when you come to, it takes a while to return to life, to breathe again, in and out ... and then a different silence begins. One that does not make you anxious, in which there is no threat from the past, no foreboding from the future; there is only the now, which is slowly expanding in all directions. You are back. Something is humming around you, and the hum unravels into sounds and then into voices, which are distilled into words and meanings ... And by now I can hear voices, evermore distinct, coming in from outside and, from the cage, the sound of a bird moving around, and on the other side of the door a cat is scratching, and soon, perhaps, I will hear my housekeeper's footsteps, and a few moments later, life will again be like home, and that unbearably anxious feeling will disappear, and it will all be as it was before ... But will it really be? Will it be at all?

'Calm down. All of it, including all of you, is just an illusion, a nightmare,' the supposed dreamer again speaks up. 'Everything I am experiencing, everything I am saying, is all a dream, and for some unknown reason, I can't wake up from it. But the moment I smell bacon, fried eggs and frothy milk, it will mean the valet has set my breakfast on the night table because he knows I got completely sloshed last night and if I'm going to even try to crawl out of bed, I have to put something in me first. When I open my eyes a little later, I'll be blinded by the bright midday sun bursting into the room through the gaps in the curtains, and then I'll hear the valet's footsteps, and he will come up to the bed with a fortifying tonic, after which the bell in my head will stop chiming.'

'Babble, babble, babble – nobody's listening to you,' someone says.

'My fear is we'll all go mad,' a voice is heard.

'Fear is beside the point – we're already in the midst of madness,' comes another voice.

'So what now?' And they all look at each other.

SYNCOPE

So what now? But there's a whole string of nows that have to slip smoothly, pass from one to the other snugly, with no gap in between ... Gaps are dangerous, they can swallow the thinker, so I have to think hard ... When the housekeeper enters the room and asks, 'Oh, sir! Are you already awake?' I answer, 'Not already, still ... I am still awake ...' Because I must stay awake. And I tell her that if she sees me nodding off she should wake me up right away. 'What are you talking about? You never sleep any more,' she replies. 'Ever since you got back from that trial, you're constantly writing about some fellow named Kostanšek, and you say strange things when you write ... You talk to yourself as if you weren't the only person in the room ...'

'This isn't my usual work; it's something entirely different,' I reply. *'It's like nailing up the door from the inside so the wood on the entrance does not give way and it does not burst into the room ... doesn't burst into my head and happen ... When a question flashes in my head, sometimes there's no answer or the answer comes too late, and meanwhile the gap widens, and through it the void lunges at me, the void wheezing and breathing beside me ... in and out, in and out ... which is why I'm writing like crazy ... a stream of thoughts is flowing through me, and I can't stop them and they aren't mine and haven't been for a long time ... it's as if I'm swimming, battling the waves ... oh, I'm swimming, I'm swimming very well, and it helps me stay above water, so I'm not carried off ... not pulled under ...'*

Beneath the castle window, Kostanšek again demands, 'Release my daughter! Buy back my farm, and I'll leave this very day!'

'Who are you to be setting conditions on us, your liege lord?' the castle lord bellows down at him.

'Somebody who's still alive, and if you don't meet my demands, you won't be when evening comes!' Kostanšek yells back.

'Impudent peasant! God will punish you!' the castle lord answers back, trying to keep his dignity despite his fear.

But when the giantess leans over the castle wall and plucks a few soldiers off it like dandelions and then crushes them between her palms, one of the others in the room says, 'Enough is enough! We'll release your daughter to you and His Lordship will pay you for your farm, but only under the condition that you disappear today and take all your unholy monsters with you!'

'Are you mad? He's not getting off that easily, not with me!' the castle lord, offended, stands his ground. His intention was at least to fight for the appearance of authority. But when one of the council members pokes him in the back with a fork, he grits his teeth and, realizing that the judicial council would sooner do away with him than gamble on their future, he stammers, 'Let the girl go and toss the peasant four sacks of gold from my treasury.'

'Seven sacks,' Kostanšek says.

'Five,' the castle lord makes a counter-offer.

'Seven!' Kostanšek insists.

'Six,' the judicial council ventures.

'Seven, or the giantess tears down the castle wall, marches into the castle and flattens all of you, one after the other.' Kostanšek will not give up.

'All right, then, seven!' one of the council members hisses. 'Release the girl, bring up the sacks of gold, anything to put an end to this carnival of madness and horror!'

Cooling Down

The populace was observing these last scenes on their knees with their hands clasped in prayer. They lifted their heads and looked up at the castle balcony and then fixed their eyes on Kostanšek's daughter, who with a bloated face and swollen limbs, and supported by two bailiffs, was brought to her father.

'Daughter of mine!' When Kostanšek embraced her, the girl cried out in pain. 'They have broken your bones, but your bones will heal. Even if you limp for the rest of your life, even though it's not clear if you'll ever walk again, still, you are alive.'

When the castle steward, accompanied by guards, placed the bags of gold into Kostanšek's hands, one by one, the last bag was intercepted by the dry hand of the black-haired foreigner, who took it as payment for the sorcery he had performed.

When the purchase was concluded, the procession, slowly and with a thundering sound, left in the direction from which it had come. As it passed by them, the populace, in two lines, some still kneeling, others standing, crossed themselves and, still muttering prayers, turned their heads and examined the apparitions carefully.

'Don't you think the giantess looks a little familiar?' one of the populace asks.

'Familiar? Familiar from where?' They all look at each other. 'Who has ever before seen such a big and horrifying woman?' a voice is heard.

But the first voice persists, 'Look at her foxy hair, look at her face – doesn't she remind you of somebody?'

'Who are you talking about? Remind us of who?'

'You mean her?'

'You mean that woman?'

'You mean that widow who consorted with the devil and was justly punished for it a few years ago?'

'You think that woman ... you think she came back to take revenge on us?'

'From the grave?'

'From the grave, from hell – what's the difference? She has obliterated everything we have!'

'Do you think we punished her ...?'

'Unfairly? Were we wrong? Only God can judge that.'

'And he will, too. But what if we were unfair as judges and executioners?

'It happens. To err is human. But God is infinite in mercy and ready to forgive even the worst errors.'

'Sure, fine, but before God forgives, he punishes. That giantess crushed the executioner and trampled down a fair number of soldiers and peasants ...'

'The priest, too, only barely survived ...'

'And she knocked down the bell tower with that gigantic bum of hers ...'

'And trampled our fields ...'

'What if it was her ...'

' ... and she was in the right and we were in the wrong?'

'What stupid questions! After all, she wasn't the one who destroyed our chapel – it was the cannonball from the castle, when the giantess dodged it ...'

'But if anyone can so nimbly get out of the way of cannonballs, it has to be ...'

'Like those seven oddities – they don't look like people either ...'

'So do you think it's over now?'

'And there'll be peace from now on?'

'There'll be peace for a while, but then no doubt someone will turn up, and it'll be a foreigner, maybe not even human, at least a Turk or a Lutheran, a preacher or a Leaper, someone who brews potions, who's a woman ... There's always someone.'

'But what was all this?'

'Who knows? First let everything calm down, and then, eventually, we'll give it some thought. People will talk, people always talk, they talk a lot, so it's hard to know what's true and what isn't, what actually happened, or even if something did happen ... But there's no way we're simply going to forget this. Once it seems that this event, where everyone who was accused got off without punishment, is in the distant past, then we will organize and strike back. Not necessarily in a few weeks or months; it could be a year, or a few years, or a few centuries. But we will destroy them all – sorcerers, Jews, bad women, foreigners, gypsies, Turks and the ones from the Caw-Caws, too. And if some Indian from the East shows up in our land, we'll kill him as well, and if we can, even some New World Indian ... It will be a pogrom! A big pogrom!'

'Just so long as we don't get it wrong and kill somebody by mistake. And then there's this: what if in the distant future the world has changed so very much that many of the things that exist today won't be around any more, and instead there will be other things, things we can't even imagine?'

'What wouldn't exist?'

'Well, us, to begin with ...'

'But surely our descendants will still exist centuries from now, with our blood and with ways of thinking that won't be very different from ours, since they will have been passed down from generation to generation. Oh, yes, we will exist, we will definitely still exist! We, the populace, will go on living through the ones who come after us ...'

'But what if in a few centuries the ones who come after us don't exist? What if God is no longer happy with this world and destroys it?'

'But he won't. Our God is good; he won't destroy us just because he feels like it.'

'But what if in the future *he* doesn't exist any more either?'

'Who?'

'God!'

'God? God is eternal! As long as we're still around at least, God will be, too. Even when there's no more earth, and everything returns to darkness, just as it came out of darkness, we will be fairly and justly arrayed all the way from heaven, through purgatory, to hell.'

'But what if not even that ...'

'What? Who said that? Step forward at once! ... Well, who was it?'

Like some immense organism, the populace swings its tail left and right. 'Who was it? Come on! Show yourself, whoever is saying and thinking such things! Because God sees everything; he hears everything, even what's still forming in your head ... And sometimes he doesn't make distinctions. And if in one place there are too many such thoughts, he doesn't pick up his sieve and sift out the sinners from the righteous; no, instead he punishes by demolishing everyone without exception ... So, who's saying this? Come on! Step forward!'

'Nobody! Nobody is saying it! It's just some strange, almost incomprehensible echo ... Nothing to worry about. That's the sound of poorly deflected, meaningless thought.'

'And it's best it stays that way, too, best for everyone, because otherwise there will be punishments, pogroms, bloodbaths ...'

SYNCOPE
There is nothing left. Not God. Not religion. Not love. The world has slipped off its bearings. The edge of the world is not the divine beyond, but the unbearable edge of the world, beyond which there is nothing. Only emptiness. An abyss stronger than words.

Once I had to try with all my might to imagine a world without God. Now, no matter how hard I try, I cannot think of a world in which God might exist. I would give anything if only I could believe again. In anything. In God, if nothing else. Or at least that a miracle might happen to me. It could be the miracle of love – although love is a trap in which nature basely ensnares humans so they reproduce and the human race continues into the future. Nature doesn't give a damn about humans. Even our spiritual and mental abilities, the noblest features of humanity, it exploits for its own vulgar propagational purposes.

I would give anything to slip back into that form of exalted madness when I was inundated by the feeling that everything is possible and there is no reason to be afraid. But I have nothing. I have no strength to live, no strength to kill myself. I have no desire for life and none for death either. I am afraid of life and I am no less afraid of death. I am afraid to kill myself. But also afraid to live and grow old. I am folding in on myself. I can't any more ... I can't ...

EASY ... THERE WAS
SIMPLY NO OTHER WAY

Before he left, Kostanšek kneeled down in the field, scooped up a clump of rich, still rain-sodden earth and lifted it to his face. This was the smell of his land, the land he would not be taking with him to wherever he was going. Where that was he still did not know, but he imprinted this smell on his memory, and memory preserves what no longer exists as well as many things that never really were.

The same late afternoon, his daughter sat down in the over-packed cart, which the two farmhands had loaded, and the maidservant sat down next to her. Kostanšek petted the cows, the sheep and the goats and placed the dog, still quivering from the sight of the giantess, by his daughter's feet, and then the foreigner, now beardless, sat down beside his daughter, and finally the two farmhands sat down in the cart and then he sat down. The farmhand at the front of the cart started the two horses, and the cart drove off, and following behind it, with lumbering steps, were the seven labourers and the giantess.

Where they went, nobody knew. Well, almost nobody. Nobody in the town saw them, so they must have gone around the town. But apparently, the odd procession was spotted by a group of pilgrims who then secretly followed it.

'We were coming to your church,' the pilgrims later told their story, 'for it is said that Mary works miracles at the mysterious fount, but then, on the way there, a miracle happened to us. What else could we think when we saw giants lumbering along after a cart? We were terribly frightened, but curiosity impelled us to follow them, as if we were a little bewitched. The procession stopped beside a pond. Then this gaunt man, a foreigner – well, he looked like a foreigner – climbed out of the cart and ordered the seven giants to undress and go into the water, and then he gestured to the giantess, who obediently followed the seven. And when the seven giants and the giantess were all in the water up to their knees, that peculiar foreigner waved his arm a few times towards the reddish light of the setting sun – no, he wasn't making crosses; his gestures were abrupt, a little circular, too – and he uttered some of the strangest and most incomprehensible words we have ever heard. Meanwhile, the peasant was standing on the bank of the pond, with two farmhands next to him, and two women, too – one was young, maybe his daughter, and the other was older.

'And then a big bird flew out of the branches of a leafy oak tree, and its wings blotted out the sky above the pond as if a heavy granite curtain had fallen over the water. And all around it went quiet, like right before an eclipse of the sun. The frogs stopped croaking, and the other animals were silent, too; even the wind died down, and other than the sorcerer's arms flapping in the air, everything was still. It was as if eternity had spread its wings above the pond,' the pilgrims said, looking at each other and nodding. 'Not very long before, it had been evening, with a reddish-orange light seeping out of it, and then, a moment later, it was that indefinable part of the day, neither day nor night but something in between, as if time had cracked above the shallow pond.

'We were genuinely frightened,' the pilgrims continued. 'We hid there in the bushes and waited to see what would happen. A cloud came and hovered over those weird creatures, who were standing in the middle of the pond; it descended to the surface of the water, and then seven truly wondrous rays of violet light shot out of their bodies and wrapped around the band of golden light that was whirling out of the giantess, and together the light formed a seven-petalled flower with a centre as dazzling as the sun, and it was so radiant we had to shield our eyes with our hands. As the blinding light began to harden into grey, with only a trace of it remaining in the air, the seven giants and the giantess became dimmer and dimmer, until their bodies lost shape and collapsed like sand into the pond, and in their place a small island was formed.'

'And then?'

'Then, there was nothing. All the others, who had been standing by the cart, climbed back on it and left. There wasn't anything after that.

Kostanšek and his family were never seen again. There were lots of different rumours: that he had gone east and made a home in the Ottoman Empire; that he had gone to the Holy Land and was living on the outskirts of Jerusalem or, even more likely, by the Sea of Galilee in the town of Tsfat, which the populace found particularly interesting because the name reminded them of *plaits* and it was said to be the home of many Jewish sorcerers who knew how to weave the kind of magic Kostanšek's bearded accomplice had woven. Some said that Kostanšek had gone on further, all the way to India, or maybe even China, to the very edge of the ocean, and that edge of the ocean is far away, so very far away, in fact, that it could well be the edge of the world. Others said that he went to Northern Europe and in Flanders boarded a ship and sailed to the New World. Or maybe not, maybe the ship turned south to Africa. In many stories, Kostanšek moved from place to place all over the world, so that some people began to doubt that he had ever lived in these parts at all.

There were also different stories about what had actually happened that day and who those seven giants were and where they had come from.

As time went on, fewer and fewer people believed they had come from the Caw-Caws, a place nobody around here had ever heard of until it was mentioned by some Turk. And there were fewer and fewer who claimed that the seven were not actually people. It's true they were enormous, but perhaps not so enormous as not to be human. It's also true that they did not speak our language, but to say they were mute is not entirely accurate either. When you met them, they would greet you (as some remembered) and not in a foreign language but in our own local Slovene language, which everybody understands. And if you asked them how they were, they would answer that they were good. That was a word they knew – oh right, we heard them say it (more and more people started to remember). And if they knew at least one word, and especially if that word was *good*, then they couldn't be so terribly bad and maybe not even as foreign as might have seemed to some. The stories differed, too, as to whether there were exactly seven of them or maybe one or two more, or fewer.

'But what about that giantess who appeared from God knows where and started crushing people?'

'Giantess? What giantess?' people were wondering a few years later.

'The one whose bum knocked the bell tower off our church?'

'What are you talking about? That bell tower was old and simply collapsed after a storm.'

'What about the people the giantess picked up and squeezed in her fist like grapes, back then in the castle courtyard, where they had set up a pyre to burn Kostanšek's daughter at the stake?'

'Burning at the stake in the castle courtyard? The lord of the castle would never burn someone at the stake in front of his own nose. There's a special place for that on the edge of the village where they also put the gallows and the breaking wheels they tie criminals on.'

'But the pyre of wood – there was a pyre, wasn't there?'

'Oh yes, there was a pyre, and it was a great big one.'

'But Kostanšek's daughter, who was accused of doing magic and witchcraft – she managed to avoid it, yes? She escaped?'

'Whose daughter? You mean that dolled-up heavyset girl who had been sick and then suddenly got better, and then she became good-looking and rich? The one who lived on the farm where those foreigners were working? What was her name? Kostanšek, was it? And wasn't the house called Orehek? Oh, no, she never went anywhere. She died here, because she was a witch, and they proved it, too. They arrested her one day and took her to the castle, where they interrogated her. It wasn't long before she broke down and confessed everything. And she wasn't the only one who burned that day. There were also a few others, mainly women, but some men, too, including a blacksmith. Then there were two midwives, a woman with six children, another woman as well as her son, who was black as coal, and then there was an entire family almost – father, mother, the mother's brother – all sorcerers. But there, next to the pyre, despite the stench – oh, we'll never forget it, so horrible and moving was that scene, with an almost heavenly beauty about it – there was a very young girl kneeling, and she had a swollen belly. In the midst of the screams – the executioner had not taken pity on them and was letting them all burn alive – that very pregnant girl, on that late September day, was kneeling and praying with clasped hands for their souls, which, despite her prayers, are now frying in hell, for they had done not only sorcery but many other wicked things as well.'

'But what about the Jew with the long beard, which fell off in the middle of his incantations? Who was he? Was he even a man? Or was he actually a woman?'

'What Jew? There haven't been any Jews in our province since 1515 when we drove them all out.'

'But what about that little island of clay in the middle of the pond?'

'It's always been there ...'

'No, it hasn't. Old people say it wasn't there in the past ...'

'Then nature must have made it, or maybe it was some ancient force still lingering in these parts, at least from when our people first settled here, if not before. Since we were not the first people here. Living here before us were the people whose tombstones were washed up by the river. Maybe these people, whose customs are unknown to us, still exist in our bodies and live through us, even if they worshipped different, ancient goddesses, who had a temple right there on that little clay island – who can say?'

'But does that mean these ancient forces are still with us? Because if they are, that's not good for us Christians. So why don't we erect a little chapel to our Mary on that island so nobody turns up again who worships the wrong gods? Because we've heard that there are some pilgrims who go there and bring gifts and flowers to the old goddesses.'

'That's not a bad idea. Let's build a chapel there to cover up the memory of pagan times. Heretical tales should be covered up by Christianity; this will make it less likely that the dark forces reawaken and trigger events that bring bad things. And require sacrifices. And blood. And human bodies. And lives. And we don't want that. We are good people. Peace loving. We hate violence; we've had too much of it.'

So the populace erected a little chapel on the little island dedicated to the Virgin Mary, and people would come there and dip themselves in the water, just as they had once gone to the fount by the other little chapel, which had since become filthy (no one remembered why) and its water was no longer holy or even clean and drinkable. Because Mary is good. There are only good and beautiful things in her story. And Mary protects us, and we are also good.

But on that little island, little clay statues of women soon started appearing next to Mary's chapel; they were similar to the figurines that had appeared there earlier. Neither then nor now had they appeared on their own, probably, or maybe they had. Who knows? Nobody ever saw anyone bringing figurines or other gifts there. But ever since the chapel has stood on the island, people have been bringing flowers there, to Mary.

The castle gentry and the Church authorities were fuming that sorcery had to be beaten out of people's heads and that the tales the populace were going on about didn't have a shred of truth in them. A few of the tales had grown up among the populace themselves, who knows when or why. But others had been jotted down, and even more had been invented, by that deranged scrivener.

Written documents tell us that the witch trials lasted for more than two months. The first judge had died tragically from lumps in his abdomen. His successor, however, convicted twenty-three suspects, who were all burned at the stake on the same day. When Archduke Ferdinand himself, who had received news of the trials, sent envoys to put a stop to them, it was you, the populace, who insisted that everything needed to be thoroughly cleansed. Let's look around one more time, you shouted, and see if maybe we haven't forgotten something! Let's look inside ourselves one more time and dig out anything that is rotten or bad.

That unfortunate scrivener, who had poisonous juices flowing in his body, had scribbled some nonsense about man-made creatures until eventually his brain gave out. After that, Mayor Volk Falke looked after him and sent him away to somewhere near a lake. No, the scrivener's problem wasn't magic and sorcery, but melancholy. Even so, it's good he got away from here. He just suddenly disappeared. We don't hear much about him, only that he spends his days walking by the lake.

'Has he started writing again?'

'Oh no, the scrivener doesn't write any more.'

In fact, we hear less about the scrivener than we do about that noble widow whose husband had been so rich – and, by the way, it wasn't us who denounced her; that was the Jesuits. The witch had attacked them just when it looked like she was going to pledge herself to widowhood and donate all her property to the Society of Jesus, who would then use it for their college and dormitories, but instead they set up the college in the Franciscan monastery. She had put a spell on one of the young Jesuits. Nor was he the first man she had bewitched. Before him, she had attacked an elderly Jesuit brother, but he did not suffer such terrible consequences as the young Jesuit, who developed festering lumps first on his mouth and later in his throat, and then there was nothing more anyone could do for him. When authorities arrived at her house early one morning to arrest her so she could be given a fair trial in the provincial court, she was already gone. She had escaped them by a whisker, for her rooms still smelled of her perfume. We hear she has it pretty good where she's living now, even better than when she lived in our land. She makes her home on one of the loveliest islands in the Venetian lagoon. They say she even gives singing lessons and has no lack of male company. But she will get her just deserts – if she escaped them here, they'll find her somewhere else, maybe even in that Venetian palace of hers. Perhaps she will get one of those diseases from a man so she wastes away and dies in madness. Maybe the plague will attack her right in her home, or maybe one of her acquaintances will squeeze her neck so hard it snaps. It would be good if something like that happened; it would be justice, for her and for all of us. Because it's not fair when somebody breaks the law and does bad things and then it's as if she is even being rewarded for her wicked deeds, with things going better for her than they do for us, who could hardly wait to see her tried. Because we don't often have the chance to see some fancy tart get the kind of punishment that can come down on us at any moment.

We are careful about whom we need to obey and whom we can offend without consequences. The worst ones to offend are the provincial authorities – and, of course, the lord of the castle. Offending Mayor Volk Falke is not as bad. He made a lot of big talk about defending his town – that's what he said, 'my town' – but when it came down to it, under pressure and threats that the provincial authorities were going to arrest the ladies of the town for supposedly dealing in witchcraft, he relented, and when Bishop Thomas Chroen arrived for his visitation, the mayor kneeled humbly before him, repented and swore allegiance to the Catholic Church. That's how he managed to avoid that 'week of grace', which we, the rural populace, were so much looking forward to. We sincerely wished to see the townsfolk quivering for their lives, especially since they've always entertained themselves at our expense and also because we're Catholics and they are Lutherans. Well, they aren't any more. Almost all of them have sworn allegiance to Catholicism. The obstinate few who refused to give up their Lutheranism have had to sell their property and move out of town and out of the region.

Nowadays, if you're going to offend anyone, it's best if it's the Lutheran gentry, whose time is running out in these parts. Preachers don't come here any more, and the few parish priests who give communion in two kinds, do it secretly. We're also thinking more and more about whether we even need the feudal lords, who seem less and less an unquestionable part of our lives. But we still don't have the courage to oppose the Church authorities; we still don't have the courage to live without God, not yet anyway, but in the future ... who knows? Maybe we won't need God any more either. Who will we then put on the altar (because we can't imagine living without altars)? That, we still don't know.

There aren't many Turkish raids any more, only now and then along the borders of the provinces. The plague still visits us, but whenever somebody appears, as they do on occasion, and starts berating us, the populace, telling us that the plague is God's punishment and it won't leave us alone until we brutally destroy everyone we recognize as heretics, as guilty of anything, we first try to shut him up peacefully, and if that doesn't work, we quietly get rid of him with our own hands. Don't let anyone insult you, someone once laid on our hearts. So now the only ones who are allowed to do this are the prince, the sheriff and the various provincial commissioners, as well as patriarchs, vicars, parish priests, deacons, bishops and prince-bishops – but nobody else!

Who knows, maybe one day in the future we'll rid ourselves of those masters, too. But until that day comes, we'll get by with what we know and what we can do. And we know a lot. Oh, we the populace are never short of knowledge and methods for getting by.

BEFORE DEPARTING

Julian opens the door cautiously, and an ashen-faced shadow with watery, bulging eyes steps into the room. The young man's right hand traces an elegant circle in the air and comes to rest pointing at a comfortable chair upholstered in light blue. The guest sits down and gazes at the bed.

'You don't look very good, probably not much better than I do,' Wolfgang says to his guest.

The man next to the bed is silent.

'It's true, isn't it, Friedrich? In the end, everybody vanishes, and we have no one left but each other – frustrated friends and occasional enemies. Still, if we didn't see each other now and then, especially on such an important occasion as death, it just wouldn't feel right. What love this is! All that lofty nonsense about love is a lie, just as love itself is a deception. It appears out of nowhere and clouds a man's vision, to make him think life is full and worth living. "Why, life is wonderful, after all!" he says. People make everything so complicated, but if you only relax a little, it all becomes simple, and then anything can happen. Yes, all sorts of things, even love sometimes. It sneaks into your life without warning and makes itself comfortable, and, when it tires of its temporary lodgings, it moves on to other victims, seduces them and leaves them in pain, with a barrage of questions that follow. But why did this happen when it seemed it would last forever? Forever? Hahaha! Love last forever when man is threshed like straw by time? He can barely take a deep breath and make plans for something a little long-term, and already he's worn out, his breathing shorter and shallower. Love – what an immensely base deception by nature! That scrivener was right, you know; in his writings he let himself feel it unreservedly and, so I hear, wrote that love is a deception by which nature induces man to reproduce, and then everything cracks apart and she sets

347

her trap for other wide-eyed innocents. Sometimes, very rarely, love remains, but usually only with those poor souls for whom it never gets past words, never reaches the body, because of the many obstacles that keep the lovers apart. If the strumpet persists in such cases, it is merely so she can torment a heart sucked dry from yearning and pain.

'Habituation, Friedrich, is a stronger and longer-lasting emotion than love, if habituation can even be ascribed an emotion. Over the years a person acquires habits and becomes attached to certain surroundings, places, objects, words, phrases and people. Which is all insipid, but even so it counts for something.

'If death doesn't take you by surprise and your end is similar to mine, your nearest and dearest will be milling around you in turns, so they can check to see if you're … if it's finally over … Dying is exhausting, almost as much for the loved ones as for the dying man. But I've made arrangements: my devoted Julian will stay with me to the end; otherwise, lying in this bed all by myself I'd go mad, like that scrivener, from fear and loneliness … But say something, Friedrich. Now that you're here, you may as well fill my final hours, because if I'm just going to look at you – well, I haven't felt that sort of desire for you in a long time. It's like I placed a mirror by my bed and am looking at myself, a living corpse who's only waiting for the door to open and a scythe to come through it. Fritzi, say something for God's sake! Anything! Be what you've always been – vulnerable and naïve and with a very special talent for kind-hearted, dull-witted foolishness.

'What? Nothing? Julian' – with great effort, the prince-bishop raises his arm and gestures to his assistant – 'bring the count a hearty snack and some wine. A red wine, heavy, so it warms him up, because he looks cold, even waxen. The only thing that convinces me he's alive are his eyelids, which close every so often over that dead-eyed gaze, which is glued to me like a physician's leech. But be quick, Julian, so he doesn't die on me next to my deathbed.

'You see, Fritzi,' the dying man continues, 'they say money can't buy happiness – but it can buy devotion, and there are moments, such as these last ones, when that is a great happiness. What can I say? It broke you. But as I told you very clearly, power is not the same little game we played when we were children. Politics demands that the ruler take care of others, but mainly that he take care of himself. Your debacle was even worse than Spitzenberg's. He kept kicking right to the end and meanwhile forgot about his own well-being because he believed that a person's views and convictions are more important than physical survival, that it's a person's way of thinking that makes him special, maybe even exceptional. And, indeed, Spitzi drawn and quartered departed this world a hero. But you, Friedrich, you've always lacked the talent for authority. You had the chance to bring everything off quite elegantly, and then you could have left your inheritance to your wife and descendants and perhaps withdrawn to some peaceful, exotic clime. Even your sister would have been better at handling power, although given her proclivities – which she recognized in time and ran away from that tight-fisted merchant to the seaside – she would surely have burned at the stake. And you would not have been able to help her. So you would be blaming yourself for her death, too. Damn it, Fritzi, if you don't say something I'll use my last strength to slap that woebegone face of yours so hard that blood will flow.'

'You're right, power is not for me. And this time I completely failed. All I could do was watch helplessly as events flared out of control. Some of the victims I knew personally and felt sincerely sorry for them. I was amazed and surprised by some of the executioners, while others did exactly what you'd expect. Here.' He places a bundle of written-over sheets of paper on Wolfgang's bed. 'In all the confusion, the mayor passed this on to me.'

'Oh, the mad writings! It's good, it's very good, that you and the mayor got them off the scrivener. If Volk hadn't sent him away, the authorities would have certainly gone after him, too. He was denying the existence of God, of himself, of everything. A courageous fellow, I'll give him that! If I had any life left in me I would tidy these writings up a bit and make sure they were published. Madness or no madness, from what I've heard about his writing, that young man simply crackled with thought – and then he literally cracked, whether from mind or from madness and delusions, it's all the same. But my life is running out, and besides, I'm not proficient in the scrivener's language, in which, as far as I know, nothing has been written other than catechisms, hymnals and Bible translations. But it is a very fine thing for a language when something is written in it that serves no purpose other than the pure and impractical pleasure of expression and thought. If this is enriched by the scrivener's philosophical bent and imagination, so much the better. If only he hadn't been so infatuated with that conceited cow, who had far less intelligence than people initially credited to her. The way she outmanoeuvred the Jesuits was more due to circumstance than well-planned strategy. There had long been whispers in my circles about that young Jesuit, who, it was said, had contracted a disease from somewhere (a man, of course) and then, out of pure self-preservation, calculating that God would stage a miraculous cure for him, he recast himself as a ruthless soldier of the Lord. The disease no doubt fried his brain. It's a pity the scrivener was so irrationally besotted with that arrogant tart, who changed overnight from victim to annihilating bitch. But time will deal with her. I hear that in Venice she has thoroughly disencumbered herself of moral prejudices. They say she gives singing lessons but that her own singing is so off key it makes your head hurt. Apparently, she's more in tune when it comes to bodily communication. In a few years no one will give a damn about some ageing, embittered *frottolara* from Carniola. But I'm curious to know if the scrivener ever managed to go beyond chatting and philosophizing with that Triestine merchant-woman, for whom he provided courier services. If he had tried a little harder he would definitely have succeeded, regardless of the mayor. When you're young you can be choosy and toy heartlessly with admirers and favourites, but in your mature years, whether you want to or not, you become more forbearing; you can no longer be sure that someone will even notice you. Mayor Volk is a man of refined and somewhat elevated tastes. He would rather be around educated women than giddy young flirts. I understand that. As the years pass, you get tired of pretty faces, which begin to look more and more alike until you can hardly tell them apart. And what's more, while you watch these juicy young sprouts blithely surrendering to passion, your own body is already creaking, stiff where you'd rather it wasn't and too soft where it should be stiff. And the more you observe that idiotic adolescent fervour, the more you realize that you yourself are getting older, that you are ever closer to death. Over the years, such scenes become harder and more unbearable to watch.

'I hope Julian will take my advice and go to Asia or the New World. With letters of credence from me, he'll have no trouble finding a position anywhere. Maybe before he goes he can put the scrivener's writings in order: some of them, mainly the philosophical writings, are in Latin, and some in Slovene, which is Julian's mother tongue, just as it is the scrivener's. Several pieces are quite lucid, or so I've heard, but towards the end, more and more of them are engulfed in madness. Maybe Julian could edit the Latin writings and translate the Slovene ones into German and then, on the way to his ship, he could stop somewhere, preferably in Paris or Amsterdam, and give them to someone who would oversee their publication. Or perhaps somewhere far away, on the other side of the world, Julian might have them translated into the local languages, so that the thoughts, world views and colourful barbarisms all get mixed together a little. In India, I know, they sacrifice people, kill babies of the weaker sex and bury widows alive with their dead husbands. Let them read about our customs, which are no less brutal and cruel, how we offer up people and burn them to appease our own dark gods (although officially this is the state). So, before I die, I'm encouraging Julian to promote an exchange of customs, traditions and practices.

'Well, are you ever going to speak, or will you just keep sitting there in a daze like some withered New World Indian head or a millennia-old mummy?'

'I have nothing to say,' Friedrich replies in a desolate voice. 'I regret everything that has happened. It would have been better, I expect, if I had done nothing and simply waited for them to attack and be done with me and leave the others alone. But I've always been too much of a coward for heroic deeds. Even in my youth, when we were raising hell among ourselves and all around, it wasn't courage that spurred me on but only my carnal juices. Once the events in my fiefdom got going, it was impossible to stop them. Even now I smell the stench of burning flesh. And I see the faces relishing it. I see the victims crippled by Fabjančič's torture, and I see the hatred and fear and desire for vengeance, which would have gone on and on if the rumours of the slaughter, which spread as far as Graz, had not compelled the prince himself to send his officials with the army and put a stop to it.'

'But our age has become inured to all these things – why haven't you?' the prince-bishop asks.

'I'm not the only one. Even the mayor was shattered by this,' Friedrich replies.

'Oh, surely not Volk Falke. Whatever accolades people have woven around his charm, his good sense, his prudence, when he finally understood that the provincial authorities were not joking and that they intended to burn not only that wealthy widow but his own wife and daughters, whom they said their mother had corrupted with her witchcraft, when he saw they were planning a pogrom against his town, he put his tail between his legs, swore allegiance to Catholicism and resigned the mayorship. As if there was really such a great gulf between the papist religion and Lutheranism! As if the whole issue was truly about God, when it was only about power and privileges, about self-image and the illusion of one's own strength and omnipotence.

'It was very clever how they went after the town by threatening to accuse women of witchcraft. Supposedly, that provincial commissioner really did believe in his "apricotters", a notion the Jesuits had devised for him. That's the way it's done, Friedrich. That's how you rule. Without emotion. With a piercing, cold mind. Look, were there any victims in the town? Did anybody die? No. And that's because when the Provincial Estates came to realize that the story of your domain could be reprised in the town, they sensibly gave in. And if you, Friedrich, had taken my advice and carried out properly just one single witch trial, with just a single stake and one well-chosen victim to serve as a reminder to both the town and your fiefdom, it would have all been different, with no other unnecessary burning.'

'But right from the start the single victim multiplied into other victims. People really came to life the moment they saw an opportunity to go wild.'

'That's because you weren't vigilant and allowed the mayor to install that lacklustre criminal judge, who naturally had to be removed. A trial with a single victim was conceived as a ritual to cleanse the town and your domain. But then that little big-bellied minx showed up out of nowhere and staged her own personal revenge on the level of the Roman Inquisition. There's nothing new about people getting excited at the scent of blood. Which is why I'm constantly telling you: keep your fiefdom on a short leash.'

'How did you manage to "remove" the judge?' Friedrich asks.

'Same as always. It was easy. We combed through your staff and found people who at the mention of money agreed without hesitation. We couldn't let this part of the prince's lands, which has no reputation for obstinacy, be infested with germs of rebellion,' the prince-bishop says, as Julian places a tray of food and wine on the table.

'In the lands of Inner Austria, the Provincial Estates have been defeated,' he continues, 'and a similar fate awaits the Bohemians. Day by day, Catholic Habsburg dominance is being consolidated, and this may even have positive consequences. The Provincial Estates, including most of the nobility, have renounced Lutheranism – out of self-interest, to be sure, but also from an awareness that only a country which is united in every aspect, with religious unity between the prince and the Estates, can provide a united, firm defence. And this gives the populace a sense of belonging, a sense of security, as well as other, similarly practical illusions. But let history be the judge. Although it won't be. History won't be doing all that much judging. The more these events recede into the past, the more they will be described in coldly rational terms. No one feels sympathy for victims who have been dead for more than three generations. And yet, something very interesting happened here, which historians may have trouble explaining. I wish I could be there when they try to clarify and debate why the Provincial Estates, which, in fact, possessed remarkable strength, never stood up to the prince – to Archduke Ferdinand. If they had all defied the Habsburgs, the prince would not have been able to defeat them, not even with mercenaries. Had they persisted with their demand, he would not have so easily subdued them. The Estates could have compelled the archduke's consent simply by kneeling down – a seemingly cheap gesture of self-abasement. They could have fallen prostrate on the floor in order to remain upright – upright in their faith and in their freedom. Instead of the lands of Styria, Carinthia and Carniola being forced to their knees before the archduke and, with fear and trembling, swearing an oath of allegiance to him, they could have kneeled down before him with resolve and stubbornly remained kneeling until he finally lost patience and yielded to their demand for religious freedom. But they didn't do that. The Provincial Estates clung to the notion that the prince was their father and they themselves his sons. And so they gave in, bowed down and stood up humiliated. And then, endlessly and pointlessly, they kept meeting and going to Graz to entreat the archduke, without ever shaking off the image of themselves as disobedient sons rebelling against a father, who, however strict he may be, is still their father. Milksops! Cry babies! Little boys who didn't have the stones to stand up for themselves and defy father! Spitzenberg, on the other hand, I admire. He took a chance, even though he knew he was alone in his endeavour and would almost certainly meet the fate that later befell him. Oh, by the way, what happened with those Triestine merchants?'

'Not long after the young widow left, they all vanished in a single night,' Friedrich replies.

'That was smart. I hope they'll do the same in the future, in similar situations, but it's just as likely they won't. I've always found it extremely curious that when victims are told from every quarter that they're under the threat of death and should leave as soon as possible, they just go numb and inexplicably wait to be killed. But now, I hear, plague is in the town again …'

'Not much news comes to us from within the town walls, but I've had guards posted along the borders of my domain, and they're not letting anyone enter.'

'Very wise of you. But do you know if Volk is still alive?'

'I don't know, and I don't ask …'

'Still, in the midst of all the death in your fiefdom, I hear that new life has also occurred – two new lives, if I'm correctly informed.'

'Yes, it's true. Not only was it a surprise, this time it really was almost a miracle, which the physician hurried along a little. Twins. A boy and a girl,' Friedrich tells him.

'So what do they look like? Fair skin, dark eyes, maybe red hair?'

'They don't even look like each other, but that's hardly important. They are both healthy, and so is the countess.'

'And the scrivener? Where is Nikolai Miklavž Paulin?' the prince-bishop asks.

'Supposedly in Bled, staying with a distant relation of the mayor's.'

'I'm very glad to hear it. I truly felt sorry for Nikolai. By the way, did you ever notice his lips? They are not heart-shaped (heart-shaped lips I've always found repugnant) but gently rounded, with a little thin moustache stretching above them. And then there are his bright, greyish-brown eyes, which would sometimes laugh in harmony with his full lips, and Miklavž's narrow hips, his nicely curved, firm buttocks ... aaah ... and his strong, long legs and those wonderful shoulders with their long muscles – I expect he enjoyed swimming ... oh ... aahhh ... Well, dear Friedrich, now we must take leave of each other,' the prince-bishop grimaces. 'The pain is back again. Julian, bring me the opium tincture ... Bring me everything, all the painkillers and potions we have.'

'Take leave? But how?' Friedrich stands up and – probably for the last time, he anxiously realizes – gazes at the dying man on the bed. 'How do I take my leave from you? Should I say, "Till next time, Wolfgang"? Should I say "Farewell"? Tell me.'

'Neither would be accurate. But go now. Whatever has been between us, whatever we had and whatever caused us to go our separate ways in life and then draw closer again, I have always enjoyed knowing you – partly because, time and again, you have genuinely brought a smile to my face.'

'Knowing someone is not the same as friendship, and we haven't been friends in a long time, or have we?'

'That's not important. Nothing is important any more. You may go, Friedrich. From now on, I am alone.'

Before the Abyss,
Before the Emptiness
– Nothing

I am lying in my bedroom and thinking out loud. Julian sits next to me, writing down my spoken thoughts; he alone has been unconditionally loyal and has never betrayed me. I myself have betrayed many, but if anyone is counting on me getting my just deserts when I die, they are mistaken. There will be no settling of accounts after death. No punishment, no reward. Drenched in rancid sweat, I lie in bed and burn with pain, which the past two weeks I have been alleviating with an opium tincture so I can talk and think in the intervals between screaming and delirium. The opium tincture sharpens my mind; it makes me see things more precisely, more clearly. More clearly than ever before, I peer into the blind spots that eluded me in the past, for whenever it seemed necessary I would always look away. When I close my eyes, all that I have ever seen and known starts being compressed. I collapse into what I was sixty-one years ago. I collapse into nothing. But from my birth to the end that now approaches, I have been many things. I have been much – much more than most would ever dare dream, and, mainly, I have been less than I thought myself to be. Was I aware of that? Yes, I was, but at the same time wasn't. I perfected the skill of avoiding vantage points from which there was a chance of my seeing myself as something I didn't like. I always found a way to look at things, to look at myself, so I wouldn't disgust myself. And I might have done. At times I catch a shadow of disgust in Julian's eyes. And you, too, Julian, like me you have intentionally turned your eyes away. So are you less guilty than I am? Yes, you are. But are you entirely without guilt? Are you pure? No. You have served me faithfully, although you could have easily hired yourself out to somebody else. The scrivener, wandering through his insanities, could not have done that. I'm not at all surprised he went mad.

At this point, Julian, I am going to claim privilege and preach you a sermon. Not one of the sermons I preached because it was my vocation. Most of what I said in those sermons I had my doubts about. But did I enjoy it? Oh, absolutely. Verbal incontinence has given me at least as much pleasure as all the carnal pleasures I have claimed for myself.

Time is running out for me. Only a trace of sand remains in the upper bulb of my life's hourglass, and when that sprinkles through, I will be no more. I am hot beneath this thick blanket and also chilled, as if burning ice is moving through my veins, and my sinews and flesh are quivering. It is the end of November, and November was always my least favourite month. At the beginning of autumn, as it extricates itself from the summer, I so often wished that nature would stop, that time would stand still in the colourful treetops of yellow and red, whose fleeting beauty has terrified me for as long as I can remember. Anything but decay, anything but winter; when the hour of my going arrives, let life discard me from time in some long-extended moment, but let it happen aesthetically so I may slip through that moment without pain and with no awareness of my own evanescence. In nature, winter is followed by spring. But I am so completely plucked out of nature I cannot accept the notion that for me the cycle of the seasons is ending, and once it gets cold that is all there will be.

My entire life I have been addicted to heights – the blaze of sensuality, riches, admiration, power, precious jewels, noble metals, the beauty of the material world in a string of pleasures. My insatiable drive, my ravenous nature … my self could never get its fill of things, most of which were not even possible to digest. I had much, in part because I knew how to take, and more than a few times I took by force, with no consideration for the other and his pain, and now that I am reduced to decaying matter, I have nothing left except memories. But then, so the Church teaches, a new life follows. Because then, so I once proclaimed, comes judgement. Punishment and payment. When the cold hand touches the back of my neck, then, I once believed, that *then* appears, all by itself, and metaphysics opens up and, with it, faith in the afterlife. But I miscalculated. My reckoning – counting on faith blossoming right before the end and carrying me over into eternity – has, sadly, not come out even. Where is the light that, after all my physical and mental torments, should carry me safely away to ... wherever? Where is God, in whom, to be honest, I never fully believed, but still I hoped that at some point towards the end he might show up? I have lived my life without God, even if my mouth was full of him. My faith was the religion of pleasure. I was a bigger heretic than anyone I ever denounced and sent to death.

I remain alone with my expiring life. The cold damp seeps into the room, the withered leaves beneath the trees are decomposing, the warm piles of manure emit a putrid odour, mud is everywhere, people are in foul mood and look like they are ill – this is November, caught between the sharp, cloying smells of autumn and December's icy chill. This, despite the pine branches and the celebrating – whether in expectation of the birth of Jesus or of the winter solstice, when the wolf-nights swallow the sun and the ancient gods steal through the shadows, it's all the same. Life and death, death and life, a repetition that is almost eternal. I lie in bed with a bloated abdomen, in which a lump is getting fatter and poisoning my blood. When I breathe, my belly rises and falls as if it were not mine.

Is this disease punishment or accident, and just the way nature shuffled the cards? But I don't think about this.

I have never concealed my vanity and it is with vanity, too, that I depart the world. I would like to leave at least something behind: my testament, which, if it came into the wrong hands, might lead to my being buried in unconsecrated ground – although as nobody would wish to cause a scandal, I expect that in any case they'll bury me with full episcopal honours.

I am afraid of death. Unbearably afraid! Not of being punished – there is no punishment after death – but of having no vantage point from which I can look back at my life. I am terrified of disappearing utterly. I am appalled by the idea that at a certain moment there will be no trace of me left, that I will simply vanish, even as – so I'm told by my physician – my nails and hair will continue to grow for a few days more. That nothing will be left of me except a rotten body, and probably all memory of me will soon begin to fade. I have neither family nor offspring. Most of my life I've had more enemies than friends, and they will very likely retain me in their memory longer than my friends, most of whom have not been my friends for a long while now.

In the end, I have only my faithful secretary, who has stayed with me despite having to witness things that were repugnant to him. But that is his story, not mine. My story is that in my last years I had beside me a man on whom I could rely and who will see to it that after my death my affairs are handled as I wish them to be. There's nothing special, just a few small things that need putting in order, that's all. If you offer someone the opportunity to wait, immobile, for death, he will experience the strange feeling that he can do something good, for no special reason, simply out of pure kindness. So that his final painful hours are easier to endure, perhaps because he believes that doing some good deed will lighten the pain, even if he knows this to be an illusion. But illusions make it easier to live. And easier to die. And anyway, we are all dying, moment by moment.

My entire life, my mouth was full of God. Such was my vocation. I truly believed in him when I was young, but later less and less. After all, no matter what I did I was never punished, and meanwhile I watched innocent people suffering and nobody heard them – neither God nor any other divinity, and not people either. God is not someone I'd like to meet, because if he can allow such things without blinking an eye, if he doesn't even listen to the most heart-wrenching cries for help ... what sort of God is he? He's like a child who had trouble putting the world together and then lost interest in his toy, lost control of it, so ever since he's just been torpidly watching what happens and even glancing away from the mechanical monster, which lives its own senseless life. And what could be more naïve than to ascribe some essential connection with goodness to an infinite being! And, finally, how do we know that other worlds don't exist, worlds that are parallel to ours? Maybe the bad things in our world are good for those other ones?

And even if I wanted to meet God, I wouldn't be able to, and for a reason that is at least as terrifying as any irrational belief in him. Namely, I know that God does not exist. Most people believe in him out of fear, or self-interest, or for no other reason than that it's easier to live when you feel there is something greater than you. Maybe fate exists, which is no more than what the Ionians believed, atoms colliding in bodies in empty space, and maybe that's how I came to be born into a wealthy noble family, became the prince-bishop and lived the life I did.

In fact, I don't give a damn what they do with my body. They can give me a big funeral or bury me with the murderers – for I was that, too, and it was what my vocation demanded of me. Many of the things that seem normal to us today will be considered barbaric a century from now, just as today we find the rituals of other climes and countries to be barbaric. The world in which we invented God, just to keep ourselves from going crazy, is cruel and unjust.

My great desire to travel to the other side of the ocean and forget everything I have been, to forget even what a long time ago I once wished to become, did not come to pass. Life simply ran out on me. The truth is I was a bigger coward than I have ever been prepared to admit. Julian, are you writing this down? That I'm a coward? Write it. Write everything I am saying, literally every single word! Most of my life, I even considered myself to be brave, but, in fact, I was merely arrogant and conceited, which is also a way of dealing with fear. Maybe when I'm gone this confession, which Julian is scrupulously recording, will be all that remains. Memories of me will very soon fade, and it's not very likely that history will speak of me. I simply was not that important.

I am probably one of the very few people who understand what happened to the scrivener. He went mad in the way that sensitive, kind-hearted and well-educated melancholiacs go mad. The way only a very few do.

Sitting there all those nights in front of his fireplace, quill in hand, he eventually split in two, into body and mind, and ever since he has been unable to paste himself together again. And in this bottomless chasm, the scrivener, too, discovered not God but the self-deception of his own thought, the mental constructions by which a man shifts his perspective on what is and what isn't, in order to survive more easily. The scrivener, too, through an intellectual daring that I myself never possessed, was unable to fill this emptiness with either a benevolent God or meaning; he could only fill it with nothing. He marched into a territory only a few have dared to enter and from which they either did not return or returned unrecognizable. He tumbled into an abyss from which he will not be able to extract himself, unless ... unless, perhaps, a miracle happens, especially the miracle of love. However much love might be an illusion, it nevertheless has healing effects and can, at least temporarily, make even the most splintered creature whole. But will he ever be able to return to those meditations of his which pushed him over the edge? Could he ever start writing again? I doubt it.

I have been close to the edge a few times myself. I've seen cracks in linear time, which went beyond the known explanations (mainly platitudes), and I didn't know what to make of them. I never told anyone about that phenomenon a few months ago on the road, when a steel-red landscape opened up into some parallel world. I didn't have the words for it. But I also knew it was better not to think about this experience, so as not to be pulled in by the density of the absurd, because that blackness, that alienness, which suddenly opens inside of you, carries an immensely stimulating power which seduces you with an openness of being and existence that transcends the here and now, but when you gaze into it, it will not let you go and slowly sucks you in. When you experience such things, it's best you close your eyes, turn around and walk quietly away. Most people are unable to endure what the scrivener saw. And should this happen to him again, I wouldn't be at all surprised if he killed himself.

Injustice, justice, honesty, goodness – these are orphans without parents, inventions through which humanity finds meaning and order and so more easily survives. Meaning is consolation, even such a banal idea as that worn-out saying that everything has its good side. Does it really? The reason so many people, including children, did not survive my brutality is that nobody grabbed them out of my hands. As for me, my survival instinct always took me where it was best for me, even if it meant trampling, beating and crushing someone to get there. I could even say I've had happiness in my life. But only a few times was I truly happy, as a child – later, however, from my boyhood on, after that crime in the never-finished palace of Charles V, when I felt mightier than God, the God the Jesuits had been feeding us, the knowledge was already ingrained in me that all experience was merely a substitute for happiness, a necessary substitute, so I could live my life and avoid the yawning abyss of meaninglessness. Something was constantly whispering to me that, whether God did or did not exist,

I could live my life differently, with no counterfeits, pure, as I had a very long time ago, a life I lost forever that night in Granada. And not because I was forced to do what I did but because, unlike Friedrich, I never regretted it later.

All of my personal effects I bequeath to my loyal secretary and companion, Julian; everything else the Holy Roman Catholic Church can take. Because, Julian, were I to leave you anything from my lands and treasures, know that you would not be able to use it at all. The vultures are outside my door, waiting to swoop down and take whatever they think is worth taking. So for your own sake, I hope you will heed my advice and with my letters of credence and with the money and personal valuables I am leaving to you go some place where, as the years pass, your homeland seems more and more a dream and less and less a memory. Not because anywhere else might be significantly better, but simply because it will be different. And because sometimes it's good to draw a line under your life and start over.

If you think that anything I am leaving you would be good to give away, give it away; it makes no difference to me. That's all I have to tell the world upon my departure, but let me end by saying one more time: there is no God! There are only the cold laws of nature. And injustice and pain. There are pleasures, too, sometimes many pleasures, and there is even a bit of love, but, as the end approaches, there are mainly illnesses and at the very end, death. And after death, nothing.

Water, Julian. My stomach is burning. And put some ice on my belly and hand me that little bottle. Bring me everything; from now on, we won't worry about dosages; from now on, the right dosage is the one that's too much. When I won't be able to speak any more or even move my lips, and my eyes will be only slightly open, but my enormous belly will still be rising and falling, dribble some cold water into my mouth and smear dark resin on my tongue so I don't go mad and burn with fever. What scares me most is that I might be burning with pain but won't have any way of showing it. Julian, don't leave me, not even when I've lost consciousness and am unable to tell you I'm in pain. I don't remember ever asking anyone for anything. Ever since I was a young man, other people, whether sincere or fawning, have asked me for things, while I merely gave orders and handed out indulgences, mercy, cruelty. Stay with me just long enough for me to die and then ... then you are free ... And now, while there is still time, I'm going to say something I haven't said in a long time – the last time I said it in all sincerity was probably as a child, to my parents; any time I said it later, I never meant it. I know I have sometimes caused you pain and been unfair to you, and you've borne it surprisingly well, and I know that being with me has not always been easy for you. Although you never showed it, I wasn't blind; I saw it. I beg you, Julian, now that I am completely powerless, do not take revenge on me. Whatever wrong I have done you, I needed you by my side and, in a way, even loved you. So for everything, for whatever I did or did not do, Julian, I beg you, forgive me.

Report from the Bishop of Laibach, Thomas Chroen, to the Holy See

The Archduke of the Lands of Inner Austria, Prince Ferdinand II, established the Reform Commission in the year of Our Lord 1600 and placed me, Bishop Thomas Chroen, at the head of it. By my side are: Georg Lenkowitsch, the Governor of Carniola; Joseph von Rabatta, Sheriff of Carniola; and Philipp Cobenzl von Prossegk. We have been given a military escort of several hundred soldiers.

The Reform Commission began its work on the Twenty-second of December in the year 1600 in the Diocesan Building in Laibach (Ljubljana). Every day from Christmas to the Twenty-seventh of December, we gave sermons on the errors of Lutheranism. I myself gave sermons in Slovene in the cathedral, while sermons in German were given at the Jesuit College by the rector, Father Henricus Vivarius. On the Twenty-ninth of December, the Commission burned eight carts of Lutheran books in Laibach's main square; a fortnight later we brought three more carts of such books to the square and burned them to the great bewilderment of the heretics, who managed, however, to rescue a few books and take them into the Provincial Building.

In 1601, throughout the month of January, we were engaged in converting the Laibach Lutherans. For three or four hours a day, I explained the truths of the Catholic religion to the burghers we had summoned. Everyone was given the opportunity to swear allegiance to the Catholic faith. Anyone who declined was condemned to be banished in six weeks and three days, before which time he was obliged to declare under oath all of his wealth and to pay a tithe. Of all the burghers, only fifteen registered as Lutherans and refused to swear the oath of allegiance, and so they were banished from Laibach.

That same month I reconsecrated the Hospital Church of St Elizabeth and gave orders for the Protestant cemetery to be demolished.

The bodies of the preachers, including the corpse of Superintendent Spindler, I had cast in the Laibach River and gave the Church of St Elizabeth to the hospital.

At the beginning of February I went to Upper Carniola, accompanied by my retinue. On the Eighth of February, the Commission began reforming the town of Stein (Kamnik). The Commission went carefully through all the houses and that same day burned a large number of heretical books in the main square. After that, I gave a speech in the Town Hall. The obedient burghers soon capitulated and swore allegiance to Catholicism; the four who persisted in Lutheranism we banished. We continued our work at Kreuz Castle, near Commenda, where the Lutherans had a prayer hall and a cemetery. Both of these we blew up. Three days later we were in Krainburg (Kranj); from there we sent back to Kreuz for the Lutheran peasant Krische Mikusch, who is called Luther; the night after our departure from Kreuz, his sons murdered a Catholic Town Councillor in Krainburg named Lauretitsch, a scales-maker. After our interrogations and investigation of the murder, the Commission arrested and imprisoned several people and razed Krische's house to the ground.

The next day I gave a long speech in the house of Mining Judge Michael Harrer. All but one or two agreed to take the Catholic oath. On the Thirteenth of February, the Commission sent Christoph Harrer with six horses, a hundred and fifty peasants and several other reliable persons to the market town of Neumarktl (Tržič). There every last burgher swore the Catholic oath. In the meantime, in Kranj, I solemnly installed Johannes Friedrich Clemens as the new town priest and ordered the Lutheran books we had seized to be burned in the square not far from the pillory.

The cold has begun to let up, thank God, and the Seventeenth of February was the first day this year that one could feel spring in the air.

On this same day we went to Bischoflack (Škofja Loka). Here, Andreas Albrecht von Seidelshofen, the administrator for the Bishop of Freising, with several horsemen, came out to meet the Commission; he received us with a salute of honour and hosted us well and grandly. The next day in the castle I preached to ten heretical burghers. All ten took the Catholic oath. We burned the heretical books we had confiscated and that same day returned to Laibach.

In late February, in Laibach, I again summoned the Lutheran burghers, several provincial officials and quite a few mothers and widows as well. We had no difficulties. Several hundred took the Catholic oath without resistance. They are forbidden under threat of punishment to consume meat dishes on fast days, and on Sundays, Mondays, Wednesdays and Fridays they are commanded to attend sermons at the cathedral or go to the Jesuit Fathers, where there will be a discussion of the chief controversial points of religious doctrine.

On the Seventh of March, Philipp Cobenzl and I returned to Upper Carniola, where we undertook reforms in the village of Vigaun (Begunje). On the Tenth of March, we blew up the so-called Lutheran Synagogue there with gunpowder (it had previously served as a barn and wine cellar); whatever remained, we burned. The wall and stones, weighing four quintals, exploded in all directions and almost damaged the nearby Church of St Ulrich. Of the two hundred and fifty people who were present to watch the event, none was harmed.

On Sunday, the Eighth of March, I preached in Radmannsdorf (Radovljica), after which the burghers were interrogated. All the men swore obedience, but to our great surprise the burgher women refused. On the Thirteenth of March, we spoke to the peasants and the heretical populace in the vicinity. The obedient ones took the oath; the disobedient were punished with monetary fines and imprisoned – the latter included a man named Gevacz, with a fine of 150 gulden, and Jurij Prescheren, with a fine of 100 gulden. The blacksmiths of Kropp (Kropa) also swore loyalty to the Catholic Church and asked me for their own separate parish with a permanent parish priest. I gave them my assent. Of the blacksmiths there were, however, three who refused to submit. Two we condemned to banishment, while the third we placed in the pillory with an open Lutheran book; less than a day later he came to his senses.

The Commission sent authorized delegates to Kronau (Kranjska Gora) and Weissenfels (Bela Peč), while we ourselves went to Assling (Jesenice) to see the Bucceleni mines. The refractory people of Weissenfels, including a certain man named Nastran and his wife, were summoned before the Commission and swore obedience; the Weissenfels administrator, however, I had arrested and taken in chains to Radmannsdorf. As he persisted in his obstinacy, I sent him to the rector of the Jesuit College in Laibach, Henricus Vivarius, after which he was at last willing to convert.

On Sunday, the Eighteenth of March, the church in Radmannsdorf was dedicated. I myself held Mass, and I gave a speech on communion in one kind – with bread alone. The next day I finally received the oath from the burgher women of Radmannsdorf. On the Twentieth of March, the Commission went again to Krainburg, where we demanded a report from the town judge on the implementation of our directives. On the Twenty-first of March, we summoned the Lutheran women of the town to appear before the Commission to take the Catholic oath. After this, Cobenzl left for Carinthia and, on the Thirtieth of March, returned to Laibach.

Our work is going well. We are very satisfied with what we have done so far. The work of the Reformation Commission has been peaceful, without violence and thorough.

Let It Last, If Only in
Syncopated Rhythm...

A south-westerly breeze gently stirs the newly green branches of the lindens and chestnuts above the lake's slightly rippled surface. Beneath one of these mighty trees, a cob has furiously, threateningly, spread his wings and is charging at a younger swan, a rival. Meanwhile, the pen, with her three tiny swanlings in speckled, fluffy down, glides slowly towards Mlino, where the lake decants into a stream, next to which washerwomen are talking in loud voices, at times laughing out loud as they rub their washing against the washboards. From somewhere the smell of fried fat fills the air and mingles with the smell of boiled milk, as the fragrances of linden and chestnut blossoms, not yet fully open, give way, defeated by these other smells.

'Well, I'm done my wash ...' one of the washerwomen says; she uses masculine forms when she speaks, which, in fact, is how the local women talk. When and why they started talking this way, who can say? But when somebody visits here from a town, especially for Assumption Day in the middle of August, when pilgrims assemble at Lake Bled from all around, then some of the women, who rent out lodgings to the pilgrims, use feminine forms, the way Slovene is properly spoken. Thus they avoid snide comments about them being mannish or having more beneath their skirts than their men have in their trousers. But most of these women pay little attention to the visitors; they say, well, we have to stand in for our husbands, who never came back from the army, who fell beneath Turkish sabres, who were mowed down by plague and other diseases, who saddled up their horses one morning, first putting a Lutheran Bible beneath the saddle, and then rode off to the north, from where they never returned. And because so many of us guys ... I mean, us girls ... were left on our own to take care of children, grandchildren and parents on both sides of the family, we're the ones who count the pennies and pay the taxes, and some of us who live by the lake also pick up the oars and, on Sundays and holidays, ferry pilgrims back and forth in our boats to the Church of the Assumption of Mary, which stands on the little island in the middle.

The sound of barking dogs is interrupted by the screeching and wailing of cats. It's that time of year when the young toms are still brawling with each other, still sniffing around females, most of whom are already pregnant, in the hope that one of them might still be able and willing – since in the natural order of things they have had to yield precedence to the older males, who, as the mating season drew on, performed their natural duties with increasingly tattered ears, bloody noses and damaged paws, injuries acquired in courtship fighting. Now, maybe, it's finally our turn, the restless young cats think, driven by nature's law; if not this spring, then this autumn our time will come; we'll fatten up over the summer and get bigger and stronger. And those old farts had better be ready! Sure, they're more experienced, with piercing eyes that are hard for a young cat to withstand, and their slow stride might tell us to get out of the way this instant or fur will fly, but more and more, to us young toms, those lords of the turf, in fact, seem mostly toothless.

From barns you can hear the lowing of cows with taut udders, and now and then the whinny of a horse, which is answered by a donkey; somewhere a dog starts barking, and then all the dogs in the village add their voices, if they are not out rambling just then, on heat; the ewes in the walled pastures, meanwhile, are bleating, calling out to their lambs, who hop over to their mothers and suckle at their teats.

But the sounds of the animals dissolve in the syncopated rhythm of a rustic cart, rattling as it makes a slow curve around the lake. The driver turns towards a bench on the shore, where a male figure sits motionless.

'Miklavž, it'll be supper soon … We don't want to have to wait for you, and we don't want our Zef flying off the handle like she did last time, throwing pots of food everywhere because the gentry were late getting back from the hunt.'

The man on the bench gives no sign of having heard, so the driver repeats, 'Miklavž, you haven't had another bad turn, have you? Come on, get in the cart and I'll take you home.'

But Nikolai, who around here is usually called Miklavž, just keeps sitting there, motionless on the bench, and as the cart slowly rumbles past, he realizes that the lake has begun to take on an inviting, fresh, green colour. Maybe, after the past winter and spring, which he has spent sitting or, rather, lying, in his room by the soot-covered stove in a manor in Zagorice, in Bled, he will start swimming again. He does not remember much about the past eight months. And there has been nothing worth remembering since the end of last summer, nothing good to remember. In all this time, he has never asked his benefactors, who took him under their roof at the request of Mayor Volk Falke, what happened in the town he left without remembering how he came to leave it. Somewhere he also left his writings there, and writing – oh, this he does remember – had brought him inexplicable satisfaction. Never in his life had he felt so utterly alive as when he was writing. While he was writing. Until everything started getting tangled up, became more and more knotted, until in the end it was all knotty and frayed ...

In the distance he saw a boat with three, or maybe four, people returning from the island. The two cobs had evidently come to an understanding, since the family of swans was now swimming in unison past him: the pen behind, in front of her the three fluffy swanlings all in a neat row, and at the very front, the cob, who every so often would turn his head towards Nikolai and give him a sharp look as if to say, 'Don't even think about messing with me and my family. My beak is hard, but my most powerful weapons are the ball-shaped elbows on my wings, with which I can strike the invader so hard he'll never get out of the water again.' 'All right, all right, I understand,' Nikolai returns his gaze. 'I know this language well. It's not so very different from the messages men exchange with each other in my human world.'

'Your hand ...' he suddenly hears a voice behind him. 'Show me your palm ...' He sees an older woman beside him; she has very dark skin, a wrinkled face, long black hair mixed with strands of grey and, surprisingly, light-blue eyes. He has seen her before. He noticed her a few times walking around Bled. Sometimes she's alone, sometimes two young women are with her, with dirty, barefoot children hanging around them. The younger women, too, had dark faces, which were concealed by their long, shaggy black hair, so black that it seemed dark blue in the sunlight, and their light-coloured eyes were even livelier than those of the woman who is now in front of him. They had been young, very young. And beautiful, remarkably so. And terribly wild. When he once caught the eye of one of the younger women, she didn't turn away bashfully but cemented his gaze to herself, so he could not take his eyes off her.

'Look away!' His host, the Knight von Rauschenberg, who at the time was sitting next to him in the cart, poked him in the ribs with his elbow. 'These gypsy girls are fun, but they're as dangerous as the devil. They can put a spell on you, and you don't even know it. Watch out for them, Nikolai! Don't look at her, because she's got her eye on you already. No matter what, don't go near them! Now that she knows you're soft, the witch is sure to try again sometime.'

'Young sir, give me your hand,' the woman in front of him invitingly motions with the fingers of her right hand, but then, without waiting, she grabs his hand herself and lifts it to her face.

'I don't have any money,' Nikolai answers weakly, 'and I don't believe in fate.'

'I know you don't have money – it's my profession to know things. And not believing in fate is part of your fate.' The woman continues to use the familiar form of address with him. 'You're sitting here with a closed heart. Somebody broke it. And a limestone crust has formed around it. But it wasn't just your heart that broke, was it?' The gypsy peers into his eyes and then looks at his palm. 'Poor boy,' she says, pressing her lips together and shaking her head. 'Come on, let's see what it was.' With her left hand she pulls a deck of cards out of her pocket and lays them down one by one next to Nikolai on the bench. 'I see death, and more than one; I see many deathly scythes, and one of them is directly above your head. But I also see a good arm moving your head out of the way just in time, so the scythe swings past it. And I see you,' she says, laying down a few more cards, 'who then tumbled into emptiness, into a place where there is neither light nor lamp. Darkness. Oh, shit! Nothing but pure, thick darkness!' She looks at him and squeezes his hand sympathetically. 'But where the hell were you, poor boy? Where have you been?' The woman shakes her head, while Nikolai, as if spellbound, keeps his hand between her two hands.

'You're lucky I stopped to talk to you, but, of course, it couldn't have been any different, because, young man, it's fate. I am here to tell you that your horrors and terrors are over. I see another heart, too,' she says, turning over a new card, 'one that was never touched by your heart, and that's how it wounded you. But you yourself are to blame. She wasn't the one. She wasn't your destiny. The love between you was your own invention, nothing more. So this woman, who, like you, also had a scythe swinging around her head, but now, as the card shows, she's not doing badly at all – you shouldn't condemn her! You'll be doing all right, too, from now on.' The gypsy runs her left hand across the mesh of lines in his open palm. 'You'll see; things will be very good for you!'

'Nothing will ever be good again …' Nikolai says gloomily.

'Be quiet, young man! You know nothing. What Kamala has told you – it all happened. Remember that,' she says and lays three new cards on the bench. 'A new woman will be coming into your life. She's beautiful, young. A good woman. You already know her. You see her every day, but you don't really see her. That's because your heart is closed. But when you open it, your life will blossom. You will love her, infinitely. And she will love you the same. Not here; you will live somewhere else. First in a great city, where I see lordly carriages, palaces and big houses and ladies in very elegant clothes. And later' – she pulls four cards from the deck – 'I see some very unusual houses and a lot of water. Not a river or lake, it's more like the sea. And a strange sort of fruit is growing there. What sort of fruit is that?' She looks at him in surprise. 'There's nothing like it in our land! And your woman – I see she has a very elegant look, too. And I also see you – you're writing something … But I don't need my gift to tell me that your tender little hands have never done serious work.'

'I will write again?' Nikolai perks up.

'Yes …'

'Books, philosophy, stories?'

The woman examines his palm, picks up another card and, with a doubtful smile, shakes her head. 'Hard to say. What I'm seeing look more like official documents … But it will be a good, reliable job, and you'll be happy!'

'Happy without writing … without real writing? No, never.'

'You'll be happy with the woman who'll be your wife, and happy with your children. I see three of them. All healthy. Two girls and a boy. And there's an enormous cat moving between their legs – such big cats we don't have in our land! And there are enormous strange lizards crawling around … Shit, I've never seen anything like them, not even in the cards! Interesting, boy, very interesting,' she looks at him, sizing him up. 'You're handsome, well-built. If you smiled a little, those two girls of mine would be all over you. That's why I want to protect you from them. You're too good for them, and you've been through too much. You deserve a beautiful love. My two are God's punishment to scoundrels and brutes. And my girls do the job with brutal efficiency.'

'Love?' Nikolai looks doubtfully at the woman and shakes his head.

'Love. Yes, love. You'll see. Believe me! Kamala is always right! I can look into the past and the future. I see things other people don't.'

'I used to think that way myself …'

'And you will again, too. Oh yes, you'll be doing a lot of thinking, only …'

'Only not writing, not like I was last year. So I won't be doing that again?' Nikolai asks the gypsy, now with no more doubts, now very trusting.

'You know yourself that these are dangerous things for you …'

'But even so!'

'Well, maybe you will do some writing, too,' she says out of sympathy to instil a little hope in him. 'If not in this life, then in some other. In your next life maybe or a parallel one.'

'Miklavž!' A voice is heard from behind them, as well as the whinny of a horse. Nikolai turns around and sees the knight's daughter dismounting.

'Miklavž, we are worried about you. Our man wasn't sure if you even heard him when he drove past. Supper is about to be served – the roast trout you like so much, and millet porridge with vegetables. And Zef's made a tarragon roll for dessert. She'll be furious if we're late for supper; you know how she is …'

Nikolai looks at her from head to toe and smiles. It occurs to him that this is the first time in a long, long while that he has smiled. 'You rode here in trousers?' he asks the girl.

'I ain't so daft as tuh go ridin' in a skirt,' she replies in the local dialect, and at once covers her mouth with her hand and corrects herself. 'It's extremely awkward to go horse riding in a skirt or dress, which is why I prefer trousers. And these are my own trousers, I'll have you know.'

The gypsy is watching the scene with a smile on her face, and when she lets go of his hand, she nudges him lightly with her shoulder and her eyes motion towards the knight's daughter, a signal noticed by the young lady.

'Leave him alone, Kamala. You have no idea what the poor fellow's been through …' the young lady says.

'Girl, you're insulting my profession! Who knows better than Kamala what did, will and is happening at this very moment! Because from now on, Izidora, things are going to be good for him, excellent even.' The gypsy winks at the girl.

'Oh, Kamala! You and your sorcery! … All right, here you go,' she says, and drops a couple of kreutzers into the woman's hand.

'Thanks, Izidora. It will be given back to you many times over. Kamala is never wrong!' Then the gypsy turns to Nikolai and, with a single tug, plucks a silver button from the middle of his overcoat, where it is buttoned over his chest, and, even before he can look down in surprise at the now vacant spot, she tells him, 'So there, boy, it's done. Your heart is open again. The button is for me, and love is for you.' Kamala laughs, gathers up the cards and shoves them in her left pocket. 'From now on you'll be able to give so you can get,' she adds as she is leaving, 'so be careful what you let into your heart!'

Izidora half-smirks, half-smiles, and then rolls her eyes and climbs up on the dark-brown stallion, who is still warm enough that steam is coming off him. She motions to Nikolai to join her. And, because he hesitates, she backs the horse up to the bench, and Nikolai climbs on from there, grabbing the saddle firmly in both hands.

'You've never mounted a horse before?' she asks in a mocking tone.

'Sure I have; I've ridden horses. But not for months …'

'I can see you're out of shape. And no wonder. You spent the whole winter in a daze by the stove. You've got to get stronger, Miklavž.' As they start off towards the manor in Zagorice, it dawns on Nikolai that this is the first time Izidora has, at least partly, used the familiar form of address with him.

'I'm going to start swimming in a few weeks. Maybe you could join me ...' Izidora says.

'You swim, too? But surely not on your own!'

'Of course! All on my own, all the way to the island and back ...'

'Most of the women I know wouldn't even know how to swim.'

'I swim almost every day in the summer, when the weather's good.'

'But how?'

'Well, definitely not in a skirt!' Izidora turns around as they ride and laughs. 'I even have a book on the art of swimming.'

'*De Arte Natandi*?'

'Yes, that's it. An illustrated handbook by the English theologian Everard Digby.'

'And you're not at all afraid?'

'There's not much that scares me. Well, of course, I am afraid of the Turks and all these anti-Reformation round-ups. But you know, Miklavž, we still give communion in two kinds in secret. Even today, there's a preacher visiting us from Lower Austria who will be holding a service for our family and a few others – but, of course, you mustn't say a word about this.'

'But I am a Catholic ... or at least I used to be.'

'You worked for a Protestant mayor, so you know about these things.'

'I don't know what I know any more ... Everything's fallen apart, disappeared; I don't know anything now ...'

'Oh, Miklavž, the past is the past. You have to forget about it. Anyway, Kamala predicted a very good future for you,' Izidora smiles. 'Do you know that the name Kamala means "goddess of love"? But it's all complete nonsense, of course. She told me that I would meet a stranger right here at home and fall head over heels in love with him, and then we'd go off some place, far, far away, and live there happily ever after with our children. Oh yes, and she saw some sort of bird in the cards' – Izidora gives a sudden laugh – 'a great big bright-coloured bird, Kamala said. Such birds we don't have in our land, she told me. But it's utter foolishness! As you can see, I'm still here ...'

A peculiar warmth starts to spread through Nikolai's body. Strange, he thinks. I haven't felt such a peculiarly pleasant feeling in a very long time. I didn't think I'd ever feel like this again.

'We need to hurry up a little. It's getting dark, and I don't want to keep them waiting at home, not when we have an important guest; also, people are coming from all over the area to hear him preach. You don't need to keep gripping the saddle, you know! Put your arms around my waist and hold on tight, because I'm about to make Whitey go faster …'

'Whitey? Why Whitey when he's such a dark, chocolate colour?'

'Chocolate! I've never had chocolate. Have you?'

'Only once. There are several places you can find it in town. But why do you call your horse Whitey when he's as black as coffee?'

'Well, Kamala is called Kamala, but she's not the goddess of love …' she says, laughing as they ride.

'Who knows?' Nikolai says softly, wondering when he had last touched a woman's body. A body as soft as this and yet so firm – never. Is he only imagining it, or does her long, fair hair, gathered in a bun, from which a few somewhat wavy strands have escaped, actually smell like chocolate? And honey, too, perhaps, and linden – or is this simply the fragrance of the year's first warm evening in May mingling so happily with the smell of her sweaty, pliable, giving body? Oh! Nikolai thinks, startled. How can I even think of this? It's as though I'm seeing her today for the first time when I've been living alongside her all winter and spring …

'Miklavž?' Izidora says.

'Yes, Izidora?' He realizes that he was about to say '*dear* Izidora' but omitted the word just in time.

'There's something I've been wanting to ask you for a while now. May I?'

'Of course, Izidora. You can ask me anything,' Nikolai replies and thinks, Kamala was right. Here, inside my chest, something is beating again, furiously. Not like in the past, in times of anxiety and terror, and also very different from the restless rhythms with which it would shake whenever I saw that widow … And it's not just that this some-thing is beating again; there's a sweet warmth pouring through my body. But if I bring my lips too close to her neck, then, oh God, the tightness in my loins makes riding painful ...

'Miklavž, is it true they tried to cure you with some strange fish that make people shake?'

'Yes, but I don't remember it very well ...'

'But how do the fish make you shake? Is the shaking very strong?' Izidora asks.

'It's fairly strong, if I remember correctly, but like I said, the last few months are all a strange blur.'

'Hmm,' Izidora thinks for a moment. 'I would like to see those fish. I might even bring myself to touch one of them, but only one. It's too bad we don't have them here. You know, there are times when I dream about going away. I don't mean just from Bled either but from Carniola. First I would go to the coast, and from there to the other side of the ocean. I've read that the people who live across the ocean are very different from us with entirely different customs ... They're called Indians, isn't that right?'

She is splendid, Nikolai thinks, finding it ever harder to breathe. She's utterly wonderful ...

'And then I think, what if I went to Japan or maybe China, where they have a big, long wall? If I were a man, I'm sure I'd go away, at least for a few years. If I were a man, I'd maybe even apply for work at some company overseas ...'

Keep dreaming, dear beauty, and I will dream with you – the thought flashes through Nikolai's mind. Kamala was right, and I, too, have a feeling that things will be better from now on ...

'So what do you think about this, Miklavž?'

'I used to think about these things, too ...'

'Really? That's amazing!' Izidora says in surprise. 'I've never met anybody who wanted to go farther than the German or Italian lands.'

I haven't either, Nikolai thinks. I've never met anybody who is at all like you. You are exceptional, extraordinary, my dear, beautiful girl, he thinks and rests his face against her sweat-soaked back, when suddenly it occurs to him, but is any of this, what's happening to me now, is any of it real? What if at a certain moment, when I was sitting on the bench by the lake, I suddenly fainted and fell into the water and this is all some pre-death vision I'm having, just before I'm completely engulfed in darkness? Or maybe I'm already on the other side and this is heaven, and instead of St Peter it's the sorceress Kamala who stands by the gate with a deck of cards in her hand, and she's handed me to an angel, who has pulled me up on a horse and now we're flying through the air like Elijah?

I am floating, I am floating with infinite ease … Let it last … Oh, God, or nature, or whoever is in control of it all, please let it last, even if it's some syncope, some swoon, that has toppled me completely and I really am dead … Even if my drowned body is already being worked over by trout and carp, please let it last; let these moments or seconds or any other units of time stretch into infinity … Because what is, is good, and it was never better! So utterly wonderful! So supremely wonderful! I'm at a loss for words!

First published in 2017 by
Istros Books (in collaboration with Beletrina Academic Press)
London, United Kingdom
www.istrosbooks.com

Originally published in Slovene as *Kronosova žetev* by Beletrina Academic
Press, 2016

© Mojca Kumerdej

The right of Mojca Kumerdej to be identified as the author of this work has
been asserted in accordance with the Copyright, Designs and Patents Act, 1988.

Translation © Rawley Grau

Edited by Stephen Watts

Cover design and typesetting: Davor Pukljak | www.frontispis.hr

ISBN: 978-1-908236-333

Printed in England by
imprintdigital.com, Seychelles Farm, Upton Pyne, EX5 5HY, UK

This Book is part of the EU co-funded project *"Stories that can Change the
World"* in partnership with Beletrina Academic Press | www.beletrina.si

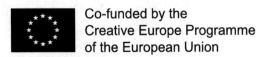

Co-funded by the
Creative Europe Programme
of the European Union

The European Commission support for the production of this publication does not constitute an
endorsement of the contents which reflects the views only of the authors, and the Commission
cannot be held responsible for any use which may be made of the information contained therein.